HEAVENLY

Divine Creek Ranch 3

Heather Rainier

MENAGE EVERLASTING

Siren Publishing, Inc.
www.SirenPublishing.com

A SIREN PUBLISHING BOOK
IMPRINT: Ménage Everlasting

HEAVENLY ANGEL
Copyright © 2011 by Heather Rainier

ISBN-10: 1-61034-379-4
ISBN-13: 978-1-61034-379-4

First Printing: February 2011

Cover design by *Les Byerley*
All art and logo copyright © 2011 by Siren Publishing, Inc.

ALL RIGHTS RESERVED: This literary work may not be reproduced or transmitted in any form or by any means, including electronic or photographic reproduction, in whole or in part, without express written permission.

All characters and events in this book are fictitious. Any resemblance to actual persons living or dead is strictly coincidental.

Printed in the U.S.A.

PUBLISHER
Siren Publishing, Inc.
www.SirenPublishing.com

DEDICATION

To my husband, my own heavenly angel.

Thanks to the girls, Christi, Jennifer and Tonya.

Thank you to the anonymous handsome cowboy at the grocery checkout counter. It's because of your flirting that Angel's character and the Divine Creek Ranch Collection sparked to life.

And a special thank you to Diana, Alison, Elisa, Caroline and all the incredibly talented staff at Siren Publishing.

HEAVENLY ANGEL

Divine Creek Ranch 3

HEATHER RAINIER
Copyright © 2011

Chapter One

July…a few weeks before Grace's wedding

Teresa Palacios bit her lip ruthlessly as she turned into the entrance of the Divine Creek Ranch. Her heart pounded a little at the boldness of what she was doing. She honestly didn't know where she'd gotten the guts to come out here. Grace kept telling her to seize the day, and that's what kept her foot on the gas as she slowly ventured down the long, curving driveway. As she drove past the house, she didn't see Grace's or any of the men's vehicles parked beside the large ranch house, so she continued on back. Seeing her dear friend might have bolstered her courage a bit, but she knew what Grace would say if she was here.

"What are you waiting for?" Teresa murmured to herself out loud.

Slowly she pulled through to the first barn and prayed hard she would see Angel amidst all the other cowboys and hands working on the ranch. Jack Warner, Ethan Grant, and Adam Davis had their own businesses to deal with and left much of the ranch operations to Angel Martinez, their long-time friend and ranch foreman. The man she had come to care a great deal for in the past several weeks.

He'd been shot in the abdomen earlier that summer by the woman who had been his girlfriend. Bravely, Teresa had visited him in the hospital, and he'd explained that situation to her and asked if she could overlook his error in trusting such a person. Of all people, she knew what it meant to be judged for the actions of others. She'd reassured him he could not hold himself responsible.

Since Angel's recovery, Teresa couldn't help but notice he frequently showed up at the store, always searching her out to say hello wherever she might be. A couple of times he'd brought her a sweet tea. He always took the time to visit with her and then made his excuses and returned to work. He'd been by three times this week alone.

His masculine presence no longer made her as nervous as it had the first couple of times he'd encountered her. When Grace had introduced her to him, she'd been unable to speak until after he was long gone. It was almost painful to maintain eye contact with him though she longed to. Every time she thought of it afterward, she wanted to kick herself for being so shy. His handsome facial features hinted that, though he was Hispanic, he probably had Native American blood flowing in his veins. She thought he was the most handsome man she'd ever seen.

The second time she'd encountered him had been the day Jack had come in to shop for Grace. Angel had flirted then, too, but she'd felt more self-confident behind the jewelry counter, in her element so to speak. She'd been able to carry on an actual conversation with him while she'd waited for Jack to return with his wallet. It had still been painfully nerve-wracking for her, especially when he'd made a point of asking if there was a man in her life. He'd seemed to not come on quite as strong, and when she'd looked into his topaz-colored eyes, she'd felt reassured rather than starstruck.

Squinting her eyes, she looked out through her windshield hoping for a glimpse of his characteristic long-legged gait or his distinctive Native American-looking profile. If nothing else, the long, silky black braid would identify him. She groaned when a ranch hand yelled something and pointed at her car. She prayed the hand was calling for Angel to come see to the visitor.

Please, oh, please, don't make me have to go looking for him! How many acres were in this ranch? He might not even be in the vicinity! Thrusting the thought away, she rolled to a stop near the barn. She could almost hear Grace now.

Seize the day, Teresa!

She looked up and heaved a great sigh of relief even as her heart pounded. Angel strode toward her car, dressed in very faded jeans that made love to his muscular frame, dusty cowboy boots, a thin, worn plaid shirt, and a straw cowboy hat. He loosened the ties on his leather work gloves, and she watched as he peeled them from his large hands. Watching him working those weathered gloves from his sensual fingers made her mouth water and intimate parts of her quiver and grow warm. She'd noticed lately that he had that effect on her, and it always disconcerted her and left her wishing she were a braver woman.

When he got close enough to the car, he recognized her and hesitated for a fraction of a second, breaking his stride. Then a wide, knowing grin split his tanned face. She smiled back, albeit a little timidly. He continued in his approach, and she noticed in the distance several of the ranch hands stopped what they were doing and stood watching. He put his hand on her door and squatted down beside her car, facing away from the men, and looked at her. He was tall, so even squatting like this, he was at eye level with her.

"Well, hello, Teresa."

She shivered pleasantly when he said her name. He always used the traditional pronunciation. They were both Texans through and through, but when he reverted to his traditional Hispanic upbringing and said her name the way she heard it when she was little, it did something to her insides.

"Hello, Angel." She returned the favor, using the traditional pronunciation of his name, which dropped the soft *G* in favor of an *H* sound. He smiled softly at her.

"To what do I owe this pleasant surprise?" His fingers curved over the door as if he wanted to reach out his long fingers and stroke her arm. She could touch his hand with nobody else seeing if she wanted to. Her trembling fingers remained curled together in her lap.

"I-I've brought you something. I made you a pie. I hope you like pecan pie."

"I'm a good Texas boy, ma'am. I love pecan pie. Matter of fact, I'll bet your pecan pie is about to become my favorite."

She felt warmth spread over her cheeks as she reached for the cardboard box the pie sat in on the passenger seat.

He leaned closer. "Wait. If you hand it to me here, I'll have to share with all these men."

"What should I do? Maybe I should come back later?" She suddenly felt very skittish. More heat rushed over her cheeks, and the butterflies in her stomach took their aerial maneuvers to a new level. Maybe this was a dumb idea and she should've called him first. Yeah, like she could ever have gotten the nerve to call him on the phone.

In a conciliatory tone, he said, "No, no. Would you mind driving on to the foreman's house, down there at the end of this long drive? That's my place. It's all right, sweetheart. Just turn off here and drive down there. Pull in beside my truck, and I'll be there in a minute."

Her eyebrows knitted together in worry, but she nodded, and he backed away to allow her to pull off on the side road. She was grateful for his direction because it effectively shielded her from driving right by the barns where all the ranch hands now gawked.

* * * *

Angel ambled back toward the barn, beating his hat on his jeans. He groaned at the knowing smiles on the ranch hands' faces as he returned to the cavernous structure. No wonder she was so nervous. She'd seen them all watching her.

"What? You've never seen a beautiful woman around here before? Where are your manners, for crying out loud?" he hollered good naturedly to them as they all turned to go back to work. He spouted orders for a few seconds then jumped on a four-wheeler and headed down to the house where she'd just pulled in.

He reached the car in time to open her door for her and held out a hand to help her from the vehicle, noticing her bright blush as she took it. Her slim fingers felt soft in his big, callused palm.

Teresa was dressed for work in a shin-length black skirt, dainty high heels, and a pretty, body-hugging top. When she stepped from the vehicle, the wind caught her skirt and pressed it to her body. He was able to make out her gorgeous curves in the sunlight before the wind died down again.

She was looking around and didn't notice him ogling her, which was probably a good thing. He wouldn't want her to be embarrassed. He did his best to ignore the semi-erect state of his cock and prayed she wouldn't notice, either.

"I made the pie for you last night, so it's cooled off. You might want to put it in the refrigerator. It will probably keep better that way." She sounded a little nervous as she moved around to the other door and unknowingly gave him a glimpse of her cleavage as she bent to retrieve it. His cock decided it was no longer content being ignored. He needed to get himself under control before she caught on to how she affected him and bolted like a scared rabbit.

Instead of taking the pie from her, he waited for her at the steps that led up to the covered deck in front of his ranch-style house and held out his hand to take her elbow. Hesitantly, she allowed him to help her up the steps. He knew she probably hadn't intended for the visit to lead inside his home, but he didn't want her to leave yet.

"Your porch is deep. I'll bet it's nicely shaded in the afternoon," she murmured.

"Yes, it is. I like to sit out here in the evenings." He'd done a lot of that lately by himself.

He opened the front door and hoped his modest home met with her approval. She stepped in and turned to him after looking around with appreciation in her eyes.

"Your home is so neat and tidy." She sounded impressed as she stepped into the kitchen and opened his refrigerator. She began to slide the pie on the top shelf then stopped and turned to him.

"Would you like some now?" She looked in his eyes then blushed and looked down, something she did frequently. He wished so much he could set her at ease. Removing the pie from her hands, he placed it on the kitchen counter and turned to her. Teresa glanced up at him again, looking uncertain, and took half a step back.

"In a moment, yes. I need something else right now." He prayed that he wasn't about to royally screw up as he reached out a careful hand to her cheek. Lightly tracing the delicate structure of her cheekbone, he tucked a stray strand of hair back and noticed the way she swallowed nervously at his touch.

She looked up at him timidly, and he could see her pulse pounding at the base of her throat. Slowly, his fingers slid to cup the back of her head beneath the thick hair that reached past the middle of her back. Teresa had the look of a scared doe and closed her eyes as if afraid when he pressed his mouth gently against her soft lips. He inhaled her floral fragrance as he kissed her for the first time. He kept his kiss chaste so as not to frighten her. She made a sound that was a cross between a whimper and a sigh, and he groaned when she parted her lips for him and allowed him inside. He didn't push her boundaries too far as his tongue caressed hers and barely sought entrance. He continued the kiss and felt triumphant as she relaxed a bit. Her hands slowly slipped around his waist, tentatively seeking his closeness.

* * * *

Teresa was dazed by the feel of his lips against hers. He released her and smiled down at her with tenderness. She had a stray thought that, although he was an unrepentant flirt, he understood that this kiss was not a casual thing for her. She looked up into his eyes, drugged by his kiss, and felt a tiny shudder go through her body as he held her close. His kiss touched every part of her, even her soul. Looking up at him uncertainly, she saw the desire that radiated from his eyes and the smile of appreciation on his wonderfully full lips.

Teresa smiled back at him and rested her head against his chest as his arms enveloped her and pressed her close to him. She smiled to herself when he released a contented-sounding sigh.

"Teresa?"

"Yes, Angel?" She listened to the sound of his racing heartbeat. "Would you have dinner with me sometime? Or would you like to bring Michael out and the three of us could have dinner together here?"

"I could get a babysitter for Michael. I think for now that might be best, if you don't mind."

Ever practical, Teresa didn't want Michael around until she was sure of Angel's intentions. Angel had given her no reason to assume he had anything but honorable intentions toward her and Michael, but she did not want Michael to become attached to Angel until she was sure of where this was going. As a single mom, she had to be careful and had plenty of long, lonely nights to think out what she would do. Until she met Angel, she'd never had any interest in any of the men of Divine. None had attracted her attention the way this lethally handsome man did. Angel nodded and seemed to understand her plight.

"That sounds fine. Could I pick you up on Friday at seven thirty?" At her silent nod, he continued, "Good. I'll look forward to it." He kissed the top of her head, and she heard him inhale as he held her close again. He didn't hold her tightly, but she thought she could feel the hardness of an erection against her abdomen.

Heat stole over her cheeks when her body responded with a rush of dampness to her core, and her nipples hardened into little pebbles. His kiss had affected her just as strongly. She was thankful for the brightly printed top that would camouflage her reaction to him. Taking a bold chance, she tilted her lips up to him, and he hungrily met hers in another bone-melting kiss, teasing her lower lip with the tip of his tongue. It was only the second kiss she'd ever received from a man in her whole life.

Chapter Two

Teresa went through her work day in a daze. She helped customers and tidied displays, distracted by the constant humming in her body. Angel came to mind repeatedly. When she thought of his kiss and the heat of his body when he'd embraced her, her heart would pound again. She had a full work day to get through, and at this rate, she would be thoroughly exhausted by the time the store closed and she could leave.

Today was already Wednesday, so she was lucky she'd been able to arrange for her neighbors' teenage daughter to watch Michael on Friday evening. Marissa loved her two-year-old, Michael, and came over to play with him while Teresa did housework and laundry on the weekends for the fun of it. She was young, only fifteen, but her parents' apartment was right next door, and Teresa trusted them with Michael.

Teresa was sitting on a stool behind one of the gemstone display cases, rearranging and cleaning the interior. The memory of the smile on Angel's face when he realized it was her in the car that afternoon came to mind.

She blotted the sheen of perspiration off her forehead as she rested her elbow on the inside edge of the display case. Somehow she was going to have to survive the next two days of anticipation. Why did she do this to herself? Get so worked up over him? He was just a man. That was probably exactly what Angel would say. He wouldn't have intended for her to become so worked up.

Beyond the lone disaster of the past, she'd never had a real date. Her parents had sheltered her rigorously when she was growing up and raised her with strict, moral standards which she could appreciate. But she sincerely wished her mother would've had some heart-to-heart talks with her over the years to help prepare her for the real world. She missed them both terribly sometimes, despite their old-fashioned ways and faults. She wished she could visit them so they could meet Michael, but that just wasn't possible.

A fresh wave of guilt over leaving them in the care of strangers, in a nursing home, came over her. It was necessary. A clean break and no ties was what she'd needed for both her and her baby. She wondered what Angel would think if she told him the whole sordid tale. She felt more guilt with the knowledge that he'd come completely clean with her about Patricia long before he'd ever asked her out.

She'd heard from Grace that Angel had been interviewed by the police and other investigators regarding Patricia and her general state of mind. The less Teresa was involved with that whole situation, the happier she was. It only increased her respect for Angel that he had esteemed her enough to tell her about his part in the upsetting story.

Teresa remembered Grace's voice, filled with stress and worry as she explained to her on the phone what had happened to Angel, knowing Teresa was interested in him. Teresa knew she needed to fill him in on her past. She hoped he'd appreciate how difficult it would be to share that story with him. She reached in the case and replaced the display boards. She smiled when she heard a familiar female voice behind her.

"Well, isn't that a pretty blush you're sporting, Teresa? You must have a lot on your mind. A little birdie told me you have a date with a certain hotly handsome cowboy," Grace said, snickering. Teresa smiled and hid her hot face in her hands. "Word travels fast on the ranch. Angel told Jack. Did he kiss you? I heard you brought him a pie. Aww, look at that blush, he *did* kiss you didn't he?" she whispered then giggled. Teresa knew the last thing Grace would want to do was embarrass Teresa within the hearing of others. Grace understood her.

"Yes, you bad girl, he did," Teresa said in a barely audible voice.

"Mmm, did you like it?" Grace asked as Teresa stood from the low stool behind the counter. "That's a dumb question. I can tell you did. So he's a good kisser?"

"Wonderful."

"Good. It's about damn time he made a move. Are you looking forward to your date?"

"I'm a nervous wreck."

"What are you going to wear?"

They chatted for a few minutes, and Grace reminded her about her bridesmaid dress fitting the following day. Teresa went back to work, and Grace returned to the embroidery shop.

* * * *

Teresa looked in the mirror nervously and wondered if the outfit she chose was all right. Angel was used to women in tight jeans and revealing tops, with big hair and long, manicured nails. She only owned one pair of jeans, and she didn't think they fit the way Patricia's had. She'd seen Patricia a time or two in the store before her arrest. Teresa remembered her being very thin, wearing a lot of makeup, hair teased and sprayed, almost plastic and fake in her perfection. No, Teresa would keep the dress on. It was feminine and nothing like anything Patricia would have worn. Maybe that was why Angel asked her out because she was nothing like that other woman.

She clasped a necklace around her neck and put on her earrings, checking the clock. It was seven fifteen. Her heart lurched a little. She smiled, hearing Michael giggling with Marissa in the living room of her small apartment. On her salary, it was all she could afford, but it was clean and in a safe neighborhood, which was more important. Her heart jumped again a few minutes later when she heard Angel's big pickup pull into one of the parking spaces outside her building. It was a diesel and hard to miss with the way it rumbled.

She giggled when she heard Michael make a rumbling motor noise while he played on the floor with his trucks. "Truck! Brbrbrbrberb!"

She primped one last time and waited for the doorbell to ring. When it came, she took a deep breath to calm her nerves and walked to the door to open it. There he stood, handsome as could be, with a bouquet of pretty Gerber daisies in one hand and her pie plate in the other, empty and clean.

"Hello, Teresa."

Heat rushed over her cheeks when she noticed him taking her in from head to toe. He was dressed in dark, pressed blue jeans, a white dress shirt, black snakeskin cowboy boots, and a fresh straw cowboy hat which he removed as he entered her home. She welcomed him into the apartment and took the pie plate and flowers from him and felt her cheeks heat again when, once her hands were full, he leaned in and kissed her on the cheek.

"Cowboy! Yee-haw!" Michael yodeled from his spot on the living room floor with Marissa. Teresa smiled at Angel and laughed softly.

"Angel, you remember my son, Michael, and this is my neighbor, Marissa."

Michael had come with her on a brief visit when Angel was still in the hospital. Angel squatted down to Michael and nodded his head at him and smiled. Michael grinned at him and made a pretend gun out of his chubby fingers and pointed it at him and fired, making sound effects. Angel grabbed his chest in mock agony, and Michael laughed outrageously at him. Angel rose up and greeted Marissa politely.

"Thank you for the flowers. They're beautiful."

"You're welcome. The pie was delicious. Your pecan pie is my new favorite."

"Thank you. I'll make it again for you some time. Did you share?"

He shook his head negatively. "No. I ate it all myself."

She smiled when he rubbed his hard, flat belly. He must have burned it off because it sure wasn't stored anywhere on his muscular body.

"Ready to go?" he asked.

She kissed Michael on top of his black curly head and reminded Marissa of his bedtime before they left. He walked her out to his truck, and she hesitated when he opened the passenger door and turned to her. She was wearing a shin-length, flowing dress, and his truck was a little farther off the ground than she could probably manage in it. She hadn't thought of that when dressing.

Turning to him in embarrassment, she said, "Perhaps I should change into slacks?"

Perhaps you shouldn't waste your time on a loser like me.

He shook his head. "You look beautiful. I don't want you to change. Would you allow me?" He held out both hands.

Oh no! He wanted to *lift* her? People would see him trying to lift her! He'd hurt himself, and she'd be *humiliated*! He didn't wait for her assent. He placed her arm around his shoulder and slid his arm around her back. He reached behind her and lifted her under her knees. He smiled at her sudden intake of breath and slight whimper.

"Don't worry, beautiful. I have you safe."

He deposited her in the passenger seat and helped her with the seatbelt. He smiled down at her and grazed a knuckle over her heated cheekbone as she thanked him. He must be very strong because he'd lifted her as if she were as light as a feather. While he walked around the front of the truck, she took a deep breath and exhaled slowly. This was just a date. Just a date, maybe. But it was her first date. She was twenty-seven years old on her first date! He pulled open the driver side door and hopped in, smiling at her before he turned to buckle himself in.

"You okay, sweetheart?"

"I'm fine." She was a *basket case*, thanks to all her helpful self-talk.

He covered her hand with his rough palm. "You sure? I'm sorry if I embarrassed you. I like what you have on, and I didn't want you to go back in and change clothes. I didn't mind lifting you. You're light as a feather."

"I—Well, it, um…you did take me by surprise. I'm sorry. I'm just being silly." She sighed softly and paused before confessing. "I don't date. I'm not used to this."

* * * *

Angel lifted the hand curled in her lap and wrapped his around it. He took a deep breath and let it out slowly. He remembered his conversation with Grace a few weeks before. She'd warned him Teresa did not date, and she'd asked that he not trifle with her. Teresa was not someone he could date casually.

He knew she was feeling nervous and flighty, more so now after he lifted her up into the truck. She probably thought she was too heavy for him to lift. He liked her petite but voluptuous form and wouldn't change a thing about her. He still thought that was a good move, but it definitely took her by surprise. She'd need time to settle now. She'd blushed more for him in the past five minutes than Patricia had in the entire time he'd known her.

"I'd planned on taking you out to O'Reilley's and buying you a steak dinner. We could still do that, if you'd like, but I have another idea. Rudy's is open for supper, and by now his early crowd will have been served. We could go over to his place, have dinner, and talk. It'll be quiet, and nobody will bother us. Would you rather do that?"

He asked because he knew O'Reilley's would be busy right now. They were well known for their excellent food and service, but it was also the place where people went to be seen, and he knew a lot of people in Divine. It was practically guaranteed that people he knew would see him out with a new woman and want to stop at his table and say hello. He wouldn't mind that at all but doubted Teresa wanted to do that on their first date. If he was lucky, this was only the first of many.

Teresa looked up at him and smiled sweetly because she understood what he was offering. He could practically feel the relief rolling off of her in waves.

"We could get dessert and coffee, too, and just talk. I promise not to keep you out late." He hoped that by telling her this he would convey to her that he had not made any assumptions.

She squeezed his hand and replied, "Rudy's sounds wonderful. Thank you, Angel. I'm not sure I'm up to all the excitement at O'Reilley's." Angel remembered the "excitement" Grace had to endure when she was out with Jack, Adam, and him at O'Reilley's the night of the shooting. Her engagement to Jack had been broadcast by a well-meaning friend of his to the entire restaurant and had drawn an unfriendly response from one nosey individual. He understood completely how Teresa would feel being under scrutiny, even if it was friendly. Many of Patricia's friends lived in Divine. He couldn't necessarily guarantee it would be all friendly.

"Then that's what we'll do."

They sat in the corner booth at Rudy's, and true to his prediction, the restaurant was quiet with only a trickle of customers coming and going. When she asked, he told her about his work and how he'd come to know Jack and the others. She told him about Michael and her work. When he asked about where she came from, he could sense her reluctance to talk about her past, and she spoke in broader terms. He backed off to safer topics and gave her a chance to get comfortable again, which she did.

He noticed it was difficult for her to make steady eye contact with him. Angel had always looked upon that as a weakness in someone's character, as if they had something to hide. He didn't feel that was the case with Teresa, and he didn't become impatient with her for being that way. It was one more question whose answer would have to wait until she trusted him more. He'd earn her trust, and then she'd feel comfortable looking into his eyes. Her eyes were a deep chocolate brown, and he was willing to bet they were almost black when she was angry or aroused. Not that he could picture her angry, but he'd love to test his theory with his lips and hands to see if he was right. If he earned her trust, maybe he'd have that chance.

The only facts she parted with were that her parents were elderly and that she was born to them late in life. She was raised by loving but strict old-world parents. That might explain why she habitually averted her eyes.

Blushing, she told him when he asked that she'd never been allowed to date as a teenager. Right about the time she'd looked forward to a little more freedom and possibly attending college, both her parents' health had taken a downturn, and they'd needed her to stay home and help them. This had allowed no time at all for socialization with men her age, and he wondered secretly if maybe they'd preferred it that way so they would always have someone to care for them. If they were as old world as she let on, it would be a natural assumption to make.

When Angel asked about Michael's father, she shut down on him. She hadn't even blushed at the question but had paled a little and changed the subject. Angel got the message and backed off again. He hoped one day she would feel comfortable enough to confide in him, to trust him with whatever it was that weighed so heavily on her that she paled at the thought.

"Michael's father is not in the picture, nor will he ever be." Teresa glanced nervously at her watch. "It's nine. I think it's time I got back home. I have to work in the morning," she said a little tersely.

Whoa, he'd gone and done it. He'd pushed too far. "I'm sorry Teresa. Yes, I—can take you home," he answered contritely.

He slipped from the booth and held out a hand to help her rise from the seat. She took his hand and gracefully rose, making momentary eye contact with him. He wanted to kick himself because he caught a glimpse of pain there. His line of questions must have stirred distressing memories. The last thing he wanted to do was upset her. He didn't release her hand as they walked to the cashier's stand and paid the bill.

They left the restaurant and walked out into the humid Texas heat. The sun had finally set, but the warm air closed in around them like a smothering blanket. He walked her to the passenger door of his truck and opened it then turned to her, smiling wryly. She looked up at him in the twilight, and he noticed it was easier for her to look directly at him in the dim shadows. Once again, he lifted her easily into the passenger seat. She tensed a little but didn't seem like it frightened her as much as the first time. Had she really thought he might drop her?

"I'm sorry I've upset you, sweetheart. I'll admit to being curious whether or not there is a man coming around to visit Michael, someone who has ties to you. I'd never want to purposely upset you, and I can see that I did. Can you forgive me?" The last thing he wanted was for this date to end on a negative note. He might not be able to get her to go out with him again if it did. He also did not want her to fear that he would spend the next date asking her more personal questions.

"There's nothing to forgive, Angel. You have every right to know whether or not Michael's father comes around. He doesn't, and he never will. He is not…part of my life. It's just me and Michael, on our own," she murmured quietly. "I'm not upset with you."

She had not referred to Michael's father as her ex-husband. How had she come to be a single mother in light of her sheltered upbringing and her cloistered young adulthood caring for her parents? It wasn't that her story didn't add up, but there were a lot of blanks left in it. Perhaps she was ashamed of the circumstances, or maybe she had been a victim of abuse. Both things she would have viewed as inappropriate topics for conversation with him on their first date.

He didn't back away and close the door. He stood there, braced against the doorway, his lips hovering inches from her face as he spoke. "I know I've intruded into your personal life asking all these questions. But maybe it would help if you knew why. Besides the obvious answer that I want to know everything there is to know about you, I want to know if another man is in my way."

His words had a noticeable effect on her. In the fading light, her eyes met his. "Oh," she said and looked at him hesitantly when he smiled at her. Her eyelids slid closed when his head dipped down, and his lips brushed hers in a kiss.

* * * *

Teresa's body trembled all over at the gentle touch of his lips on hers. His scent was clean and manly, inducing a warming response in her core. He slid his hand up her forearm, and she shivered as he stroked her lightly, stopping at her inner elbow. She was sorry she'd called an early end to the evening now. She wanted very much to spend more time with Angel. She wanted the butterflies and the nervousness to go away. She felt comfortable out here in the twilight, looking up into his eyes in the dim light, and thought it helped.

He drove her home to her apartment and lifted her down from the seat. "Teresa, will you let me take you out again sometime, or have I made a royal mess of things?"

"Angel, it's my fault. I'm not used to dating and flirting and making small talk. I'm not very good at this."

"You did fine, honey. I'll call you, and we'll get together again soon. I imagine Grace has you busy in your spare time, getting ready for the wedding."

"Yes, there is a lot to do. I'll look forward to hearing from you sometime." She wondered what he would do now.

Would he kiss her? He kissed her before, so it wasn't like she expected him to ask permission. She looked up at him after gathering her purse off the seat. Angel drew her into his arms, and her heart soared at the contact with his tall, hard body. He tilted her chin up with his long fingers and pressed his warm lips to hers. Instinctively, she tilted her head and angled into his kiss. She parted her lips for him, and he stroked her tongue with his, not plundering but seeking to be close to her.

She leaned into him slightly and slid her hands around his waist and up his back, holding on to him as a light wave of dizziness swept over her. Her heart pounded, and the heat coursing through her veins kicked up a notch as the throbbing in her pelvic region grew in intensity. She felt dampness between her thighs and both an aching fullness and a desperate emptiness there inspired by his kiss. He swept his hands down her back, holding her to him. His hands strayed to the tops of her hips, and pressed against him, she could feel the hard ridge at his groin.

Finally, he released her and offered her his hand. In a daze, she took it, and he led her to her apartment door. She removed her house key from her purse and turned to him.

He tilted her chin up to him, kissed her once more, then whispered, "Goodnight, beautiful."

"Goodnight, Angel," she responded breathlessly.

She slipped in and smiled at him still standing there, making sure she got in safely, before he turned and sauntered back to his big truck. After conversing with Marissa for a few minutes, she paid her and watched as she returned to her parents' apartment next door. Teresa leaned back against the front door after closing and locking it and let out a deep breath, willing her heart to slow its pounding rhythm. He called her beautiful.

Chapter Three

Teresa had just delivered Grace's wedding gown, which had been at the dry cleaner's for pressing. Angel had kindly carried the long dress bag in for her. Teresa watched Angel saunter out the backdoor of the Divine Creek Ranch house, the sun glinting off his long, jet-black braid.

What she wouldn't give to run her fingers slowly through those silky strands. Teresa could almost feel his hair against her fingertips. He'd kissed her and nuzzled her throat before saying goodbye. Talk about sensory overload. Who knew such an unassuming spot could be that sensitive to his touch? Tingles raced up and down her spine at the memory of his lips behind her ear.

She found Grace in Jack's bedroom sorting through lists. Teresa plopped down on the end of the bed then hopped up and sat in the upright chair standing by Grace's dresser. Grace grinned and rolled her eyes, not even asking, knowing what Teresa was thinking. That was the bed that Grace shared with her men, and Teresa shouldn't be sitting on it.

Sheesh! Where had her parents gotten all the ideas they raised her with? She huffed rebelliously and bounced right back out of the chair and came and perched next to Grace on the edge of the bed. Grace looked over at her, a surprised smirk on her face.

"Wow. Angel must be a good influence on you. He's really into you, you know that?"

"Huh?"

"Did you hear what he said? He would 'look forward to seeing you come down the aisle'?"

"He said that to me out on the porch earlier, too."

"He said that *twice*? What's on his mind, I wonder?" Grace said knowingly, looking at Teresa. "Are you going to let him teach you to dance, risk-taker?"

"He said he would. I hope I don't step all over his toes."

"Oh, don't worry, Teresa. You have a natural, graceful way of moving. I don't think you'll have any trouble at all. You really like Angel, don't you?"

Teresa sighed and smiled, shivering delightedly at the memory of his lips brushing beneath her ear. "Yes, Grace. I do."

"Does he still make you nervous?"

"Like a long-tailed cat in a rocking-chair factory, but it was better today than it was on our date. Maybe I'm getting used to him?"

"Maybe. He deserves someone sweet like you."

* * * *

Angel stood at the back of the church greeting other guests he knew, waiting to take his seat until the last minute. He greeted Evan and Wesley Garner and Rosemary Piper, whom he knew from Cheaver's Western Store. She was her Uncle Randy's right hand running the big operation. He finally seated himself on the end of a row, next to the aisle. He wanted to have a clear view of Teresa as she came down the aisle.

Movement could be seen through the stained-glass windows on either side of the closed wooden doors. The music changed tempo, and the musicians began to play a slightly different melody. Sunlight streamed through as the doors were swung open again. Everyone turned in their seats expectantly, him included. Haloed by bright sunlight, Teresa stepped into the doorway.

Angel's heart pounded in his chest. He wondered if it could be heard by anyone else, it was so loud in his ears. She blushed, but her were not downcast. She moved forward, and he was glad he'd chosen to wear a sport coat over his dress shirt. It would serve to cover the swelling erection he had when it was time to stand for the bride.

Holding her head high, she took measured, unhurried steps forward. She scanned the crowd until she found him, he noticed, and then her eyes stayed on him until she came abreast of him. He took it as a good sign that she did not avert them, hoping it meant she was growing more comfortable near him.

The silky fabric of her dress caught the fading rays of sunlight as she moved, framing and accentuating the curves of her hips and thighs. The bodice of the dress framed her lush breasts in a way that was pure torture for his hardening cock. His hands and cock twitched as he wished he could touch them.

* * * *

Teresa's heart pounded as she moved through the doorway. She took deep, calming breaths and proceeded slowly down the aisle. She sighed in relief when she found Angel on the end of a row about two-thirds of the way down the center aisle. His golden-brown gaze felt like a caress, and he smiled when their eyes met. Her cheeks tingled in response to the subtle heat in his gaze. The aisle was not very wide, and if she wanted to, she could've touched him as she passed. Teresa kept her hands on her bouquet and proceeded forward, wondering if she'd actually felt his body heat or if it had merely been a trick of her mind.

Moving forward to the head of the aisle, she felt a shiver run from her shoulders, down her spine, over her derrière, and down the backs of her legs and knew he was still gazing at her. She reveled in the sensation, for the first time proud of what a man thought of the way she looked. She wasn't all that surprised as the surging current of desire she now associated with Angel's nearness ran through her core. She climbed the shallow steps and walked to the designated spot and turned to face the congregation and the open doors at the back of the church as Grace's irrepressible sister, Charity, made her way down the aisle next.

Across the altar, Grace's official husband-to-be smiled kindly at her. Jack understood how big a deal it was for her to be standing before people like this. Even under such benign scrutiny, it was a stretch for her. Charity made her way up the steps, giving her a sneaky thumbs-up and a wink before she also turned to face the congregation. The volume of the processional increased slightly, and the wedding guests stood as Charity's husband, Justin, led Grace in her gorgeous gown to the doorway.

She glanced at Grace's men, tears coming to her own eyes at the sight of the undisguised adoration on their faces. She was not surprised when Jack quickly reached up a hand to wipe away a stray tear. Grace was so beautiful she *should* bring tears to their eyes. Teresa wiped her own tears, watching Grace's radiant face as she moved down the aisle on Justin's arm.

Teresa looked out on the congregation and caught the smile Angel directed to her. She smiled back and sent a prayer heavenward that someday she would have love like Grace had for her men and she would no longer let fear rule her life.

After the ceremony, all the well-wishers crowded forward to congratulate Grace and Jack. Teresa was standing with Charity when she felt a warm hand slide around her waist. She knew immediately who it was.

Leaning into her a little, Angel whispered, "Jack asked me to shoot video of the binding ceremony. May I give you a lift over to the mansion?" He took advantage of the opportunity to nuzzle her neck a little with his nose, and she heard him inhale. She didn't realize she'd closed her eyes until she opened them and caught Grace and Charity grinning at her.

"I—um. I don't know. Grace, do you need me for anything? Should I go on over?" She wanted to kick herself. He was a man, she was a grown woman, and she had nothing to be ashamed of if they were attracted to each other.

"It would be a good idea for everyone participating to get over there quickly, so the other guests don't have to wait very long for us. Why don't you go ahead with Angel?" Grace whispered to her.

Teresa let Angel lead her by the hand back up the aisle of the church. Once outside, he turned to look at her as they walked. "Sorry if I embarrassed you back there. You're gorgeous in your gown, and I couldn't resist temptation. I like your hair like that." He fingered a chunky ringlet that fell to her shoulder. Her hair was rolled and finger-styled then pinned up artfully on her head. She wore roses in her hair at the crown that matched the deep red roses of her bouquet.

"You're looking handsome yourself. Thank you for offering me a ride." She smiled up at him.

He drove them to the Victorian mansion and helped her carefully up the back stairs that led straight to the second story. The other specially invited guests arrived, and soon Grace and her men came up the stairs.

Teresa allowed the tears to flow during this much more intimate ceremony, especially when Jack, Ethan, and Adam knelt in turn to pledge themselves to her and Ethan and Adam received the rings. Without drawing any attention to her, Angel pressed his clean white handkerchief into Teresa's hand. She smiled at him gratefully and blotted her cheeks.

Later, during the reception, Grace surprised Teresa with a live floral bouquet. "I wanted you to have this but knew you'd never do battle for it like some of these gals would." Grace hugged her then turned Teresa in Angel's direction and whispered, "Seize the day, baby!" She pushed her in Angel's direction.

Her responsibilities as a bridesmaid were finished, and Grace was releasing her to Angel, that much was clear. Angel smiled broadly when he saw her headed his way, her nose in the bouquet Grace gave her.

"What have you got there, beautiful?" he asked, smirking.

"Grace tells me I won the bouquet toss. Isn't it lovely?" she replied.

He dipped his nose to it and nodded, but his eyes stayed on her. "Let's put it with your purse and my coat at the table, and then I'll make good on those dance lessons."

He led her to the dimmest corner of the dance floor, and without making a big show of it, taught her to two-step and waltz. She took right to it and laughed softly as he spun her into his arms, and they set off around the dance floor with everyone else. He was a graceful dancer and led well, never stepping on her toes even once.

"I heard on the news last night there's going to be a meteor shower visible next weekend. Would you like to drive out away from the lights and watch it with me?"

"That sounds wonderful, Angel. Should I pack us a picnic supper?"

"If you'd like. Make sure to bring a jacket, in case it's windy." He caressed her back as he danced with her, and the warmth of his hands was like a brand through the fabric of her dress.

"I'll look forward to doing that with you." She could feel the powerful muscles of his shoulder under her hand as they continued around the dance floor together. A slow dance began to play, and the lights on the dance floor dimmed a little bit. He wrapped his arm further around her waist, and his masculine scent invaded her nostrils as she rested her cheek against his chest.

"Teresa. I wanted you to know something. You never asked but I—I just wanted you to know."

"Yes, Angel?" She looked up at him in concern. He suddenly seemed unsure of himself, which she'd never seen since meeting him.

"You are the only woman I'm dating. The only one I *want* to date. I'm hope that pleases you and that you feel the same way."

The tables had turned because Teresa felt confident in her next words as she beamed up at him.

"Angel Martinez, are you asking me to be your girlfriend?"

"Yes, that was my amazingly clumsy attempt at asking you to be my girlfriend," he said with a laugh. "So will you?" he asked, his easy smile made her knees want to melt.

"I would love to be your girlfriend."

Chapter Four

Late August

Angel checked his watch as he climbed down from his truck. He was right on time as he walked into Stigall's Department Store. He wandered around until he found her kneeling on the floor in the baby department, restocking a shelf. She was busy sorting packages and didn't hear him sneak up behind her and squat down.

He placed his hands over her eyes and whispered, "Guess who, beautiful?"

She giggled playfully. "Um, Gerard Butler?" At his growl, she giggled again. "John Cusack? Chris O'Donnell? Or, could it be? *The man of my dreams*? My Angel?" she teased, putting her soft fingertips up to his hands as he kissed the top of her head. She looked up at him and smiled happily as he offered her his hand. She tucked the last package into the display and allowed him to lift her to her feet.

"I'm here to take you out to lunch for your birthday, unless you're already expecting Mr. Butler," he teased.

In the last few weeks, the more time they spent together, the more comfortable she became around him, gradually revealing her quick wit and sense of humor. The change he liked best, however, was that she no longer averted her gaze from his as a matter of habit.

Nonchalantly, she waved her hand and said, "Oh, no. Gerard called, he even begged, but I told him he was too late. I'm already taken."

"Yes, you are. I've brought a surprise for you. It's out in the truck. Can you get away for lunch now?"

"Yes, let me get my purse and let Margie know I'm leaving. I'll be right back."

He nuzzled her cheek before kissing it. It made her blush, which he loved about her. She disappeared through the stockroom doors, and he slowly made his way to the front of the store.

"Well, if it isn't Angel Martinez," he heard a seductive voice say as a woman moved up beside him.

He looked down at her in surprise as she reached up and slid a hand down his arm. Chills went up his spine as he recognized Patricia's best friend, Clarissa. He didn't want to be rude to her but backed away several inches. It didn't seem to deter her because she closed the distance between them again.

He kept his tone carefully neutral. "Hello, Clarissa. How are you?"

"Fine, busy with work. I heard about Patricia. Have you talked to her?" she asked, showing either her utter ignorance or stupidity, or both.

"No, Clarissa, not since she *shot* me," he replied flatly, arching an eyebrow.

"Oh, well, no. I guess you wouldn't have, would you?" She rolled her eyes before looking him up and down like a juicy steak she wanted to sink her teeth into. "So, I see you're all better."

"Yes, I've made a full recovery, thank you."

"I was wondering if you were dating anyone. Maybe you'd like to go out. I always had a thing for you."

Just what I always wanted. To go out with my psycho ex-girlfriend's ultrapromiscuous best friend. "As a matter of fact, I am dating someone."

Her smile widened, and the look in her eyes was calculating. Her tongue flicked out and licked her lip. "Oh? Well maybe we could get together sometime, you know? Have a good time?" The seductive way she said it made his gut clench. He frowned darkly at what this young woman suggested and how Teresa would react to the idea. He suppressed a growl as he looked up and saw Teresa approaching. She was close enough by now that if she was listening, she would be able to hear what Clarissa was proposing. The look in Teresa's sweet eyes indicated she heard but didn't understand. Her delicate eyebrows were knit together in dismay as she slid her little hand into his.

"No, Clarissa. What you and Patricia called fun was not something I ever participated in with her or condoned. You have the wrong idea if you think that's something I would want to be involved in. Take care." He led Teresa from the young woman, who blushed angrily as Teresa looked her in the eye. Angel wrapped his arm around her shoulders, and they walked out into the humid August sunshine.

"That was interesting," Teresa ventured carefully.

"That's an understatement. That was a friend of Patricia's. They used to run around together, before…you know." He decided to say as little as possible about Clarissa. If Teresa didn't understand the gist of what Clarissa was offering, he wanted to keep it that way.

Patricia had made many assumptions based on what she knew of his upbringing and had pestered him endlessly about a threesome with Ethan. Her fixation with the notion had taken an obsessive turn when Grace had come into Ethan's life. She completely rejected the idea that there was an intrinsic difference between what Ethan had with Grace, Jack, and Adam and what she wanted from Angel and Ethan. In her mind there was no difference, and he could never persuade her otherwise. Her quest had not ended successfully.

"Yeah." She smiled up at him and patted his hand on her upper arm, and, bless her heart, she changed the subject. "So, what did you bring me?"

"It's a surprise. You'll see it in a minute." He helped her into the truck before he climbed in. "I'm taking you for a nice lunch at O'Reilley's. Is that all right?"

"That sounds wonderful."

He drove them over to the restaurant and parked in the shade of an oak tree. He reached in the glove box and pulled out a square box. Smiling at the surprise in her eyes, he handed the box to her.

"Open it. Tell me what you think." The suspense was killing him. She opened the hinged box and gasped in surprise. He smiled with pleasure.

She removed the large locket from its box. It was sterling silver on a pretty silver chain. The front of the locket was an intricate scrollwork design, and embedded in the center was a vibrant, oval-cut peridot, her birthstone.

"Peridot? How did you find this?"

"I didn't. Clay made it for you."

"Mr. Cook made this for me?"

"Yes, I had him make it for you, beautiful. Happy birthday."

"Thank you, Angel. It's lovely." She handed it to him, and he unclasped the chain and put it around her neck. She lifted it and looked at it. He pushed the catch on the side and showed her the interior of the locket.

"I'm glad you like it, Teresa. It looks beautiful on you." He sighed with satisfaction when she impulsively threw her arms around him.

Unbuckling her seatbelt, Teresa wrapped her arms around his shoulders. She brushed her lips against his, and he pulled her more closely to him. His hand held the back of her head, bracing her for his gentle assault. He could've stayed with her like that for the whole hour, her full breasts pressed to his chest, but then he heard her stomach growl. Their kiss parted with a chuckle from them both.

"Let's get you fed, beautiful. I don't want you starving."

"Not much danger of that. My fat stores will sustain me through a few skipped meals."

"Hmmm. I like you exactly as you are, so don't waste away on my account." His gaze roamed over her curvaceous form before climbing out of the driver side door.

"Sweet talker," she whispered shakily to him as he opened the truck door and lifted her down on account of her dress. They walked hand in hand through the parking lot.

"Just telling the truth."

"Thank you, Angel. I appreciate that."

"Should I tell you what I have planned for tonight? Or should I surprise you?"

"I love your surprises. Do I need a babysitter?"

"No, not tonight, if that's all right."

"That's fine," she replied easily as he pulled open the front door and held it for her.

* * * *

Teresa dressed in her blue jeans and boots and pulled her hair back into a long ponytail. She dressed Michael in his little Wranglers and cowboy boots, which got him all riled up.

"Gonna be a cowboy! Pschew!" He pointed his imaginary six-shooter and fired before hugging his mama's leg. "Mama's a cowgirl!"

Angel gave a soft wolf whistle when she answered the door. He kissed her cheek, and then he squatted down to give his buddy, Michael, a high-five. Michael went right to him, and he lifted him onto his arm.

"You ready, beautiful?"

"I sure am."

"Mama's a cowgirl!"

"She sure is, buddy." Angel gave her a sexy wink over Michael's head.

He drove them out to the Divine Creek Ranch and spent the next hour showing her and Michael around the horse barn. The horses were all huge, and they'd both enjoyed the awe in Michael's eyes when Angel showed him Languir and Esperer. Angel taught Michael how to say their names, but the closest he could come to the proper pronunciation was "Long-ears" and "Air-air."

They smiled at his cackle of joy when he saw the two newly born foals in their stalls with their mamas.

"Hossie babies!" Michael cooed and clapped his chubby little hands together.

They stopped by the office in the first barn, and Angel came back out with Michael still on his arm, wearing a pint-size little straw cowboy hat, just like the one he was wearing.

"Mama, I got hat, jus' like Angel!" He clapped his hands again. "I cowboy!"

"You sure are!" she murmured, chucking him under his chubby little chin. "Thank you, Angel. I hope that wasn't very expensive."

"I'm glad it fits him. I had to guess on the size, and Rosemary helped me out with it. Looks good on him, and it will keep the sun off his head when we take him riding. Are you hungry, honey?"

"*I* hungry! Wanna corndog. You got corndogs, Angel?"

"We'll have to see what they have, buddy. Let's take Mommy out to eat for her birthday."

They both laughed when Michael sang "Happy Birthday to You" at the top of his lungs while Angel helped them back into the truck and drove into Divine for supper.

* * * *

Teresa smiled as she looked at Angel in the dark movie theater. He was watching the movie, and Michael was sound asleep in his lap. It was Michael's first movie theater experience seeing an increasingly rare G-rated movie. He'd loved it but had fallen asleep in Angel's lap halfway through. They watched the whole movie then strapped the sleepy boy into his car seat, and Angel took them home. Michael remained sound asleep while she changed him into his pajamas and tucked him in for the night. Then she joined Angel in the living room.

She took a detour through the kitchen, got glasses, and filled them with ice.

From the living room, Angel said, "Mom called today to see how I've been. She asked about you, also."

"She did?" Teresa asked as she poured him a glass of iced tea. She liked his mother and admired her feistiness. She wondered sometimes what it would be like to be fearless and impetuous.

"Yeah, I think she took a liking to you when they were up here a few months ago. The dads said to tell you hello, too. One of my brothers may be coming out for a visit. He's been thinking about making a permanent change and moving up this direction. Jack's talked to him about coming on full time to help with the breeding operation. I could use the help with the stud service and training Coraggio and Valiente, the new colts. You'd like Joaquin. He's very easygoing."

"Is he a flirt like you?" she asked as she sat down next to him after handing him a glass of tea.

"He's worse if you want to know the truth. Very charming," Angel said with a teasing glint in his eyes. "He and I are a lot alike."

"Uh-oh. Tell me he's married," she said with a giggle then sipped from her tea glass.

"Nope, single and free."

"What will the ladies of Divine do? They'll have another handsome flirt to chase after. You'll be running stray women off from the ranch every day."

"Oh, no. I'm definitely more handsome than him." He chuckled as he nuzzled her throat and pressed his lips to her flesh.

She chortled and said, "I've seen your parents, Angel. They could only make beautiful children." She turned into his kiss and rested in his embrace. He was always free with his affection but never demanding, so she had gradually learned to relax in his arms. He seemed to know where her limits were by instinct and never put her in an uncomfortable position.

"Well, you'll have to see for yourself whether or not you think he's handsome."

"I'd hardly notice with you around, Angel." She snuggled into his chest where her head fit perfectly into the hollow above his strong pec and below his collar bone.

She shuddered lightly as his hand slid over her hair and down her back. She was content just being with him like this, sitting quietly and enjoying each other's touch. There were times, like now, when she sometimes wished for more than a touch.

Angel lifted her chin, and she gazed into his golden eyes. He licked his sensual lips, and a stab of desire traced through her body at the simple gesture that bore just a trace of self-consciousness tonight.

"I love you, Teresa." He smiled at her gasp of pleased surprise and kissed her again. He stroked her throat where her pulse now pounded and pulled her closer for another tender assault. "Yes, honey. I really do love you." His voice was husky with sincerity.

Her lips trembled as he smiled at her, and his eyes twinkled. "I love you too, Angel. I love you so much." She allowed him to pull her closer and kiss her soundly before she added, "This has been a wonderful birthday, the best ever. Thank you."

"You're welcome. I'd better go. I know you have to get up early." When he came over, Angel made a point of never staying late at her apartment.

"I'll talk to you tomorrow, beautiful. Happy birthday."

They kissed goodnight, and he left for the ranch. As she got ready for bed, she could not recall a time in her life when she was this happy. He told her he loved her for the first time tonight. Her heart felt full and contented, and of course, there was always that undercurrent of arousal she now associated with Angel. He never pushed the limits there, which only served to increase her trust in him.

The time never seemed right to tell him about her past. She knew it needed to be soon. She'd never want him to feel like she held something back because she didn't trust him. Maybe she would ask him over tomorrow night for the sole purpose of telling him so she'd stop worrying about it.

* * * *

Early September

Teresa smiled when she looked at the caller ID and pressed "talk." "I was just thinking about a devilishly handsome man."

"I've missed you, beautiful."

Angel's voice made her quiver with longing. She heard his soft sigh and wished she were right there with him. Work had kept them both hopping lately.

"I've missed you, too," she murmured as she sat back down on the couch in the empty break room at Stigall's. "How are things with work? Are you still shorthanded?"

"I hired on two new hands today, both of whom have experience. One of them, a guy by the name of Ash Peterson, is qualified to take on the foreman duties. Jack got to meet him while he was here and agreed. If it works out, I could take on the breeding operation full time. It would make life less complicated. He seems like a real nice guy. We'll have to see if it pans out. How are you doing?"

"The same. I like having the extra hours since Margie got put on bed rest, but it means I won't have much spare time for a while," Teresa said, unable to hide the wistfulness in her tone.

"Is Michael adjusting to your extra hours all right?"

"I think so. He's learned to be flexible at an early age. I miss him most when I'm at work when I'd normally be at home with him," she replied honestly. The extra money would help so much, and the hours were temporary.

"Maybe I'm overstepping my boundaries a bit, but I could help you with him. I could pick him up after I'm done with work, and he could hang out with me, you know? Eat a corndog and watch a movie?" Angel offered carefully.

Teresa paused for a second, closing her eyes, and smiled as she envisioned the two of them hanging out at the foreman's house, playing, talking, and looking at the horses. Angel would have him up in a saddle in no time, she imagined. But Angel's hours had been brutal lately, and he needed his rest as much as she did in order to deal with it all. She'd meant to have a talk with him on Monday night, but he hadn't been able to get away, and she didn't want to have that conversation over the phone. The following morning, Juliana had called her in to see if she'd like to fill in for Margie, who had been put on bed rest by her obstetrician.

"I think that you are the sweetest man I have ever known. I know Michael would enjoy that, but you need your rest in the evenings, and I wouldn't want to put you out. He can be a real handful."

"I'd have the benefit of getting to see you, so you know it's not all one sided. But I understand that's a big step. I want you to remember I'm available for you if you get in a pinch." She felt a little guilty at the disappointment in his voice, but she knew what it was like to deal with the little dynamo on a daily basis.

"Thank you, Angel. I'll remember that. I hope I can see you sometime soon. I need to talk to you about something."

"Do you need me to come over tonight? Do you want to talk about it now?"

"Well, I wanted to talk in person. I'm on a break right now. I'll be at work until at least six o'clock. Maybe call me after then, and let me know if you have the time tonight."

"I'll do that. Is everything all right?"

"Oh, yes. Everything is fine. I just want to talk to you about some things I think you have a right to know about. You deserve to have answers to the questions you were asking on our first date. Nothing is wrong, though."

"All right. Remember, if you need help—Teresa, can you hang on for a minute? That's Grace calling in on the other line. Hold on, sweetheart."

"Sure."

He was only on the other call for a few moments.

"Honey?" The tone of his voice set her on edge immediately. "There's been an accident out on FM 709, at the bridge. Rachel Lopez was involved in a collision. It sounds like she was injured pretty seriously."

"Is there anything I can do to help?"

"I don't know. But I'll call you later, regardless."

"If anyone needs food brought over, I can take care of that."

"I'll ask and see about bringing Eli something to eat and drink tomorrow, since I'm sure he won't leave her. It's nice of you to think of that."

"I don't know Rachel that well, but any friend to Grace is a friend to me. I'd be happy to bring him breakfast and lunch tomorrow if that would help."

"I'll let Grace know. Thanks, sweetheart. You and I will have a chance to sit down and talk soon. I promise. Be safe."

"I love you. I'll pray for them. Be careful."

"I love you, too."

Chapter Five

Teresa rose very early the following morning and got to work in the kitchen. After the carne guisada was simmering, she set about making fresh tortillas. She thought of her mother and remembered when she taught her to make tortillas. Her mother told her it was easy to make them yourself, and they tasted better when the person who made them loved you. Smiling at the memory, she rolled them out one at a time with her little roller pin. She made an extra large batch of carne guisada so she could take some breakfast tacos out to the ranch after stopping in at the hospital to bring Eli his breakfast.

When she spoke with Angel on the phone the night before, he told her Rachel was stable. The doctors were fairly certain Rachel would suffer no lasting damage from the accident, but her injuries were extensive.

Teresa got herself ready and loaded Michael for the trip to his daycare. After kissing him goodbye, she drove to the hospital. She found Eli dozing upright in a chair in the ICU waiting room.

Even in slumber, his handsome features were tense, his stress and exhaustion apparent. His long legs were stretched out in front of him, and his head rested against the wall, propped up on one hand. Teresa imagined he had not been asleep for very long. She sat without disturbing Eli to give him time to rest while he was able to. After fifteen minutes, a door chimed down the hall when someone came through it, and he shifted in his seat, gradually waking up. He looked over at her blearily, and her heart went out to him.

"Eli? I'm Teresa Palacios. I've brought you breakfast tacos and something to drink."

Eli's voice was deep and gravelly as he spoke. "You're a friend of Grace's?" He sat up and rubbed his eyes. "I remember you. You're Angel's girlfriend, right?"

Teresa smiled and said, "Yes, I am." She opened the paper bag she'd placed his breakfast tacos in and held it out to him. She'd put five in the bag for him. Now she was glad she'd packed him extra because he was probably starving. "I made fresh carne guisada this morning."

He smiled and took one from the bag and opened it. He groaned when the succulent aroma of the breakfast taco rose to his nostrils.

"This smells incredible, Ms. Palacios. Thank you so much."

"Call me Teresa, please." She smiled as he took a big bite and groaned then started chewing voraciously. "Good?"

"Uh-huh," he said, taking another big bite. After the third taco, he sat back and sighed deeply. She closed the bag and set it on the table with his coffee and orange juice.

"I'm glad I brought you extras. There are two more in there for a snack later."

"Thank you, Teresa. Those were delicious. Angel is a lucky man. You're a good cook."

"Thank you. I'll be bringing your lunch, too. Do you like barbecue or hamburgers?"

"Wow. I hope you're not inconveniencing yourself too much?"

"Not at all. I know I wouldn't want to leave Angel's side if he was the one in ICU right now. I take my lunch break at one o'clock, and you can expect me a little after that. So which do you prefer?" she asked and grinned when he removed a fourth taco from the bag. He removed his wallet from his back pocket and handed her a twenty dollar bill.

"I'm easy to feed. Get whatever you prefer, but I insist you allow me to pay for it. Let me buy you lunch to thank you?"

"All right, if you insist. Has Rachel awakened yet? Have they allowed you to see her?"

"No and yes. She had internal injuries and bleeding. It was touch and go for a while yesterday afternoon but they tell me she'll recover. It will just take time."

"I'll keep praying for a speedy recovery. Is there anything I can get for you? I can bring whatever you need at lunchtime."

"No, I'm fine. Thank you again for the tacos."

"You're welcome, Eli. I have to make a big taco delivery to Angel and his hands at the ranch, so I'm going to leave now. This is my phone number," she said, handing him a slip of paper. "If you need anything else, let me know."

"Thank you, Teresa." He smiled tiredly at her as she rose from the chair.

She placed a hand over his and said, "God bless you, Eli. Try and rest some more, if you can."

* * * *

Teresa parked by the first barn at the ranch and lifted the picnic cooler from her backseat. She was swamped by giddiness when she looked up and saw Angel's lean frame striding toward her. *He is really something else.* She sighed longingly and enjoyed the sight of him. When he got close enough, her cheeks throbbed with sudden heat at seeing the outline of his hardening erection through the worn denim of his blue jeans and bit her lip.

"You keep looking at me that way, beautiful, and *everyone* will know what is on my mind." He took the cooler and set it down then wrapped his long arms around her and hugged her close. She giggled and allowed him to kiss her.

"I brought you breakfast tacos."

"You did?" he said in surprise. Angel had already discovered that Teresa liked to cook and eagerly lifted the cooler with one hand and put the other arm around her. "Jack and Ethan are in the barn, and I'm sure they'd like to say hello. Why don't you come on in with me for a minute?"

"Are you sure? I know you're busy. I don't want to distract you from your work."

"You're a sweet distraction and a welcome one. This cooler feels full. How many did you bring?"

"Enough for hungry working men," she replied as she allowed him to lead her to the barn. "I wasn't sure how many to make for all of you so I made a bunch. I just came from the hospital."

"How's Rachel?"

"She's in the ICU. It sounds like she'll be resting there for the day, and then they'll know more tomorrow when she wakes up."

"How's Eli?"

"Tired and hungry."

"I wouldn't want to imagine how it must be for him." He leaned to her and kissed the top of her head.

"I do, a little. I didn't know you well when you were shot, but I remember how I felt when Grace told me about it. I remember what it was like when I came to see you."

Teresa had felt terrified the first time she'd walked into his hospital room. He hadn't looked like himself at all, but she'd felt so relieved that he was alive. So relieved.

"You worried about me?"

"Seeing a big, strong man like you hooked up to IVs and monitors and lying in a hospital bed was scary."

"I enjoyed your visits so much. I understand now what a big stretch it must have been for you to come to the hospital, to take that step."

"I was afraid you would be amused by such a shy little mouse coming to visit you."

Angel chuckled at her description of herself. "Hmmm, a shy little mouse? Is that how you saw yourself? I remember thinking you were an angel, coming to me like that."

"Wow. You are such a smooth talker." She giggled as his hand slid possessively around her hip.

"I'm being completely honest." He hugged her to him and kissed the top of her head again as they entered the cool shadows of the barn door.

* * * *

Early December

Angel patted his couch, and Teresa sat down with him and looked into his light brown eyes. He still seemed a bit concerned about her going out with the girls for Rachel's surprise bachelorette party.

"You're sure you want to go tonight?"

Teresa smiled at him reassuringly. "I do, Angel. Rachel is my friend, and I want to celebrate with her. Adam said he'd get me a seat right behind him, so that I wouldn't need to worry about the dancers touching me. I think it will be fun, and I'll stick close to him. What about you?"

"I was worried you might be jealous of me going to a strip club, sweetheart. It would be understandable."

"I don't mind if you want one of the girls to dance for you, Angel. I know you're not going to do anything…physical with any of them," she said. Adam had also told her that the club they were visiting had a strict hands-off policy. If the men touched the dancers, they were ejected from the club.

"I appreciate your trust, but…" It was rare for Angel to be at a loss for words.

"But what?"

He lifted one of her hands to his lips and kissed her fingertips. The simple gesture garnered a big response. His lips left a slightly damp trail of kisses over each pad of her fingertips. Her inner core blossomed with heat. "I want a lap dance from only one woman. Any other would feel a little like cheating." He lowered her hands and grinned sheepishly when she gasped at what he was insinuating. "I hope I didn't offend you."

Her heart raced at the thought. She looked up into his eyes and saw the heat and desire there. "You're *imagining* me doing that with you right now, aren't you?" She surprised herself by giggling. How did one "give" a lap dance?

"Well, I am a man. And I am in love with you. It only seems natural, sweetheart."

Her core melted at his open honesty. She kissed him again. "I can't believe I'm able to talk to you about such things and not go up in flames or rush from the room in embarrassment."

"I like that you feel more at ease with me, and you can look into my eyes more comfortably now than before. You were raised with quite a few burdens placed on you, and then the hand life dealt you couldn't have made it any easier."

She'd come out to the ranch a couple of nights before, after leaving Michael with Marissa for the evening, and showed up at his door a little agitated. He'd just gotten out of the shower after a long day. He'd answered the door in nothing but a pair of blue jeans, his hair still dripping, towel in hand. She'd told him that continuing their relationship without him knowing about her past was verging on dishonesty. He'd welcomed her in and told her he would accept whatever she had to tell him about her past, but that it wouldn't change how he saw her.

"I'm sorry for not confiding in you sooner. I was afraid to tell you everything at first. I think I had begun to believe what people told me back home, that I had done something to bring it on myself. Once I realized I could trust you and that you wouldn't judge me like that, it never seemed the right time. Then other times we had Michael with us, and I couldn't tell you with him around because he understands more than he lets on. Then work got so hectic with all those extra hours for both of us and Rachel's accident and planning Rachel's wedding, it was just never the right time."

Chapter Six

The story Teresa had told him hadn't shocked Angel, but it had made his heart ache for her. Given her previously skittish nature, especially around men, Angel had begun to understand that the events surrounding Michael's presence in her life were probably painful and traumatic for her. He understood now why she was as shy and nervous around him as she had been at first.

Her father had hired a home renovation contractor, Ranulfo Ferraro, to install a wheelchair ramp on their front porch because her mother had been confined to her wheelchair. As it had turned out, Ranulfo's parents had been old friends of her parents, and they'd known each other well before either couple had children. He'd asked Teresa out several times and had even spoken with her father about it. Her father had given his approval, and she'd had lunch with him one time. She'd told Angel that Ranulfo had been nice enough, if a little pushy and macho. He'd wanted to kiss her and to go out with her in the evening alone to his place to watch a movie. Even as sheltered as she'd been, she'd known better than to do that.

He'd told her he loved her long hair and would run his fingers through it, which she didn't care for at all. The way he'd done it had made her feel tethered. Ranulfo had become more persistent about her going out with him, and she'd found herself making excuses. He'd moved too quickly for her, and she'd told him so. The construction project had dragged on, and she'd wondered if he was allowing it to take longer on account of her. Late one afternoon, she'd just refused his most recent invitation to a date and had told him she simply wasn't able to see him anymore. He'd accepted her decision, though she knew she'd angered him. Two days later, the ramp had been completed. He'd called several times, asking if she was seeing someone else. Finally, she'd told her father that Ranulfo's pursuit of her bordered on stalking. Her father had called Ranulfo's parents in the hope they might be able to talk him into leaving her alone. They'd seemed offended but had said they would speak with their son. The call hadn't had the desired effect.

Mr. Palacios had taken Mrs. Palacios to bingo every Tuesday night in Tillman. Because of her declining health, it had been her only social outlet besides church. Teresa's elderly father had his own health issues, as well, and it wouldn't be too many years before they would need full-time care. It had worried her because she'd hoped to go to nursing school the following year. Fifteen minutes after her parents drove away, the doorbell rang. She'd answered it, realizing too late it was Ranulfo. He'd looked sad and ashamed, and he'd begun to apologize. She'd felt bad for him and had accepted his seemingly heartfelt apology.

It had been very hot outside, and she'd foolishly invited him in for a glass of iced tea. She'd brought them both glasses of iced tea, and he'd asked if she had an aspirin because he had a terrible headache. She'd returned with it, and he'd thanked her kindly and took it. He'd apologized again and seemed so sincere. Uneasy with his repeated apologies, she'd sipped her glass of tea and had waited for him to wind down so she could end the conversation and ease him out the door.

In telling the story, Teresa had gone quiet for a few seconds, seeming to gather the nerve to tell Angel what had happened next. Angel had done his best to be a quiet, comforting presence sitting next to her, not asking her a lot of questions. He'd already surmised what came next.

She'd told him her memories were blurry, as she'd recalled for him, watching Ranulfo smile wolfishly and take the tea glass from her slackening hand.

She'd returned to consciousness some time later in terror and horrible pain. At first she'd been so scared she couldn't even move, but eventually she'd called out, and no one had answered.

Teresa had sat up, shocked by her nudity and in searing pain. She'd looked down and had seen blood smeared over her thighs and between her legs. Her breasts had ached and so had her right shoulder. She'd pulled the top sheet from her bed, shocked when she saw more blood smeared on the pink sheets of her bed. When she'd been able, she'd stumbled painfully to the bathroom and screamed when she'd seen her reflection in the mirror. Her breasts were covered with bruises, her nipples were raw, and she'd seen teeth marks. She'd also discovered a painful bite mark on her right shoulder where his teeth had left a perfect imprint where they'd broken the skin.

Her next words further stoked the fury inside Angel. She'd blushed and looked right into his eyes when she'd said them, which humbled him because he knew how hard it must have been for her to tell this story. "He raped me on the bed I'd slept in every night since I was a little girl. I was a virgin…and he raped me."

She'd stayed in a hot shower until the scalding water had finally run cold. Because her parents had never allowed her to be exposed to programs or information that dealt with traumatic topics, she didn't know that was the worst thing to do in case of rape. Her sobbing efforts to erase his painful assault washed away all the evidence of his attack.

Scared and afraid of frightening her mother into another heart attack, she kept the assault to herself and prayed for guidance in what to do. She'd contacted a friend from school who was now a sheriff's deputy under the guise of having questions about neighborhood children playing in the drainage tunnels near her parent's home. He'd paid a visit the following afternoon. When she would have brought up the subject of what to do about Ranulfo, her father had come outside and gotten involved with the conversation about the drainage tunnels.

She'd never been able to ask him but had a feeling Allen knew she'd wanted to talk to him about something else. Realizing her father would not leave her alone, a single woman talking to a single man, she'd finally taken the card Allen had offered. He'd written a private cell number on the back of it along with a short note, *Call me if you need me, Teresa*, and then he'd bid Mr. Palacios and her a good evening. Pocketing the card, she'd reassured her father when he'd mentioned her unusually quiet demeanor of the last couple of days.

At the grocery store one afternoon, she'd run into Allen. He'd greeted her, discreetly asking her is everything was all right with the drainage tunnels, arching an eyebrow at the reference so she would know he understood there was some other underlying reason she'd called him. She'd wanted to tell him what had happened to her, but she'd come to realize she had no real evidence.

He'd intuitively asked her about Ranulfo and if she had dated him. She'd gripped the handle of her shopping cart with white knuckles. Allen had caught on, even though she hadn't answered any of his questions, and he'd reminded her he was there if she needed him and would she *please* call him when she was ready. She'd nodded, and he'd reluctantly backed off.

Six weeks after the attack, feeling fatigued and suffering from violent nausea, she'd made a visit to their family practitioner only to discover she was pregnant. She'd been confident her doctor had upheld his obligation where her confidentiality was concerned, but someone else who worked in his office leaked the information. Overnight the whole town knew she was a single expectant mother with no father in sight.

The final straw had come the night Ranulfo's mother had called, offering to buy the baby. She'd told Teresa once it was born she'd pay cash for it whether it was a boy or a girl. Mrs. Ferraro had hinted insultingly that she would know whether or not it was really Ranulfo's baby with one look at it. When Teresa had recovered from the shock of the woman's offer, she'd vehemently refused to consider it and had told the woman neither she nor her baby would have anything to do with Ranulfo and his family. Ranulfo's mother had gone on to insinuate that Teresa might not have a choice in that matter and that it was always possible she might find herself declared an unfit mother. In which case the child's paternal grandparents would of course step up and do the "right thing" and claim the poor, unfortunate baby.

The thought of that woman raising her child in the same way she'd raised his father horrified Teresa. She'd been certain that she'd made a monumental error in not contacting the police the night of the first attack. She'd been naïve and ignorant in her response to the attack because she would have had all the evidence she needed. Now she had the end result of the attack to deal with. What mattered now was that she'd had to get away from Tillman. Angel had understood why she'd never gone home for a visit.

She and her parents had a long, painful conversation at the dining room table that same night. Teresa had told them she was leaving and where she would go. She'd had a good friend from school who had moved to Divine, which was three hours away. Juliana had talked with her recently and offered her a job at the store she managed, if she ever needed one. Teresa had called her before sitting down with her parents, and Juliana had offered her a place to stay, as well, after she shared the circumstances with her. Juliana had promised she would not tell anyone she knew in Tillman that Teresa would be coming to stay with her.

Her parents had tearfully promised they would not reveal her whereabouts to anyone. Teresa had contacted an old friend of her mother's whom she'd known all her life and could trust. Teresa would need an alternate way to communicate with her parents besides the usual means. She'd called Allen and told him she was expecting and that she was leaving. Teresa had given him her address and new cell phone number. She'd told Angel that she would never forget how sad he'd sounded at her news.

She'd packed that night then loaded her car with her belongings and left Tillman before the sun had even risen. Juliana had welcomed her with open arms and allowed her to stay until she'd found a small apartment that would be affordable and safe for her and the baby once it arrived. Teresa could never find it in her heart to blame the baby for the radical changes that had been thrust upon her. It wasn't the baby's fault that the one who made him had no conscience or heart, nor that she had been assaulted.

She'd fit in well at Stigall's Department Store. At first it had been hard talking to strangers, but need was a powerful motivator, and before long, she'd begun to feel like she fit in Divine. Teresa made a good friend in Grace Stuart who was a kindred spirit of sorts with her own set of domestic challenges in the form of a good-for-nothing, live-in boyfriend. As if to make up for all the pain she suffered at his father's hands, Michael's birth and infancy were joyous events.

"Do you hear from your parents often?"

"Yes, my father calls me from their nursing home on a monthly basis. He and my mother share a room. Her health is not good, and her mind has begun to wander a lot. I hear from Delores on a regular basis, and Allen still checks on me every so often. He told me Ranulfo is in trouble right now for contracting and taking payment for jobs he never finished and with the IRS for getting creative with his tax returns. This is one situation his parents' money may not be able to get him out of. So, that's my story."

He'd held her that evening and smiled as she'd told him she felt like a ton of bricks had been lifted off her shoulders. She'd said in the long run she'd gotten the only redeemable thing out of the whole ordeal in the form of her precious little son. Michael was the spitting image of Teresa's father and looked nothing at all like the man who had brutalized her.

Bringing them back to the present, Angel said, "We're going to have a good time tonight. Later you and I can dance once we return to The Pony if you'd like."

"I'd love to. I was wondering if we could do that. I wanted to spend time with you, too. Not just go our separate ways for most of the evening."

"We won't be at the clubs that late. It's Saturday night, so we can do whatever you want to, beautiful."

Chapter Seven

Late December

Teresa sat cross-legged on the area rug in the little living room of her apartment, wrapping presents for Christmas, which was just two days away. Her hours were long and very busy ones, but even more so this Christmas season while she was covering for Margie's bed rest and maternity leave, which had segued right into the busy Christmas season. With the extra income, she had been able to build up her savings account. It had also made Christmas not quite so stressful for her in the gift-buying department. She wrapped a new straw cowboy hat she'd splurged on for Angel, enlisting Grace and Rosemary's help to find out what size he wore and what style he preferred.

She smiled tenderly, her hands stilling on the box after laying it on the large sheet of wrapping paper. She'd taken the hat out to look at it the evening she'd brought it home. Michael had wandered into the room and asked, "Is that Daddy's hat?" She'd made some comment about it being for someone else to throw him off the trail, knowing he'd tell Angel the moment he saw him, guileless toddler that he was. But his innocent little words kept ringing in her ears.

That was the first time Michael had referred to Angel as "Daddy," but Teresa was honestly surprised he hadn't said it before now. Angel had helped her out several times, caring for Michael when she'd been asked if she could stay late to help during busy evening hours and once when her daycare provider had gotten sick. Michael would tell her all about riding the "horsies" when she picked him up. Angel told her Michael was turning in to a good little rider.

Angel had been busy around the ranch, working with other horse owners who brought their mares for breeding. He was never too busy, however, when she needed his help. Grace told her on the occasions when she saw Michael with him that Michael was usually riding on Angel's shoulders or getting piggybacked, even when other horse owners were around. Thinking of the loving care he showed her son made her heart bloom with tenderness for this man.

Angel had asked her the week before what her plans were for Christmas morning. After ascertaining that she hadn't made plans, beyond watching Michael open his Christmas presents, he'd asked her if she would spend Christmas morning with him. She'd been surprised, but she'd happily agreed. She had assumed Angel would probably want to spend it with his brother who would arrive sometime soon or possibly go home to spend the day with his parents and siblings. Honestly, she couldn't think of any place she'd rather be Christmas morning than with the two most important men in her life.

Teresa tidied up and got herself ready for bed. Angel had asked if he could have Michael during the day on Christmas Eve. He had the whole day planned for the two of them while she went to work on the wildest shopping day of the year. Their plans included having supper ready for her when she got off work the following evening. She fell asleep looking forward to seeing Angel in the morning.

Teresa woke early and got ready while she listened to holiday music on her stereo. Michael chattered excitedly while they ate breakfast about getting to go with Angel for the day.

At one point, he got a little serious, and then he asked, "Mama? Is Angel my daddy?"

She was standing at the sink, rinsing her cereal bowl. She paused then shook her head. "No, honey. Angel is Mommy and Michael's good friend." No, Angel wasn't Michael's father, but he was the kind of father she would have wished for. She attributed it to the sentimentality of the season and missing her parents when tears filled her eyes and a large lump formed in her throat. Her heart pounded a little at the thought that this was the question on his mind, right before Angel picked him up and spent the whole day with him. She hoped he didn't put Angel on the spot, asking him more questions along that same line.

"Mama cryin'?" Michael asked softly, sympathetically. She smiled, noticing that he had developed Angel's habit of sometimes dropping the "g" at the end of words.

"No, I'm fine. Mama just loves you so much." She got up from the table and kissed the top of his head and allowed him to pat her cheek before nibbling his neck and making him giggle. A few minutes later, he came screeching from his bedroom when he heard Angel's big dually pickup truck outside.

Angel took one look at her face when she opened the door and smiled when she immediately went into his arms for a hug and Michael tugged on his leg and babbled.

"What's the matter, beautiful?" he whispered in her ear. She could hear the concern in his voice. The lump reformed in her throat, and she shook her head. Teresa gathered Michael's backpack and cowboy hat, and Angel lifted Michael up onto his arm to carry him out to the truck. Michael loved being outside when Angel's diesel truck was running.

"Berbbbbbbbbb!"

Teresa held Michael while Angel installed his car seat, and then he buckled the little boy in. After handing him his hat, Angel closed the truck door and turned to her. She'd had a minute or two to compose herself and will the lump trying to reform in her throat into submission. "Are you all right?" He brushed away a wisp of hair the chilly wind blew in her face.

"I'm fine, Angel. Just feeling sentimental, you know? Michael is so excited about spending the day with you. Thank you for taking care of him for me."

"We men are going to have a good time." Then focusing the attention back on her, he murmured, "You looked sad when you answered the door. What's wrong, sweetheart?"

It was difficult to speak through the thick huskiness that formed in her throat as she battled tears. "Nothing is wrong, Angel. I feel…very blessed," she said as her lips trembled, "like my cup is running over. It got to me, I guess."

"All right," he replied, smiling down at her with a look of understanding in his eyes. "Don't bother packing a lunch because me and the little man are going to bring your lunch up to the store. I know you only get a few minutes because of the rush, so we'll stop by with it then you can eat whenever time allows."

"You are the most thoughtful man I've ever known, Angel."

Angel smiled flirtatiously. "Wait until you meet Joaquin."

"Is he coming today?" They still hadn't heard for sure when he was planning to arrive.

"When I talked to him this morning, he said he was tied up. When he calls later today, I'll have a better idea of what time he'll arrive. He tends to be more spontaneous. I should know something by the time you get off of work. Now, you don't work too hard today." He wrapped his arms around her and leaned down to kiss her.

They both laughed when they heard a loud squeal from inside the cab of the diesel. He released her and opened the driver door.

"What's all the ruckus in here for, boy?"

"Mama kissin' Daddy!"

Teresa's hands flew to her mouth in utter mortification. Angel roared with laughter then gathered her into his arms, flaming cheeks and all, and kissed her again for good measure.

"Angel, I swear I didn't teach him that or encourage him to say it!"

He laughed softly, the sound resonating in her ears like a reassuring caress. "I know. He's been calling me Daddy for at least a month when we're together at the ranch."

"He asked if you were his daddy this morning. I think he sees other daddies picking up their kids from daycare and wondered where you fit into our lives."

Angel nodded in understanding, filling her heart with relief. "Out of the blue one day last month, while I had him on one of the mares, he called me Daddy. I saw no reason to correct him or confuse him further, so I let him. Don't worry, sweetheart. It doesn't bother me." He tilted her head up for one final kiss. "I know you need to get to work. I'll see you around eleven with lunch, all right?"

"All right. Thank you, Angel. It will give me something to look forward to in my hectic day." She backed away when he closed the door and buckled up then backed out of the parking spot and drove away.

* * * *

"Mama sad?" Angel asked as he tuned the radio to a country station then glanced back at Michael in the middle of the backseat.

"Yeah. Mommy *looooves* Angel. Kissing is *yucky*!"

"Naw, not when you love someone like I love your mommy. Ready to run errands?"

"Running errins? Gonna go get Mama's ring?"

"Yeah, but you're gonna keep the secret, right?"

"I not telling! Angel gonna be my Daddy!" he screeched at the top of his lungs and clapped his hands. Angel smiled at him in the rearview mirror and fought the lump that was growing in his throat. That's what the expression on her pretty face was about. Michael must have dropped a hint, and it was on her mind when she answered the door. He smiled, knowing the time had finally arrived.

* * * *

"Pretty Mama, you planning on untying me sometime today?" Joaquin drawled, feeling way too comfortable tied to the woman's bed. She returned to the bedroom totally nude, brushing out her long, wavy blonde hair. His naked hips flexed lustfully as he watched her full, pink-tipped breasts sway slightly with her movements.

"Mmm. Maybe I want to keep you under my thumb as long as I can, cowboy," she murmured sexily as she admired her handiwork with the ropes.

Joaquin growled hungrily and stretched his shoulders. "Well, if you're gonna keep me here like this, you might as well put me to good use." He gazed at her through half-shuttered eyelids. His lazy smile was an invitation for her to mount up on the cock that was rock hard and begging for attention from between his thighs.

She giggled as she slowly climbed onto the bed and prowled over him like a jungle cat. "Cowboy, I sure do like this big, thick cock." Lifting his heavy shaft from his abdomen, she stroked him, her little hand unable to wrap around his entire girth. "Someday you're going to make a woman real happy with this beautiful monster of yours." She licked her lips and smiled. He groaned as her lips descended over his cock in a slow up-and-down sucking motion, engulfing him in her moist, hot mouth. He pulled against the soft ropes that were tied securely around his wrists and ankles and thrust upward into her mouth, groaning.

He'd met her in El Paso the day before. They'd gone out that night and had a good time then came back to her hotel room and had an even better time. They both had to head out that morning. He was expected at his brother's place later that day, and her family was expecting her back in time for Christmas in Colorado, which meant she was going to need to leave soon. Even then she'd have to haul ass and hope for good weather.

She'd told him she didn't normally hook up with strangers but wanted to enjoy herself a little while she was away from home, and she felt attracted to him. Joaquin had assured her the attraction was mutual, and she'd said she was clean and always used condoms.

Joaquin had been perfectly willing to saddle up for an adventure, and they'd shared a few exciting memories last night. He figured they had time for one more before she hit the road in her fire-engine red dually pickup and horse trailer. His truck and trailer waited outside parked next to hers.

She straddled his hips and held his cock, sheathed in an extra large condom, and slid down onto him. He laid there and enjoyed the view as he thrust into her slick pussy. Her eyes glittered with pleasure as she rode his cock in sinuous strokes to an orgasm that left her panting with ecstasy. She kept up the rhythm for him and pumped him to a growling orgasm.

Afterward, she reached over and untied the knots, one handed. She allowed him to kiss her before he got up to lose the condom and take a shower. He appreciated that she didn't try to make small talk, nor did she become clingy or sentimental. She jumped in the shower after he was finished and then got ready while he checked on their horses.

When she was ready and the hotel room was cleared out she said, "Well, cowboy. Maybe I'll see you again sometime. You're always welcome in my bed if we cross paths again." She leaned in to kiss him but made no move to hold him or hug him. It was just too intimate now.

"You drive safe, darlin', all right?"

"You bet. You, too."

He appreciated the clean break. No promises or requests to call. She called him cowboy, he called her darlin', they never exchanged phone numbers, and he had no idea where in Colorado her ranch was.

Joaquin climbed into his truck and headed southeast to Divine. His tumbleweed lifestyle was uppermost in his mind on the lonesome drive. His pretty face and easygoing, flirtatious manner got him all the free pussy he wanted on the circuit, but he had grown weary of living out of a horse trailer and a duffel bag, even if the lifestyle did have its perks. He hadn't seen Angel in a couple of years and looked forward to stopping for a while, see if any roots took hold in Divine.

* * * *

"Purty, purty," Michael whispered in awe when Angel opened the small, leather-covered box and showed him the pretty platinum and diamond engagement ring and wedding band he planned to propose to Teresa with the following morning. Michael sat comfortably in the crook of his left arm and reached out a chubby little hand to touch the rings. "Mama loves you. You be my Dad. Everybody's happy!" he crowed enthusiastically. Clay and the other female showroom employee grinned at the little boy's happiness.

"Proposing tomorrow?" Clay asked him in a deep Texas drawl.

"Yep. Lord willing, she'll say yes." Angel handed him his debit card. He'd been saving for that ring for a while and hoped she would like it.

"Ride the horsies now?"

"In a little while. Let's go see Rosie and get Uncle Joaquin a little something."

"Yeah! Go see Rosie! Wah-keen needs a cowboy hat, too?" Then he very dramatically clapped his hand over his mouth.

"Uh-oh, kid. I think you let the cat out of the bag, didn't you?" Angel chuckled at the look of consternation on the boy's face. He was too smart for his own good. He put his chubby little hand over Angel's mouth and put his other index finger to his lips and said, "Shh! I in *big* trouble now."

Angel and Clay both had to fight laughter when Michael not so subtly changed the subject. "Then we go see Gracie?"

"Sure. We can stop in if you want to."

"Good. We go see Rosie and 'Dette now?"

"Yes, Rosie and Bernadette can help us out. So you think he needs a hat, huh?" Angel asked as he waved to Clay and his sales clerk and strode out the front door into the mild December chill.

At Cheaver's, they found a nice, black felt Stetson for Joaquin. Angel set Michael down for a moment and whispered to Rosemary to wrap up a set of spurs and authentic leather chaps for itty-bitty boys they had on display, for Michael.

"Anything else we can't live without, Rosemary?"

"Well, now that *you* mention it. Let me show you something that I happen to know Teresa likes. Come with me."

Angel smiled, knowing he'd asked for it.

Rosemary led him to another rack and lifted a top from the rack in her size and said, "This would be gorgeous on her with her long black hair and dark brown eyes. I know she liked it but wouldn't buy it for herself because it wasn't on sale. It will go perfectly with the skirt she purchased."

He smiled and nodded. "And of course, there's a necklace or some other trinket that is perfect with it also, yes?"

Rosemary's eyes twinkled with merriment. "I like how you think, Angel. Of course, I have just the thing. It's right over here." She happily led the way to the jewelry counter. When Rosemary finally let them out of the store, Angel was loaded down with the Stetson, Teresa's blouse, a pretty necklace and earrings set done in shimmering onyx stones, and the chaps and spurs. He reminded Michael that secrecy was absolutely necessary for the Christmas gifts he'd found for Teresa, and Michael promised happily.

They stopped in at Rudy's to pick up lunch for Teresa, ordering her favorite food, and then drove over to Stigall's. The parking lot was full to bursting, and they wound up parking at the curb on Main Street. Michael grabbed his cowboy hat and popped it on his head, imitating Angel. Angel carefully lifted the container with her food in it and held Michael's hand as they walked across the parking lot and approached the glass doors. Angel caught their reflection in the glass.

Michael walked beside him like a miniature version of himself, his little chubby hand held securely to his own, and it wrenched his heart when he thought of how much he wanted that boy to be his own and call him Daddy, for real, for *good*.

Angel sauntered through the store with Michael walking just like him by his side. Teresa was floating today, working wherever she was needed. Angel found her tidying up the dressing rooms in the menswear department, one arm loaded with clothing.

When he spotted her, Angel released Michael's hand, and he ran to her. "Mommy! We bring-ded you some lunch! Your favorite!"

"You bring-ded me lunch, huh?" She squatted down to give him a hug then stood to hug Angel. Her face glowed when she smiled up at him. It was all he could do not to take her in his arms right on the spot and lay a hot, wet kiss on her in front of the whole store. Then he remembered this was the spot where they had been introduced to each other the previous spring by Grace, back when she worked there on the weekends. Dang, but he was sappy today.

"There are beef fajitas, fresh tortillas, extra guacamole, and pico de gallo in the bag. We also brought you a sweet tea. You look like you're busy, so we won't stay long."

"Angel, thank you so much for doing this for me. It's a real treat on a crazy day. I'll look forward to it and be thinking of you. What are you going to do now?"

"Well, we have presents to wrap, and Michael wants to stop in and say hello to Grace. I thought I'd let him take a little nap after lunch and then take him for a ride with me this afternoon."

"Don't need no nap. I'm good to go," Michael said reasonably, giving Angel a thumbs-up, then yawned hugely.

"Uh-huh," Angel replied, smiling, "you want to ride horses with me, buddy, you'll take a little rest first. I don't want you worn out when your mama gets home. She doesn't want you to be a cranky boy, you know?"

"Uh-huh." Michael said with his little lip stuck out as he held out his arms for Angel to lift him up.

"Wow, you must have had a busy morning, if he's this subdued already."

"We had a few errands to run." He grinned at her curiosity. "We also had last-minute shopping to do. I needed to get something for Joaquin for Christmas."

After saying goodbye, he leaned in and kissed her cheek then let Michael do the same. He glanced back at her as he walked with Michael to the main entrance, and her cheeks flamed adorably when he caught her ogling him.

Chapter Eight

Angel was on horseback with Michael riding in front of him when his cell phone vibrated in his pocket. He smiled when he saw the caller ID.

"Hey! I was beginning to wonder what had happened to you."

"Oh yeah? Remember how I told you I was…tied up in El Paso?" Joaquin chuckled suggestively.

"Too much information, little brother. Are you on your way?"

"Yeah, I just stopped in San Angelo to gas up and get a bite. I should be there right after supper time."

Angel shifted the reins and placed his forearm protectively in front of Michael as he squirmed in Angel's lap. "Listen, I have some news for you. You're going to be here for a special occasion."

"This have anything to do with the 'perfectly lovely young woman with the perfectly gorgeous long hair and perfectly perfect hourglass figure' that Mom has been going *on and on* about?" Joaquin asked with obnoxious emphasis in an imitation of their mother's voice. If she'd been there, she'd have popped him good for his disrespect.

"Mom has been talking about her? She only saw her a couple of times at the hospital after I got shot."

"Yeah, about your records with girlfriends—?"

"This one is completely different. What did Mom tell you?"

"That she was shy and innocent, respectful and *very* beautiful."

"She's all of those things. I'm riding with her precocious two-year-old right now."

"She has a baby?"

"Long, long story. So Mom liked her?"

"Yeah, I think that's another reason why she was nudging me to visit with you."

"Nudging you? Why?"

Joaquin chuckled. "Why do you *think*?"

Angel was taken aback by the thought, though not necessarily offended. He recalled his mom hinting to him when he was in the hospital that Joaquin might be taken with her also if he were to meet her. His only concern was how Teresa would react, knowing that his mother was suggesting that she might like Joaquin *also*.

"You still on the horse?"

"What? Yeah! I'm just wondering what *she* would think about that. She was raised in a sheltered environment."

"Yet she has a two year old? Boy or girl?" Joaquin asked with interest.

"Boy. He's a real pistol, too."

"Awesome. So you're going to ask her? When?"

"Tomorrow morning."

"I'm looking forward to meeting her. I'm glad you found a nice one. That Patricia was an evil bitch."

"Wish I'd known how evil. I would have given her the boot before she had a chance to use her gun on me and Ethan. Speaking of which, the guys are looking forward to the visit. Jack talks like you're already working here, and we damn sure could use the help."

Angel grimaced at the little intake of breath from in front of him. "Um! You said a *bad* word."

Joaquin snickered into the phone. "You're going to have to watch your mouth now, Daddy."

"Sorry, buddy," Angel said to Michael then to Joaquin he said, "Yeah, I am going to have to watch it." He didn't respond to Joaquin's crack about being a daddy now because he didn't mind one bit. Despite the years and miles, Joaquin was close to his brother and immediately picked up on that.

"Man, she must *really* be something."

"That's what I've been trying to tell you. You'll see in a little while. She's good friends with Grace. That's how we met."

"Jack, Ethan, and Adam's new wife?"

"Yeah, she's *another* keeper."

"From the sound of it, you must be rolling in available women. I may fit in just fine out there."

"One thing. She's shy, so no teasing. Give her a chance to get to know you."

"Gotcha. Does little mister like horses?"

"Loves them, why?"

"They've got a western store here that I've stopped at before. I thought it might be nice to not come empty-handed for Christmas, you know?"

"Sure. What did you have in mind?"

"Hat?"

"Covered."

"Boots?"

"Covered.

"Chaps?"

"Covered that today."

"You probably got spurs, too?"

"Yep."

"Horse and saddle?"

"Funny."

"Belt?"

"Bingo. He's two years old, average size."

"How about your lovely lady? Jewelry?"

"Sure. Surprise her. You're gonna make all kinds of brownie points around here. So I'll see you after supper?"

"Yeah, depending on how busy the store is right now."

"Be careful. You remember how to get here?"

"Yeah, I think so," Joaquin said sarcastically. "I'll call if I get hung up."

Angel ended the call, and Michael asked him if it was "Wahkeen" calling. They talked about Angel having a little brother and the kinds of things they liked to do when they were little boys growing up.

"You ride horsies?"

"All the time."

"I gonna be a cowboy just like you, Daddy," Michael stated, sat back against Angel, and was still for a while. They rode the fence line, and Angel showed him the creek that ran through the back of the property and told him sometime when he was a little older, they could go fishing in it. Michael liked that idea.

Angel and Michael headed back to the barn and took care of the mare. Afterward, he got Michael settled watching a video and started preparing supper.

Teresa arrived after six thirty looking a little dazed. With concern, he asked her if she was all right. She said she felt like she'd been hit by a truck. A *big* truck. Michael greeted her with a kiss and went right back to his movie, and Angel convinced her to go lay on his bed for a while and rest. She made him promise that he wouldn't let her oversleep.

* * * *

Teresa awakened later to the feel of sensual lips trailing over the flesh of her throat and shoulder and a big hand stroking her hip. The combined sensations made her feel a little shaky as she gradually awakened and realized it wasn't a dream. She shuddered and panted lightly when his warm fingers stroked her lower back above the waist of her slacks. A restless ache invaded her core, and the juncture between her thighs throbbed. It was seldom that Angel touched her so intimately, and she was usually conscious when he did so, so she was prepared for the sensations. But waking up like this, her need slammed into her, swamping her with waves of desire. That hot, quivering spot pulsed when the tip of his tongue and his lips brushed the flesh beneath her ear. She was utterly defenseless when he paid attention to that spot.

She reached for him, and he gathered her to him and held her close. She wrapped her arms around his shoulders, and her fingers slid into his hair, which was down loose today. He stole her breath with his kiss, and she moaned when he finally released her from it. Angel's eyes were full of desire, and his hands were gentle as he stroked her ribs and hip. He swept her hair over her shoulder and kissed the other side of her throat.

Teresa reached for his hand, her heart pounding in her throat, and slid it down over her breast. Her breath hitched at the contact. Her nipples tingled as his hand cupped her breast and stroked a hard peak through the lace cup of her bra. She heard Angel groan against her shoulder. This was the first time she'd ever directed him to touch her so intimately, and the long wait made it all the sweeter.

"I love you so much."

"I love you. I want you, need you." She whimpered, clinging to him. On the verge of something huge, Teresa looked up at him, not bothering to hide the need she felt. A deep, enthralling tremor swirled and built up in her pelvic region. His only response was a soft growl in her ear, and a sudden tension built rapidly inside her. Gathering her to him snugly, he kissed her as though he were ravenous. He slid his hand down her hip, over her derriere, touching her there for the first time. His hand slid farther until it cupped the back of her thigh and pulled her to him so that her core was pressed more intimately against his hip. Her breath rushed out in a shuddering pant, and a pulsing started deep in her depths, gathering heat and momentum. A great pleasure bloomed inside her, and in that split second, she knew what she needed. One more little touch, one more little sound. *Just one more.*

"Mommy? Wanna eat?" Michael called from the living room.

She closed her eyes, swallowed hard and sighed. The swirling tension building inside her shifted from anticipation to frustration and became almost painful. He rested his forehead lightly on her collarbone, which happened to put his lips near her breast. He pressed a quick kiss there and sat up as she released him. He grinned when she made a little whiny sound in her throat.

"I *did* come in to let you know supper is ready. Grace called earlier and said she was bringing some presents for Michael to open in the morning. Joaquin will be here in a little while, too. How do you feel?" he asked, stifling a groan. Teresa smiled sympathetically, having a good idea how he was feeling.

"Mommy?"

"I'm coming, honey. We'll eat in a minute." She looked up into Angel's eyes, "I feel much better. Maybe better than I've ever felt in my whole life." She smiled ruefully at him. "I'm sorry about the interruption."

"It's okay. Let's get some food in you." He helped her sit up. In the dark room, somehow her hand landed lightly in his lap, and she gasped when she felt the size of his erection.

"Oh! I'm…sorry, Angel." She removed her hand and apologized again when he groaned quietly. "I…you're *so big*, Angel," she whispered in a shaky voice, not even sure where the ability to speak had come from. She relaxed a little when she heard him chuckle.

"Well, thank you, beautiful. See the effect that you have on me?"

"Wow," she whispered. She wanted so much to know what it was she'd just barely missed. She'd been so, so close. Her core trembled in agreement.

* * * *

Angel did his best to ignore the throbbing ache in his groin and helped her sit up without further incident. He was pleased that awakening her like that hadn't startled her or frightened her.

He'd set the table nicely to celebrate Christmas Eve with her. The food was already on the table, and all they had to do was sit down. "This was so thoughtful of you, Angel, to go to all this trouble for us. After a day like *today*, it's wonderful to come home to all this."

Angel smiled at her mention of his house as home and held the plate while she chose her steak.

"I'm glad it made you happy. Come on, Michael. I've got a nice, thick phone book for you to sit on." He held out a hand to Michael, and he ambled up onto the chair and plopped down. His head was still a little low at the table. "I ought to pick up a high chair for when he comes over here."

"You're very thoughtful, Angel. Mmm. This steak is perfect."

"Thank you. So it was crazy at the store?"

"Yes! Two little blue-haired ladies who have been friends for years were fighting over a marked-down purse!"

They enjoyed the meal, and Teresa entertained him with other stories about shoppers that let the last-minute shopping anxiety get to them. After they'd finished eating and she'd helped him clean up, she put a plate together for Joaquin, in case he was hungry, and placed it in the microwave. Teresa was putting a Christmas movie in the DVD player when the doorbell rang.

Chapter Nine

Teresa happily flung open the front door, ready to wish Grace a Merry Christmas and give her a big hug.

"Merry—!" The rest of what she would have said ended with a quiet rush as she suddenly exhaled. She was gazing upon possibly the handsomest man, barring Angel, of course, that she'd ever seen. In fact, at first glance, he could have *been* Angel. The sparkle in his eyes was the same, but they were a different color. A heated rush bloomed through her body as she speechlessly took in the sight of him. He leaned into the doorframe, a sexy smile forming on his full lips.

"Well, hello, sugar. And who might *you* be?" he asked in a deep Texan drawl. The naughty grin he bore spread to his clear green eyes with a mischievous twinkle as he waited a few seconds for her reply, which was lodged in her throat. He was well over six feet tall, tanned, and hard-muscled just like Angel. The only other difference was his hair, which was shorter, hung loose, and reached past his shoulders.

Teresa finally mustered a soft, "Hello." Her heart pounded in her throat, due in part to being startled, but she also felt a little flustered as she continued to stare at him speechlessly. He exuded overabundant charm and animal magnetism. She could hear her heartbeat in her ears and felt her cheeks grow aflame as that pulse was echoed somewhere else a little *lower*.

Michael chose that moment to summon her from her stupor. "Wah-keeeen!" he screeched happily like he was Michael's long-lost friend. "Mama!" he said loudly as he tugged at her pant leg. "Angel's brother!" Feeling like an idiot for staring, she backed away from the door and welcomed him inside. Angel approached with a big grin on his face and arms held out. Joaquin chuckled, set his bags down, and grasped his brother in a full-on bear hug, slapping his back and laughing.

* * * *

Angel couldn't help but grin at him after witnessing the whole deer-in-the-headlights experience Joaquin had with Teresa. She wasn't used to Joaquin's magnetic personality, so she wouldn't have noticed he had a similar reaction to her. He just hid it better behind his notoriously flirtatious exterior. Right now she was on the receiving end of double-barrel bedroom eyes and looked in need of rescue. He noted with satisfaction that she didn't avert her eyes. That in itself spoke volumes to him.

He turned to Teresa, twining his fingers with hers, and said, "Sweetheart, this is my brother, Joaquin. Joaquin, this beautiful woman is Teresa Palacios, and this little guy is her son, Michael." He lifted Michael with one arm, not releasing her hand, and said, "Buddy, this is Joaquin."

Teresa greeted Joaquin while Michael chirped something that sounded a lot like "Pleased to meet you" before he started babbling on about cowboys and Christmas.

Joaquin gestured to his duffel and another bag. "Where should I put all this? I have more packages in the truck."

"Here, let me have it." Angel lifted Joaquin's duffel bag. "You're going to use the other bedroom. I'll show you real quick then I'll help you bring everything else in. The gifts can go under the tree."

His bags put away, Joaquin followed Angel out to the truck and horse trailer. Joaquin handed him the wrapped gifts from the backseat and looked around as if to see if Teresa was nearby. The front door was still open, but he could hear her inside the house talking to Michael.

"You weren't kidding, Angel. She is beautiful," he said quietly.

Because Angel knew Joaquin so well, he noted immediately the lack of playful banter, bragging, and teasing that was innate to him. He was never at a loss for something witty to say. Now, after meeting Teresa, his thoughts were limited to seven words? Interesting.

"Seeing is believing, little brother, and sweet as honey, too. Now you know why I'm proposing."

"You're lucky you've claimed her already. Otherwise I'd go after her."

Angel observed Joaquin. At any other time, Joaquin would have said the same exact thing, but he would have meant an entirely different sort of pursuit. A pursuit, and conquest, of a more temporary kind. He was quiet and thoughtful, which confirmed Angel's earlier assumption.

"We'll talk more tonight. Let's unload Deseo and get him squared away."

After they brought the gifts into the house, they unloaded Deseo and walked him a bit while Angel showed him around. After getting him settled, they walked slowly back to the house. Joaquin was still distracted and contemplative. When he finally spoke, Angel wasn't all that surprised by his words.

"Angel, if you need privacy, I can get a motel room in town or stay up at the ranch house for a few days. I don't want to throw a monkey wrench into any of your holiday proposal plans."

Angel noted Joaquin's respectful offer to back off and allow him time alone with Teresa, which would also give Joaquin the chance to reconcile his attraction to Teresa and the fact that she was off limits. He appreciated the offer but knew it was unnecessary.

"Joaquin, all the plans *include* you. No way would we let you leave again tonight. We've all been looking forward to your arrival, even Teresa and Michael." Angel grinned at him and clapped his hand on his brother's beefy shoulder. "I saw your reaction to her when she opened the door. She inspires all these...protective instincts in me. I think you surprised her, but once she gets her bearings with you, it will be easier for her to talk to you. Give her some time. Michael's a riot, isn't he?"

Joaquin chuckled and said, "He's pretty cute. He seems comfortable with you."

Angel grinned, thinking of his ride earlier that day with the little boy. "Yeah, he's even been calling me Daddy."

"No shit? What did she say about that? Has she heard him say it?"

"Yeah, a couple of times. I think she was worried it would upset me, but I told her it was fine."

"Wonder what she made of that?"

"I'm more concerned how she *feels* about it. When we first started dating, she was so skittish. She was protective of Michael, and we didn't even spend that much time with him until she got more comfortable around me. She's a good mother to shield him like that. We've been taking our relationship very slow and gradual."

"Slow and gradual is code for what?" When Angel didn't respond, Joaquin turned to him in shock. "You mean you—*you* haven't—?"

"Don't act so surprised. Teresa's story is a complicated one. Someone from her past did her some real serious hurt, so it's not easy for her to trust. That's why I suggested you not tease her too much about being shy. She's nothing like *any* other woman we've ever known."

"And shared?" Joaquin hinted in his oh-so-subtle way.

"We're gonna have a serious talk about that later. I can see the interest in your eyes, but there are things you need to know first. Do not bowl her over with all your charm. Go easy and let her get used to you."

Angel and Joaquin were close to each other growing up, separated by less than a year. Many people mistook them for twins. Joaquin had his mother's green eye color, and Angel had his father's light-brown eye color. Though all three fathers claimed all their children equally, it was obvious looking at Joaquin and Angel that they were both biological sons of the eldest brother, Eleazar. It was under Eleazar's guidance they developed a talent for handling horses and horse breeding.

That was how Jack met the two of them. His father invited Eleazar to visit the Warner Ranch many years ago when the Martinez Ranch had fallen on hard times, to teach Joe and teenagers, Jack, Ethan and Adam, what he knew about horses. He stayed at the ranch for almost a year and worked with the breeding stock Joe had purchased. He taught them what he knew and sent his earnings home to his family.

During the summer months, Angel and Joaquin were sent to visit and work while they were out of school. The teenagers took a liking to each other and remained friends over the years. When Jack bought the ranch and knew he'd need someone with experience in control of it, the only people he thought to call were Angel and Joaquin. Joaquin was already on the rodeo circuit, but Angel preferred a more stable life and took him up on the offer.

It seemed almost inevitable to Angel that Joaquin would be attracted to Teresa. He supposed that was because he'd not been raised with any stereotypes about a woman belonging to just one man. He knew that if Joaquin wanted to make a commitment to Teresa, she would be very well cared for and cherished by both of them. Her needs would be their first concern. He and Joaquin had sewn some wild oats in their twenties, sharing a few uncommitted, one-night-stand threesomes, but that was in the past and had no bearing on the present situation.

They walked back to the house, talking and joking, and were on the porch when they saw lights coming down the driveway that led from the main ranch house. "That must be Grace bringing Teresa and Michael their Christmas presents," Angel said as they turned and came back down the porch steps to help her as she parked the SUV.

"So *this* is Grace?" Joaquin said in obvious anticipation to finally meet the woman Jack had been going on and on about anytime he talked to him the last few months.

"Hang on to your hat, brother. *She's* a flirt." Angel smiled, remembering a time when Grace was almost as afraid of her own shadow as Teresa had been. Grace popped the rear door on the back of Jack's SUV and climbed out.

"Hi! I'm sorry…or…at least I *was*…about not coming down to drop these off sooner. Wow, Angel, it's like you have a yummy twin! Can we *keep* him?" She giggled enthusiastically when Angel groaned.

"Grace, this is my brother, Joaquin. Joaquin, this irrepressible blonde is Grace Warner." He turned to an unrepentant Grace and shook his finger, unsuccessfully hiding his grin. "You behave or he may not stay. You made him blush and *nothing* makes this cowboy blush."

Joaquin gave her a crooked little grin and turned up the high beams on his charm. "Grace, up until now, I thought everything I was hearing about you was fanciful rumors. It turns out you're every bit as precious as Jack, Ethan, and Adam have been bragging about."

Grace's eyes twinkled with merriment and good humor as she redirected their attention. "He's a sweet-talker too, I see. Okay, boys. The presents are in the back, and the one in silver paper is very fragile. I'm going to run in and say hello to Teresa and Mini Me."

"Mini what?" Angel lifted a large gift wrapped in brightly-colored paper.

"You know, 'Mini Me'? Michael? He's your little 'Mini Me' in his cute little cowboy hat," Grace said, giggling gaily. "I saw you in the barn earlier. He's watching you close, Angel. He even tries to walk like you."

Warmth suffused his chest at her comment. "Really? I hadn't noticed. I'll have to keep my eyes open for that."

Grace reached for the gift wrapped in silver paper. "Every little boy needs a good male role model in his life, Angel. Michael is lucky to have you. So is Teresa. I think you are so good for each other. Joaquin, have you met Teresa yet, or did you just arrive?"

"I got in a few minutes ago, but we have been introduced to each other."

"Isn't she *beautiful*? She's a dear friend and one of the best people I know." They climbed the stairs to the deck carrying all the gifts.

Teresa opened the door and smiled happily. "I thought I heard your voice, Grace. Michael, look who's here. It's Aunt Gracie."

"Gracie-*baby*!" Michael crowed and came running.

Teresa tilted her head and grinned at Grace and mouthed "Gracie-baby?" at her and raised an eyebrow.

Grace giggled and said, "He heard Jack call me that in the barn the other day, and somehow it must have stuck." She handed Teresa the gift and lifted Michael into her arms and received a big, wet kiss. "Merry Christmas, Michael-baby!"

"Merry Christmas!"

Grace left a few minutes later after she wished them a good night and reminded them to come for the party the following evening. Teresa reheated the plate she'd set in the microwave for Joaquin while they put the gifts under the tree then sat down to visit for a little while before she took Michael home. Joaquin thanked her gratefully, and they had a good time talking. Angel and Joaquin did most of the talking, with interjections here and there from Michael. Angel noticed Teresa said little but observed much.

* * * *

Teresa noticed the two handsome brothers shared some mannerisms. Such as the little sideways, twinkling eyes and grin, which made her so nervous when she and Angel first met, but she now loved to see. The nerves she felt when she was on the receiving end of it from Joaquin was nothing like Angel had had to deal with back when he'd first asked her out. She supposed that was progress of some sort.

Joaquin was almost the same height as Angel, maybe less than an inch shorter. His hair was the same ebony black as his brother's, the length being the only difference. It was thick and had a little wave in it. He dressed the same, in faded blue jeans, denim shirt, and the requisite cowboy boots. Another similarity between the two was the smile lines around their eyes and mouths. He was as easygoing as his brother, and she was willing to bet he'd left many a yearning heart behind when he'd come to Divine.

She loved listening to them talk. The deep, resonant quality of their voices was soothing after her long day. Michael drifted off after he climbed sleepily into her arms. She kissed the fragrant top of his head and smoothed her hand down his little back. She needed to get him home soon and ached for a moment to know what it felt like to not have to gear up to go home after an evening at Angel's house. She glanced up and caught them both gazing at her.

Angel's eyes were filled with deep tenderness, which made her smile. The look in Joaquin's eyes was warm and open. There was a soft desire there that she would have been a fool not to notice. She looked away in embarrassment when a response stirred within her core. The heat of her blush spread over her cheeks, and her nipples tingled, her breathing came faster. The folds between her legs swelled and throbbed in response to his gaze. She looked up at Angel, embarrassed, and whispered, "I should take him home."

Angel rose from the couch and lifted Michael's limp little body from her arms, grazing her cheekbone with his lips as he did. She looked up at him, confusion probably apparent on her face. He smiled at her and cuddled Michael against his chest as he offered his other hand to her to help her rise. She turned to his brother and said, "Joaquin, it's been a pleasure finally getting to meet you. I—I'll see you in the morning when we get here." Joaquin smiled and responded in kind. He watched from the door for a few seconds as Angel helped her get Michael into his car seat before closing the front door, allowing them their privacy.

Once Michael was settled, Angel closed his car door carefully, trying to not disturb him. He turned to Teresa and pulled her into his embrace. He looked into her eyes and tucked a loose lock of her long hair behind her ear.

"Angel, are you sure you want us to come early? You might enjoy having some time alone to visit with your brother."

"I'd be disappointed if you didn't come in the morning. We'll probably be up late getting caught up tonight, so don't you fret about that. If you come early, I can make breakfast for you, which is what I was hoping to do. I'll be up by five taking care of things around here. If Michael is usually up by six or six thirty, why don't you bring him around seven, unless you can get him to sleep in a bit?"

She chuckled and replied, "I don't have that kind of luck. Michael has always been an early riser. I'll see you around seven then, but we'll both need a nap by mid-morning." She emphasized that thought with a little yawn behind her hand.

A sexy smile spread over his handsome face, and he murmured, "That's fine. I'll tuck you in for a nap when you get sleepy. Of course, I'd also take responsibility for waking you, too."

"Really? Like earlier?" she asked breathlessly, smiling at his nod. "I wouldn't complain, I-I don't think."

"I love you, beautiful." Angel cupped her cheek and kissed her tenderly. She felt a pulse between her legs as she wrapped her arms around his neck and allowed him to lift her off her feet and press her body to his. She moaned against his lips and stroked his tongue tentatively with her own, eliciting a soft growl from him. He set her down carefully.

"I love you, too, Angel." She rested her head against his chest, listening to his strong heartbeat. "I love you so much it hurts sometimes," she whispered as she stroked his biceps.

"But it's a good kind of hurt, isn't it?"

"Yes, it is. I'll see you early in the morning." She sat down in the driver's seat of her car. He closed the door and leaned in to kiss her again after she lowered the window.

"Sweet dreams," he whispered.

Yeah, like she was going to be able to sleep at all.

* * * *

Angel stayed up late into the night talking with Joaquin. Angel sensed her unease and imagined she thought she betrayed her love for him by feeling an additional interest in Joaquin.

Taking him into strict confidence, Angel told Joaquin everything Teresa told him about her past and how she'd been when they first started dating six months before. He was gratified by the anger in Joaquin's eyes as he imparted the details of Teresa's horrific experience with Ranulfo, the pain and terror he'd inflicted on her.

"So now you can understand why we've taken our relationship so slowly. Her only sexual experiences were painful ones. The last six months have been all about taming her fears and earning her trust."

"Do you know where the bastard is right now?"

Angel explained what Teresa had told him of Ranulfo's whereabouts. Angel smiled at the need he saw in Joaquin's eyes to set right this wrong and knew it mirrored his own feelings on the matter.

"I'm asking her to marry me in the morning. I want you to know that as far as I am concerned, there's room for you within our family. If she says yes to me, that is. She would have to want you and welcome you also."

"Damn, Angel." Joaquin swore softly, taken by surprise.

"You'd have to make it permanent with her. I won't allow you to come and go or treat her love casually. If she'll have you, you stay permanently. Remember the only experience with polyamorous relationships she has is what she sees between Grace, Jack, Ethan, and Adam. She knows about our family, but she was raised differently.

That would be a major hurdle for her to jump, wrapping her mind around two men loving her. She's probably confused by her reaction to you, and I'll need some time alone with her to talk to her about it tomorrow. Give her time to get used to you, and you take some time to decide if this is what you want."

Joaquin retrieved beers for both of them from the refrigerator and handed one to Angel. "I remember talking to Adam when he called one day after he got engaged. He went on and on about Grace and how he fell in love with her the moment he set eyes on her. I gave him a hard time about it. Now I'm eating my words, because the moment I laid eyes on her, I—I just *knew*."

Joaquin ran his hands through his hair and scrubbed his whiskered cheeks with his palms. "I laid eyes on her one second and…wanted to take her in my arms in the next. It felt like she reached into my chest and stole my heart from me while I was busy staring at her like a calf at a new gate. I'm going to have to confess all to Adam now and let him laugh at me this time, because I'm *smitten*." He rubbed the center of his chest. Angel grinned at the action, familiar with the feeling.

"Do you think you could love her the way she deserves? Make her your first priority? Consider her son as your own?" Angel had seen the answer in Joaquin's eyes all evening but needed to voice the question point blank.

Joaquin mulled the question over, his eyes hooded as he thought before answering, "Yes. The question is can she love me and learn to trust me, the way she does you? And what about when she finds out about my life on the circuit? I mean, I wasn't exactly a priest."

Angel smirked sarcastically. "So I gathered from your little *predicament* this morning. Big *bunny-slut*."

Joaquin swore but also had the grace to blush. His reputation amongst the buckle-bunnies that followed the rodeo circuit was legendary.

* * * *

Teresa woke to the sound of excited screeching coming from the living room. She smiled sleepily and looked at the clock. It was 5:45 a.m. It was a good thing they hadn't stayed up too late last night. She knew he'd be up early no matter what time he went to bed. It brought happiness to her heart to know that Angel was already up, as well. That thought, of course, brought his handsome brother to mind. She'd gone to bed troubled last night.

Her heart belonged irrevocably to Angel. She'd been attracted to him since the day she met him. Where the attraction to his brother came from, she didn't know. Was it because of the resemblance? Was it the long look that passed between them at the door?

Her mother always told her the eyes were the windows to the soul. Perhaps she should have followed her mother's teaching and averted her eyes when she'd first seen him, then she wouldn't be having these feelings. Last night, he'd seen straight into her soul as deeply as Angel ever had. That didn't sit well. Angel had patiently earned her trust and the right to see that deeper part of herself.

He'd encouraged her to hold her head high and told her that she had nothing to be ashamed of. He'd told her once that her mother was wise in her teaching, but perhaps averting her eyes had become a way to hide from even those who cared about her and intended her no harm. She knew he was right.

Any way she looked at it, she was confused. She didn't feel violated for having allowed Joaquin to look in her eyes—that would be silliness—but she worried about what he saw there that made him respond to her.

She groaned and rose from the bed and donned her bathrobe. Maybe everything would be fine this morning. Maybe it was her exhaustion that made her feel that way last night. Maybe he was noticing and concerned because she looked so worn out from work. *Right*, that would explain the desire she saw plainly in his eyes last night. She hoped if Angel noticed her reaction to Joaquin that he wasn't mad at her for acting so silly at the door. He was not one to take offense easily. Maybe she was worrying for nothing, or maybe she was a loose woman needing her head checked.

She walked into the living room and couldn't help but smile, watching Michael in his cowboy hat and pajamas, astride the rocking pony. He rocked back and forth on it with one arm up high in the air. She picked up her camera and started taking pictures. After jumping off the horse, he brought the little play tool belt to her, needing her help to put it on. When it was secure around his little hips, he turned to her and said, "Now me and Daddy are gonna build you a house." She pulled him to her and hugged him close as tears stung her eyes. He had such a tender, giving heart.

"You play, and Mama is going to get ready so we can go to Angel's house."

Those were the magic words. "Angel's house! Angel's house! We gotta go!"

"Slow down, you have time to play. Mama is going to make herself pretty then get you dressed, and we'll go."

"Take my tools?"

"Sure, baby."

Teresa texted Angel, and he called her right back. She handed Michael the phone, and Michael said, "Angel! Santa came! Santa came! He got me a horsie! Yeah, a rockin' horsie. Yeehaw!" Michael screeched as he rocked on the horse. "Yep, I'm a cowboy just like you!" he crowed. "We comin' over soon. Bye!" he yelled and handed the phone back to Teresa.

"Good morning, Angel. Merry Christmas."

"Good morning, sweetheart. You coming over?"

"We'll be there as soon as we can. Michael was so excited. He wanted to call you and tell you about the horse."

"A cowboy's first horse is a special thing. Sort of like first love. I'll finish up here and get breakfast going. I love you."

"I love you, Angel."

Chapter Ten

Teresa stood beside the couch watching Michael trot around the living room dressed in his chaps, spurs, cowboy boots, and plaid shirt that looked so much like the ones Angel wore. Over the shirt, he wore the little denim vest Grace had given him. His cowboy hat was perched on his head as he rode his little stick horse. She looked up at Angel standing beside her, his arm around her and his hand resting on her hip. Her heart was so full it felt like it would burst.

Angel said, "Why don't we take the little cowpoke in the backyard and let him run that horse a little. I want you to open my gifts now."

"But Joaquin—"

"Joaquin will come out with us and keep an eye on Michael." He gathered several boxes and twined her fingers with his. "Come on." He pulled her to the back door that opened onto the covered porch built onto the back of the house. His backyard was fenced, and the fence was lined with mature trees and shrubs.

Joaquin found a rope and showed Michael how to tie it to the stick horse. While the toddler held the rope, Joaquin galloped in a circle around Michael, hollering "Yee-Haw!" Michael cackled ecstatically at Joaquin's antics with the toy. She imagined what Michael would look like in years to come if he stayed within the loving shelter of Angel and Joaquin's guidance here on the ranch, if Joaquin stayed. He'd probably grow up to be an expert horseman, strong and hardworking, just like them. Though she hadn't seen him work with the animals yet, Joaquin's reputation had preceded him on the ranch.

Teresa watched appreciatively as Joaquin interacted with her son, unable to ignore the strong, handsome lines of his muscled body or the noble profile that was currently turned to her. Like Angel, he was poetry in motion. He talked and joked with Michael easily, judging by their combined laughter at something Joaquin had said. She feasted her eyes on the way his faded blue jeans clung to the backs of his thighs as he bent to help Michael adjust the little chaps that were strapped on him. Her body responded to the sight, as well.

As her eyes roamed over Joaquin, Angel took a gift from the stack on the table near the porch glider. She turned her attention guiltily to him as he handed it to her, and her cheeks felt like they must be beet red. She wondered how she could act and think like that when the man she loved most in the world sat beside her. To make matters worse, she had a feeling that he *knew* what was going on inside her.

Grace lived a life of utter happiness with her three men, and Teresa had never questioned the rightness of it because of what Grace had gone through to find that happiness. She could admit to a spark of curiosity over what it would be like, and she knew about the unique family Angel was a part of.

But she'd met Joaquin less than twenty-four hours ago. She had no business thinking about him as anything other than a possible future brother-in-law down the road.

This attraction for him was the newness of his arrival, with some hormones thrown in for kicks and giggles. The fact that she was even daring to stare at his body appalled her. That was not like her at all. She turned her full attention on Angel, feeling inexplicably blue. Casting her eyes down, she smiled at the contents of the first box. She looked up at him, an eyebrow arched.

"Rosemary took you shopping, didn't she?" She smiled up at him, thinking what a generous man he was.

"Yes, she did point me in the right direction. She said you liked that top. I agreed with Rosemary that it would look pretty on you."

"I love it. Thank you, Angel. You spoil me." She tilted her lips up to him as he leaned in for a kiss.

"I'm only just getting started, darling," he drawled as he handed her another box. He smiled at her gasp as she opened the long, rectangular-shaped velvet box.

"Angel, this is lovely." She touched the shimmering onyx facets on the teardrop necklace and earrings with her fingertip. "Just lovely. Will you help me put it on?" she asked excitedly as she removed the pieces from the box and handed him the necklace. He stood and clasped the necklace as she lifted her long hair from her shoulders. Then she put on the earrings. "How does it look?"

"It's a pale shadow compared to the one who wears it."

"You are such a sweet-talker." She hugged him and kissed his chin.

"You've met my dads. You know where I get it from."

"Thank you. You must have spent a fortune on it." She touched the stones that rested at the base of her throat.

"To see you look so radiant and happy, it was well worth the cost."

Teresa wondered if he would still think that if he knew what her earlier thoughts had been about. The guilt gripping her heart twisted a little further.

He handed her another box, which contained a spa gift set from Madeleine's Day Spa.

"I love gardenias!"

He smiled. "Grace told me you would like this."

"Thank you, Angel. I don't know what to say. I feel like you've showered us both with so many gifts." She gestured out to Michael in the yard, still running happily, the fringe on his chaps flapping in the cool breeze. His little straw cowboy hat bobbed on his dark head as Joaquin chased him. Her hands caressed the glittering stones at her throat. She felt so unworthy of this man.

Angel's fingertips lifted her chin, and she looked up into his loving eyes. "There's one more." He reached into his jacket pocket. He took her hand in his and kissed her knuckles before placing a little square box in her hands. His eyes never left hers as he spoke to her.

"Everything in my life that is good, you make even better just by being here." He rose from the glider and got down on one knee as the tears brimming in her eyes overflowed in a sudden flood.

"Marry me, Teresa. I promise I'll devote myself to loving you, caring for you, and protecting you and Michael." He lifted her hands, which still held the unopened box, and kissed them again. Her heart burst with love for him, and she cupped his cheek with one hand and kissed him tenderly.

"Yes, Angel. I'll marry you. I want to be your wife, and I want you to be the man who helps me raise Michael into the man he is supposed to become."

He kissed her cheek and wrapped his arms around her, brushing his lips over her throat. Her body quivered at the sensation, which reminded her, as her husband, he would do much more. "I can picture you coming down the aisle to me in a white wedding dress."

"You're very romantic." She would have thought most men would want to go to the courthouse and get it over with as soon as possible. "We could have the wedding here. Maybe Grace could help me."

"We'll talk to her tonight and see what she thinks. My mother is going to be beside herself." He paused and chuckled. "You haven't even seen your rings yet. You may not like it and decide you don't want to marry a bum like me."

"I doubt you could ever be a bum. I already know you have excellent taste in jewelry." She touched the necklace she wore again and thought of the locket he'd given her for her birthday. She opened the box, gasping at the beautiful diamond engagement ring and wedding band that were nestled in the box. The engagement ring had a large, square-cut diamond with two smaller diamonds on either side, set into a wide, polished platinum band. The narrow wedding band was studded across its top with smaller diamonds. "It's simply beautiful."

"You've made me a very happy man." His voice hitched with emotion as he looked into her brimming eyes. He lifted the engagement ring from the little box and slipped it on the ring finger of her right hand. They were startled from their cozy little bubble by cheering from the backyard and Michael screeching.

"She said yes! She said yes! *Angel's gonna be my Daddy*! Yeah! My *Daddy*!" he yelled at the top of his lungs as Joaquin cheered along with him. He lifted the happy boy to his shoulders and trotted up to the porch. Teresa smiled up at them happily, noting the genuine warmth in Joaquin's eyes for her without a trace of envy. He squatted down and let Michael off his shoulders so he could hug his mommy then his daddy-to-be.

Joaquin leaned down to her, and she was disquieted by the way her heart leapt in her chest as he came near. She could feel his body heat as he kissed her cheek. His scent was clean like soap and his own masculine essence combined. His kiss, pressed up against her upper cheekbone, did not feel like a brotherly peck. It felt like the caress of a lover. It sent a shot of shameful desire straight through her core. Heat tingled in her cheeks and she gave herself a mental kick to not read anything into that sensation quivering inside of her. It was the excitement of Christmas and becoming engaged. She was in overdrive. Yeah, maybe overdrive to have him *kiss* her again. She looked up in time to see Angel nod slightly at Joaquin.

Joaquin said, "Michael told me he's hungry and wants to try using the potty like a big boy. I'm going to fix him a snack and help the little dude out if he needs it. You two stay out here. You probably have a lot to talk about and want to be alone for a while. Don't worry about us. Right, Michael?" He held out his palm to Michael as he walked to the back door, and Michael slapped it with his open palm.

"Yeah," Michael nodded casually, pulling up his britches, "we got this," and stepped over the threshold as Joaquin opened the door for him.

She nodded and watched silently as Joaquin smiled at her again then closed the door behind them. Angel returned to his seat beside her.

He stroked her knuckles. "I've been watching you, beautiful." Her heart hammered with unease. "I can see that you're feeling... conflicted."

She ducked her head, and a hitching sigh escaped her lips. He'd noticed her reaction to Joaquin. She was now his wife-to-be. Was he about to lay the law down?

As if he sensed her sudden nervousness, Angel tilted her chin with a fingertip so she had to look into his eyes. His gentle gaze chased the fear away that had leapt in her heart. He was a totally different sort of man from any other she'd ever known. He caressed her chin with the pad of his fingertip. "You feel something stirring between you and Joaquin. Like there's an attraction there?"

Her eyelids slipped closed, no longer able to gaze at his handsome, loving face. Pain stung her chest, and tears flooded her eyes as she nodded. A hitching sob escaped her, and Angel quickly took her in his arms and held her tight as another sob came and shushed her before he continued. "Now, now. None of that on our happy day. The *last* thing I am is upset with you. You haven't done a thing wrong. What you feel doesn't upset me, although you probably think it does. Do you feel as if you are being disloyal to me?"

He cupped her cheek in his palm and waited until she looked up. She shook her head negatively because her love and loyalty to him were without question. Then she nodded because her attraction to Joaquin was undeniable, and given time, she knew she would feel as loyal to Joaquin. He was kind to her, but that budding loyalty was driven by the way he treated her son and the easy way he had with him. It put her at ease with him as much as any particular kindness he paid her.

"Remember, meeting my parents at the hospital? You know that our dads are brothers. Eleazar met and fell in love with my mother first. Being very close to his brothers, he could tell when they met her that they fell in love with her also. Loving all three of them, he proposed the unique arrangement. Joaquin told me he laid eyes on you and knew he loved you, standing there in the doorway last night. I could see it happening for myself. He could sense last night that you were uneasy. The last thing he wants is for you to be uncomfortable around him. I have no problem with the attraction Joaquin obviously feels for you, neither do I take offense that you feel the same way.

"It's my right to tell him to back off, as his elder. But I confess that I've always wondered what it would be like to raise a family and love a wife with the brother I've always been so close to. He hopes you'll permit him to spend time with you, to allow you to get to know him. He tells me that what he feels for you is completely different from a passing physical attraction. He's never put down roots anywhere, but he's seriously considering making Divine his permanent home. If you allow him into your heart, he would make a lifelong commitment to you and Michael."

He paused a moment and studied her face, she assumed to see how well she was handling everything he'd told her so far. "It might help you to talk with Grace about this. She probably experienced a lot of the same feelings after meeting Ethan and Adam. She could give you insight that she's been keeping to herself, not wanting to shock you. You know there's not a thing those men wouldn't do for her if she asked." Teresa smiled and nodded at that thought. Those men were unquestionably devoted to Grace. What must that be like?

Angel's eyes twinkled as he said, "It would be the same for you with both of us. You'd have two men to help with Michael and two men to protect you and provide for you." His lips brushed her cheekbone and kissed her temple before murmuring, "Two men to love you." A soft shudder rippled through her as the mental image of both of these handsome men holding her and loving her together swam through her mind. Her core throbbed at his words and his touch.

She was relieved, and she told him as much. "I could not understand why I would feel that way toward your brother when I love you so much. Especially given my past and the way I was raised. I looked in his eyes and..." She left the thought incomplete because she had no words to describe what happened. It still warred within her. Her love and loyalty were supposed to belong exclusively to Angel. But Joaquin was like a powerful magnet to her steel.

"I placed no implied boundary between you and Joaquin. I told him a little about you on the phone yesterday, including that I was planning to propose. That would have been the time to warn him off if that was how I felt. If he thought that I was not willing to share, he would have ignored any attraction he felt and declared you off limits. We were not raised by men who were jealous of each other. Eleazar allowed Mom to get to know his brothers and to consider them as possible suitors. It worked out well for them, most of the time, anyway." The last he added with a chuckle.

"Most of the time?"

"My mom is a firecracker, as you can imagine."

It helped to know that Angel was still the one in the driver's seat where the relationship was concerned. It also helped to know that Joaquin would have done the right thing if sharing wasn't an option for Angel and would still do the right thing if she wouldn't consider him.

"If Joaquin had known you would not...share me, he would not have *allowed* himself to be attracted to me? And it's all right with you? What if he tries to kiss me?"

"I haven't released him to do that. I wanted to talk to you first, sweetheart. He wouldn't make any move toward you until you told me you would consider him and I had given him the right to touch you. You wouldn't have to *leave* my arms if I sensed you wanted to go to him. I would release you to him. Remember I grew up watching my mom interact lovingly with three husbands. From my point of view, it would seem weird if you *didn't* kiss him or if you felt guilty for kissing him in front of me."

Teresa trusted Angel implicitly and knew she needed some answers to put her growing concerns at ease.

"What about…sex? How would that work? Would I have to switch off who I slept with?" How was she going to keep all that straight? His hands still held hers, and he rubbed her palms to reassure her but allowed her to finish.

"I have no experience, Angel. Are you sure I could even handle it? How can I please you both when I'm not used to pleasing one?" As she grew increasingly agitated, he lifted her easily into his lap. She rested her head against his strong shoulder and felt safe as he rubbed a hand up and down her spine.

"Are you really asking if I would make love to you while Joaquin was in bed with us?" Angel asked bluntly. At her nod, he continued. "A lot of that depends on you. If you allowed us to love you together, you might find that you'd prefer it to two separate beds. Our first priority would be making you happy.

"You've always been very modest around me, but I want you to know how it would be so you won't get the wrong idea. Your men would introduce you to a whole new world, beautiful. When we make love to you together, we would show you how many ways a man can bring a woman pleasure."

She tried to picture what he was talking about, and the more the image of the three of them together entered her mind, the more it intrigued her. "When you say you would make love to me together, what exactly do you mean? I don't know *anything* and Grace and I have never gotten into detail…about…you know." She knew her cheeks were bright red.

"And you see that as a problem, don't you, sweetheart?" He squeezed her reassuringly. "It would be our pleasure to teach you how to make love to us. That's not something to be embarrassed about or ashamed of."

Angel shifted subtly in his seat and cleared his throat. As he moved, she could feel the hard erection against her hip. He'd never once nudged her to touch that part of him, and it had been months they'd been dating. Her cheeks grew hotter as she hoped sometime soon she could touch him there. Hot moisture rushed to her core in response to that thought. She wished she knew what to do for him.

"When you say both of you loving me together, how does that work, exactly?"

"What I'm talking about right now is both of us being in the same bed with you. We'd kiss you, stroke you, and make love to you, one at a time. There are other possibilities that we can try down the road but only if you are willing and have a desire to…be more adventurous."

As he spoke, she felt his erection grow even larger and harder. Her curiosity grew along with it, and for once, feelings of trepidation didn't follow, just a desire to be with him in a more intimate setting to explore what he talked about. She liked the idea of them kissing her and stroking her. The thought of them making love to her while they were all together in bed made her feel naughty, which she found she enjoyed just a bit.

"I'll answer any question you have, even if you think it's a dumb question. You can also ask Grace how things work." He became thoughtful for a second, and there was a twinkle in his eyes as he looked into hers. "Let me put it this way, if you ask her and she tells you about something you'd like to try, I can guarantee we'll be willing to try it with you. There's just one stipulation, which I'm sure you will agree with."

"What's that?"

"They are a foursome, a ménage à quatre. We would be a ménage à trois, a threesome. We would never welcome a fourth party into our relationship with you."

"Oh! So what you mean is I don't need to worry about *another* of your brothers showing up and falling in love with me?"

Angel laughed out loud and hugged her. "No! Luka and Matthias are much too busy sowing wild oats. Besides that, they are only in their early twenties. Sweetheart, if you're asking all these questions, can I assume you're going to give this idea some thought?"

"Yes, I think I will consider it, but I have more questions."

"What would you like to know?"

Teresa brought up the other issue that concerned her. "From time to time, the men have felt the need to defend Grace's honor. I deal with the public like she does. I'm not a person who is good with quick comebacks or deflecting the questions of others. People can be so mean, especially when they feel self-righteous."

Angel nodded. "People will always have opinions, but I take encouragement from Jack and the guys. They keep their marital status with Grace a private issue but don't try to hide it like it's a secret. If you'd like to keep working, we'd do as Grace does and only acknowledge one spouse and allow the public to draw their own conclusions. We'll always be respectful in how we treat you publicly."

His brows drew together thoughtfully as he pressed on to the real issue. "We'd take a dim view of anyone insulting you, and protecting you would always be our top priority. Keep in mind that Jack, Ethan, and Adam would also be very protective of you, the same as I would be toward Grace, or any of her female friends. It would not be just me and Joaquin looking out for you."

"Thank you. I've never thought of it that way, but it's nice to know all of you care that much about us."

"So, I can tell Joaquin you would be willing to consider him?" Angel sounded formal asking that question.

Chapter Eleven

Angel stroked her shoulder as Teresa considered his words and nodded without hesitation. In the small span of time that this had become a possibility, he'd emotionally invested himself in the idea and was surprised to realize how disappointed he would've been if she'd said no.

"Yes, but make sure Joaquin understands I'll need time to…catch up?" she asked as she stroked his hand. "I need to know him individually before I can consider the commitment you're proposing. And also, he may discover I'm too timid and not want me after all."

Angel laughed at her last comment and said, "I think there's a side to Teresa Palacios that is anything but timid. Could you imagine having this conversation with me six months ago?" At her laugh and the fervent shake of her head, he continued. "I think the more pressing question is what happens when you discover you like Joaquin better and that I am a gigantic ass."

She laughed with him. "No way. I already know I'm madly in love with you. So this puts off our wedding date for a while?"

He didn't miss the disappointment in her tone. "I would prefer to be your husband today, but I would rather start out together than bring him into our relationship later. It would've been nice if he'd had the last six months with you also."

"The Teresa you asked out on that first date would have run screaming at the first sign you were both interested in me and would have fainted dead away at the mere thought of sharing a bed with you. It's interesting, the changes being with you've brought about in my life, Angel."

"I could say the same about you, beautiful."

Angel rose from the glider after helping her stand and folded her into his arms, relieved at the relaxed smile that had replaced the look of confused embarrassment she'd worn perpetually since meeting Joaquin. They went inside and found Michael and Joaquin at the dining room table, eating re-heated brisket.

"This is purty good, Daddy!" Michael chirped through a full mouth. They chuckled, and Joaquin looked up at them both with guarded hope in his eyes. Angel smiled as he watched the way Joaquin's eyes drank in Teresa's beauty while her attention was on her son. It was plain to see that his brother was enthralled by this woman who so easily held both their hearts in her delicate hands.

She smiled self-consciously at Joaquin and said, "I think we should open more presents. There are gifts under the tree for Angel and Joaquin that they haven't opened yet, aren't there, Michael?"

"Yep!" He hopped down with no hands from the thick phone book on the chair and ran into the living room to the Christmas tree while she went after his grubby little hands and face with a damp dish cloth.

Joaquin rose as Angel stopped beside him and said in a low voice, "She asked for time to get to know you, but she's willing to consider you. She asked for you to be patient with her. She had quite a few questions, which I take as a good sign." He clapped Joaquin on the back and chuckled at his relieved smile. "Let's go see what Teresa and Michael brought us."

Teresa handed a small package to Michael and whispered to him. He grinned and brought it to Joaquin and climbed up in his lap and watched him expectantly as he opened it. Teresa brought the large square box wrapped in red-striped paper to Angel.

"Hey! It's a cell phone case, isn't it? Look, bro, hand-tooled leather." Joaquin proudly held it up.

"Yeah," Michael chirped. "Now you got someplace to keep your phone, right?"

"That's right, buddy. Thank you."

Angel smiled when Michael turned in Joaquin's lap and gave him a big hug. Joaquin looked over Michael's head at Teresa, and his eyes were filled with affection as he whispered, "Thank you," to her and kissed the top of Michael's head before he jumped down to go watch Angel open his gift. Angel smiled at the exchange, knowing firsthand what it felt like when that little boy reached in your chest and stole your heart. He'd felt it, too.

Teresa nodded and smiled back at him then whispered, "You're welcome, Joaquin. Merry Christmas."

* * * *

As Joaquin sat in the living room opening gifts with Angel, Teresa, and Michael, he spared a thought for the young woman he'd been in bed with the morning before. Recalling the way they casually parted ways afterward, he hoped she'd made it home safely. He felt embarrassed he intentionally never asked her name but most certainly had known her intimately. He looked over at the beautiful woman sitting next to his brother. His brother had patiently wooed her for six months and barely done more than kiss her.

Teresa's warm brown eyes and her blushing cheeks had changed his outlook on life. Her scent still lingered in his memory from when he'd kissed her cheek earlier. The memory of wild sex with that nameless girl hadn't even stirred a tingle, but the look of hesitant attraction in Teresa's eyes had his cock ready to shatter diamonds right then. He had a feeling that horndog was going to be howling for a while before it got any relief.

Joaquin looked on as Angel sighed in appreciation when he opened the hatbox. Inside was a pale-wheat-colored straw hat. Joaquin watched the way she leaned into Angel as he wrapped his arms around her lovingly and kissed her. Her dark lashes swept down across her cheeks as she tilted her full lips up to his. The kiss was brief because her son stood nearby, but Joaquin didn't miss the love in her eyes as she looked into Angel's eyes. She was too beautiful to be real. Joaquin was dragged back to reality when she spoke.

"You like it?"

Holding it up to admire it, he said, "I love it. That's a very fine straw hat."

"Put it on." Michael said, leaning against Angel's knee. When Angel complied, he said, "Nice, Daddy. Looking good! Merry Christmas!"

"Merry Christmas, buddy." Angel wrapped an arm around him and kissed his forehead. "Thank you."

Joaquin was finally able to rise from the couch without embarrassing himself and retrieved the gifts he'd brought with him from San Angelo. He handed Michael a gaily-wrapped package and chuckled as Michael shredded the paper and opened the box.

"Hey! I got a cowboy belt!" He pulled the small, tooled leather belt from the box and handed it to Joaquin to thread through the belt loops on his blue jeans. "Thanks, Wah-keen! I love it!" he exclaimed and hugged him again.

He caught her eye and said invitingly, "I have something for you too, Teresa." He held the gift-wrapped velvet box in his hand and watched as Angel guided her around him on the couch to sit between Angel and Joaquin. He caught the reassuring smile Angel gave her. He appreciated the way Angel released her so easily to him, and he hoped Teresa would quickly become comfortable with him. She tucked her black hair behind her ears and settled onto the couch next to him, her bare feet folded underneath her. She radiated a combination of innocence and sensuality as she settled with her hands folded in her lap. Angel stroked her back.

Joaquin handed her the rectangular package wrapped in heavy silver paper. She smiled shyly up at him and turned back to look at Angel briefly as he watched her unwrap the package. She glanced up at Joaquin in surprise when the velvet box inside was revealed. She hesitated briefly and then opened the lid.

Her eyes popped open wide, and she gasped. "I-I don't know what to say. This is beautiful, Joaquin, but *so* expensive." Her lips trembled as her fingers lightly traced over the blue stones. He hoped he hadn't just screwed up royally. She seemed embarrassed. That wasn't what he'd been going for with this purchase.

When he'd seen the matched set in the jewelry counter at Harrelson's in San Angelo, he'd thought he couldn't go wrong.

Angel looked over his shoulder and gave an appreciative nod of approval. There was a chunky turquoise necklace, set in sterling silver, with a shorter silver chain set within it from which dangled smaller turquoise charms, a heavy bracelet made from the same color turquoise with silver beads and crystals mixed in, and matching turquoise dangle earrings. She looked up into Joaquin's concerned eyes and whispered, "Thank you, Joaquin. It's lovely. I'm overwhelmed." She quickly wiped away the tear that slid from her eye.

"Teresa, I didn't mean to upset you with the gift. I wanted to bring you something nice. I wanted to make a good impression on you." He slid his finger along her jawline until his fingertip rested under her delicate chin. Her skin felt like satin.

She looked into his eyes and smiled. "You accomplished that before I ever opened this gift, Joaquin. I love it." She placed the opened box on the couch and hugged him. He took her in his arms and stifled a groan when he felt not a trace of stiffness or hesitation in her voluptuous body. Her delicate scent filled his nostrils. He unashamedly buried his nose in her fragrant hair and inhaled deeply. She bowed her head and leaned into him, resting against his chest.

He looked up at his brother, and Angel smiled at him then glanced down at the turquoise jewelry and raised an eyebrow. "I think someone stole my thunder," he muttered good-naturedly.

She giggled. "Nobody is stealing anybody's thunder. I have never been so spoiled with gifts and attention like this," she said as Joaquin reluctantly released her. She lifted the box to her lap and turned to

Angel and placed her hand on the black onyx necklace. "Would you mind if I tried it on?" Then she turned her back to him and lifted her hair from her shoulders. He removed the necklace and helped her put the turquoise on. "How does it look?"

"Beautiful," both men said in unison then grinned at her and each other.

Joaquin and his brother watched as she gazed at herself in the mirror and stroked the turquoise stones. She seemed lost in thought for a few moments as she stood there. Sunlight shown in through the glass storm door and illuminated her hair, causing the strands to glisten in the light. The light reflected off the mirror onto her face, giving her an almost ethereal glow. He thought she was the most beautiful woman he'd ever seen. Joaquin glanced at his brother and noticed a sappy look on his face that probably matched the one on his own. Teresa looked over to them, and Joaquin saw the happiness that shown from her eyes.

She didn't look away and didn't cast her eyes down but held their gazes. Joaquin envisioned him and Angel introducing her to pleasure like she'd never known before. Given her history, the only reason she was so open to them both now was because of the groundwork Angel laid over the last several months. He'd shown her he was a man of integrity. Joaquin knew he needed to spend some time alone with her so she could see what he would bring to their relationship. It would give her a chance to develop trust in him, as well. With less than a day elapsed since they met, he was encouraged that she was open to him at all.

They opened the rest of the gifts under the tree and talked and laughed. Joaquin and Angel watched Michael's antics in amusement, smiling as he wound down like a clockwork toy toward lunch time. Angel made him a grilled-cheese sandwich while Teresa reheated some of the leftover brisket Angel smoked earlier in the week and made sandwiches for the grownups. Michael yawned intermittently throughout the meal and agreed to take a nice, long nap on Angel's bed when Angel promised him he could ride a horse that afternoon, but only if he got his rest.

* * * *

Teresa tried to keep from laughing out loud when Michael did the Jell-O-neck head bob in his seat and lifted him from his perch on the phone book and carried him back to the bedroom.

She lay down with him for a little while as he drifted off. She breathed in Angel's scent from his pillow, desire flooding her senses at the recollection of being in his bed yesterday evening. She stretched languorously and fantasized about him lying beside her, kissing her lips as Joaquin lay closely behind her, his body pressed to hers as he nuzzled her throat.

Michael's light, whistling snore roused her from her fantasy. She carefully rose from the bed and piled the pillows around him in case he rolled around in his sleep. When she came out of the bedroom, Angel met her in the hallway. She recognized longing and desire in his topaz-colored eyes but saw something else in his smile and wasn't quite sure what it was. Pride, maybe? Was he proud of her?

He tilted her chin up and gently brushed his lips against hers, pressing her against the wall with his hard body. The desire she saw was confirmed when she felt the rock-hard shaft pressed against her abdomen. Her body responded as the muscles in her sheath clenched with need. His arms encircled her upper body, and he groaned as their kiss deepened and she opened for him. She tilted up to him, stroking his tongue with hers, giving him all she had and holding nothing in reserve. Her hands were clinging to his shoulders as she arched her back and pressed her belly against his erection.

Their breath came in quiet gasps as he finally released her lips with a growl. If they had been completely alone, that might have been the moment when they made love for the first time.

He rested his forehead lightly against hers. "Thank you."

"For what?" she whispered, breathing in his spicy, masculine scent as he pressed his lips to her forehead.

"For being willing. For being so receptive to Joaquin. I've never seen that look in his eyes or the hope that's there. Thank you for loving me and trusting me."

His words filled her heart with pleasure. "No matter what, I'll always love you, Angel. And I'm glad Joaquin feels that way." She nuzzled his lips with her own. "That makes me hopeful it will work out." She couldn't process the desires she had and didn't even try. She wanted to stay like this with Angel, but she wanted Joaquin, too.

"I told Joaquin I would be out of the house for a little while. I released him to touch you if you want him to. He'll allow you to make the first move. He will not touch you or kiss you unless you reach out to him first. He's concerned about scaring you."

Knowing that only served to increase her tender feelings toward them both. "I'm not scared of him, or you. I'm a little scared of what I'm feeling."

"I'm sure as time passes that feeling will ease. Kissing him will probably help. It won't bother me if you want to kiss him," he murmured, kissing her again.

He led her down the hall to the living room and turned to Joaquin. "I'll check on Deseo while I'm in the second barn."

"Thanks, Angel," Joaquin said simply but also saying so much.

Teresa went to the stereo and tuned in a country and western station, turning it down so it played softly in the background. Blake Shelton's "Who Are You When I'm Not Looking" began to play as she filled the sink with soapy water. She washed the dishes by hand, even though Angel had a dishwasher. Joaquin came in the kitchen, picked up a clean dishcloth, and began drying them as she rinsed them and placed them on a towel. They worked in companionable silence for a minute or two before Joaquin finally spoke.

"Why don't you tell me about your work? I think that would be a good place to start." His face was an open book. He wanted her to become comfortable with him. Teresa told him about Stigall's and how Juliana helped her when she moved to Divine. She also told him that Grace introduced her to Angel and even how she had reacted to him at first. She talked about visiting Angel in the hospital after the shooting and that Patricia was in state custody, in a mental facility being treated. She confessed to him that sometimes she worried that Patricia would be released and show up on Angel's doorstep with the intent of taking revenge. He asked questions here and there but mostly just let her talk.

She was surprised that once the words started flowing, she told him much more than she would have normally shared with somebody she'd just met. She stopped short of telling him about Michael's father but answered all Joaquin's questions. He asked her about where she lived and how she managed on her own. She was honest with him and told him it was hard. It made her feel stronger for taking care of Michael on her own, but that it was lonely, too. Joaquin commiserated with her, and she asked him to tell her about his life, his family, their ranch, and his life on the circuit. Was he still happy living from town to town?

He showed her the scar on his hand, received when he was thrown from a bull and trampled. "I love it, but it's a hard life, and injuries can be real serious. I don't want to be crippled before I'm fifty. The money can be good, but I'm not seriously pursuing a national standing, and living like a gypsy can get old. I may compete locally for the next few years, but that's probably it. I'd like to settle down, start working with Angel again, and begin building a solid foundation."

"I see. So you'll be helping Angel with the horse-breeding operation?"

"Yes. Angel told me they've been busy lately."

"Yes, he has. I know he's been looking forward to having your help with it."

After finishing, she dried her hands on his towel and hung it up. Joaquin looked down at the floor and stuck his hands in the front pockets of his jeans. She turned to him, and he looked up at her with encouragement in his green eyes and said, "I know you're still nervous, but I promise to behave. Let's just talk, okay?" He gestured to the living room with a tilt of his head.

She smiled hesitantly and followed him out of the kitchen. It had been easy to talk to him while washing the dishes because it occupied her hands, and she had to keep her eyes on what she was doing. Now they were face to face, and she felt a little breathless.

He sat on the leather couch, and she perched mutely next to him, her fingers twining in her lap. His body was intimidating, wrapped in lean muscle. He exuded a caged, masculine strength that made her long to reach out to him, but her mind told her to hold back from touching him. She knew once she made the first move, she would be lost to him, whether he wound up being good for her, or bad. He looked like more man than she could handle.

"You must love my brother an awful lot." He watched her face carefully.

"Why do you say that?" She looked up at him from her hands.

"You must if you're willing to consider for even a moment that there might be room in your heart for me, as well. It must seem foreign to you."

"I'm wondering if I'll be able to make you happy and if…I'll be able to keep up with you." She knew that was an excuse. Grace looked like she had no problem "keeping up," and Teresa knew they pampered her and helped with chores around the house. She didn't look haggard or ill used.

"Are you referring to the work of running a household or to the physical aspect of such a marriage?"

She realized he was using euphemisms to increase her comfort level. She recognized a difference between the two men just then. Angel tended to use plainer language. She was raised in a household where her parents talked around certain subjects. It wasn't necessarily better, but it was what she was comfortable with.

"Both."

"It would be a high priority for us that you were not pushing yourself too hard, in either way. It's not *supposed* to be more work, and it would be *us* trying to make sure you're satisfied. We wouldn't want you to approach it as trying to keep up. If your needs are being met, then we'll be satisfied, whether we loved you every night, every other night, or once a week. I want you to be happy. I certainly don't want you to feel like a workhorse."

"Joaquin, you've known me less than a day. What is it about me that makes you think you might want to settle down here with us?"

"Well, I heard about you from my mom. Mom has always been very intuitive. She likes you very much, by the way, and Mom…does not like everybody. Then, talking with Angel about you, hearing how…reverent he sounded, like you were precious to him." Teresa's cheeks heated at his words.

"When you flung open the door last night, your eyes were unguarded and excited. When you realized it was stranger, there was a glimmer of fear there. It brought out an instinctive part in me. I wanted to protect you from what scared you, and I wanted you to not feel scared of me. Then Michael went and broke the ice for us, didn't he?"

She chuckled. "Yes, my son knows no strangers. He likes you a lot. That's definitely in your favor because if Michael doesn't trust or like someone, that raises a big red flag with me. You seem to be comfortable around small children. Thank you for helping him with the potty, by the way."

"We helped Mom when we still lived at home, with Luka and Matthias. Me and Angel had them both potty trained before they were two. It's a bit of an incentive when you see that your big brothers don't wear diapers and get to do cool stuff like pee outside. Michael seems to enjoy horses and spending time with Angel. I hope he takes to me as easily."

"I doubt that's going to be a problem. Do you miss your family and your home?"

"Yes, but I'm closer now than I have been in months. It's just a few hours there and back. I'm sure I'll probably head down there for a day or so sometime soon. Were you planning to see your parents over the holiday?"

"No. I love them and miss them, but it's better if I stay here in Divine. I talk with my dad every so often and send pictures to them through a friend. For now, that has to be enough."

His eyebrows had drawn together in concern. He drew closer to her on the couch and settled back against it, facing her. "You sound as though you *can't* go home, Teresa. Do you not feel safe going there?"

Biting her lip, she shook her head. "No, I don't. And…"

"What?" Joaquin leaned toward her.

"I can't risk taking Michael there. It's not safe for either of us." It was going to take some time before she could share the whole story with him.

As if he sensed her discomfort with the subject, Joaquin backed off and said, "Angel and I will protect you, regardless of whether it works out between you and I or not. You'll be my brother's wife someday soon, and I would help protect you from anyone who would threaten you or Michael. You have us now."

"Thank you. It's hard to let down those walls. I suppose I could go back home now if I had to. It was never an option when it was just the two of us. I've never been away from Michael overnight, although I know I could leave him with Grace, Rachel, or Rosemary if I needed to. There have been so many changes in my life this year, and it's a lot to process. Now you're here and I have all these feelings toward you."

He grinned sympathetically at her. "Feel like you are at war with yourself?"

"No, it's not negative like that. It's more like a seesaw that's moving too fast. If I could get it to slow down, I could get my balance in the middle."

"Are you still feeling uncomfortable around me? Since we've been talking?"

She looked up at him and smiled. "No, I feel better. Talking to you helps. I think we understand each other."

"Would you like to maybe lay down with me on the loveseat recliner and watch a movie? Just sort of—" he paused and cringed and started again, tripping over his words, "I don't mean *lay down*— well, yeah I do. Okay, let me start again. Let's pick a movie and watch it laying down on the reclining loveseat, you want to?" he finally blurted with a grin.

She smiled and felt her cheeks tingle but looked into his brilliant green eyes and playfully said, "You're funny when you do that. Yes, I would love to watch a movie with you—on the loveseat—laying down with you—right beside you," she said, speaking in teasing, choppy sentences.

He chuckled. "Angel is rubbing off on you. You were flirting with me just now."

"Was I? Well, you were so cute. I think you even blushed for a second." She giggled as they looked at Angel's DVD collection of pop-culture iconography.

He scoffed in disgust. "Holy crap, what is Angel doing with a copy of *Twilight*? No self-respecting—"

She poked him in the chest with her finger and got a little sassy. "Hey! That's mine, and *no* disrespecting Bella and Edward. That's a deal breaker right there, cowboy." Then she popped her hand over her mouth and giggled at the look of incredulity in his eyes.

He arched a brow and held up his hands in mock surrender. "*Kitten's* got claws. Has Angel watched those with you?"

Somehow her hand found its way to her hip, and she was sure that was Grace's influence on her. "As a matter of fact, he *has*. I won't make you watch them with me if you don't like them. Just remember I have a soft spot in my heart for Bella and Edward…*and* Jacob," she added and giggled. They looked at each other and both burst out laughing.

They put on a movie, and Joaquin opened the recliners on the loveseat so they could lie down and watch it. Teresa missed the whole first fifteen minutes of the movie, wondering if it would be okay if she came closer. Joaquin behaved himself like he promised and watched the movie. If he noticed her distraction, he didn't comment on it. His forearms were tucked behind his head, which made his bulky biceps even more tempting. His body language was completely open, welcoming her to do as she wished.

Here goes nothing. She sat up and shifted her pillow to his side. She gave him a shy smile before lying back down and tentatively laid her hand on his chest. He put his arm around her back and stroked her forearm and the top of her hand and fingers with his other hand. She could feel his heart beating underneath her palm.

Chapter Twelve

Joaquin smiled and closed his eyes, sighing silently in relief as she lay down right next to him and got comfortable. The next hour and a half were a sweet combination of bliss and torture for him. Halfway through the movie, she drifted off to sleep. He appreciated that she felt comfortable enough with him to do that, but she *moved* in her sleep, getting more comfortable. She *snuggled*. Damn it. He wondered if he should stuff his hands in his pockets again so he wouldn't be tempted to let them rove over her delectable body as she sighed happily in her sleep.

By the time she finally settled, she was curled up to him, her head all the way on his chest, one arm flung across his torso and the other curled adorably under her chin. She turned more toward him, slid a knee and thigh over his, and pressed the other thigh along the length of his leg. When she shivered lightly, he realized her body temperature must drop when she fell asleep and she was drawing close to him for warmth. Luckily, there was a throw blanket on the arm of the loveseat, which he carefully unfolded and draped over her. She stilled immediately and fell deeper asleep.

He watched her as she slept. Her lush body, growing warmer, cuddled up to his. She was so beautiful his hands ached to touch her. His cock hardened as the evocative image of her sleeping naked snuggled to him like this flitted through his mind. He pressed his lips carefully to the top of her head, inhaling her clean, natural fragrance. He did his best to ignore the erection tingling behind his zipper.

He must have dozed at some point, too, because he woke when he heard Angel come in quietly and noticed that the beginning menu for the movie was back up on the television screen. He looked over when Angel came in the living room and saw them on the loveseat.

Angel smiled at him and whispered, "She's like a sick kitten to a hot brick when she falls asleep, isn't she?"

Joaquin nodded and gave him a big, satisfied grin.

His brother studied them for a few seconds and murmured, "I'm glad to see she's growing more comfortable with you. I'll check on Michael." He returned a minute later and mouthed, "Still snoring," and came into the living room and picked up the remote. He scanned the satellite channels looking for something they could watch while Teresa and Michael finished their naps.

* * * *

Teresa awoke from her nap slowly, realizing she was toasty warm under a blanket and wrapped in Joaquin's arms. Motionlessly, she opened her eyes and took stock in her surroundings. Uh-oh. She was laying half on top of Joaquin, and he was sound asleep, judging by his regular breathing. What time was it? She needed to get started on the food she was bringing to Grace's tonight. Unmoving, she looked over at the clock and noticed Angel on the couch. The television was on, but he was watching her, his eyes alight with love and contentment. He smiled at her when he saw that her eyes were open. She smiled back and blew him an air kiss.

"What time is it?" she whispered.

"A little after three."

Joaquin must not have been deeply asleep because he stirred and woke up. His muscular body vibrated with strength as he stretched and grinned down at her when he saw she was awake. "Hey, it's Sleeping Beauty."

Teresa yawned and stretched but didn't sit up or move away from him. She felt too comfortable under the blanket, snuggled up to his body heat.

"Not ready to get up yet?" Joaquin asked.

She curled up to him and shook her head, yawning again. Joaquin kissed the top of her head and his arms once again settled around her, seemingly content to stay there with her. She didn't want the moment to end, instead wishing there was room for one more on the recliner.

Angel grinned and said, "Grace got a nice surprise from Santa this morning."

"She did? What did she get?" Teresa stretched one more time, arching her back. She thought she heard Joaquin groan faintly, but when she looked up at him, he smiled at her as Angel answered her.

"A brand new BMW Z4 convertible, electric blue. Little two-seater."

Joaquin whistled softly in appreciation. Teresa giggled and sat up finally. "How did she react?"

Angel chuckled. "She told me she screamed twice and then *fainted*. Adam had to carry her back in the house. Made poor Ash come running to see what the ruckus was all about."

Teresa laughed and asked, "Did you tell them our good news?"

"No, I wanted to do that when we were all together. They will be thrilled about our other development, as well, I'm sure."

"Good, then I'll call her in a bit," she murmured, sitting up and lazily stretching her arms over her head. She looked up at Angel and caught the unguarded desire in his gaze. He grinned crookedly and put his hands on hips as he grunted appreciatively at the view. Unapologetically, too. She bit her lip when her gaze landed on the bulge growing at his groin, which he did nothing to hide. She glanced away then looked back again, drawn by her curiosity and the tingles of desire that stirred at the sight. She glanced at Joaquin and found that he, too, was watching her, a similar desire warming his gaze. What would she do if she had the chance? She *really* needed to talk to Grace.

"I need to get started on that casserole and the tortillas."

"Mmmm, you're *making* tortillas?" Joaquin asked admiringly, like she'd offered to strip for him then give him a lap dance.

"Yes…why?" She teased, "Would you like me to make some special for you?"

"Please, baby?" Angel wheedled as he helped her rise from the loveseat. He turned to Joaquin and said, "I'll deny it if you ever repeat this to our mother, but Teresa's homemade flour tortillas are the best I've ever had. *Way* better than Mom's. Try them, and you'll see what I mean. She has magic in her little fingers," he added as he kissed said fingers.

Joaquin arched his brows and grinned. "Magic fingers, huh? Is there anything I can do to help?" He closed the recliners and followed her into the kitchen.

"I'll let you cook the chicken breasts and grate the cheese if you want. That way I can start the tortillas."

Angel said, "I'll get the little man up and see if he still wants to ride."

"*If?*" she asked with a chuckle. "Ask him if he needs to potty first."

"Sure, baby." He kissed her temple and went down the hall.

She looked up at Joaquin and said, "Thank you for my nap. You're comfy to snuggle up to." She came to him and put her arms around him. He encircled her in his arms and pressed his cheek to the top of her head. She thrilled at how good it felt to be held against his muscular chest, his strong arms wrapped around her. He smelled wonderful. They both chuckled when they heard a still-sleepy Michael down the hall in the bathroom, chirping about "riding horsies." After the toilet flushed, Michael cheered and came running down the hall.

"I dry, Mama. Gonna ride horsies with Angel, okay?"

"You be careful, and do what Angel says, all right?"

"Yes, ma'am."

Joaquin smiled at her when she turned to Angel and mouthed, "Thank you," to him. Angel kissed her, squeezing her hips. After they left, she looked at Joaquin. "I'm teaching him good manners, but it sure helps when there's a man backing me up. Especially when teaching him how to talk to ladies. He forgets, or I forget sometimes. You and Angel can help him remember to be a gentleman. So now that I've been reminded, I'm dying to know."

"Know what?" he asked.

"Did you do the pee-pee dance with him earlier?" she asked, giggling as she imagined this big cowboy doing the dance.

"Yes, ma'am, I did. I felt like I was on *Dancing with the Stars*. He showed me how to do it and criticized me until I got it right," he said, and they both laughed together.

She made some tortillas and set them aside on a plate under a dish towel. She spread butter on one and rolled it up, then gave Joaquin the first bite. He moaned rapturously as he stirred the chicken while she took the next bite.

"You like it?"

"Please marry me!" He opened his mouth for another bite.

She held it back, teasing him. "What about my cooties?"

He gave her a devilish grin. "I like your cooties. Give me more, please," he begged. She held it up for him, and he took another big bite. "Angel was right," he said over the mouthful. She blushed with pleasure that he liked it so much. He turned the chicken and covered the skillet with the lid. "He said you were a good cook, and he wasn't exaggerating. Who taught you to make tortillas?"

"My mother. She also taught me how to cook. When I left Tillman, she gave me her recipe book."

"She did? Wow."

"Yeah. She was pretty wonderful, old fashioned. I'll show you her picture sometime. I have some from when she was very young after she married my father. She was beautiful."

"How is she now?"

"She has dementia, Alzheimer's," she said matter of factly. "My dad shares a room with her in their nursing home. His health is declining, as well."

"What's wrong with him?'

"Nothing except old age."

"Would they like to move to Divine?"

"I don't know. I suppose I could ask him."

She smiled and chuckled a little to herself as memories of her parents came to mind. When he looked at her expectantly, she giggled and said, "I can remember when I was a little girl, my father would come in the backdoor while she was cooking and tug on her apron strings. He would sing 'Besame Mucho' to her and use them to pull her into his arms and dance her around the kitchen singing to her. She would giggle and blush, but I know she loved it. He made her very happy." Her chin quivered, and her vision blurred with unshed tears. The pain of missing them the last three years was suddenly a heavy weight on her heart.

She sniffled and allowed him to pull her into his arms. He patted her back, and she sighed. After a minute, she wiped her eyes and smiled up at him. "Thank you. I'm so emotional today."

"Don't apologize. It must be hard to be away from them, especially during the holidays. I hope you won't think ill of me, but I tended to tune my mother out when she went off in Spanish, and my dads hardly ever spoke it around us kids. When she spoke Spanish, she was usually yelling, or maybe even cursing, who knows? What does *besame mucho* mean?"

Teresa turned to him incredulously. "You're kidding right?"

"No, ma'am. I'm a Texas boy. I speak English and Texan. Angel knows some Spanish, but I was never a good student."

"Well, *besame mucho* means…kiss me, *a lot*." She giggled when he smiled big. "I have it on a CD. I'll bring it so you can hear what it sounds like. It's a beautiful, old romantic love song."

"Do you like to dance?"

"Yes, but I haven't gotten much practice. Angel taught me how."

"I would love to dance with you some time."

Her heart felt open and unfettered as she turned to him and looked up into his handsome face. "I'd like that, too." Feeling brave, she rose on her tiptoes and kissed him. Her hands slid up his broad chest, over his shoulders, and into his silky hair. She shivered when his lips and tongue stroked hers. He slid his large hands over her ribs, holding her lightly. She could tell by his touch and his kiss how careful he was being to not come on too strong. He allowed her complete control of the moment, so she took her time.

Her heart pounded, and her nipples hardened against his chest, tingling almost painfully. The heat of desire washed through her core. That sensitive spot between her legs throbbed in pleasure, and her panties were suddenly damp. His masculine scent filled her nostrils, and she moaned softly against his lips.

They were brought back to Earth abruptly by the smell of a burning tortilla. She used a fork to hurl it in the sink then quickly applied another one to the cast iron griddle. He smiled, watching her fingers work the next tortilla. She grinned up at him and leaned her head against his arm as he stirred the chicken and turned the heat off.

"Did I surprise you?"

"I'll say! Surprise me as often and as much as you like, sugar."

* * * *

Along with Angel and Joaquin, Teresa pulled Grace and her men aside at the ranch house that evening and told them the good news, including that Teresa was considering making it a threesome with Joaquin. Angel said they were postponing setting a wedding date so that Teresa could take her time getting to know Joaquin. Joaquin told them he wanted her to have all the time she needed.

As he said the words, Teresa knew he was giving her an out in case it didn't work between them, but she already knew she would love him. It would just take a little time for her to be sure.

Michael asked Joaquin if he wanted to watch his video with him. Joaquin grinned at Teresa and Angel and lifted Michael onto his back and gave him a piggyback ride to the living room where *The Aristocats* was currently playing. They grinned when they heard Michael singing along.

"*Everybody! Everybody wants to be a cat!*"

Grace admired Teresa's ring, and they went into the kitchen to finish setting up before everyone arrived. The mild temperatures meant that people would be able to flow in and out of the house, making use of both the indoor and outdoor spaces.

Teresa kept a closer than usual eye on Grace as the Christmas get-together got into full swing. She observed with new eyes the way Grace interacted with her three men. They were always classy in the way they showed affection toward her. A simple touch, a whisper in her ear, a sweet caress or pat depending on the body part, and it was easy to see why she was so happy. She moved easily through the crowd, mingling with their guests and paying attention to all three of them.

Teresa noted a marked lack of stress in her features regarding the party, the mess, *or* the clean up. The men made sure the food and drinks were set up and kept the food coming and the beverage coolers full. They were the ones handling the electric knife, carving the beef brisket, and cutting up the sausage and pork tenderloins. They were the ones with pot holders in hand, removing heated items from the ovens and placing them on the buffet table. If Grace helped at all, it seemed incidental.

Teresa's cheeks heated a little as she observed Grace and Ethan conversing across the room. The two of them were standing together, and he was whispering something in her ear, a wickedly sexy smile on his handsome face. Grace's eyelids slowly closed, and her cheeks bloomed a rosy pink as his fingers traced over her cheekbone. *Wow.* Whatever he was telling her, she was enjoying a lot. Grace reached out a hand to Ethan's shoulder to steady herself. He wrapped his arms around her waist and kissed her lips adoringly like nothing else was pressing at the moment.

Ethan looked up and made direct eye contact with Teresa. He smiled at her and winked before leading Grace over to the buffet table and put the things she pointed at on a plate. He led her by the lit fireplace and sat down in one of the overstuffed chairs. Grace joined him, comfortably curling in his lap. They fed each other bites of food from the same plate, but not in a way that made them a spectacle for those around them.

"They look like they enjoy doing that, don't they?" Joaquin whispered, startling her a bit, but also sending a pleasant shiver down her spine. "We would want you to feel that kind of freedom between us. Have you noticed how they care for her? She hasn't had anything to drink or eat all night because she's been socializing." Teresa nodded, still watching the couple but very aware of his warm proximity. "I'm sure he wants her to feel cared for. At the end of the evening she'll be happy and ready to give him and the others the attention they crave."

The thought of what kind of attention they craved could have filled her with apprehension. Instead, a wave of desire for Joaquin flooded her with its hot intensity. She released a quivering sigh when he traced his callused fingertips down her inner arm, stroking the sensitive skin of her inner wrist.

"Does it turn you on to watch the way they interact so tenderly with her and imagine us the same way?" he asked, smiling down at her when she groaned and nodded, leaning into his chest a bit. Her body bloomed with arousal, responding to his scent and his body heat. He stroked her back and she swayed against him and felt the hard shaft that pressed against her through his blue jeans. A sudden tension grew within her, familiar to her now from her experience with Angel on Christmas Eve. She felt a tingle as though she were being watched and located Angel across the room. He watched them with a contented smile on his face and love in his eyes. Michael sat in the crook of Angel's arm still dressed in his cowboy outfit as Angel talked with Evan and Wesley Garner and Rosemary Piper.

She smiled back at him, vaguely noting her own absence of worry at what he thought of seeing her interact with Joaquin so intimately. Angel excused himself from the threesome and made his way over to the two of them.

"It's getting late, and the two of you look about ready to combust. Would you like to say goodnight and go back to the house?" he asked while Michael was distracted in his arms. Joaquin looked down at her, and she nodded.

Chapter Thirteen

Michael yawned hugely and laid his little head against Angel's shoulder as they climbed the steps onto the front porch and went inside. He would be sound asleep in a matter of minutes. Teresa had planned for this possibility and packed pajamas for him to wear. At Joaquin's urging, she took him to his bedroom and laid him down half asleep and changed his Pull-Up and put his pajamas on. He revived enough to want to use the potty when Joaquin asked him and then returned to Joaquin's large bed. He said his prayers with them, and they tucked him in and propped pillows around him, smiling that he was snoring again before they even left the room.

Angel was in the living room. He patted the couch between him and Joaquin as his brother joined him there. She went to them and climbed onto the couch, her calves and feet tucked under her, sitting back comfortably, looking from one man to the other.

"What a wonderful day, from beginning to end. And I don't mean just the material gifts. I also mean the way you treat me and the way you are with Michael. I feel especially blessed."

Angel caressed her thigh. "The day did turn out even better than I expected. We wanted you to feel special, and we want you to know that you can trust us. You know neither of us would take advantage of you." In her heart, she knew he spoke the utter truth. The trust was there for both of these men.

"You wouldn't have been as kind and sweet to me as you've been for the last six months if you didn't intend to keep my trust in you intact. I love you," she said, reaching out a hand to Angel's biceps before turning to Joaquin. "And I think you know I'm falling for you, as well, Joaquin. I would be a fool to deny what I can plainly see and feel. Maybe I'm foolish to give in so easily, but I trust you, as well, with…everything. Maybe more importantly, I trust you both with Michael."

Angel leaned in and kissed her then backed away slightly as Joaquin leaned in and kissed her, as well. Angel was thoughtful for a few seconds and then asked her a question.

"Beautiful, tell us where you want to go from here."

She pondered that question for a few seconds. Teresa thought about watching Grace in Ethan's lap. She smiled, a vision of exactly where she wanted to go from there in her mind. She was about to live up to Grace's advice and seize the day.

"I want to go wherever it was Grace went, to get to where *she* was tonight. She's so happy, content and so in love with her men it radiates from her. I want to be cared for on that level. I want to love you like that, and I want you to teach me what to do, so you look as satisfied as her men do. And I'm ready to get started when you feel the time is right." She grinned at the surprised expressions on their faces and added, "We don't have to do anything tonight if you don't want to, but I'd be open to the possibility." Her body clamored eagerly for them to do something tonight.

Angel touched her cheek. "What happened to the shy, nervous Teresa I flirted into speechlessness?"

Placing her palm over his hand, she answered his question. "I can't have what Grace has by continuing down the path the old Teresa was on, ruled by fear and doubt. If I want what Grace has, I need to forget the past, let go of the fear, and learn to trust someone. Well, *two* someones." She smiled at Angel, touching his cheek with her fingertips and reaching out to Joaquin to do the same.

Angel looked up at Joaquin, and she perceived some sort of silent communication between them as she went to Angel and wrapped her arms around him and felt his arms envelop her. They must not have anticipated this change in her so soon. She wondered if maybe she was moving too fast. She decided she could move slowly toward her goal or take each step without hesitation. She stood from the couch, knowing her next destination.

"Will you listen for Michael while I take a shower?"

"Yes, sweetheart. My robe is on the back of the bathroom door. You're welcome to it."

"Thank you. That's perfect." She went to Angel's bedroom, thankful now that Joaquin had suggested putting Michael in his bed. She used her new gardenia body wash in the shower then borrowed Angel's shampoo and conditioner. After rinsing off, she toweled the moisture from her warmed skin, noticing that she was copiously wet between her legs. Trembling with anticipation, she wondered, even hoped, they might touch her there tonight. She had no idea what to expect, but she was going after what she wanted. She wrapped herself in Angel's thick fleece robe, feeling enveloped in his clean, woodsy scent. Pushing the long sleeves up her arms, she gathered the length to exit his bathroom.

Lit candles were placed on the night tables on either side of his king-size bed, providing the only illumination in the room. Angel rose from the bed and went to her. "We left Joaquin's door closed, so our voices won't disturb Michael, but we should hear him if he calls out or cries." She hugged him, respecting him even more for placing Michael's needs and her job as his mother before his own pleasure.

"He's a sound sleeper, but thank you for telling me." He took her hands and drew her to the bed where Joaquin reclined against the pillows.

"I know it took guts to ask for what you need, to pursue what you want now that you're sure. I talked to Joaquin while you showered. You know that we desire you in a fierce way."

She didn't doubt it, judging by the desire glittering in his eyes and the tremendous bulges at their groins.

"We look forward to making love to you someday soon. But we don't think we should start there tonight. I don't want you to look back and regret rushing into anything, and I think we'll know when the time is right. We want to show you how it would feel to be pleasured by a man as you deserve."

"Oh," she whispered, biting her lip.

Angel closed his eyes and breathed deep for a second. "We want to remove the robe and just look at you. Will you let us do that?"

"Yes." She allowed him to untie the belt but then stayed his hands. "But please be patient with me. I'm not toned and taut like what you're probably used to. Short and dumpy is a little more like it, and I have a scar. I don't mean to destroy the mood. I don't want you to be disappointed."

Angel responded, "The scar, is it the result of an injury?"

"No, Michael was delivered by C-section."

Desire and love still shown in their eyes.

"You've never been like this with a man who truly loved you, beautiful. We desire every luscious inch of you, even the parts you think are flawed."

Joaquin came to the edge of the bed. They were both shirtless and barefoot but still clad in their jeans. She understood this was so she could touch them, but not be frightened by their total nudity. She appreciated Angel for thinking of that. He was taking things a step at a time and not throwing too much at her at once.

Joaquin reached for the robe as Angel did. They slid it from her body with a heavy sigh from them both. She was glad the candles made the room dim, so she wasn't so self conscious of her blushing.

Angel slowly sighed as he looked her over. "Teresa, all the times I ever fantasized about you, my imagination never did you justice." he murmured.

Joaquin's voice was a velvety whisper. "Every inch of you is lovely, sugar."

Joaquin feathered his fingers through her hair, stroking her neck, and then slid his hand down over the curve of her spine, drawing a shiver in the wake of his fingers until he reached the top of her hip and paused there. His thumb stroked the inner curve of her hip, and the small but intimate touch almost made her knees buckle.

Angel gazed into her eyes, and his fingertips lightly slid from her cheek down to her throat. Her breath hitched as his fingers continued their motion past the hollow at the base of her throat and slowly trailed between her breasts.

The backs of his fingers brushed the underside of her breast, and he whispered, "Like silk." Then he stroked her nipple with his thumb.

She stifled a moan as Joaquin's fingers stroked at the base of her spine. The folds between her legs flooded with moisture and pulsed.

"She's trembling," Joaquin said.

She allowed him and Angel to draw her with them onto the sheets. Joaquin helped her to the middle of the bed and kissed her, still stroking her.

"How do you feel?" Angel asked before tenderly kissing her.

"Wobbly and excited. Nervous." She lay back with Joaquin's help.

They lay down on either side of her and continued to stroke her, their body heat and nearness reassuring her. Their hands were so gentle on her arms, her face, and her abdomen and down her thighs and calves, and the trembling deep inside her increased. They stroked her breasts, delighting in her nipples that were tight and ultra responsive.

Joaquin murmured, "Her skin feels like warm satin. I'll bet she tastes sweet as honey."

She laid her head back and sighed blissfully, swamped in the eroticism of the moment. Listening to his sexy drawl made her even wetter. He wanted to taste her? As in *lick* her?

Angel brushed his lips against her forehead while his he cupped the underside of her breast. "Sweetheart, we don't want to make assumptions, so I'm just going to ask. Do you know what an orgasm is?" Teresa nodded mutely, trusting him fully. "Have you ever had an orgasm before?" She hesitated, "Have you ever come before?"

She shook her head. No, she never had.

"To come, or have an orgasm, are two different ways of saying the same thing. It's a climax of pleasure. You're going to have *at least* one tonight," Angel murmured playfully as he kissed her lips again.

"Oh?"

"Do you like us both touching you at the same time?" Angel asked, smiling when she nodded vigorously. "It doesn't scare you?"

She sighed shakily and whispered, "No. I l–like it a lot."

He smiled as she gazed up into his sensual, golden gaze. "Good. We want to taste your skin, is that all right?"

Like he had to ask? She nodded breathlessly.

The place between her legs throbbed as they put their lips on her skin. Joaquin tasted her throat, his lips and tongue sliding over her collarbone in teasing, feathery touches before his hot lips settled over her nipple and her back bowed off the bed. She felt, once again, like she was on the crest of something huge, like riding a tidal wave. Angel's lips and tongue caressed her other nipple, and she was overwhelmed by the erotic onslaught. They tongued the underside of her breasts then looked at each other and smiled at her.

"You are delicious, both your scent and your taste," Joaquin whispered to her before his mouth and Angel's continued down her abdomen and kissed her C-section scar one at a time before moving over her hip bones. Angel growled softly before moving on to her thigh, whispering, "My mouth is watering for your little pussy."

His words inflamed her, and her sheath pulsed achingly as she trembled under their lips. She thought she might explode at any moment.

Angel whispered to Joaquin, "She's about to go over. Help her, then I want to taste her. Joaquin is going to touch the place between your legs, your clit. Will you come for him?"

She nodded, her breath came in high-pitched pants as her back arched, waiting for Joaquin's touch. Angel kissed her as he rubbed a nipple between his fingers and whispered, "It will feel *so* good you'll want to cry out. Don't hold back, beautiful."

Joaquin's exquisitely gentle fingers slid between her lips over the aching bundle of nerves at her apex. She let loose a shuddering gasp as one of his fingers slid into her entrance.

"So hot and wet." He growled deeply as he stroked in and out.

Teresa's body drew up tight, and her breath turned to rapid, sobbing pants. Angel's lips descended on hers, muffling her cries as the tidal wave crashed over her, around her, and within her. Joaquin stroked her through the first orgasm she'd ever had. Her sheath clutched at his fingers as she thrust against his hand in a rocking rhythm her body instinctively knew.

When the pulsing waves receded, she opened her eyes and looked up in wonder at Joaquin. She was mesmerized as she watched him slide his fingers into his mouth. He closed his eyes slowly, licking every drop from his hand as if it were nectar.

"Sweet, like I knew she would be," Joaquin murmured as he moved to her side and stroked her abdomen with a warm hand. "Angel wants to taste you, here." He stroked over her mound, his fingertips in close proximity to her sensitive clit, which drew a gasp from her. "Will you let him?"

She nodded, as Angel lifted her thighs and placed them over his shoulders. This was not a position she'd ever thought she'd be in, but the thought of his mouth on her, down there, was so powerfully erotic her body drew up with tension again. He cupped her buttocks, lifted her to his mouth and slid his tongue over her slit, drawing a trembling cry from her. She pondered for a millisecond why he would want to taste her down there and why she'd never known what she should call that place before now.

Her pussy. He laved her pussy, flicking her clitoris with the tip of his tongue in a way that had her once again rising on the crest of *that* wave. Faint, rumbling sounds came from his throat as he slipped one finger slowly into her entrance. Her pussy tightened around his finger, drawing up steadily harder and higher. Joaquin stroked a nipple before latching onto it and suckling. He reached for the other peak and lightly tugged on it. Feeling like she might soar away, she held onto Joaquin's muscular shoulder.

She flexed her hips against Angel's hand, rising higher still on a wave of another climax. He pulled out and slid two fingers into her opening and continued the same slow pumping rhythm. The increased tightness was unbearably pleasurable, and when he bore down on her clitoris and suckled tenderly, she came for him with another muffled cry of ecstasy.

He continued, pumping his fingers deeper into her pussy. She arched tightly and cried out again as a third orgasm slammed into her, taking her by surprise with its almost painful, burning intensity. She found it exhilarating that he made a feast of her as the last pulses faded away, licking the evidence of her orgasm from her.

"*Oh*," she murmured in a shaky voice, her breasts heaving as she tried to catch her breath. Her body trembled with aftershocks created by his tongue.

"Yes, beautiful. *That* is what it's *supposed* to be like," Angel whispered softly but emphatically. "*That* is what we wanted to give to you. To show you how *we* would love you." His voice was deep and intense with emotion. Tears flooded her eyes at the love she heard in his voice.

"That's only the beginning of what we want to do for you, sugar." Joaquin kissed her lips again. "I'll be right back." He climbed from the bed and went in the bathroom, and a moment later she heard the shower running.

She reached for Angel, and he held her securely as she shook and sniffled quietly. "I never knew it could be like that, Angel. It was so *beautiful*," she murmured as he stroked the tears from her cheeks.

"Yes, baby. It was like that for us, too. I love you." He kissed her, and she tasted a hint of herself. It made the moment all the more intimate.

"I love you, too, Angel."

A few minutes later, he rose from the bed as Joaquin returned. Joaquin slipped under the covers and spooned to her, smelling fresh, like soap. He nuzzled the hollow under her ear, and she realized he was nude and so very warm.

"Sleep now, sugar. We've worn you out. I've got you," he whispered, his hand sliding over her bare hip and abdomen. She snuggled back to him trustingly.

Sleepily she whispered, "You gave me something precious tonight. I'll remember this night for the rest of my life. I love you, Joaquin." She felt cocooned in safety, and a tranquil ripple of bliss slowly washed over her.

He brushed a lock of hair from her cheek, kissed her there and whispered back, "I love you, too, Teresa. Your heart and your son are safe with me, sugar."

After his shower, Angel returned to the bedroom and blew out the candles. He slipped into bed and cuddled up to her. She noticed he was nude, also, as she felt his bare hip before he pulled the covers over them. She rested her hand there and tilted her head up and kissed him goodnight.

* * * *

Joaquin woke at five o'clock ready to start the day but unable to move from the bed. Actually, unwilling might have better described the way he felt. He looked at his brother, who was also awake and watching Teresa sleep. Unaccustomed to rancher's hours, she was deeply asleep. She had shifted between them during the night and now lay flat on her back with her head still pillowed by Joaquin's biceps. The fingers of her left hand were feathered in Joaquin's hair. Her right forearm was curled around Angel's right arm, holding it snug to her chest. Her right knee was drawn up with her thigh resting open against Angel's hip.

One of them had kicked the covers off during the night, so she was exposed down to the other knee where the cover rested. Joaquin lay motionless with a thick, twitching cock eager for action and watched her like a sap with his first crush. Angel was in similar straits. They needed to get up and dress before she saw them in all their erect glory. They lay there a few minutes longer, watching her peaceful face and gazing at her lush form as she dreamed on.

She sighed and smiled in her sleep then rolled to face Angel. Still holding on to his arm, she wiggled her ass against Joaquin, snuggling to him. She was deep enough asleep she didn't feel his hardened cock against her. Nor did she realize how precariously close she was pressing her pussy to his cock. He bit his lip and stifled a groan as the damp lips of her pussy glided against the length of his throbbing shaft. Joaquin was afraid if he moved against her for even a second, he'd embarrass himself. Hating the thought of leaving her satiny, damp heat and not wanting to disturb her sleep, Joaquin carefully inched away from her, putting some safe distance between them.

He sat up with a shudder and hung his head for a few seconds, breathing deep, wanting badly to return to her and slide into her delectable pussy. He drew the covers up to cover her and finally rose from the bed, stretching the kinks from his muscles. His cock twitched in angry rebellion as he walked into the bathroom.

Joaquin took another shower, needing to tame the beast that throbbed between his legs. He stroked himself under the hot spray as he remembered watching her come for the first time. He remembered the awe in her eyes as she gave in to the sensations they'd built inside her. He bit back a deep groan and fisted his cock. The cum jetted from his shaft as he remembered the passionate sounds she'd made. He imagined sliding into her hot, tight pussy as the last of his cum pulsed hotly from his cock. He showered and toweled off then left the bathroom, only marginally satisfied.

The dim lamp was now on in the bedroom. Angel still lay beside Teresa, and she was now awake, speaking to him in soft tones. He caressed her hip through the sheet lay that lay over her, covering her nudity but revealing the sensual line of her curves. Her cheeks were a rosy hue, and as Joaquin drew close, he saw the tears in her eyes and peaceful contentment on her face. He crawled on the bed dressed only in his jeans from last night as she reached for his hand.

She turned her dark gaze to Joaquin and said in a voice husky with emotion, "I told Angel I'm falling in love with you."

Joaquin turned to his brother. "You already know she holds my heart in her little hands. Is everything else all right?"

"Yes. These are happy tears." Angel caressed her cheekbone. "Sweetheart, we'll be back in a little while. Right now we need to check the barns and make sure chores are getting started. It's still dark outside, so you should try to sleep a bit longer."

"All right. I'll adjust eventually to your hours if I'm going to be a rancher's wife." She yawned behind her hand and stretched happily.

Joaquin stifled a groan, and the desire to dive under the sheet with her, then said, "I'm sure you will, but for now you rest, sugar. Angel, can you loan me a shirt?" Joaquin asked. "My other clothes are in my bedroom, and I don't want to disturb Michael." Angel rose from the bed, walked across the room naked, and retrieved a plaid flannel shirt from the closet and handed it to him. Joaquin smiled when he noticed Teresa blush at Angel's nudity, but she didn't avert her eyes. Angel slipped into the bathroom to shower.

Teresa's words from last night came back to him. She wanted what Grace had, but she couldn't get it if she kept doing things the "old" way.

She wrapped the sheet across her breasts and scooted closer to him at the edge of the bed where he sat slipping into his socks and boots, still naked from the waist up.

He glanced back at her and smiled as he pulled on a boot. "How do you feel this morning, sugar? Any regrets?" he asked, kissing her as he turned to her.

She shook her head. "None. Do you have any regrets? Still sure you want me?" She drew closer and pressed her cheek to his shoulder.

"No, no regrets at all. And I'm even more certain I want you. Thank you for trusting us last night, sugar. Giving you your first orgasm meant a lot to me. Waking with you all snuggled up to me was the best feeling. I want to feel that kind of peace and satisfaction every morning." He smiled like a big sap when her arms slid around him. Her firm, full breasts pressed against his back with only the sheet between them, and he wanted to purr and rub against her for about an hour.

She kissed his ear. "When I woke up this morning, I thought for a second I'd had the most amazing dream then opened my eyes and realized I was really here with you. Last night and yesterday really happened. You really love me, Joaquin?"

"Yes, sugar, I do." He lifted her hand from his biceps and kissed her knuckles.

"Ready to go, Joaquin?" Angel whispered as he slipped from the bathroom, completely dressed.

"Angel, do you have a T-shirt I could slip into? In case Michael gets up before I'm dressed," she murmured, yawning.

"Sure, beautiful." Angel pulled open a drawer and pulled out a navy blue T-shirt that looked like it would reach her knees. He handed it to her, and she slipped into it, burying her nose in the fabric after she had it pulled on. She glanced up at them watching her appreciatively and blushed.

"You look good in my T-shirt. Back under the covers with you," Angel said as he went to her and wrapped his arms around her where she knelt on the bed and kissed the top of her head.

Joaquin came to her and hugged her also and kissed her lips. "We'll make you breakfast when we come back in a little while."

"If you insist."

"We do," they both whispered, smiling at her. They quietly passed down the hall and out of the front door.

The ground was covered with a light layer of frost and the grass crunched under their feet. On the walk up to the barn, Angel asked, "Shower help any?"

"Yeah, for about five minutes. Her beautiful, sleepy face and the way she pressed her breasts to my back…It seems like I'm hard anytime I'm around her."

In all seriousness, Angel said, "Thanks for not giving into temptation earlier. I appreciate you that. I know it must have been hard not to…go there."

"Angel, you loved her first. You'll be the one who makes love to her the first time. Thanks, by the way. Watching her come for the first time was…damn."

"Now you've got me thinking about it, too. I'm going to be hard all morning, knowing she's in our bed," Angel muttered as they entered the second barn.

* * * *

Teresa curled up with their pillows and breathed in their combined scents, slipping back to sleep in the dim predawn darkness. She slept lightly, and dreams of Angel and Joaquin swam through her mind, swamping her with arousal and unparalleled joy. They were *her men* now.

Joaquin stood in front of her, holding her to him loosely at her hips while Angel stood behind her, one hand sweeping her hair away from her neck to kiss her there while the other hand stroked her belly. Angel's fingers dipped down over her mound then slid into her slit, teasing the sensitive lips of her pussy. He stroked her clit with a fingertip, and she moaned as Joaquin kissed her passionately and slid his hands over her ass.

Her clit pulsed, and her panting breaths were trapped in her throat, so she couldn't make a sound as her arousal flew higher and higher. Angel's persistent fingers continued to stroke her pussy, and his lips at her throat sent shivers down her spine. His other hand strayed to a bare nipple and tugged, dragging it teasingly between two fingers. Joaquin's lips suckled on the other nipple, drawing on it with torturous skill.

Angel whispered in her ear and told her she was precious and he loved her. Her hands strayed between the two of them, back and forth as they loved her with their lips and their fingers. Finally, her hips flexed against Angel's questing fingers, and her orgasm washed over her in a convulsing wave. She came awake as the orgasm pulsed gently, realizing her head wasn't on a pillow but against Joaquin's shoulder.

Chapter Fourteen

Teresa felt Angel's warmth at her back and knew it was his fingers she'd really felt as her dream orgasm had rushed over her.

"I thought I was dreaming."

Behind her, Angel chuckled. "You were, until we helped it become reality."

"I fell asleep thinking about you. You were making love to me. How long have I slept?"

"It's almost seven." Joaquin pressed kisses to her collarbone. "The little cowboy is still snoring in the other bedroom. We wore him out yesterday."

"I need to go home, shower and change." She felt morose at the thought of leaving them after what they had just shared. "And, um…I'm also wondering…I mean, the two of you were so good to me last night and just now. Shouldn't—"

"Shouldn't what?" Angel asked.

"Shouldn't I be—I don't know? Reciprocating?" she asked weakly, unsure what it was she could do for them. She *so* needed to talk to Grace.

Smiles stretched across both their lips, and Angel shook his head. "Sweetheart, it's awful nice of you to ask about that. We think it might be better if we took making love with you one step at a time. There will be plenty of time later to show you ways you can make us your devoted slaves. Why don't you let me take you home? Michael can stay with Joaquin, if you feel comfortable with that. You can bring him a change of clothes, and he can bathe here later. It would also be a good idea to bring a few things to leave here for if you need them some other time. I have plenty of room in my closet and dresser."

"If you don't mind. I'd like that."

"While we're there make sure and bring something to change into for tonight because we'd like to take you dancing at The Pony. I asked Grace, and she said she'd babysit Michael for us."

For them, not just for her. It sounded good when he put it that way.

* * * *

Angel had just closed the door to her apartment when there came a knock at it. Teresa smiled wryly at Angel and whispered, "See? They are a *little* bit protective." She held two fingers close to each other and giggled quietly as she went to the door and opened it. There stood a couple in their late forties, a look of concern on both their faces.

"Hello, Martha. Hello, Frank. How was your day yesterday?" she asked.

The older woman responded to her smile, glancing over at Angel, and said, "It was wonderful, Teresa. How was yours? We were a little concerned when you didn't come home last night." Martha stole another glance at Angel. "Hello, Mr. Martinez. It's good to see you again." But she said the last sentence as though she weren't certain it was a good thing they were seeing each other again.

Angel nodded at the couple in a friendly, open manner but allowed Teresa to respond.

"My Christmas was wonderful, the best in some ways. Frank, this is Angel Martinez. I don't think the two of you have met before."

Angel smiled and shook Frank's hand in a firm, friendly fashion.

"I have news for you," Teresa continued and held out her hand to Martha, so she could see. Martha's eyes bugged a little looking at the platinum and diamond engagement ring. Frank looked over his wife's shoulder, whistling in admiration, then glanced up at Angel speculatively.

Martha began talking a mile a minute, barely giving Teresa time to answer all her questions. The men grinned and made small talk for a minute before Frank got Martha's attention. They congratulated them one last time before excusing themselves.

"Michael and I will be home late tonight because we have plans, but we will be home. You don't have to worry about me with Angel. I'll be in good hands. See you later."

"Sure, sure." Frank waved as they retreated to their front door.

Teresa closed the front door and went giggling into his arms. "You see? They worry about me, plus they're a little nosy. Did you see the way Frank looked at you after he saw the ring?"

"I got the feeling it set his mind at ease." Angel was glad. He wanted anyone who felt kinship or responsibility for Teresa to know he was more than capable of taking care of her.

"I'll get fresh clothing and take my shower." She backed the short distance to her little bedroom. Pointing to the coffee table she said, "There's the remote if you want to watch TV, or do…whatever. Make yourself at home."

* * * *

Angel smiled at her newfound zest for life. He wondered if she would welcome a little company in the bathroom. After a few minutes, he knocked at the bathroom door. She called out hesitantly, and he turned the knob and peeked in. The room was steamy, and the floral fragrance of her body wash hung intoxicatingly in the humid air.

"May I come in?" he asked the shadowy image behind the translucent shower curtain. He couldn't see much, but he could tell she was facing away from the shower head, rinsing her hair. He could make out the lush mounds of her breasts as she raised her hands to her hair to squeeze the rinse water through it.

"Um, yes. Of course you can, Angel."

"You told me I could do whatever, and I was wondering what my options were?"

He was hypnotized by the curves of her body, illuminated by the light shining through the window. When she moved her arms, her breasts tipped forward and he could see the silhouette of her nipples. "I could stay in here and talk with you, or…I could join you." He wanted a little more than just to see. He wanted to taste.

She gathered the edge of the shower curtain away from the tiled wall, and peeked out. Her wet hair was slicked back and water beaded and dripped down to her chin. Her cheeks bloomed with color, and she smiled shyly at him, but he thought he saw the hint of a playful twinkle there, too.

"We'll be married soon, right?" she asked so faintly he had to strain to hear her over the shower running. He swallowed hard, and his cock, already at a semi-erect state from ogling her through the shower curtain, sprang to joyous life and pressed hard against the zipper of his jeans.

"Yes, we will. Very soon, I hope." He didn't make a move but waited for her response.

"You can join me if you'd like. I'm nearly finished," she said as he unbuckled his belt and began removing his clothing.

"Good. Just in time for me to get started," he murmured with a chuckle as she retreated behind the shower curtain.

"I'll hurry so you have plenty of hot water for your shower."

"No, I mean to get started with *you*, sweetheart. But it's nice of you to so considerate. What I want in the shower is *you*."

He parted the shower curtain at the other end of the tub. She was rinsing her hair again, so he had a moment to feast his eyes on her voluptuous beauty. Her eyes were closed and her head tilted back under the showerhead. She wiped her eyes and smiled when she saw his face.

Determined to do nothing to scare her, Angel asked, "Teresa, have you ever seen a man naked before?"

"I got a glimpse of you from the back this morning. I know what a man is supposed to look like, but I've never seen a totally naked man before…now." She gave him a tremulous but encouraging smile. "I know you must be very large from touching you accidentally the other day. Are you…?"

The innocent desire in her voice sent a electrifying bolt of lust from his tailbone to the nape of his neck, and his cock leapt forward, seeking her. "Erect? Yes, extremely so, sweetheart. I wanted to…prepare you," he said, feeling a foreign nervousness of his own at her reaction when she saw him the first time. Was this the right time? Or was he about to blow six patient months of wooing?

Surprising him, she asked, "Will I like it, Angel?" She seemed reassured by his sudden hesitancy. It leveled the playing field somehow.

Her innocent words served only to stiffen his cock further. His heavy, blood-engorged shaft twitched and stung as it hardened almost painfully.

"I hope so, beautiful," he said, his hand poised on the cool tile of the shower.

"Well, then, why don't you just show me?"

* * * *

Teresa knew Grace would tell her to seize the day, and that thought put the words in her mouth that made his face light up with anticipation. Her heart beat a rapid rhythm in her chest as she gazed into Angel's eyes. He stood poised at the edge of the shower curtain, about to move it aside. Part of her shifted in fear, ready to run, and another part of her knew that was an irrational thought. She loved and trusted this man and had come through so many hurdles to get to this point. She wrung the washcloth in her hands and held it clutched to her breasts as he slid the curtain aside, and one muscular calf came into view. Her gaze shifted to his face as he stepped into the shower.

Teresa drank in the sight of his hard-muscled chest. The hairs that grew there collected moisture from the shower and gradually narrowed down to a damp trail that led over his abdomen and past his navel to the dark nest between his legs.

Her pussy clenched in a pleasurable spasm, and her breath caught in her throat. She glanced up into his eyes then back down again as her eyes grew wide with awe. He was so big and thickly erect. Moisture trickled from her pussy as another ripple flow through her inner muscles. This part of him would be hers? Unconsciously, she licked her lips and reached out a tentative hand to touch him.

She pulled back her hand when she heard his shuddering breath and glanced up for encouragement. His face was taut as he braced a hand on the tile wall. He glanced up at hers, and she shivered at the intense desire that burned in his eyes, then extended her hand.

"May I touch you there?" She wondered if it was painful for him to be like this with her. "Will it hurt?"

His features broke into a vulnerable smile and he chuckled. "No. It'll feel very good if you touch my cock right now. Good like it felt when we stroked your clitoris last night."

"Oh! Really?" She felt emboldened by his explanation. "If I touch you, will you come for me, too?"

Chapter Fifteen

Teresa's innocent tone and tempting words worked at the tight reins of Angel's control. He prayed for self discipline and hoped he'd last at least a minute before he exploded. Angel was more experienced than this, but he felt like an untried teenager standing in the shower with her now.

"Yes. If you stroke me, I'll come hard for you." He groaned and fisted his hand against the cold tile wall, watching her soft hand come closer and closer.

"Show me what to do?"

He gritted his teeth as all his fantasies of what he'd like her to do came rushing to the forefront of his mind.

"Just touch me, baby. Explore if you want to. Then I'll show you what to do if that's what you want." His cock twitched hungrily for her touch, and his release boiled up inside him. He clenched his jaw and stifled the deep growl that threatened to rumble from his chest. He wanted her to have this moment to satisfy her curiosity, and he wasn't going to spoil it by coming at her first touch.

Her fingertips made contact with the heavy, throbbing head and circled his girth, causing him to hiss sharply at her light touch. She hesitated briefly but stepped closer to him. Wrapping her delicate fingers around his shaft, Teresa slid them down the length then up to the head. Her full lips parted, and she made a small mewing sound. In the heavy steam of the shower, the scent of her arousal came to his nostrils. Her body and mind were making the connection with the action of her hand on his cock. A quavering moan escaped from her lips. He gritted his teeth again as she stroked up and down. He groaned when her palm caressed the head. She glanced up at him before she continued.

He nodded in encouragement. "The head of my cock is very sensitive. That gentle swirling of your hand is heaven right now."

"Is that what I should call this part of you? Your cock?"

He smiled at the innocence of her words. "Yes, baby. But you can give it any nickname you want if you'll keep doing that to it!" He groaned as she squeezed just a bit. She had great instincts. Her thumb smoothed over the droplet of pre-cum escaping from the tiny slit in the head. Her other hand came to rest on his chest as she continued stroking him with growing confidence. He groaned softly before murmuring, "When I come for you, my seed will spurt from that opening."

"Oh. Your seed?" Her encircled fingers slid down his thick, pulsating length. "It's so hard and hot but like silk at the same time. Will it feel good inside me, Angel? As good as last night?"

He couldn't help the deep growl that rumbled from his chest at the mental image her words conjured. "Oh, sweetheart. When my cock slides into your little pussy and I make love to you, it will feel better than anything you've experienced yet. I *promise* it will." He held onto his control by the thinnest of threads.

"You're so big, Angel," she whispered hesitantly. "Are you sure I'll be able to…?"

"We'll make sure that you're ready for us. We'll be slow and careful with you and give you time to adjust to us. But I think you'll love it. And yes, it'll fit. I promise." He hissed again as her hand stroked back and forth along his length. He leaned his temple against the forearm braced on the wall. "I stay this way just being around you or thinking of you."

"That must be uncomfortable."

"Torture," he said shakily as her fingers strayed into the bed of crisp curls around his cock and farther south to the heavy sack that hung between his thighs. At her touch, they drew up, and he moaned.

His eyelids slid shut in ecstasy while she caressed his sack carefully. As talented as her innocent hands were, he remembered this was still a learning experience for her.

"Those are my testicles, my balls. I love it when you do that. Your touch is heaven, baby." She carefully caressed him with her fingertips, swirling over them again as he moaned.

"I want to know what it's like for you when you come, Angel," she whispered as she feathered her lips against his chest. "Will you come for me?"

He breathed deep, fighting the losing battle for control as lightning shivered up and down his spine. He poured a little conditioner in the palm of her hand and wrapped it around his cock. He began a slow stroking motion, establishing the rhythm for her and tightened his hand over hers a tiny bit. He was engulfed in the delicate scent of her arousal as he allowed her to stroke him. He braced one hand against the wall behind her head and leaned into her a bit, her scent spiking his arousal to volcanic proportions. His breath came in short, choppy gasps.

His release gathered momentum as she increased her rhythm. "Your hand feels so good."

"Can I use both hands? Would it be too much?"

"Oh, *fuck yes*, baby!" He moaned as she wrapped his shaft with both her slippery little hands. "You're doing it just right." He groaned, flexing his length into her hands. He was about to explode.

* * * *

Teresa felt her pussy swell and weep for him as she thought someday soon he would slide this gigantic cock into her pussy. She knew she'd love it, every hard inch of it. His big body loomed over her, his cock pistoning through her stroking hands, and she wasn't intimidated by his size and unleashed strength in the least. She moaned at the thought of being the recipient of their lovemaking, of *fucking* with her men. He flexed hard into her hand, perhaps responding to her sounds. He growled deeply and began pumping even harder. His breath was loud panting, and she knew he must be very close.

She imagined how it would feel to have this tremendous organ sliding in and out of her hard and fast like this, and she moaned again. Her pussy clenched rhythmically as her body *begged* to be filled with his. She looked up into his tortured golden gaze and whispered, "Soon, I'll let you fuck me, and you'll come inside of me. Soon. Come for me, my Angel. Show me what it's like for you."

His eyes filled with love and wonder, looking into hers. She could feel the transformation inside her happen as she brought him to an explosive orgasm. He threw his head back and cried out loudly. She moved a little closer and allowed his cock to brush against her abdomen. His seed spurted from him in hot, jets onto her belly and over her fingers. She continued stroking him as more of his cum poured from his cock. His other arm wrapped around her shoulders, and his forehead rested lightly on the top of her head. His breaths were deep and rasping as he recovered.

"*You're* the angel," he said at last and stood to look breathlessly into her eyes. Teresa smiled up at him, her cheeks warm as she released his sated cock.

She looked at her hands covered in his seed, and he cursed softly as he watched her slide her index finger into her mouth. All she wanted was a taste. If they liked what came from her, perhaps she would like what came from him. She was surprised as her mouth watered for more. He was salty and musky. She could taste his unique essence there, as well, what made him Angel.

He gazed down at her cautiously, awaiting her reaction. She beamed up at him and slid her middle finger between her lips next, letting him know she liked it. A hitching laugh came from his lips, and he crushed her to him in relief. He kissed her lips, and she wondered if he could taste himself there, too. Her clit throbbed, and moisture slipped from her pussy at the sweet eroticism of the moment.

"I love you, Angel." Her voice shook with the depth of her happiness.

"You are everything to me, Teresa. My whole world. Thank you." He breathed out in a shaky voice.

"If we hurry, there should be enough hot water to get cleaned up," she whispered as she scooted to the side to share the showerhead with him. He rinsed his semen from her abdomen and her hands then rinsed himself off. His hands strayed down her back to her buttocks.

"I love this luscious ass. It's beautiful," he murmured, squeezing her cheeks. One hand strayed around her hip to her mound, and his fingertips began a downward quest to her pussy. He teased through her black curls before sliding into her slit and she clutched his biceps when his slippery finger found her clitoris. Her pussy was on fire for him.

"It's going to feel so good to slide my cock into this little pussy. Were you imagining what it will feel like while you stroked me?" He held her securely as he continued to stroke her clit. More moisture seeped from her at his words.

"Yes, I was. I wanted it so much my body was crying out for it."

"Let's get you dried off then, and I'll give you some loving. It's the least I can do for the stroking you just gave me. I want to taste your cum, too." He turned off the water, reached for her towel, and wrapped her in it then began drying her. "Do you know what a G-spot is?"

"No," she mewled distractedly as he paid special attention to drying her inner thighs, licking her pebbled nipples as he did so.

"It's your G-spot. A place inside your pussy that's very sensitive to the right touch."

As he said the words, his eyes twinkled with devilishly at her monosyllabic reaction to that thought.

"Oh."

He toweled himself quickly and lifted her in one smooth motion and carried her to her neatly made queen-size bed and laid her on it. The December sun shone brightly outside, streaming in through the mini blinds on her bedroom windows. He climbed onto the bed with her and palmed aside her thighs as he took up his position between them. The light in the room left nothing in shadow, and she asked, "Should I close the drapes?" She thought he might like it dimmer, more intimate.

He smiled at her from between her thighs, glanced down at what lay before him in such close proximity that she could feel his hot breath on her pussy as he chuckled. He said with obvious relish, "I love being able to see every inch of you, every little dip and curve." His tongue flicked out and licked at the hollow between her inner thigh and the curls of her mound, stealing her breath.

"Oh," she said shakily as he rose over her and kissed her. "I'm far from perfect."

He smiled understandingly at her. "You're beautiful. I love you." The truth was in his eyes as he kissed her again. She smiled up at him and relaxed, allowing her head to rest on her pillow. He caressed her collarbone and then both breasts. She gasped as he rubbed her nipples lightly between his fingertips then cupped the underside of each breast and licked one nipple then the other. Her back arched when he suckled one as she watched in the bright daylight.

A low growl rumbled deep in his chest as he tasted her flesh, and she felt a gush of moisture in response to the sound. Her clit throbbed almost painfully, begging for a touch. He stroked her waist with his big, strong hands, and tremors rocked through her core. His thumbs traced lightly over her mound, and he leaned down and pressed his lips there while his fingers skimmed over her hip bones. He slid a hand behind one of her thighs, which he lifted and placed over his shoulder then did the same thing with the other one. His mouth was poised over her pussy, and she could feel the heat of his breath. He gazed hungrily on the most intimate part of her, seeing her clearly in the bright morning sun.

He stroked with a single finger over her wet entrance. "This is a delicate, beautiful treasure, sweetheart."

Angel slid his tongue into her slit, teasing her. Her head fell back, and her back arched at his loving touch. His words touched her heart, and the last of her inhibitions slipped away. He wrapped his hands around her thighs, and used his fingers to splay her outer lips open. She knew he could see every bit of her.

His velvety drawl was like a caress. "Your clitoris is swollen, beautiful. Your lips are parted for me. I think I'll kiss them." Teresa moaned as she felt his lips and tongue on her pussy. The tightening sensation that she now knew signaled an orgasm began inside her as she stifled a groan. More moisture flowed from her as he stroked her.

"Your pussy juices are like honey on my tongue. I love it. You like what I'm doing, don't you?" At her mute nod he added, "I can feel you trembling."

"Yes, baby, I love it. You're so good to me." Her voice shook with love for him and pleasure at this communion between them. "I like it when you talk to me, while you do…what you're doing."

"Good. There's plenty more where that came from." He slid his tongue into her slit again, flicking at her clit. She moaned and flexed against his mouth. He laved her with his tongue over and over, taking her higher with each pass of his tongue until she was writhing in his hands.

He glanced up, and she saw the utter enjoyment that danced in his eyes as he played with and loved her. Teresa smiled back at him and cried out when his tongue slid into her entrance as he slid his thumb over her clit. Her body tightened up, and she was certain that she was going to come any moment. Her back arched, and the wave she was on crest even higher.

Angel rose over her, spreading his knees and lifting her thighs and wrapping them around his hips. He smiled down at her reassuringly when her eyes flared, wondering what he planned to do next in this very intimate position. She wanted to thank him when he placed his thumb over her clit and began a slow but insistent stroke.

Angel slid a thick finger into her pussy and Teresa moaned and slammed her eyes shut, imagining that it was his cock he gave her. Then he slid in another finger and pumped in and out a few times.

The gripping tightness of her pussy on his fingers made her want to scream with pleasure. If it felt like this with only two fingers, how would it feel when he thrust his much larger cock inside her the first time? Oh, ecstasy! He would consume her! As always, Angel was incredibly gentle, but the sensations he evoked in her were explosive.

His voice sounded strained when he spoke again. "The sounds you make and the way you move makes me want to come again. Just feel for me." He ceased the pumping motion and stroked inside her pussy. Clutching the bedspread in her hands, she felt like she was soaring. The pleasure he was building inside of her expanded outward. Her eyes opened wide, and she panted quietly.

"That's your sweet spot I'm stroking. Do you like it?" He chuckled as he asked the stupidest question in the universe.

She laughed then moaned. "Yes, baby. I'll be your slave. *Please* don't stop!"

"I'll take good care of you, beautiful."

He continued and once again to stroked her aching clit. He sent her higher and higher, surpassing anything she'd experienced the night before. Her body trembled hard, and the muscles in her pussy drew up impossibly tight as he continued stroking both places.

"That's right, baby, unlike anything you thought possible, right? I love you so much, Teresa. It's me who is your slave. I want to taste your cream." He replaced his thumb with his mouth and firmly tongued her clitoris, holding her to him carefully as her back arched off the bed. Pressing his lips to her, he suckled her clitoris.

The wave broke in a magnificent crescendo as her body bore down hard and came explosively for him. Her hand clapped over her mouth to stifle the rapturous scream that escaped from her. She moaned and shuddered in bliss as his lips and tongue lapped and slid over her drenched pussy.

As she came back to Earth, she could hear him growling softly as he feasted on her pussy, just as he said he would. He sounded like he was enjoying himself. Her cheeks felt like they were on fire, and a blush spread over her whole body, making her nipples tingle fiercely. A hazy warmth crept over her as she listened to the sounds he made, still licking her.

His next words floored her as he gazed up at her from between her thighs, his lips and chin wet with the evidence of her orgasm. "You taste like spun honey. Joaquin is partial to spun honey. You're going to have a hard time keeping panties on. I may not get any work out of him." He chuckled at her when she flung a forearm over her eyes and giggled.

"That sounds like a good problem to have. I'm wondering if you'll be able to share, though."

"Oh, don't worry. We share very well where you're concerned." He punctuated the end of his statement with one last long lick up the entire length of her slit.

"Oh, goodness," she said a few minutes later as she tried to sit up but fell back limply on the bed.

"Feeling good?"

"A little better than good. I though last night was incredible, that it couldn't get any better."

"Wait until it's my cock sliding into your pussy. We've only scratched the surface, sweetheart. I promise."

She moaned at the image he'd just described and turned in his arms, stroked his firm, muscled chest and said, "Thank you for being so patient with me. My fears were all so foolish. I was *afraid* of becoming intimate with you for *nothing*."

Teresa rested her chin lightly on her hand and tears filled her eyes as she looked up into his honey-colored eyes. He pulled her to him so her head was on his chest and held her trembling body in his arms. His work-roughened hands felt perfect on her skin as he stroked her back.

Once she had quieted some, he said, "This is what love is supposed to feel like, beautiful. This good, this special. Yeah, we're working up to bigger and better things, but it's all supposed to feel this good. I'm glad you've left the fear behind."

She wanted nothing more than to start her life as his wife. She didn't want to come to this empty apartment tonight, not when the solace of his arms was so close. Waiting to get married didn't make sense when her heart and instincts told her there was no point, considering she felt the same way about Joaquin.

"I want to marry you as soon as we can, as soon as Grace and I can put it together."

His eyes flared a little at the change in subject, and he said carefully, "Couldn't you give Joaquin a little more time? It will be better if he has a chance to prove himself to you, and we can start our marriage together."

"Angel, I want you both. I *want* to be married to you both. I don't want to be away from you any longer than I have to. Going home with Michael by ourselves tonight is looking less appealing all the time."

Excitement gleamed in his eyes. "You're sure? You're sure you're ready?"

"I know I am. I've never felt so sure in my life. Soon, please?"

"I'll talk to him. He'll want to propose to you, too. Can you give him a day or two to find your ring?"

"Of course. I'm looking forward to my afternoon with him. Tell him before then, all right?"

"You are about to make a lonesome cowboy extremely happy, honey. Hell, two lonesome cowboys, for that matter!" He wrapped his arms around her snugly and rolled with her on the bed until she was beneath him.

Feeling perfectly sheltered, she tilted up and kissed him, sliding her tongue between his full lips. As he drew her tightly to him, his body trembled against hers. His cock lay hot and hard once again at her naked hip.

"Do you need to…?"

He grinned, and his eyes twinkled devilishly. "What, honey?"

"Do you want me to…?"

"What, honey?" he murmured in a teasing tone.

She grinned back when she realized what he was playing at. "Do you want for me to take this *great, big, thick cock* in my hands and stroke you until you *come*, groaning and *growling* my name?" she asked in her most innocent voice.

He let loose with a sexy chuckle as he rolled onto his back, pulling her along with him. "Well…now that you mention it. I do have a need. Oh, just like that, baby," he groaned as she *took him in hand* and taught him a thing or two about teasing her.

Chapter Sixteen

Joaquin chuckled as he poured tea in glasses for the grownups and quietly said to Angel, "It's about fucking time you got back. I was ready to send a search party."

Angel leaned against the counter with the look of a man utterly satisfied by his woman on his sappy face. People said women were bad about gossiping? He could not fucking wait for some details. Whatever had happened between the two of them had left them both looking totally blissed out.

Angel grinned at him and Joaquin groaned as his cock swelled. What did they *do*?

"Don't worry. We didn't do anything serious. You and I need to talk and soon."

"Good news?"

"Fucking fantastic news."

* * * *

A few hours later, Angel and Michael left to run errands together. Teresa picked the movie and put it in the player while Joaquin prepared a snack for them. While he was in the kitchen, she dead bolted the front door and closed the drape over the picture window. He noticed the change when he returned with the snack and a glass of iced tea. He grinned at her, sat down, and pulled off his boots.

"So we can see the television without the glare coming in through the window," she explained, smiling, and then added, "and also for privacy."

He smiled at her and sidled up behind her and whispered, "I like privacy, especially if you're with me, sugar." Every note of his sexy, deep drawl sent a thrill to her pussy. His hand slid around her hip and pressed her back against his erection, and her body ached with desire. He drew her down to the recliner and used the remote to start the movie.

She'd picked a romantic comedy, and they watched for a minute or two before he picked up the plate and held it across his lap so she could see he'd made bean and cheese nachos. He lifted one from the plate and held it for her. Teresa looked up, as he waited for her to take it from his fingers, smiling down at her expectantly. She opened for him and took it.

"I hope this is okay."

"It's perfect. I love nachos."

"I brought jalapeños, if you like it hot," he added with a grin, offering the option.

"I like jalapenos, but I'd better not," she said, grinning. Not with where her mouth was planning on going later. He offered her another one, and she took it from his fingers, pausing his hand long enough to lick a little of the salt from the chips off his fingertips.

He groaned softly and then offered her his glass of tea. She took a sip, smiled, and thanked him. She took a few more nachos from him, paying similar meticulous attention to his fingers, and shared his tea with him. Neither of them was really paying attention to the movie. The growing heat between them and the languid arousal she felt became a topic of greater interest. He offered her a last sip of tea then picked up the remote and hit the mute button.

He pulled her to him firmly as though she were weightless. His lips descended on hers roughly, and her body felt swamped with desire, ready for him and whatever he wanted to do. His hands roamed up and down her back and over her buttocks while his lips nuzzled her throat and the tops of her breasts over her shirt.

After a few breathless minutes, he grasped her hips and shifted her directly on top of him. In this position, his thick erection was noticeable. She rubbed against his cock, making him growl. He drew her lips back to his and kissed her lightly to make up for his earlier forceful treatment, licking at them with his tongue. She sat up, straddling his hips, her pussy directly over his cock, and wiggled a bit. His eyes roved over her, and his sensual mouth spread in a sexy smile.

She grew bold and asked him, "Did Angel tell you about our time together this morning?"

Teresa heard another low growl in his chest as Joaquin replied.

"Yes, he did. He said it was incredible being with you. I was hoping I might merit some of your loving attention this afternoon."

"'Merit' my attention, huh?" she whispered as she unbuttoned his plaid shirt. "Yes, Joaquin. You do." Shifting her ass slightly over his groin, she enjoyed at all the hardness she felt there and the corresponding pulse in her clit. She tugged the shirt from his jeans and greedily slid her hands over his bare, muscular chest, enjoying every dip and bulge as she stroked him.

Sliding his hands over her hips, Joaquin palmed her ass, groaning as he rubbed his cock against her. He gathered the hem of her top and slid it over her ribs, lifting it higher when she bent to kiss him and drew it over her head. He smiled admiringly at her breasts, his thumbs tracing over the nipples that peeked out through the lace of her bra, drawing a happy sigh from her.

She scooted back over his thighs, rubbing every inch of his length playfully as she moved over it, so she could unfasten his silver belt buckle and unzip his fly. His hand came over hers as she grinned up at him.

"What are you up to, sugar?" he drawled as her fingers drew the tab of the zipper down a little at a time.

I'm seizing the day, baby!

"Why, giving you my attention, Joaquin. Do you mind if I play?" she asked in a mischievous tone.

"Far be it from me to not give a lady what she wants," he drawled, watching her with glittering green eyes, "especially when she asks so sweetly."

Assuming Angel had given him details about what they had done together, she believed he was hoping for the same attention, at most. But Teresa had talked with Grace that afternoon. She eagerly anticipated trying out her newfound knowledge. He lifted his hips and helped her slide his blue jeans down a bit. She paused for a moment and sat up. She didn't want to do this in half measures.

"Sugar, if you tell me what you want, I'll help," he offered, not teasing her at all.

"I changed my mind. I want it all off. Everything. I don't want anything covered up."

"Okay," he complied quickly while wearing a lopsided grin. "You gonna reciprocate, sugar?"

"Would you like that, Joaquin?" she asked, climbing off the loveseat and unbuttoning her jeans slowly.

"Yeah, then I can touch you, too." His eyes smoldered with longing as she undressed and returned to him naked, straddling his thighs again. He looked down and groaned, and she knew he saw that this position parted her pussy lips so he could see the damp pink flesh within. Cupping his balls, Teresa stroked delicately. He flexed his hips and pressed into her hand with a low growl.

A contented smile crossed Joaquin's face as he tilted his head back and his eyelids slid closed, a deep breath escaping from him at her touch. His cock was lying stiff against his abdomen, as long and thick as his brother's. She felt no fear being alone and naked with him like this. In fact, the thought of being at his mercy made her pussy clench and swell a little for him. Her lips felt hot and grew even damper with her increased arousal.

"Sugar, that feels good." He groaned as she caressed his sack again, drawing closer to him. With his eyes closed, he was completely unprepared for what she did next. She began licking one testicle then the other. She grinned to herself at the low-pitched, startled cry that erupted from him as he bucked toward her mouth.

"Fuck! Where did you…! How—" She lightly suckled one testicle and his back bowed off the recliner. "Oh fuck, baby!"

Gazing up at Joaquin, she released one testicle and then laved and suckled the other one between her lips, her nose tickled by his short, crisp curls. She watched the ecstasy that played across his features and continued while her hand slid up to his cock. He cried out again when she wrapped her fingers around his girth and began stroking up and down on his length. His fingers slide into her hair at the nape of her neck.

Finally she released his other testicle and moved a little higher, watching his face as she stroked him. His eyes smoldered as he waited to see what she would do next. He allowed his head to fall back to the recliner and begged her to do whatever she wanted to him. He closed his eyes again, an enraptured groan leaving his lips when she lifted his cock from his nest of black curls.

He shivered with anticipation as she held his substantial shaft up with one hand and continued to caress his balls with the other. Licking her lips, she pressed them to the head of his cock. He cried out at the first touch of her mouth, and she smiled with satisfaction at the sound as she licked the drop of pre-cum from the tip in a soft, broad stroke and swirled her tongue around the blunt head.

"Sugar! Oh fuck!"

Responding to his taste, her mouth watered for him. She licked her lips again and allowed his cock to slide between them, and she stroked him with her tongue as she slid his cock in and out. Her wet lips gradually descended farther over him, taking more until his head touched the back of her throat. Grasping his cock at the base, she suckled on his cock. He was enormous, and she hoped that he would be satisfied with her novice effort.

Joaquin whimpered and moaned when she allowed the head to slide from her lips with a slight popping sound every so often, so she knew this was something he liked. She slid him to the back of her throat and took him as deeply as she was comfortable several times, sucking as she drew up on him, teasing him with her tongue on the underside, especially at the sensitive head.

"Sugar, your mouth is so sweet and hot," he murmured, his hips grinding with her movements. "How did you learn to do this? Fuck, I don't care, just don't stop! Yes, suck me, sugar." Taking her time, Teresa loved the way he felt and tasted, the way he sounded so enthralled in what she was doing, and enjoyed the moment and the way her body responded.

She received pleasure from this, too. Realizing her hips were rocking, she understood what Grace meant. Giving Joaquin pleasure didn't mean she had to disconnect from what she was feeling in order to give her all to him. It all rolled into a satisfying feeling of connectedness with him. She knew this when she dipped down and her extremely wet pussy rubbed against his lower thigh. He acknowledged her presence there and lifted his knee slightly for her to increase the contact between his thigh and her pussy if she wished. She understood now.

Joaquin was building quickly to his release. She kept the rhythm the same for him until he was groaning and almost incoherent. "Sugar, you do that so well. I'm going to come soon!" His voice, while enraptured, also took on a note of concern. She knew the moment had arrived.

"Baby, if you don't want me to come in your mouth, you'd better *let go!*"

Sliding her free hand under his thigh, she held him to her. She increased the suction slightly and listened to him as he was consumed by the pleasure she gave him.

She could hear the conflict of emotions in his voice. "Baby? I mean it, let go, you *don't*—oh sugar! *What are you doing!* I'm going—I'm coming! *Oh fuck!*" He roared rapturously as she continued sucking. His body tensed suddenly, and his cum jetted from his cock into her throat.

At the first sensation of warmth, she swallowed and was dimly aware of the pulsing that grew until it ignited between her legs where she rubbed against him. She swallowed every drop as his cum spurted from him in long, hot streams while her body rode her own orgasmic wave. Rubbing her clit against his thigh hard, she rode each pulse.

Finally releasing him after licking him clean, Teresa felt a slight buzz like she'd had a couple of glasses of wine, and her pussy felt hot and wet because she'd been rubbing against him the whole time. Her clit throbbed insistently, wanting to be pushed over into another orgasm.

Teresa smiled when she heard him release a trembling sigh. His fingers were still in her hair, and the other hand cupped her cheek. She crawled into his arms as he drew her to him and tucked her to his side. She'd pleased him very much if she was going by his expression and how tightly he held her now.

"Sugar, where did you learn to do that?" He sounded astonished as he stroked her cheek.

"When I talked to Grace this afternoon, she told me how to do it."

"Told you? That was the first blow job you've ever given?" he asked incredulously.

"Mmm-hmm."

"I can't believe it. You sucked my cock like you had experience, *swallowed* my cum…like you *enjoyed* it," he said in an awed-sounding whisper.

"I *did* enjoy it. Very much as a matter of fact."

"You sure did, sugar. You are a sweet, hot thing, Teresa. That took me completely by surprise. Angel said he showed you how to stroke him."

She nodded happily. "Oh yes, he did. That was fun, too."

"So he doesn't *know* about your talented little mouth yet?"

"Nope, but I'm sure you'll tell him all about it, won't you?" she asked cheekily.

"Damn straight. That news is too good not to share."

She mewed when he tweaked her nipple before sliding in a leisurely path down her abdomen. "You were rubbing your delicate little pussy pretty hard against my rough old leg." His fingers stroked lightly over her heated flesh. "I'd better check and make sure you didn't rub too hard." He sounded very concerned about the state of her pussy.

"Oh? And what if I rubbed my pussy too hard on you?" She giggled as he turned her onto her back and loomed over her, looking *hungry*.

"Why, I'll have to kiss it and make it feel better," he replied eagerly. A low growl rumbled in his chest, and he latched onto her erect nipple. Joaquin was excellent at playing doctor.

Chapter Seventeen

Teresa adjusted the ankle straps on the dressy sandals she wore as they pulled into The Dancing Pony's parking lot. On Friday nights the place was packed, and tonight was no exception. Angel cut the ignition on the pickup and smiled at her appreciatively. She could recall a time when that same look would have sent her skittering into her frightened little shell.

"You look gorgeous. Loving the two of us must agree with you because you're glowing tonight." Angel's eyes roamed over her body, and she felt incredibly sexy. She wore the slinky, body-hugging top he'd given her for Christmas, which showed her cleavage to maximum advantage, topped off with the glittering black onyx jewelry. She'd paired the top with the long, straight, snug-fitting denim skirt and a pair of wickedly high black snakeskin heels. Her hair was pulled up in a black clip, leaving some curling tendrils around her face.

Joaquin climbed out and lifted her from the seat. Setting her down, he took full advantage of the contact as he nuzzled her throat. "I won't be able to keep my hands to myself tonight. Your ass in that skirt—*Mmmm!*" His hands strayed to her derriere and squeezed before releasing her. His playful demeanor was contagious, and her heart felt incredibly light and happy as he lifted her chin and kissed her soundly. His eyes glowed with mischief. "I'll be thinking about how you were earlier, lovely and naked in my arms, all evening long. Angel's right. You're radiant tonight."

"You make all the difference, Joaquin. Thank you." Teresa did feel different. She felt free, *really* free. She'd been reserved for so long, and it felt wonderful to release herself from that self-protection. To give her trust to Angel and Joaquin was liberating. What anybody in the club thought of her didn't mean a thing because she knew where she stood with the men who loved her.

Angel came around the truck and slid his fingers into hers, asking, "Are you ready, sweetheart?"

She slipped her forearms through both of theirs and nodded. "Yes, I'm ready."

Angel had talked with them in the truck on the way over. They hadn't been sure how she wanted to be perceived in the club. Arriving with Angel, as his fiancée, with Joaquin tagging along, would have been the best option as far as public opinion was concerned. Of course that option had a huge drawback. Other women. Feeling a little territorial, Teresa had told them she had no problem entering the club as a threesome. She was not about to watch women approach her man all night, thinking he was single and available.

Angel had questioned her, but she had defended her choice, and he'd acknowledged that she had a good point about the other women. Joaquin had seemed to enjoy the glimpse of her territoriality, judging by the mischievous twinkle in his eyes.

Joaquin pulled open the door for them, and they escorted Teresa into The Dancing Pony. Mike and Rogelio greeted them, and Angel introduced Joaquin to two of the club's three bouncers. The third, most recent addition to club security, Eli Wolf, was still on his honeymoon with Rachel.

They found a high-topped table near the dance floor, and Angel ordered drinks for them while Joaquin helped her into a tall chair. Teresa looked around the club for people she knew and noticed many admiring glances cast Joaquin's way. She and Angel came in here often enough that people knew they were a couple, but the newest member of their trio was gathering a lot of hungry looks.

Teresa had a tiny glimpse of what Rachel must have dealt with on a regular basis in the club, as Eli's girlfriend. She recognized one of the women eyeing Joaquin hungrily from the table next to theirs. It was the woman, Clarissa, whom Angel had spoken with at the store when he'd come in to pick her up for her birthday lunch. She leaned toward Angel and whispered, "Isn't that one of Patricia's friends?"

Angel looked in the direction Teresa indicated and chuckled. "Yes, it is. She's looking at Joaquin like he's a prime cut and she's starving to death. Why don't you ask Joaquin to dance with you? Maybe she'll get the message."

Teresa doubted it, but she'd give it a try. She glanced at Joaquin, who was relaxing at the table, and then back at Clarissa's group. She was still staring at him, and several of her female companions were doing the same.

Leaning toward Joaquin, she caressed his muscular shoulder. She knew in that position he'd be able to see right down the front of her top and her cleavage. He grinned ear to ear, and his eyes twinkled playfully, enjoying the view as she whispered in his ear.

"Can I ask you a question?" His shoulder was hard under her fingertips, and she couldn't resist a lingering stroke over all those abundant muscles.

"Sure, sugar." His lips sent shivers up and down her torso when he brushed them softly over her cheekbone. He whispered, "So beautiful." Her core liquefied at his intimate touch and earnest words but also felt tingles on her neck and knew she was being watched by unfriendly eyes.

She obliged him kindly by brushing her lips against his earlobe before asking, "Would I be right in assuming that you're mine?"

Joaquin laid his hand on her thigh, gave her a naughty grin, and whispered back, "Every single rock hard *inch*. Why?" His hand swept higher and higher up her thigh, sending exhilarating chills along her spine.

"The dark-headed woman dressed in black at the table behind us was a close friend of Patricia's," she said as her fingertips stroked into the silken hair at the nape of his neck. "She and most of her girlfriends are watching you like wolves eyeing a lamb wandering through the forest."

"Really? What should we do?" he whispered suggestively. A great shudder went up her back as his hand strayed over her hip and along her rib cage. She could barely think with him doing that. The devilish twinkle in his eyes sent a bolt of lust straight to her clit. She bit her lip as it throbbed in happy response to his touch.

"I'm feeling a little territorial."

He looked in her eyes. "You're feeling jealous?" He glanced at the table she'd indicated. "None of those women have anything on you, sugar. Why don't you come dance with me, and we'll give them some clues?"

"I thought you'd never ask." She slid her hand back over his shoulder as he helped her from the chair, palming her ass in the process. She glanced back at him, and he grinned innocently at her. As she stepped from her chair, she stopped alongside Angel and kissed him tenderly on the lips. He caressed her cheek and then settled back in his chair, looking contented.

Joaquin led her to the dance floor as "Remember When" by Alan Jackson began to play. She came smoothly into his arms, and he pulled her close against him. Resting her head on his chest, she closed her eyes, allowing him to lead. His hand at her hip stroked up and down from her lower back to the upper swell of her ass.

The area he stroked was super sensitive, and the way he touched her there telegraphed eloquently to the nerve endings in her clit but even more shockingly in her rear opening. She had to stifle a heartfelt moan at the naughty sensation. She opened her eyes and realized he was watching her face, his eyes filled with love and desire. He knew what he was doing to her.

She listened to the words of the song, and smiled up at him. He took that opportunity to lean down and kiss her tenderly on the lips. He released her right hand, and she reached up and threaded her fingertips into his hair at the nape of his neck and stroked him. His other hand joined the first which still caressed her lower back, increasing the sensation for her. He groaned as he released her from the kiss and gathered her to him, close enough that she could feel his stiffened cock.

"I'll never want anyone else, Teresa. Not after loving you," he whispered huskily as he executed a turn with her and kissed her again. "Especially not a woman who was friends with someone who harmed my brother. If you're feeling territorial, I say it's time you staked your claim."

She stifled a giggle, whispering, "Who gets 'staked' in that scenario, exactly?" His chest rumbled with a chuckle at her humor, so unlike her.

He glanced around. "For the purpose of our discussion, you get to do the honors *this* time." His fingers slid down her back to her ass, and she did the kissing this time. They never missed a beat in the dance as she tilted her head and pressed her lips to his. She parted her lips and stroked his tongue with her own. Her body responded to his nearness, her pussy felt swollen, and her clit throbbed in need. He hugged her tightly to him from lip to toe.

"Sugar, have I told you what a talented kisser you are?"

"Nuh-uh," she replied with a shake of her head and a grin on her lips. "Why don't you tell me all about it?"

"You start out sweet and innocent, kind of shy. Then you melt into me, and you sneak in with that sexy little tongue of yours. Soon, it's not just your lips kissing me. It's your whole delectable body. You've made me your devoted slave with those kisses."

"Well, thank you, handsome. I love the way your hands feel on me, especially when you slowly slide them down my back and over my derriere." She shivered as he mirrored what she was telling him. "That spot where you've almost gone too far is right where I like them as if you might still slide them a little lower. Yes, *right there*. Oh, *honey*." She shuddered lightly and bit her lip. "Your hands right there say, 'She's mine.' I love belonging to you."

Glancing over to Clarissa's table, she added, "Do you think they got the message? I sure hope I'm not going to be watching women approach you all night."

"Don't worry. Any decent woman can tell now that we are here together. Any others I'll turn down. It's our first time in here as a threesome. They'll get used to it." As handsome at Joaquin was, she knew he'd always attract women, whether he meant to or not.

After the song ended, he escorted her back to the table where Angel sat talking with Brice Huvell and Corina Scott, who'd just come in. Angel introduced Joaquin to them, and they greeted him.

"Corina and Brice have some exciting news, Teresa," Angel said with a smile.

Teresa smiled expectantly at their friends. "Well? Don't keep me hanging. What's up?"

Corina peeked up at Brice and said dreamily, "Yesterday, Brice asked me to marry him."

Teresa hugged her excitedly and made a big deal over Corina's engagement ring. Corina spotted the diamond on Teresa's finger and looked at her and Angel with big eyes. "*No way!* We got engaged on the same day?"

"Uh-huh, but it's even better than that Corina—" She put her lips to Corina's ear and told her she was considering Joaquin, as well. She giggled when Corina's eyes popped wide open again, and she looked over at Joaquin.

"Wow! I *never* would have guessed it. Still waters run deep. I'm so happy for you, Teresa. This has been a wonderful Christmas, hasn't it?"

"The best. The absolute best. Have you talked to Rachel and Eli?"

"Yeah, their flight gets in late tonight. They told us they would be coming by the club tomorrow night. It sounds like they had a wonderful time on their honeymoon."

The three of them chatted with Brice and Corina for a few more minutes before the happy couple finally made their way to the dance floor.

"They seem like nice people," Joaquin said as they watched little Corina peck Brice on the cheek. He responded with a gentle caress and held her close.

Teresa nodded. "They're special. Rachel introduced them to each other, and Brice and Eli have become good friends, as well. It's a nice, tight-knit group we're a part of. Most of us sort of knew each other one way or another, but Grace has drawn us all together until we're like family. Grace is also a bit of a matchmaker, too." Teresa grinned at Angel.

Angel agreed. "Yep, and God bless her for it. So, when are you gonna dance with your fiancé?"

"Right now, honey." Teresa turned to Joaquin and kissed him again.

"These lips will be right here waiting for you when you get back, sugar." He growled low to her and made her giggle when he patted her ass. She allowed her hips to sway seductively as she walked away.

Angel looked behind her as she followed him and said with a chuckle, "Joaquin's ogling your ass shamelessly, like he's a starving man."

"Really?" She giggled and turned her head back in time to see Clarissa rise from her chair and approach Joaquin. A low growl emitted from her throat, but she held onto Angel's hand and followed him to the dance floor.

"You're fierce when you're riled up, aren't you?" he asked with a sexy chuckle.

She smiled up at him a little sheepishly. "I've never felt this way about anybody before, Angel. I want to rip her hair out, every last strand of it."

"I wonder how she even got in. Ethan told me he'd banned her the same time he banned Patricia and all the others." He gestured with a lift of his chin. "There, see? Joaquin turned her down flat. No small talk or anything. He's too busy watching your lovely ass right now to care about any other women in this place." She sighed blissfully when he slid his hands down her back, clutching at her waist and her hips.

She rested her head on his chest. "You say the nicest things. Were you watching my derriere earlier when I danced with him?"

"Sweetheart, I wasn't just watching your body. I was fantasizing about it. Feel that?" he asked in her ear as the hand resting on her bottom pressed her against him. He was very hard, and her pussy responded instantly, swelling and seeping moisture for him. "You keep me that way. Even this fierce little territorial streak of yours is a turn-on," he murmured to her as he spun her on the dance floor.

"I'm glad you don't mind."

"Why would I mind? It's good to know you're wanted completely."

"That's exactly how I feel. I want you completely."

"Like we both want you, beautiful. Look at the way his eyes drink you in. He adores you every bit as much as I do." He leaned down and kissed her tenderly.

She looked over at Joaquin and smiled at him and blew him a little kiss, and then noticed a very tall woman approach Joaquin.

Never taking her eyes off of him, she said, "Angel, it's that awful woman." She watched Joaquin's face change as Dinah sat down in Teresa's chair. Joaquin's look of distaste was barely veiled as he turned to the woman who was dressed in a bloodred spandex dress. She was overly made up, and her hair was a wildly teased disaster. She gave Joaquin her best seductive grimace and spoke to him, casually pushing Teresa's wineglass across the table away from her with one long fingernail.

Teresa had seen Dinah in action before, on the night of the bachelorette party. Charity had gone to the ladies room, and Dinah had approached Justin. When Charity walked into a room, you could almost feel the self-confidence and sexiness roll off of her. She had a heart of gold, but she was *not* someone to piss off.

Charity had returned to Justin's side, taken one look at Dinah, and had told her in clear, graphic language to back off. There had been no doubt she'd fully intended to back up her words with action if Dinah hadn't moved her rump out of Charity's seat in a hurry. Dinah had wisely taken the opportunity to walk away.

Justin had chuckled and turned to Charity and said, "Baby, you are the shit, aren't you?"

She'd brushed the seat of her chair as if Dinah might have left critters behind. Then she'd sat down in it, and smiled dreamily up at him. "I am."

Teresa watched Dinah now with repugnance, knowing there was no way she would ever possess enough intestinal fortitude to confront that woman. "She touched my wineglass."

"I saw that. We'll get you a fresh drink when we return. You're staying out here with me until she leaves. Don't let her get to you."

"Well, at least I'm stranded on the dance floor with a man I love."

"And who loves you in return. Joaquin was excited to hear you'd be receptive to his proposal," he said, obviously trying to distract her.

She giggled. "I could tell this afternoon when I was watching you tell him."

"I thought I felt your eyes on me. So you saw my thumbs-up?"

"Yes, sneaky. Any idea when he's planning on asking?" Her heart pounded at the thought.

"I think he's waiting for the right moment. It'll be soon, that much I know. He may even have it on him tonight."

"Really?"

"Yeah, but I doubt he'd do it in front of all these people. You'd say yes no matter where he proposed, wouldn't you?" He smiled at her, reading her mind.

"I'd be all over him like a duck on a june bug." Teresa sighed, laying her head against his chest.

"The change in you from when we first met is remarkable. I thought you were too good to be true when Grace introduced us. Since you've met Joaquin and realized what you want in life, you've bloomed. It's amazing to remember you were the shy beauty who brought me a pecan pie. Remember the first time I kissed you?"

"I'll never forget. That was my first kiss and second." She gazed at him with love in her eyes.

"I gave you your first kiss?"

She nodded, sentimental tears in her eyes. His lips descended to hers in a tender kiss as he led her in the dance. Aching with desire for him, she wished for nothing more than to be consumed by him and Joaquin both.

Chapter Eighteen

After the song ended, Angel walked her to the ladies room and waited for her as he usually did. Tonight, Joaquin was not the only one drawing hungry looks. He didn't think she saw them, but Angel noticed that she was the recipient of more than a few appreciative stares. She was radiant tonight, even more than usual, and that attracted the attention of others.

He caught a glimpse of Joaquin across the club. Ben was at their table escorting Dinah out of Teresa's chair and away toward the bar. There was something not quite right about that woman, but Angel couldn't put his finger on it. He'd heard a few interesting rumors about her but didn't honestly know what to think about her. He was relieved she'd vacated Teresa's chair so she could take a break, though. He stepped to the bar to order another round of drinks for their table while he waited for Teresa.

Returning to the hallway where the restrooms and office were located, he thought he heard Teresa's voice. Looking in the dimly lit hallway, he could see Teresa pressed against the wall, trying to escape the close proximity of an overly friendly cowboy. Her brows were drawn together, and she spoke in clear, sharp tones.

"I told you, I am here with my fiancé. I do not want to sit with you or your friends." She didn't sound frightened, but she didn't sound happy, either.

The man was taller than her and outweighed her by a good seventy-five pounds. "Come on, honey. I saw you dancing with those two cowboys and kissing them both. You can drop the 'fiancé' line. I promise we'll treat you right. Don't worry," he said good-naturedly as he leaned toward her.

Angel tapped him on the shoulder and got his attention. "Teresa, go to the end of the hallway and wait for me there. Don't leave, just wait for me." Teresa looked up in relief and scooted past him, still pressed against the wall.

Angel turned his full attention to the cowboy who now looked a little embarrassed. "When a lady tells you no, you should accept that she means it. That beauty *is* engaged to me. If you'd checked her finger while you were ogling her, you would have seen the two carats worth of diamond she carries on her delicate finger. She's here with me and my brother. If you have a problem with that then we can go outside and have a little chat about it," he said, pointing at the backdoor.

The tall ranch hand raised his hands palm up in apology. "Sorry, man, we saw her dancing with you both and made some assumptions. That was a dumbass thing to do. I apologize. We're new in town and haven't had any time to relax in a while. No harm, no foul?"

Angel would have liked to stay angry at the guy for making assumptions about Teresa's character. It was obvious the guy had not intended to insult either of them. He seemed liked a good guy. Something about him also seemed vaguely familiar. "Are you going to apologize to her?"

The cowboy nodded affirmatively. "Sure. I didn't mean anything by it, just happened to see her waiting in the hallway on my way to the men's room and thought I'd take a chance. I'm *really* sorry."

The man was nice enough about it and willing to apologize to Teresa, so Angel decided to throw him a bone. A nice, juicy, ripe, and ready one, he figured.

"I can see you didn't mean to offend Teresa, so I'll give you a tip. There's a woman sitting at a table near ours who *is* into group encounters, but you can't mention how you know that." He followed

Angel as he walked back to Teresa. "Also, see that tall redhead in the red spandex dress at the bar?"

"Uh-huh!" the cowboy responded eagerly.

"You might want to try your luck there, too, but she likes it a little rough, I hear."

The guy got a quizzical look on his face. "Rough, huh?"

"Don't misunderstand, cowboy. She'd be the one getting rough, not you."

The look on his face told Angel that was a whole lot more kink than he could handle. "Holy shit. Point me in the direction of the other gal first, and I'll keep that one in reserve."

"First, do your duty," Angel said with a chuckle, indicating Teresa standing beside him.

The cowboy earned even more points when he removed his hat. "Ma'am, I'm really sorry I made such an ass of myself earlier. My powers of observation were seriously lacking. I can see now that you definitely are engaged to this gentleman by the ring on your finger, nor do you look like the type trolling for a group one-night stand. I'm *very* sorry. Please forgive me?" His hand was over his heart, the picture of sincerity and remorse.

Teresa looked him over speculatively and said, after smiling at Angel, "Thank you for apologizing. I forgive you. You seem like a nice cowboy. You should settle down with a good girl and not waste your time and money on loose women. But if that's what you're after, there's a whole table of them next to ours. Why don't we trade tables with you?"

"That's not a bad idea," Angel commented, "How many of you are there?"

"Three, over there." He pointed to a table with two decent-looking cowboys sitting at it. "We're working out at the Rockin' C until we can get our own place out on FM 709 started up again. We haven't been into town since we got here except to buy supplies and groceries. We'd be happy to trade tables with you. If you're in here on a regular basis, maybe you could introduce us to some decent gals, especially if they're as pretty as you are. No offense," he added deeply, glancing at Angel, who chuckled. He was starting to like this guy.

"None taken. My brother, Joaquin, is waiting at our table. I'll introduce you. I wish you luck with your ranch. We're over at the Divine Creek Ranch on FM 709. I'm Angel, and this is my fiancée, Teresa, by the way."

"The Warner Place?" the man said and got an incredulous look on his face.

"No, the Warner Ranch is farther out. But Joe Warner's son, Jack, and his two friends own the Divine Creek Ranch. You know Jack and Joe?" Angel asked with a funny feeling in his gut.

"Holy crap! It's a small world!" He held out his callused hand. "The name's Kendall. Kendall *Warner*."

Teresa's jaw popped open, and a smile spread across her face.

"My dad, Jack, was Joe Warner's brother. My brothers, Richard and Boone, are over at the table. Dad died a couple years back and left us his spread. We decided to settle down and try to make something of the old place. Jack is named after my dad. We've been meaning to get in touch with them."

"I'll be damned," Angel uttered in disbelief. "I remember meeting your father once when he came to visit Joe during the summer. He was an old man back then. He must have met your mother late in life. Joe said he lost touch with Jack over the years but not intentionally."

"He always meant to get in touch, but the years and work got away from him. Mom lives in Washington with our younger sister. So you've known the Warner family a long time?"

"Since I was a teenager. Your uncle and my dad are long-time friends. You need to get in touch with Joe and Jack. I think they'd all love to meet you. They'd probably be up here tonight, but their wife Grace is babysitting our little boy tonight." As he said it, he caught the warm look Teresa shot him and held her a little closer around the waist.

Kendall got a confused look on his face, and Teresa said, "It's complicated but all good. Listen, forget about the loose women and come sit with us. We'll call Jack and Grace and tell them we found you."

"Just…don't tell them how, okay, ma'am?" Kendall said uncomfortably.

"Only if you stop calling me 'ma'am.' I'm your age. Call me Teresa or Miss Palacios if you must."

"All right, ma'—Miss Palacios."

Angel pointed out their table, and Kendall went to tell his brothers about meeting them. Angel and Teresa made their way over to the table where Joaquin still waited.

Joaquin smiled at the look on Angel's face. "Meet someone interesting?"

"You're not going to believe this." Angel told him what they knew so far.

Teresa placed a palm on his brother's biceps. "They're going to call Jack. Wait till Grace gets a load of those cowboys. She'll be up to her elbows in matchmaking schemes. I want a dance with you, Joaquin. You've been all by yourself over here waiting for us, and I don't want you to feel neglected." Angel patted her curvy bottom affectionately as he released her to his brother and sat in his chair.

"Well then, how about you come kiss my boo-boo." Joaquin stood and grinned at Angel before he led her to the dance floor.

* * * *

Teresa stood at the stove while Michael sat at Angel's kitchen table in his little booster seat, playing with Play-Doh, when a familiar sound was heard in the distance. She smiled when Michael's head popped up from what he was doing and listened.

Angel was in the shower, and Joaquin was dealing with some issue Ash had called him about, saying he needed to talk to him.

Michael started to go back to what he was doing when the noise got louder, coming down the drive to the foreman's house.

"Wubida-wubida!" he squealed, imitating the throaty growl of Eli's Harley-Davidson motorcycle. "Eli and Rachel home! Wubida-Wubida! Eli! Rachel-Baby!" he screeched as he carefully climbed down from the booster seat.

Angel came into the kitchen dressed in a T-shirt and blue jeans as Michael went running for the front door, flung it open, and ran out on the porch hollering. "Eli! Rachel-Baby! You're home!" The fringe on his little leather chaps flapped with his movements and the stiff winter breeze.

"You're finally home from the moon! Eli! Rachel-Baby!"

They followed him out the front door as Eli rolled to a stop on his Harley with Rachel riding on the back. By the time they had their helmets off, Michael had toddled carefully down the porch steps and was running for the motorcycle. Eli's immense size didn't faze Michael a bit as Eli caught him and lifted him high in the air, still sitting on the bike. Rachel removed her helmet and climbed off then held out her hands for him expectantly. Rachel looked beautiful in full leathers. Her long hair was loose, flowing in the breeze as Eli placed a wiggling Michael in her arms.

She smiled radiantly at Teresa and said, "What have you been feeding this boy? He's grown four inches since the wedding."

She wrangled him into a hug, and he wrapped his arms around her neck and gave her a kiss and giggled, saying, "I missed you so much, Rachel-Baby, while you on the moon!"

Rachel looked at Eli, and they started laughing then she looked over at Teresa and whispered, "Rachel-Baby?"

"I know. He's calling all of our female friends 'baby' now. It started with Grace," Teresa said as she came down the steps and hugged Rachel then hugged Eli. He got off the bike and lifted Michael high on his shoulders.

"Welcome home, newlyweds," Angel said. "Did you have a good time? Do any hiking?" he asked as he came down the steps.

Rachel glowed when she smiled at them. "Yes, Angel, we did. I got some beautiful pictures of snow on the rim of the Canyon. Our lodge was awesome."

Eli nodded at Teresa's hand. "We hear you have some interesting news." he said speculatively. "I wonder if this Joaquin I keep hearing about is good enough for you, Teresa. He sounds like a bit of a tumbleweed to me," he added teasingly as Angel grinned at him.

Teresa's cheeks warmed, and she said, "Oh, he's wonderful, Eli. You'll meet him in a minute. He said he'd be right back. Did you hear about Jack's cousins turning up?"

Rachel smiled widely. "You should see Grace. She's beside herself. They're going to meet them tonight for supper then go out to The Pony. We're going to meet them there. Are you going out tonight after we eat?"

"We were out last night, so we're planning on a quiet night at home," Angel said as he slid a hand around Teresa's hip. Teresa saw Rachel's smile as she turned to him and snuggled up. There was a time when Teresa would not have made a move toward him like that with others watching, and Rachel must have taken notice.

"Well, supper is about ready. Why don't we go inside?" Teresa offered, leading the way. Eli lowered Michael from his shoulders and carried him inside giggling, slung over his hip.

"Rachel-Baby! See my big-boy chair? I big boy now. Wanna come play Play-Doh with me?"

"Sure, Michael. Were you good while I was gone?" she asked as she took a seat by his booster chair.

"I sure was! Angel gonna be my Daddy! Mommy loooves Angel." Then he giggled and added in a stage whisper, "Mommy loooves Joaquin, too, I think. They kiss, *ick*!" He wiped at his lips like it was something gross to do that.

"But I kiss Eli all the time," she teased.

"I know. That's gross, too. Here, you pick. Want my red or blue?"

Eli turned to Angel and Teresa and said, "Congratulations, you two. I mean three, maybe?"

"It's not official yet," Teresa said. "Joaquin hasn't proposed. It's on his timeframe now."

"It was a big surprise," Eli said as Teresa returned to the kitchen. "But I know they're going to take good care of you and Michael. Rachel thinks very highly of all three of you."

"So, Eli, I hear the sale on the ranch property went through," Angel said.

Eli's face split into a wide grin. "Yes! We're talking to Jack about doing the contracting for us."

From the kitchen table, Rachel said, "I can't wait to get started with landscaping plans."

"It's going to be beautiful," Teresa said as she lifted the lid and stirred the carne guisada and checked the other food.

Eli came up behind her and sighed dreamily, rubbing his belly. "Is that what I think it is, Teresa?"

Teresa turned to him with a smile. "Yes, I hope you don't mind. I thought you might enjoy it again. I have fresh guacamole, pico de gallo, homemade flour tortillas, Spanish rice, corn, and homemade pinto beans."

"Do I *mind*? I think it would be wonderful to have your carne guisada again."

"Again?" Rachel inquired, rolling a worm out with blue Play-Doh and handing it to Michael.

Eli smiled, remembering. "Yes. The first morning you were in ICU, Teresa showed up with homemade carne guisada on *homemade* tortillas. My mouth waters every time I think about it," Eli said and hugged Teresa again. He was a giant, for sure, but soft as a marshmallow for the women in his life.

The front door opened, and Joaquin came in and hung up his jacket. "Temp is dropping a little out there. Hey, Rachel!" Joaquin laughed as Rachel came to him and gave him a big hug. "How are you? Damn, you're looking beautiful, girl!"

"You're a flirt, as always," Rachel said, laughing. "It's good to see you again."

"Eli, this is Joaquin Martinez, Angel's brother," Teresa said. Eli greeted Joaquin, and they shook hands, and the three men sat and talked while Rachel helped Teresa lay out the food on the rustic dining room table. They all sat down to enjoy the meal.

Joaquin had known about the accident when it happened, but he asked Rachel and Eli all about it. Joaquin and Eli discovered a lot of topics they saw eye to eye on. The three men enjoyed talking, and Michael interjected key points, as well. The time flew, and soon they were slipping back into their jackets and readying to leave for the club where they were meeting the rest of the gang, including Rosemary and her men.

Michael cackled and crowed when Eli fired up the Harley, "Wubida-wubida-wubida!" waving at them both as they pulled away. The night had definitely gotten a lot chillier, and they quickly returned inside and began Michael's bedtime routine.

At first Teresa wanted to return home tonight to be consistent for the sake of Michael's schedule and also so that her neighbors wouldn't worry about her, but Michael had asked for a sleepover.

She'd given in and was thankful she'd brought a change of clothes over that she could wear home tomorrow. She reminded the men that she could not make a habit of it. They promised that they understood, and then she worried that she disappointed them by seeming to not *want* to stay. That simply wasn't the case. She secretly wanted to come home with them and never leave, starting today.

Going home the night before, after their wonderful evening out, had been hard but necessary. She'd had work that morning, and so she'd gotten in her car late Friday night and driven Michael home. Joaquin had followed her in his truck and had waited to make sure she'd gotten in all right.

Michael fell asleep less than halfway through his bedtime story, and she carried him to bed in Joaquin's room. She smiled at Joaquin when he retrieved clothes for the following day while she tucked Michael in and laid an extra blanket over him. She returned to the living room, feeling happy about staying.

Music played as she came into the living room, and she noticed that they had moved the coffee table aside and rolled up the area rug, lit candles all around the room, and turned down the lights. Now they had a nice dance floor complete with music.

"Beautiful, may I have this dance?" Angel asked as he held out a hand to her.

"How romantic of you." She slipped into his arms. He danced her around to the soft instrumental while Joaquin sat down and quietly watched, waiting his turn. She smiled when the next song came on, recognizing it.

"You remembered, Joaquin," she whispered as he took her in his arms and held her close while the opening strains of "Besame Mucho" played. She danced with each of them a few more times then there was a knock at the door.

It was late, and Teresa was immediately worried that something was wrong, but Angel reassured her as they answered the door. Ash stood at the bottom of the steps with Deseo saddled and ready to ride. Angel helped Joaquin bundle up a bemused Teresa, complete with muffler, gloves, hat, and earmuffs. They wrapped her in her heavy winter jacket before leading her outside.

"Joaquin, I put an extra wool blanket up there in case you want to wrap her in an extra layer or cover her legs. It's pretty chilly tonight."

Joaquin pulled his gloves on and shook Ash's hand. "Thank you for the consideration, Ash. I appreciate it. I'll take care of Deseo after we're done."

Ash nodded and said, "Have a nice ride. See you in the morning."

"Thank you, Ash," Angel said. "I appreciate you staying available to us this late."

"You're welcome. Good night." The tall cowboy strode off into the dim light cast by the security lights from the barns.

Teresa turned to Angel and then Joaquin, a questioning look on her face as Joaquin put on his new black felt hat and his heavy jacket.

Angel smiled as he tucked a stray lock of hair into her crocheted wool scarf. "It's a perfectly clear night tonight. Joaquin wants to take you for a moonlit ride, beautiful. How does that sound?"

She was awed. "It sounds wonderful. I'd love to."

"I'll stay here with Michael and watch a movie," Angel said as he pulled her jacket closed and adjusted her scarf to cover her neck fully. "Take as long as you like and enjoy yourselves."

Joaquin climbed into the saddle, and Angel assisted him in lifting Teresa carefully onto Deseo in front of Joaquin, sitting crossways on his lap. She wrapped her arms tightly around him, feeling a little nervous. It was just a horseback ride, but the moment felt huge, and she felt small and vulnerable. She looked up into Joaquin's eyes, and he smiled at her, easily controlling the horse as he touched her cheek with the soft, work-worn leather of his glove.

"Now don't you worry, sugar. Deseo loves women and won't make any false moves with you in my arms. He doesn't mind carrying the both of us. All you need to do is relax against me. Angel, let's wrap that blanket around her legs." The horse shifted slightly under their weight but made no other move. She caressed Deseo's neck and patted him.

After they had her situated, Angel went back in the house and waved to them from the open front door. She hadn't been on horseback in quite a while but relaxed against Joaquin, trusting that he would keep her safe. Deseo was a fine, beautiful animal, majestic in his stature and carriage, and she wondered briefly at the romantic sight they made riding off into the starlit night.

Once away from the house and the security lights, she looked up and sighed appreciatively at the night sky. The moon was nearly full and shown its light on their path. The night was still, and the smell of wood smoke from a chimney faintly scented the air. For a while they rode on in companionable silence, lulled by the rhythm Deseo created as he moved along at a leisurely pace.

"I think this is the most romantic thing anyone has ever done for me," she said, snuggling into him with her hands drawn under her chin. His arms around her, holding her securely, felt like home.

"We were hoping for a nice, clear night tonight, and we lucked out."

"It's beautiful tonight."

"Are you cold?"

"No, you bundled me up well, and the wool blanket helps, too. How about you?"

"Being near you keeps me warm. I'm fine."

"I adore you," she stated simply. "You make me happy."

His lips were hot, pressed against her temple. "I'm glad to hear that, sugar. Oh, look. Did you see it?" He quickly pointed into the sky.

She looked up in time to catch the streak of white light that shot across the sky overhead. "Yes! I saw it," she said as they reached the top of the rise and continued on.

"Aren't you supposed to make a wish or something when you see a shooting star?"

"Yes. You make the wish."

"I already have what I want. *You* make the wish," he whispered in her ear as he nuzzled her. Deseo continued on at the same gentle gait.

"Okay." She closed her eyes and leaned her head against his chest.

Chapter Nineteen

When Teresa opened her eyes, his bare hand was held up in front of her. In his fingers was a diamond ring. The platinum and diamonds glittered and shimmered ethereally in the bright moon and star light. She whimpered and slipped the glove from her hand to touch it.

"It's beautiful, Joaquin."

"I've loved you from the moment I first saw you, and it doesn't matter if I've know you only four days or four years. You have a beautiful heart and a sweet spirit, and I absolutely, utterly adore you. Sugar, would you do me the honor of becoming my wife, too?"

Teresa hugged him tight, and looked up at him. "I would love to be your wife. I can't imagine my life, our lives, without you in it. My son loves you and obviously adores you, also. You're about to make him one happy little cowboy."

"Would you like me to put it on?" he asked, taking her hand in his free one.

"Yes! Yes, please." She held out her hand for him. He slipped the ring on her left ring finger and then held her hand in his palm so they could see it.

"I'm glad it fits."

"I love it Joaquin. It's gorgeous. Thank you." She hugged him again, then he kissed her. His kiss was intense, with a promise of passion yet to come.

In a shaky voice, Teresa said, "I'll keep this memory, out here with you, forever in my heart."

"I decided to propose to you in a way that showed you something of me. Proposing on the back of my horse under the moonlit sky seemed to fit the bill. Want to keep riding or head back?"

"Oh, let's keep riding if that's all right with you and Deseo."

"It's fine, but you let me know when you start to get chilled, so I can take you back. Angel and I will warm you up once we get home."

Teresa knew exactly how she wanted them to warm her. "This means we can set a wedding date."

"Yes. I have a feeling this is going to be a wedding put together in record-breaking time."

"You ain't seen nothing yet." She giggled and tilted her lips up for another long kiss. "So, what else is planned for this evening?"

"Well, we had some thoughts and ideas, but you're the one in the driver's seat."

"Were you considering making tonight 'the night'?" she asked quietly.

"As in 'the night we make love to you for the first time'?" Joaquin asked, his eyes sparkling. She felt his body's response to the change in subject as his cock swelled beneath her bottom.

She smiled and her cheeks tingled as she nodded. "Angel told me he's explained what happened to me so you'd understand me better. I'll always carry the memories of the violent way Michael was conceived, but I want to break free from what happened and make new memories with you both."

Joaquin nodded. "I hope you don't mind that he told me."

"No, because it saves me from having to tell the story over again."

"If I could get my hands on him, I'd avenge you."

She smiled and assured him, "I believe in God. He says that vengeance belongs to Him, and He'll repay Ranulfo for what he did to me. Although, if he accidentally becomes the hood ornament on the front grill of an eighteen-wheeler going down the highway at seventy miles-an-hour, I wouldn't shed any tears."

Joaquin chuckled and asked, "What about Michael? Would it be inhibiting for you to have him close by and possibly hear us?"

"Michael is a sound sleeper. Once we're married, he'd be in the house with us when we made love, wouldn't he? We'll always have to be careful about being too loud. If you'd rather wait, I can ask Grace to invite him to a sleepover, and then we'd have the house to ourselves the first time. It'll be special to me either way."

"What do you want?" he asked simply, his hands sliding around her hips and holding her close.

"I want you both to make love to me tonight."

"It's unromantic, but I need to ask. Are you on birth control pills?"

"No, but I plan to get on them," she replied, thinking she probably should have already done that.

"We'd need to use condoms until you've been on the pill a month or so. Would you mind that?"

"Not at all. I want to wait a while before we start adding on to our family. Plus, we're a little limited on space right now."

Joaquin chuckled. "You're right about that. Angel has mentioned the possibility of building a new house for us once he turns the duties of ranch foreman over to Ash."

Teresa raised her eyebrows in happy surprise. "So that's working out? He seems capable and levelheaded."

"In most things, yeah." He chuckled and said, "Right now a certain redhead has got him tied up in knots."

"He has a girlfriend? Who is it?"

"Well, I wouldn't call her his girlfriend yet, but he met your friend, Juliana Meyer, at the party the other night, and she must have made an impression on him. That's what he wanted to talk to me about earlier. Plus, we needed to plan the details for our ride tonight."

"They met at the party? I never even saw them talking together. Juliana is…such a city girl. I can't imagine her with a cowboy. And Ash is *one hundred percent* cowboy."

"Not to change the subject, but—"

Teresa grinned. "Right. I'll make an appointment with Dr. Guthrie and get on the pill. Do you by chance have condoms we could use?" she asked, proud of herself for being so direct about the subject.

"Yes. We had a feeling you weren't on the pill and decided it would be better to be prepared. You didn't ask, sugar, but I always use condoms." She hugged him and nodded silently, appreciating his fastidiousness.

A light breeze kicked up a few minutes later, and Joaquin turned Deseo back toward home. "Let's get you home. I want to make love to you." Her core quivered at the prospect.

* * * *

By the time Joaquin got Teresa in the house, she was chilled. He took Deseo back to the barn to care for him while Angel helped Teresa get her extra layers off and started a hot shower for her. She was grateful because parts of her did feel a little frozen. She took her time washing her hair, exfoliating, shaving, and scrubbing nice and smooth. She thought about her conversation with Joaquin a few days before, about making love. They put her in control of when that finally happened, and she'd made her wishes known. Now ultimately, it felt like Angel was the one in control of how much happened tonight.

She heard a light tap at the door and called out a welcome as she dried off in the tub and blotted the water from her dripping hair. One of her men came in and closed the door behind him. She peeked around the curtain and smiled at Angel, figuring it would be him coming to talk with her.

"Are you feeling warmer now?"

"Yes, the hot water felt wonderful." She wrapped the towel around her and stepped from the tub onto the mat. Angel stood there gazing at her with a far-off look in his hypnotic eyes. His expression was hard to interpret. "Did I do something wrong?"

He tilted his head, and his features softened immediately. "No. You haven't done anything wrong. Why would you think that?"

"I couldn't tell from the way you were looking at me."

"I'm sorry. I was thinking. Soon I'll get to see you stepping from my tub fresh from your bath everyday for the rest of my life. It floored me."

That thought filled her with happiness. She smiled and felt like her heart was stretching from all the love for him it held. "Well, that's a good thing."

Angel glanced down at the new ring she wore on her left hand, "So, he asked, and you said yes. Did you like the ride?"

"Very much. I want to do things like that with you, too, Angel. It was so romantic out there."

"Joaquin said the same thing. He told me you're ready for us to make love to you."

She nodded, water droplets sliding along her cheek. "I am."

"You're sure you don't want to wait for the wedding night?" She wondered if he might be teasing her, judging by the hint of mischief she saw in his eyes.

She shook her head slowly. "No. Nerves, remember? I want you both to make love to me tonight."

"And Michael?"

"I'll do my best to keep my screaming at a minimum." Her cheeks tingled with heat as she giggled.

Angel gave her a lop-sided smile. "But we like it when you scream. That's how we know we're doing it right."

"Everything I've experienced at your hands has been done right, Angel."

"Mmmm, now you're just flattering us. Why don't you let me help you dry off?" He reached for the corner of the towel that was tucked in at her chest.

There was a knock at the door, and a deep voice from the other side said, "You better not be starting without me."

Angel opened the door a bit. "She finished her shower, but she's not dried off yet. We don't want her to get chilled if she comes out wet, so I offered to help her dry off." He gave her a crooked little grin. "Come in and help if you want to, or better yet, why don't we light a fire in the bedroom fireplace?"

"Oh goody!" Teresa chirped. She'd always been intrigued by the small fireplace in Angel's bedroom. A night like this would be perfect for lighting it.

Joaquin stuck his head in the doorway and eyed her hungrily. He even growled a little as he looked her up and down. "She sounds like she likes that idea. I'll get firewood and kindling, and we'll have things warmed up in no time," he said with a playful wink and closed the door.

Angel reached for the towel, and she let it fall from under her arms. A smile spread across his lips as he lifted it and began drying her off. She reached for another towel and started drying her hair.

* * * *

Angel admired the full, sexy sway of her breasts as she dried her hair. She had *no* idea how tempting she was. All she saw were the things she thought were imperfections, like her shapely, rounded thighs and derriere, and the flesh of her upper arms. She didn't see herself the way he and Joaquin did.

Those very things made her attractive to them and a tremendously hot turn-on to be pressed against.

He loved nuzzling into Teresa's fragrant flesh and that was a big part of what he was looking forward to tonight, being hip to hip, buried deep in her hot, wet silkiness.

She sighed as he rubbed her dry, seeming to enjoy his touch. Finally she put the towel down and ran her fingers through her wildly tangled locks to tidy them. He loved her fresh from the shower like this, her skin glowing and her cheeks rosy.

He looked up when she giggled. "You keep drying me, Angel, and I just get wetter and wetter."

He had finished drying her and was now just using it as an excuse to keep touching her. They heard Joaquin out in the bedroom starting the fire. Angel swept down his hand down her back and gently patted her lush ass, feeling the sexy shudder that passed through her at his touch.

* * * *

After Angel slipped out of the bathroom, Joaquin entered to take his shower. Teresa noticed that he had stripped down to his boxers and his snug, long-sleeved thermal shirt and socks. He gave her a funny pose and said, "Sexy huh?" to her in the mirror, making her snicker and cough on toothpaste. "Angel is already in the bed warming it up for you. When you're finished, why don't you join him, and I'll be along as soon as I'm done. I smell like horse." He nuzzled her cheek, and she shuddered with anticipation when his callused hand glided down her naked waist and caressed her hipbone.

In the mirror, she watched him as he undressed. His cock was rigid and standing at attention against his abdomen. She'd stopped brushing her teeth and stood there ogling his reflection. She caught his twinkling eyes watching her. "Huh? Oh, all right." She rinsed quickly and left the bathroom as he stepped into the shower.

The bedroom was lit only by the light of the crackling log in the fireplace and candles on the bedside tables. Angel lay back against all the pillows piled at the headboard, his head propped up on his forearms. He looked over at her and smiled tenderly then reached to pull back the covers so she could join him. As she climbed up into the bed, she felt the warmth emanating from the fire on her backside and the slickness of her lips as the heat licked at them.

She went into his arms and climbed in alongside his naked body. His strong arms encompassed her, and his hand moved in a slow glide over the small of her back as he tucked her to him. He slid his other hand down her ribs, over her ass, and drew her thigh across his until it rested over his erection. He hissed and shuddered a little.

"You looked lost in thought when I came out. What were you thinking about?" She sifted her fingers through the light layer of hair on his chest.

His fingertips stroked her as he said, "I want tonight to be the beginning of something wonderful for you." The emotion of his words was reflected in his shiny eyes, and she had to close her eyes and press her cheek to his chest. His heart beat comfortingly under her ear as he spoke again. "I want to make love to a woman who loves *me* and wants me as much as I want her."

She remembered that she wasn't the only one with painful memories. He needed this as much as she did and not just physically but emotionally, as well. Patricia had wounded him deeply, more than just the gunshot wound. That was a void in his life Teresa was happy to fill. Because he was so often the sexy, confident man she admired, she'd forgotten that he'd been hurt by Patricia, whether he would admit to it or not.

She whimpered a little when his hand slid up her thigh to the underside of her ass. He slid his fingers into her cleft and stroked her drenched lips. She cried out when he slid a finger slowly over her clitoris. "Angel!"

His touch lingered there another minute, drawing an assortment of increasingly erotic, needy sounds from her until she finally rose up and straddled his thighs, gazing admiringly at his hardened cock. Feeling daring and a little brazen, she reached down, encircled his tremendous girth and lifted his cock as she licked her lips. She saw his mouth fall open when he realized what she was going to do.

"Sweetheart? Oh, *baby*! Mmmm, you do that so nice." She slid her lips down his long shaft again as the head touched the back of her throat. "Baby!" he moaned, and his back arched in a way she found incredibly sexy.

She lowered herself onto her shins as she continued stroking him with her mouth, teasing the underside with lapping strokes of her tongue before sliding her lips over him again. He moaned long and low as she slowly suckled his cock in long, leisurely strokes. She heard movement from the bathroom as the door opened. Having an audience turned her on in a way that surprised her. Her arousal was skyrocketing, and she felt very wet and ready.

Joaquin strode into the bedroom, climbing onto the bed to watch. "Does it feel as good as I told you it would, Angel? She's amazing with that hot little mouth of hers and the way she takes her time." She glanced over at him and batted her eyelashes flirtatiously then turned to watch Angel as she dipped down and took as much of his length as she could comfortably and increased her suction. He moaned again and again until she finally released him, lapping her way down to his balls.

"Oh, now you're in for a real treat, Angel." Joaquin chuckled, and Teresa smiled cheekily at him as she took her time reaching her destination. "You know, one of the things I love about our little sweetheart is that she really enjoys what she's doing to us. So she wants to take her time." Teresa softly hummed her agreement with that statement.

She inched down Angel's legs and shuddered when her lips opened a little as they engorged, so ready to be taken. Gently licking his balls, she smiled at his moaned compliments. Joaquin got off the bed and came around behind her and her heart pounded as she wondered what he was up to back there. He didn't keep her guessing long.

She moaned loudly as she sucked one testicle between her lips, matching Angel's own cry as Joaquin's lips descended on hers. Joaquin nibbled at her flesh as she suckled his brother's, zeroing in on her clitoris, ruthless with his focus. Teresa moaned again when his tongue slid into her engorged flesh, and the vibration in her mouth made Angel respond loudly, as well.

Finally, Angel reached out and stroked her cheek. "You've got to stop. I don't want to finish before we've even started," he said as he stroked her shoulders. She released him, rested her forehead at his hip and panted as Joaquin continued tonguing her clit. "Is Joaquin teasing you?"

"Yes," she whimpered, stroking the head of Angel's cock with her tongue.

Angel chuckled as she playfully licked his cock again. "Mmmm, does it feel good?"

"Yes!" She flexed her hips which pressed her pussy against Joaquin's mouth. Angel stroked her hair from her face as Joaquin slipped one finger, then two, into her entrance and began stroking her sweet spot. She recognized the foreign sensation of pressure and felt the tendrils of insanity-inducing pleasure swirl through her. His fingers were a tight fit in her pussy, and the sensation communicated itself to her clit, which throbbed with her heartbeat.

"Oh, please Joaquin. Just a little more, please, please, don't stop," she whispered against Angel's abdomen, gazing up at him as he tenderly stroked her face. He smiled at her as she took her pleasure. The muscles in her pussy drew up tightly, her back arched, and her body went rigid as Joaquin relentlessly stroked her.

Joaquin whispered in a deep tone, "That's right, sugar. You're almost there aren't you? I can feel you clenching. That's right, baby. Take what you need." His hair tickled the backs of her thighs as he dipped his head again and tongued her clitoris firmly, over and over. She threw her head back, and her breath became high-pitched, rapid panting.

"Let go for him. Come for us," Angel whispered as he caressed her upper arms. Her orgasm crested and broke over her with his words. Her long, wavering moan was muffled against his taut abdomen as her pussy rocked against Joaquin's hand and lips. He didn't withdraw until she'd ridden every pulse and was thoroughly finished. Finally he released her, and she lay down exactly where she was on top of Angel. Angel brushed her hair from her flaming cheeks and stroked her shoulders as she recovered.

"Was it good, sweetheart?" Angel asked, crooning to her when she crawled into the crook of his arm, drawing Joaquin alongside her.

"Yes, I need a minute. I seem to have lost all my bones," she whispered and shivered.

"Honey, come here," Joaquin murmured as he and Angel both turned to her and snuggled her between them, covering her with the blanket. She floated in a blissful haze as they plied her with lingering kisses. When the last tremor had left her and the orgasm had passed, she'd felt sure she was done in for the night. But their kisses and whispered words of love as they stroked her face and her body, combined with their masculine scent and nearness, served to stoke the embers that burned inside her. She wanted more. She wanted them.

Chapter Twenty

Angel pulled the blanket down and allowed his fingertips to slide in a slow caress between Teresa's beautiful, blushing breasts. She shuddered and panted as his fingers continued straight down to her mound, and her skin felt like velvet under his fingertips. He slid them through the wispy curls that covered her mound, and she moaned and caught her breath. Her eyelids were half open, watching him, and she sighed blissfully as he slipped a finger into her hot, wet slit. Her moan was musical as he slid a fingertip over her clit. She kicked the cover away and arched her back as he stroked her and slipped a fingertip into her pussy. Joaquin kissed her throat, making her shudder delicately. Her pussy clenched on his fingertip, inviting him in further.

"I like that little sensitive spot very much, sugar," Joaquin murmured as teased her nipple with a fingertip before suckling it. "It's going to be so much fun spending time finding all those little hot spots on you."

Angel agreed wholeheartedly with that sentiment. He was currently exploring his favorite hot spot at the moment. Angel slid his fingers farther into her silken cunt, and a whimper escaped her lips as he stroked into her drenched heat. His cock twitched at her responsiveness. Using two fingers, he found her G-spot and stroked her there lightly.

"Oh, Angel. Oh, please, please." Her body undulated, and more moisture coated his fingers. As she took her pleasure, he couldn't suppress the growl that rumbled from his chest, which only seemed to increase her arousal.

"I love it when you do that, honey," she whispered.

"Do what?" Angel asked.

"Growl. It makes me feel…"

"Desired? Wanted?"

"Yes! Oh yes! Angel, all those things!" She clutched at his shoulders. "I want more, please," she whispered.

Her pussy rippled around his fingers as her body begged for his. He wanted to fill her with his cock and give her what she craved.

"I'm going to make love to you, sweetheart. Is that what you want?" Angel smiled sympathetically when she moaned in disappointment as his fingers retreated from her slippery cunt. He kissed her, teasing her tongue with his, and she moaned.

"Yes, Angel, please."

He reached for a foil package from the bedside table drawer, opened it, and rolled the condom onto his cock while Joaquin nuzzled her cheekbone and kissed her, stroking her torso. Teresa caressed Joaquin's face while she watched what Angel was doing.

"Beautiful, you're not afraid are you?" Angel asked as he coated the condom with a generous application of personal lubricant, stroking his cock to warm the gel to his temperature before touching her. His cock tingled and stung with the need to slide into her.

She shook her head minutely. "No, Angel. I'm not afraid of either one of you. How could I be afraid of the two gentlest men I've ever known?"

She shuddered and panted when Joaquin applied a little of the gel to her entrance for him. "This is lubricant, sugar. It'll make it easier for Angel's cock to slide in. We don't want you to be sore later," Joaquin murmured as he stroked her swollen, wet little lips.

She smiled at him and said, "Grace told me you would remember that. Thank you." As he continued to stroke her ripe, wet flesh, she murmured and flexed her hips against his fingers. Angel gritted his teeth as his cock threatened to explode if he didn't get the show on the road. He needed to get a hold of himself.

Caressing her hip, Angel looked into her eyes seriously. "Promise me you'll tell me if you get scared, or if it doesn't feel good?"

"I promise, Angel." She looked up at him from trust-filled eyes and stroked his arm as if she were consoling *him.*

Joaquin moved up higher on the bed, closer to her head, so he could nuzzle in her hair, kiss her, and whisper to her but more importantly to help Angel watch for signs she might be frightened or agitated but trying to hide it.

Joaquin stroked her cheekbone with the backs of his knuckles and said, "Angel is going to make this first time so good for you, sugar. He's going to slide real slow into your little pussy. You'll feel him moving inside you and stroking your clit."

Angel could tell Joaquin's words enflamed her because her eyes glittered with desire as she listened. Angel knelt between her thighs and spread them so he could see all of her in the muted glow of the firelight. Her body blushed for him, and the perfume of her arousal filled his nostrils. Her juices flooded her entrance joining the lubrication Joaquin had applied. Angel spread her outer lips, which made her inner lips open as well.

Another low growl stirred within him at the sight. "You have such a beautiful pussy, Teresa, so pink and delicate. Your little lips are parted for me, ready to take my cock." She moaned and arched her back slightly, and another droplet seeped from her opening. His mouth watered, and his cock twitched eagerly.

He knelt closer to her, lifting her calves so they rested over his hips, which brought his cock into prime position to enter her. He ignored the flames of wild lust that urged him to plunder her and sink into her receptive warmth. He'd walk to the ends of the Earth for her, and his entire body was filled with desire for her as he savored the first time he entered this woman he loved so completely.

He stroked her thighs and her abdomen, and the feel of her firm, full breast in his hand was nearly his undoing as his breathing became harsh and shallow. He positioned the throbbing head at her hot entrance, gritting his teeth, disciplining the urge to plunge inside in one smooth stroke. Later he would, but he'd hurt her if he did that now. His need for her was so great that hot shivers raced up and down his spine, but he proceeded slowly.

She gasped when the wide head of his dick pressed for entrance, and he could feel her tremble. Her breathing turning into rapid panting, and she bit her lip adorably as her eyelids slid closed. "Yes, please, please, Angel, fill me." She lifted her hips in his hands and flexed, offering herself to him. Sexy woman.

His cock slid in a minute, and he hissed as her satiny heat kissed his cock. In a deep, gravelly voice he barely recognized as his own, he said, "Now that is a pretty sight." He growled again and felt her body tremble in response. Her pussy flooded with juicy arousal inspired by his growl. He shuddered, knowing it was only going to get better.

Joaquin sat up and murmured. "Oh, fuck me. That is beautiful, sugar. The way you welcome him inside you."

The muscles in her pussy clamped down tightly and quivered around him, begging to be filled. A tortured-sounding moan escaped her lips, and he groaned loudly, holding back by a thin thread.

"Oh fuck!" Angel growled. "She clenched on me just now. Mmm, look at that. She's flooded. Damn, this is going to be a pleasant ride."

His beautiful Teresa whimpered incoherently, and Joaquin murmured as he looked at where they were joined, "That is amazing. She wants you awful bad, Angel." Then he returned and spoke softly to her, "Your soft little pussy is going to feel like heaven to him and to me later. I can't wait to feel your pussy gloving my cock."

She touched Angel's cheek and reached the other hand out to stroke his hand and whispered, "Please." Her hips trembled and flexed her juicy little pussy against the throbbing head of his cock.

Angel smiled down at her tenderly. His hands pressed her thighs open a bit more and began the slow, sweet glide into utter bliss.

"Oh, fuck. *Heaven.*" He ground out, fighting for control to slide in only that first inch. His heart pounded in his chest, and a whimpering moan slipped from her lips. He experienced utterly delicious heat and silkiness as her lips stretched to receive the head and he breached those muscles that clenched for him earlier. Her pussy gloved his cock tightly as her body sang with more moisture. He slid another inch deeper and felt little rippling spasms begin along the length that was buried in her.

"Oh fuck, she's so close already, Joaquin. I can feel it. She's tight like a vise on my cock. How are you doing, sweetheart?" He studied her face for a moment, searching for a trace of fear or pain. Her eyes flashed open, and she looked straight into his so he could see the truth.

She licked her lips and smiled at him. "Angel, it's *wonderful*. Please, more. I'm going to come soon. I know it. Oh, honey, yes," she whispered as he slid in another inch, then retreated smoothly, then pressed in again, gaining a little more ground. "Oh, yes, that's beautiful!" she whimpered and tried to move under him, but he stilled her hips.

Joaquin stroked her cheek. "Sugar, try to hold your climax off until he's all the way inside you."

"I don't know if I can," she whimpered, and Angel knew that only made her want it more, now that Joaquin asked her to wait. She fought his hold slightly, still trying to undulate on his cock.

"Listen to me," he said as Angel continued his slow thrusting and retreating, gaining a little ground with each wet stroke. Joaquin made eye contact with Angel, and Angel mouthed *oh fuck* and rolled his eyes, smiling a tortured smile at them both.

"If you can hold off and let him fully inside you, your orgasm will be like nothing you've experienced so far." Her eyes got big, and she smiled in wonder. "*Yes*, that good. Sugar, he's loving your pussy so much right now. Damn, that is a beautiful sight, the way his cock disappears inside you. You're doing great. Does it feel good?"

Her voice was shaky. "It's amazing. I feel how hot he is inside me. He fills me so tight. Is he all the way in yet?" she asked as she arched her back, trying to take more.

Joaquin chuckled and stroked her nipple. "Oh, no, sugar, he's only halfway slid inside you right now."

A look of disbelief appeared on her face, and she whimpered, "Oh Angel. It's so good. I'll never last." He wanted to be careful with her. He wanted her to stay still and relax for him, but she was so close to the edge. Thankfully, she took a few slow breaths and allowed him to hold her hips still. As he moved against her, her pussy felt as though she had liquefied around him, going completely slick. Never, ever had sex been this fulfilling, this satisfying, and he hadn't even come yet.

"I don't want to hurt you. You need time to adjust," he said in a strained whisper.

"It doesn't hurt, Angel. You feel so good," she whispered, as he slid out and thrust against her. He groaned in ecstasy as more of him was engulfed in her molten heat.

Angel thrust a few more times and then stopped, stroking her abdomen, cupping her breasts, his hands a little shaky. "I just need to feel you for a second," he murmured as he came to her and braced his elbows at her sides. His hands slid under her shoulder blades and pressed her incredibly soft torso to his. Shivers like small electrical shocks skittered up and down his spine as he controlled the urge to move. To *fuck*. He kissed her tenderly and rolled his hips one more time and groaned as he slid into her to the last thickest inch. "You have all of me now, sweetheart. It's utter heaven loving you."

Her blissful smile lit up every dark corner of his formerly lonely heart and made him happy beyond belief. She now occupied every part of his heart.

"You were right. You *did* fit, and it's so *good*," she whispered then flexed her hips experimentally, and they both growled at the motion. The thin thread of control he maintained unraveled. Now free of his hands stilling them, her hips undulated against him, and he could feel every inch of her satiny heat sliding over him, engulfing him. "Angel, please love me. I can feel it coming. I can't stop it this time!" She moaned, her voice gradually picking up volume and intensity as she moved against him. She parted her lips on a moan as her pussy rippled and grasped on his cock.

"You don't have to hold it back any longer, sugar," Joaquin said to her. "He's going to fuck you now. Don't hold back."

Angel rose on his forearms and pulled out a little and thrust back in then repeated the reverse motion, pulling out farther and thrusting back in again. He breathed harshly as her pussy rippled around him. He repeated the motion over and over again, pulling out a little more each time, his speed increasing with each stroke until he was pistoning into and out of her with his full length as her hips flexed and rolled against his.

"Every long inch of him is sliding into your wet little pussy, sugar. It's *incredible* to watch. You're just *glorious* fucking him, the way you move," Joaquin said, inflaming them both. She moaned again and writhed uninhibitedly beneath him.

Her breathing matched Angel's, and she wrapped her legs around his hips and began her own counter thrusting motion, taking him eagerly, hungrily in fact. Her head was thrown back on the pillow, a low, keening moan flowing from her lips.

"Angel, oh, Angel. It's so good, ohgodohgodohgod! I'm! I'm—oh *fuck* yes! I'm *coming*!" Joaquin covered her lips with his own, as she let out a euphoric wail of ecstasy. Her orgasm rippled through her, gripping his cock like a pulsing fist. Her hips rolled erotically against Angel's, sinuously undulating on his cock.

Angel ground against her, feeling every exhilarating pulse of her cunt as she came, her cream flowing copiously between them. He was overwhelmed with an almost animalistic satisfaction, knowing he'd satisfied her and she'd come hard. He rose over her, her legs relaxing from around him as she looked up in blissful awe. The new knowledge in her eyes softened the alpha sensation, and he remembered he needed to be gentle with her. He lifted her hips and began his rhythm again, seeking his own release inside her tender, sated body.

He held her as he thrust, tilting her so that his body aligned perfectly with hers and her clit slid with each stroke along his cock before colliding with his pubic bone. The tension increased within her again as her passion responded to his. He murmured love words to her, thrusting with increasing speed, trying to be gentle for her sake. Reaching out for something to hold on to, she gripped the sheet in one fist and Joaquin's hand in the other.

"It's feels so good, Angel. I'm--I'm coming *again*." She smiled joyfully, and her body took over. She established a double-time rhythm on his cock as he pounded into her. She cried out in ecstasy as she came, taking him with her. His deep growl of release was a low rumble in his chest, though he truly desired to howl in satisfaction as he came. His release pounded through him, and his cum spurted in long, powerful streams into her warm cunt.

Still entwined with her, he caressed her hip, hoping he hadn't hurt her by holding on too tight, and laid down on her, bracing himself on his forearms. Her cheeks blushed bright pink, and he kissed them both, feeling their heat with his lips. It was pure bliss to lay there with her, his cock still pulsing inside her trembling body as she recovered and caught her breath. He looked up at Joaquin and gave him a lopsided grin.

Joaquin smiled back and looked down at her. "How are you feeling, sugar?"

"Bliss," she whispered, her eyes mostly closed but moving back and forth between the two of them. "Now I understand," she said in a husky voice thick with emotion.

"Understand what, sugar?"

"Why Grace always has *that* look on her face." Her full lips spread in a seductive but satisfied smile.

"Which look is that?" Angel asked, nuzzling her collarbone.

"The one Teresa's wearing right now if I was to hazard a guess." Joaquin leaned down to kiss her when she nodded serenely.

Angel kissed the spot between her breasts and murmured, "That's how making love is supposed to feel. And you have *two* ready and willing cowboys at your beck and call."

Joaquin chuckled playfully. "Now you know what lovemaking is supposed to be like, but you haven't tasted the lovemaking of *two* men yet. That is if you're up to it," he added seriously, all playfulness aside for a second.

"I'm thirsty. But I'm definitely feeling up to more lovemaking," she murmured.

Angel licked and kissed her nipple. She released him from her ankle lock so he could dispose of the condom, and he rose over her, watching as his cock slid from her tender pussy. He touched her swollen lips with his finger tip. "Are you feeling sore? You're bright pink now."

* * * *

"My whole body feels like its singing." Teresa watched Angel as he petted her lips and drew a taste of her cream to his mouth. His eyes caught hers and sparkled with love and renewed desire. She noticed with admiration that his cock was already hardening.

Joaquin looked at Angel and smiled back at her. "You see what you do to us, sugar? We'll be hard for you on a moment's notice." He handed her a glass of water, and she noticed he was stroking his cock which was every bit as deliciously hard and thick as his brother's, standing up straight and proud.

She drank the glass of water, and he took it from her and refilled it then brought it back to the bedside table for later. Appreciating the thoughtful things they did for her, she wanted to return the favor. She rose up and crawled over to the edge of the bed where Joaquin now stood as Angel returned to the bed, watching them. Joaquin smiled at her as she reached for him. On her knees before him, she caressed Joaquin's biceps and forearms as he stroked her hips.

"You've both been so good to me tonight. Before I met you, I had no experience in what men look like or what they are supposed to *be* like. The very thought of one of these filling my pussy...I imagine it's the most beautiful thing in the world."

Joaquin chuckled as she ran her hands over his abdomen to his chest. "Teresa said pussy, Angel. Did you hear?" Teresa giggled, wondering if they'd opened the floodgates on other slang foreign to her lips.

Angel chuckled in response. "Yes, I did, and I loved the sound of it."

"I thought that was a bad word growing up, used like curse words were. Saying it now feels like...I'm taking it back. Like it's *ours*. It doesn't bother me at all the way I thought it would. I liked what you told me as you put your cock in me, and I wished I could see," she said, feeling her cheeks heat up. Would they think she'd turned into a sexual deviant?

After sharing a look with Joaquin, Angel slipped out into the hallway and returned a few seconds later with the mirror that hung beside the front door.

Joaquin stroked the sides of her breasts with his thumbs as he ran his hands up her sides. "You don't have to imagine it, sugar. You can see for yourself as I make love to you."

"Thank you. You are so thoughtful." She kissed Angel then turned back to Joaquin. She didn't know where the sudden brazenness came from, but she went with it. "Now, *about* this big, beautiful cock. Wasn't Joaquin sweet to me while you made love to me, Angel?" Both brothers looked at each other in mild surprise.

Yes, shy Teresa has a cheeky streak.

Joaquin hummed when she wrapped her hand around his thick cock and stroked as light as a feather.

Angel nodded. "He was, and he even helped you delay and intensify your orgasm," Angel added generously.

What a nice brother he is!

"Oh! That, too. I should thank him, don't you think?" She looked back at Angel with twinkling eyes, knowing he probably thought she'd give Joaquin a blow job for consistency's sake.

Maybe.

She licked the head of his cock.

Maybe not.

Angel chuckled. "I think he'd like it very much if you did. He does adore you, would do anything for you." She giggled at Joaquin's eager nod and mischievous grin.

She looked up and giggled. "Hey, you rhymed. But you're right, and I adore him, too." She patted the center of the bed. "Why don't you come and lie down here for me, so I can thank you properly."

Joaquin had a big grin when he climbed onto the bed and lay down in her spot. Teresa beckoned Angel to her and whispered in his ear. He grinned smugly and walked over to the bedside table and retrieved the bottle of lubricant.

She knelt over him, making sure Angel had a lovely view of her ass, and lifted Joaquin's cock in one hand and began licking him and stroking him with her tongue, drawing tortured-sounding moans from him. His erection twitched and pulsed in her hand, and she knew it must be difficult to control his response.

She laved him with her tongue then made her way down to his balls and lavished them with attention, as well. While she did this, Angel generously coated her pussy lips and her slit with the lubricant, taking special care that *no spot* was missed. She wiggled her ass at him and giggled while he played with her, adding more for good measure because it paid to be *very thorough*.

Joaquin looked like he was about ready to explode when she finally released his cock and laid it on his abdomen. Watching his reaction, she straddled his hips. His eyes opened wide as she aligned the rigid length of his cock with her spread outer lips and sat down on him. His lips opened wide to match his eyes, and she giggled mischievously. She slithered her well-lubricated pussy all along his hot shaft.

"Oh, fuck! I was not expecting that!" He groaned happily and shuddered. "You are full of surprises, sugar."

"Mmmm-hmmm," she agreed and ground her pussy against him, her arms rising over her head into her hair.

Chapter Twenty-one

The giggling nymph was gone, replaced by the tempting vixen. Teresa owed Grace *big time* for that move, for the priceless look on Joaquin's face. He looked awestruck as he watched her.

"Holy shit." Angel watched as she arched her back and moved slowly, establishing a rhythm that she enjoyed as she sighed happily. "Our wife-to-be is a goddess. She can have *whatever she fucking wants*."

"Oh, *hell* yeah." Joaquin groaned as she ground over his cock. "I'm so in for it." He moaned. Starting out with a circular motion, Teresa rubbed her sopping wet pussy over his cock and coating him well from balls to the head. After a minute, she leaned slightly forward and braced her hands on his hard pecs and began a sideways figure-eight swirling movement. She twisted and rotated her pelvis in a slow belly dancing move, stretching her arms over her head. He caressed her thighs with his hands, staring up at her, his face enraptured. She hoped he saw the love in her eyes for him.

"Thank you, Joaquin." She continued grinding, lowering her upper body so that her chest made full contact with his. She slid her hands under his shoulders and held him so her breasts were pressed against him. Arching her back, she presented Angel with another view of her pussy and ass. She looked back at Angel, smiled seductively into his smoldering topaz eyes and murmured, "Thank you, Angel." Her lips quivered a little because she meant thank you for so many things.

"Sugar, you're so welcome." Joaquin sounded like he was being tortured with pleasure. His head was pressed back into the pillow, and his lips were parted in ecstasy.

"You're welcome." Angel sounded like his breath had left him all together. Love radiated from his warm eyes.

Rising up over Joaquin again, she returned to her circular grind, enjoying the feel of his work-roughened hands on her hips. She rose up slightly and slid back and forth over his length until he reluctantly begged her to stop.

Angel came and lay down on the bed with them, handed Joaquin a towel, and asked Teresa in wonder, "Where did you learn to give a lap dance, sweetheart?"

"Grace got together with Charlotta and Cami from the club. She explained to me what they showed her. Did you like it, Joaquin? You sounded like you did, but did I do a good job? It's not exactly the kind of thing you can practice alone." She giggled when they looked at each other in astonishment.

Teresa sat back, stroked Joaquin's cock, then looked over at Angel. "Do you remember the conversation you and I had right before the bachelor party? I asked you what it would be like in the club you were taking Eli to."

Angel nodded, and she said, "Remember telling me there was only one woman you would want a lap dance from? Well, you have something to look forward to now."

Angel growled with pleasure. "Woman, you amaze me." Angel slid his hand over her back in a slow caress. He helped her rise from Joaquin so he could towel off the lubricant before returning to her on the bed and applying another condom.

Joaquin said, "Thanks for my lap dance, sugar. I've never had one quite that exciting, nor have I had one from a woman as beautiful as you." She lay back on the bed next to Angel, who sat against the headboard. Joaquin climbed onto the bed and drew her to his virile, hard body, from lip to toe. His heavy cock was pressed against her mound. The heat and hardness of it made her whole body vibrate with desire for him. He looked into her eyes soberly, stroking a strand of her hair from her forehead. "Do you feel up to more loving, sugar?" When he was playful, he was a devil, but when he was taking care of her, he was serious.

"I'm wonderful. Use the lubricant like Angel did, and I'll be fine. You're both so gentle with me. You could never harm me."

Joaquin drew her lips to his and kissed her. "That's something I'd never want to do."

Angel passed Joaquin the lubricant, and he applied a bit of it to Teresa's already wet pussy, making sure to slide some of it into her entrance. Joaquin smoothed some on over the condom and stroked it a few times. Watching him stroke his hardened shaft made her pussy quiver. He returned to her embrace and caressed her back. He slid his fingers over her hip to her tailbone and pressed her to him. She sighed at the feel of his hard shaft aligned to her throbbing slit. He paused briefly.

"What?" she asked.

Joaquin gestured with his chin to the mirror, which Angel retrieved. "We promised you could watch, remember? Come over here." He patted the center of the king-size bed. "Come lay down and we'll position the mirror so you can see. You're gonna love it, sugar."

She enthusiastically did what he asked, giggling when he chuckled at her eagerness. They propped her up on several of the pillows so she could relax, and Joaquin came to her, stroking his cock, smiling naughtily at her. He probably knew she liked it when he did that.

He leaned to her and kissed her deeply then left a trail of kisses down to her abdomen, stopping at her mound. She whimpered in disappointment until he grinned and slid a finger over her sensitive clit, which sent a lightning bolt of pleasure through her pussy. He parted her lips and teased her mercilessly, stroking her to a feverish pitch until she was begging for him to do something.

Much to her surprise, he lifted her ankles, and nodded at Angel, who held the mirror so she could see. Joaquin got himself in position and asked "Sugar, can you see your pussy?"

Angel shifted the mirror slightly until she could see. "Oh." She focused on looking at herself in the mirror and felt a tightening inside her pussy. Joaquin placed her feet on his shoulders. In the reflection, she could see her juices glistening on her lips and the opening to her pussy, and she bit her lip, not so secretly loving the sight of it.

Joaquin and Angel smiled at each other and her. "You like it, don't you, sugar? We love it, too, so wet and pretty. Are you ready?"

Ready? She could practically *feel* his cock there already.

At her eager nod, he said, "Watch in the mirror."

Angel held the mirror as Joaquin slid his hot hands slowly down her inner calves and thighs until he reached her lips. He caressed her stroked her clitoris again.

In the mirror, she could see that her juices ran from her opening and slid down into the cleft of her ass, adding a new layer to her sensory overload. She gasped in surprise when Angel reached out a fingertip and caught the moisture and slid his finger to the virgin territory of her rear opening.

She whimpered but never once looked away. While Joaquin continued ministering to her clit, Angel massaged her anal opening.

Angel looked steadily into her eyes and said, "Think you might like us to make love to you here someday?"

"Oh, yes."

Her pussy and asshole both convulsed at the thought of them taking her that way. There were so many more nerve endings there than she would have thought possible, and he was making contact with *all of them.* The pressure of his fingertip gave her a naughty, lustful feeling in the depths of her belly.

A low moan escaped her as his finger pressed more insistently against the tight ring of muscle at her asshole. The feeling scared her a tiny bit, but she wanted it at the same time. Grace said it would hurt a little at first if they ever breached her there, but she wanted it, all the same. The dual stimulation combined into one lustful, primal need. She wasn't sure what Angel would do next, and she glanced away from the mirror and looked up at him.

Angel kissed her forehead and murmured, "Relax. Lay your head back so you're not straining. Just feel for us." Doing as he asked, she realized how tense she'd become. She relaxed her bottom as the pressure increased a tiny bit and felt her asshole give way slightly. Part of her wanted to clench, but the other part wanted her men to have all of her.

Relaxing against his finger, Teresa moaned in surprise as his finger entered her ass a bit more. She felt the slight pinch, and her breath came in rapid pulses, but she relaxed and allowed him in another tiny degree.

"Trust us. I wouldn't hurt you for anything." He stroked in and out repeatedly as the unfamiliar sensation became more pleasurable and the intrusion became a welcomed one. Joaquin stroked her clit, and she realized he'd been giving her time to experience the other sensation. Now combined, it was explosive. Her pussy convulsed, and she moved with them. What would it be like if they were ever to *both* penetrate her. She'd die of pleasure.

"It feels good, doesn't it?" Joaquin asked as he stroked her clit with one hand and her inner thigh with the other. Her feet still rested at his shoulders.

"Yes," she whimpered.

Angel's finger slid a little farther into her bottom as Joaquin slid a finger into her pussy. They began a concerted rhythm with their fingers, one thrusting in while the other pulled almost all the way out. Her juices ran copiously from her pussy, judging by the decadent, wet sounds of their play. It generously lubricated the way for Angel so that eventually he was able to slide in all the way to the top knuckle as she watched. They gradually began moving into her simultaneously, filling her in both places at once, and the pleasure exploded inside her, her orgasm causing her to clamp down on both their hands.

Angel withdrew his finger while she was still flying high, and Joaquin reminded her to watch in the mirror. He positioned his cock's head at her opening, and she could see how erotically her pussy lips stretched around his thick cock.

The sight of him sliding into her pussy, combined with the pressure at her opening and the rolling aftershocks of her last orgasm, had her ready to come again.

"Oh! Joaquin, I feel another one coming, please. Please!" She was swamped with lust and insanely turned on by the sight of his rigid cock disappearing into her tingling pussy, filling her so magnificently. "Fuck, she's as tight as a fist," Joaquin muttered, pressing in farther. Seeing for herself the way his cock slid inside her was a huge turn-on for her, even more so when it reappeared covered in her juices. Her pussy rippled around him as he slid in again.

Angel's voice sounded tense as he said, "Teresa, can you see how your cream coats his cock? We'll never forget this first night with you."

"The first time and for the rest of our lives," Joaquin whispered. "We're your slaves now."

An incoherent moan slipped from her throat as he gained more ground with each thrust, fascinating her with the sight of so much thick, hard flesh sliding inside her yearning pussy. Finally, he was seated to the hilt.

"You amaze me," she whispered to him and tightened on him as he withdrew and pushed back in.

He gazed at her and said, "I love you, Teresa." He thrust, groaning intensely. Reveling in the sight of his cock thrusting into her pussy, Teresa thought she felt him grow slightly larger, which set her pussy to clenching. He licked his thumb and reached down to stroke her exposed clit, and the muscles in her pussy tightened down as she spiraled toward her orgasm.

Joaquin pistoned into her, and while she watched, her pussy swelled and tightened more. He stroked her clit in rhythm with his thrusting, and her juices ran from her pussy as the wave overtook her. She cried out as they came simultaneously. His big, swollen cock thrust into her one final time, and Joaquin moaned loudly as he filled her so full of him.

For a second, she thought of them someday coming inside of her without a condom and making a baby. A baby that they would love as fiercely as they loved her and Michael. She imagined her belly filled with either Angel's or Joaquin's child. It was so strong an image that she slammed her eyes shut and ground her pussy against him, completely undone by the strength of her orgasm and the power of that image.

Joaquin released her legs and rubbed them before lowering them to either side of his hips. Still joined, he lay down in the cradle her body formed and nuzzled her throat. Looking into her eyes, he kissed her while they caught their breath.

"How do you feel?" Joaquin asked, brushing his lips over her jawbone.

"Heavenly," she murmured as her eyelids drooped heavily.

"We should help you shower and then tuck you in to sleep. It's late," Angel murmured. The fire in the fireplace had died down to smoldering embers but had heated the room nicely.

Joaquin carefully withdrew from her and rose from the bed. "I'll start the shower while I lose the condom."

Angel followed him into the bathroom to wash up then returned and lifted her from the bed and carried her into the steamy bathroom. They pinned up her hair, and at their request, she allowed them to bathe her. They were gentle with her tender parts and then rinsed her off and toweled her dry. Angel gave Joaquin her silky nightgown, and he put it on her and brushed out her hair. She brushed her teeth again, and this time Joaquin lifted her and carried her to bed. They tucked her in between them, snuggled close to her, and both kissed her goodnight.

She whispered in the dark, holding onto both of them, "I love you both so much it hurts."

"But in a good way, right?" Joaquin asked quietly.

"A very good way."

Chapter Twenty-two

Teresa sat on the couch in Grace's living room and felt icy goose bumps rise on her arms as she exclaimed in a panic, "You did *what?*"

Her spa day with the girls, while the men moved her belongings from the apartment to the ranch was sounding less like fun and more like torture.

"Honey, it's not as bad as you think. It'll be *fun!*" When Grace used that cajoling tone, Teresa knew she might as well give in. But *this* was presuming a lot on a friendship!

"For who?"

"Well, *that* part won't be fun," Grace said, her elegant eyebrows knitting in sympathy, "but you'll enjoy the benefits on your honeymoon, I *promise*. And there's more to the spa day than getting waxed. We're all getting massages and facials then we're getting our nails done."

Teresa steeled herself. If she was doing this, she was going to at least negotiate for a fair deal from all her so-called friends. "I think if I have to bare my *goodies* and get waxed, everybody else should, too."

Five faces grinned at her. *Oh crud. That was their plan all along. Now they have me!*

"Okay!" Grace giggled, clapping her hands like she was looking forward to it. *Masochist!*

"No problem, babe." Charity snickered, slapping palms with Rachel.

"Heck, I might try a full Brazilian this time." Rachel said, grinning

"I'm game. I like *neat*," said Kelly, her eyes twinkling at Teresa.

Corina laughed and gamely said, "Count me in. It's good to try new things."

Rosemary patted Teresa's shoulder in reassurance and wisely said, "Trust me, honey, it's better than shaving. Your men will love it. I'll do it, too. I'm due, also."

Teresa knew they had her. "Ooh! All right! But I'm not going totally bare, Grace. How do we even know Angel and Joaquin will like it?" Before the words were even all out of her mouth, she knew she was grasping at straws now.

The girls all looked at each other and then in unison erupted in raucous, cackling laughter.

Grace giggled and said, "Well, we know because *one of us*, who shall remain *nameless*, may have dropped a hint or two and got a positive response from them. When quizzed about it, they both expressed an interest—"

"Exactly *how* do you quiz two men about what style of waxing they prefer for their bride-to-be?" Teresa demanded, her cheeks in flames.

Sagely, Charity interrupted with her usual irreverent wisdom. "Is that a question you *really* want an answer to, or do you just want to know what they prefer?"

Teresa adored Charity for her ability to see the real issue. "You're right, Charity. Okay. Give it to me straight. What did they like?" Teresa asked in resignation.

"A triangle, French wax. Bare vulva. Perianal waxing they left up to you. They don't want you to feel like you have to bare yourself like that to the wax tech the first time."

Well, how very thoughtful of them!

Teresa started sputtering, "Peri*anal*? Bare myself? *Bare vulva*? I—first time?" *More like only time!*

"Do you trust us, honey?" Grace asked gently.

"Of course I do."

"You'll get through this, and after it's over, you are going to wonder why you hadn't done it sooner, for yourself if not to please them. It's going to hurt for a few seconds, sting for a few minutes until they're done, but you'll take ibuprofen for the pain, powder the offended area, and know it was all worth it the moment your men get a good look at your—"

"Okay, I'll do it."

Charity patted her shoulder. "Trust me, honey. It takes weeks to grow back, and I don't think it hurts as much with subsequent visits. You can work your way up to the perianal, full wax later."

"No, I think I'm going to go for it. It should feel better after a couple of days, and you're *all* getting waxed, right? I'm not doing this alone," she said, looking at all of their faces for confirmation.

Rachel grinned. "Nope, we're all in."

Grace got up to retrieve the phone. "I'll let Madeleine know. Look on the bright side, Teresa. We thought about planning another bachelor-bachelorette party, but it's been less than a month since the last one, and we figured everybody was still stripper happy."

"Although I totally volunteered to go with the guys if they wanted to still do it," Rachel said with a chuckle. "Angel and Joaquin told me they weren't *in the mood*." Rachel rolled her eyes before continuing, "What a load of crap, not in the mood to see almost completely naked women shake their asses and stick their boobs in their faces. They said, and I quote, 'The girls at the club couldn't give them a lap dance that satisfied them.' Or something to that affect."

Teresa burst into a fit of giggles.

Charity caught on first and laughed with her. "Oh! They have a *private dancer* now, huh? I think I'd be shocked, but I'm too happy for you, Teresa. Those two brothers have been *good* for you."

Teresa looked around the room at the best friends a girl ever had. "You know what? *You all* have been good for me, too."

The only one missing was Juliana, who was at Teresa's apartment, helping pack Teresa's bedroom and kitchen. Grace had invited her to come today, but she'd said she'd already committed to help the men and really didn't mind. Teresa wondered if the fact that Ash Peterson was also helping with moving day didn't have some impact on her choice to help.

Grace patted Teresa's shoulder and said, "You're being a good sport about the waxing. If it's any consolation at all, when Angel and Joaquin came over for a bit on Sunday, I heard Jack talking to them both about having their first prostate exam done. They both agreed. You know what that means, don't you?"

Teresa knit her eyebrows together, afraid to reveal the fact she had no idea what a prostate exam entailed. The girls removed all doubt when they squealed almost as one, *"The gloved and lubricated finger!"*

Teresa laughed with her friends. They'd included her from the beginning, even when she hadn't known how to relate to them. It also made her happy that her men were safeguarding their health for the sake of their family.

Grace disappeared upstairs and came back down with a large box wrapped in white paper and a big frothy bow. "I called Madeleine. She said we should come an hour early, so we still have until three o'clock." The girls all gathered around.

She placed the wrapped box in front of Teresa on the coffee table. Teresa looked at her in dismay. She'd wanted to keep things simple and had told Grace so. They were all doing so much for her as it was. The wedding had been pulled together in less than a week and was going to take place that Saturday.

Teresa said, "I thought we were getting together for a planning session before going to the spa?"

Grace chuckled. "No, honey, everything is planned and under control. This was our time to get together with you and watch you open a special gift from *your men*. They adore you so much," Grace said with a tear in her eye. "They said they needed my help, which as you can imagine, they got in spades. This came in yesterday morning. Open it."

Tearing into the paper eagerly, Teresa looked at the shipping label and squealed with glee. "Hips and Curves!"

Teresa opened the numerous bundles inside. There were lingerie in every cut and fabric imaginable and even some items she had no idea how to wear. Among the panties and thongs was a beautiful, finely made pearl G-string with a double strand of white pearls and white lace waistband.

Teresa started to ask, "Where do the pearls—never mind. I'll figure it out." She was sure Angel and Joaquin would be delighted to help her figure that out.

There were bras in different designs, in lace, satin, and silk. She also found several gowns and babydoll nighties.

Grace giggled and said, "Angel and Joaquin were cute, comparing the styles and talking about the colors. They said complimentary things about your assets and your coloring. I think they made good choices."

There was a white silk corset, complete with detachable garters and halter straps.

"That one is for under your wedding dress. It has a matching G-string and lace top stockings. Bear in mind, *they* picked these things for you. I steered them in the right directions, style wise. Keep going."

Near the bottom, she found a long, white, halter-style gown. The empire waist and skirt were in a heavy white satin. The halter style bodice was a fine, sheer white lace. It had a series of thin, white satin straps that crisscrossed the back. It was the most gorgeous gown she'd ever owned. All the girls made appropriate ooh and ahh sounds.

Grace said dreamily, "They chose this for your wedding night. Look at the robe they chose to go over it."

She opened the package, revealing a sheer, white, floor-length robe made of a fine silky mesh. It was joined at the fitted, gathered bust by a simple tie in front.

"Damn, I'd wear that by itself," Charity murmured, reaching out to touch the filmy fabric.

Teresa was awed by the selections they made for her, especially this gown and robe, which were stunning.

Grace stopped her as she reached into the box and said, "Now, what's left in the box is just for kicks and giggles, and they wanted you to know that *before* you opened it. I encouraged them because they weren't sure, so you can blame these choices on me if you want."

Unsure what she was about to find, Teresa made big eyes at Grace and went fishing. The next item out of the box was a sexy, leopard-print cat suit with a discreet overlapping, crotchless opening, complete with detachable tail and a headband with kitty ears attached to it.

All the girls giggled, including Teresa who was sure her cheeks were hot pink. There was a white envelope at the bottom of the box.

"Open the card," Grace said encouragingly as Teresa looked at the mountain of lingerie piled around her. Teresa opened it and read it silently as tears welled up in her eyes. Then she read it out loud.

Dear Teresa,

By now you've made it to the bottom of the big box. We picked things we thought you might like that we'd love to see you in. But don't think for a second that we're trying to dress you up a certain way or change your style. We love you the way you are and hope you never think otherwise.

Loving you and Michael, and becoming a part of your lives has made us better men. The gift card is for just in case there was something you've been wanting from that company that you didn't get today. We want you to have whatever makes you happy.

All our love—
Angel and Joaquin

P.S. We really do love that cat suit, a lot!

Enclosed in the note was a gift card from Hips and Curves in the amount of two hundred dollars. She felt like she'd entered another dimension. Being spoiled like this was going to take some getting used to. Two hundred *more* dollars for lingerie? *More* lingerie besides what was in the box?

There was a collective gasp when she showed them the gift card.

"Wow. I—wow." Teresa was at a loss for words.

"Yes, this is what spoiled rotten feels like," Grace affirmed for her, patting her shoulder.

Chapter Twenty-three

Teresa had a chance to think on the way over to the spa and knew she'd made the right choice about waxing. If they were willing to spend that kind of money on lingerie so she could doll herself up, the least she could do was get the full triangle French wax.

She rethought her earlier resolution once she was naked from the waist down and feeling a wee bit vulnerable in the private waxing room.

The wax was spread, the fabric strips applied. Ready to start yanking, the friendly wax tech, Rebecca, put her hand on Teresa's arm before she got started.

"Trust me when I tell you I've *heard* it all in this room. Curse your fiancé, curse your friends for talking you into this, curse at me all you want. Whatever gets said in my waxing room stays in my waxing room, okay?" she said with a cheerful grin. Teresa secretly wondered if many wax techs were secretly sadists.

As Rebecca said these things, she checked the strips and found one particular one and pressed down on the flesh beneath it, holding it nice and taut before continuing with what she was saying. A cold chill rolled up Teresa's spine as she suddenly wasn't so sure about this adventure.

"I'm the best at what I do. Just ask Grace and Charity. They'll tell you. When you see how smooth and lovely you are after I'm done, you'll be singing my praises. Okay?"

In a tremulous voice, Teresa said, "Okay…?"

Rip.

Okay, that *stung*, more than a little. New strip, hold the skin taut and…

Rip.

Did not enjoy that one, not *even* a little…

Rip.

The other spots were starting to *throb,* and that last *motherfucker* really hurt! She was panting when…

Rip.

Then chirpy, cheerful Rebecca said, "Hey, you're doing really well. You must have a high tolerance for pain. *Excellent.*"

Oh no, am I seeing black spots?

Rip.

"Shit!" Teresa yelped, both at the pain and at hearing herself curse out loud. At least she was breathing again.

"It's okay, honey. Let 'er rip. These rooms are soundproofed. You should hear Grace and Charity. They shriek like banshees."

Rip.

"Son of a bitch!" Why had she agreed to the full wax? Wax and your ass *should not* be used in the same sentence, *ever*!

Speaking of which, *rip.*

"Ow! Motherfucker! Grace, I'm gonna kill you!" Teresa screamed, and like that, the dam burst open, and Teresa discovered the joy of cursing.

Rip.

Rip.

"Now, don't hate me for this last one because it's –"

Rip! "Oh, fuck!"

"—a doozy. There, all done. Breathe, honey." Teresa was seeing black spots again as Rebecca patted her shoulder. "Hold still while I apply some oatmeal powder. This will help a lot. I'll send some home with you, too. You may have some inflammation for a day or so, but you'll be fine by Friday. Take some ibuprofen, sleep bare skinned tonight, and try not to get sweaty. A cool shower would be good, too, if you can stand it, but don't chafe with the towel. That skin is a little delicate right now. Your triangle turned out pretty." She powdered the offended area and patted the neatly trimmed triangle that now adorned Teresa's mons, proud of her work.

"Thank you," Teresa whimpered. *For torturing me.*

The wax tech smiled at her and said, "I know you probably hate my guts right now, but give it a day or so, and I'll be your new best friend. See you in a month or so. You can get dressed now."

"Thanks, Rebecca." *Whimper.*

"Congratulations on your wedding Saturday. Have fun," she replied, grinning.

"Yeah," Teresa groaned. *If I can freaking walk.*

* * * *

"I said *bad* words," Teresa said with a chuckle fifteen minutes later after Grace wheedled an ice pack out of Rebecca for Teresa and Corina, who was also new to waxing. They all sat in luxurious padded chairs receiving pedicures.

"I know. I heard you," Charity said with a snicker.

"Nuh-uh," Corina moaned. "That was me. I was in the room next to yours, Charity. I was afraid she was going to kill me. That first strip was murder. The *other* one was even worse."

"*Other one?*" Charity scoffed. "What did you get, just a basic bikini line wax, two little strips?"

"Uh-huh!" Corina said pathetically.

Teresa looked over at Corina in stunned surprise as Charity snickered. "Teresa's gonna *kill* you if you keep talking, Corina. How's that ice pack, honey? Need a shot of whiskey to go with it?" she asked Teresa sympathetically.

Teresa looked at her and started laughing, and soon they all joined in.

Finally, with tears streaming from her eyes, Teresa said, "What would my poor, sainted mother say if I told her I had my *ass* waxed today? How would that conversation go? 'No Mom, not my BUTT, my ass, right up the middle!'" She giggled and made a ripping motion with her forearm and laughed hysterically along with the others. All the spa techs were giggling, as well.

"Stop, I'm gonna pee in my pants!" Rosemary wheezed, doubled over while they all sat in their chairs getting pedicures.

Teresa wiped tears from her eyes, chuckling. "I said a lot of *really bad words*. I'm appalled at myself."

"Yeah, it was you I heard," Charity said with a chuckle.

Grace's phone rang, and she answered, "Hi, honey, I have you on speakerphone. How's it going at the apartment?"

They could hear distinctive Adam's voice. "Well, we've about got everything packed up, but we've run into a little snag."

"What's that?" Grace glanced at Teresa in concern. Something about Adam's voice led Teresa to believe that the little snag was anything but minor.

Adam hesitated for a moment. "Well...Ash accidentally knocked Juliana off the seven-foot ladder in the living room—"

There was a collective gasp from all the women.

He continued, "Onto the coffee table, the one with—"

Teresa groaned. "The glass top."

"Yeah, we'd moved it into the center of the room to take out with the next load of furniture. Juliana was using the ladder to take the clock down that hangs over your front door. She didn't lock the door, and Ash came barreling through it. She toppled right on the table. When he tried to help her up, she got a *little upset* with him and started fussing, backed away from him, and tripped backward over a box and busted her head good on the kitchen counter top." They all cringed at the vivid picture he painted.

Grace asked, "Is she all right?"

Adam groaned and then chuckled. "From the *sound* of her, she's going to be fine, but *man,* that girl can *cuss.* Ash carried her, crying, screaming and cursing out to his truck to take her to the ER. She's probably gonna need a bunch of stitches. I'm pretty sure her wrist is broken, and she's got a bad knot on the back of her head. Sorry Teresa, but the table is broke all to pieces."

"I'm just glad it wasn't more serious, Adam. What are you doing now?" Teresa asked.

"Well, there's one more load of boxes to take over that they're loading right now. We thought after we dropped them off we'd go check on Ash and Juliana. They…they don't seem like they get along well, kinda *sniping* at each other all day."

"Oh, they like each other just fine." Charity snickered. "Did you see them at the Christmas party?"

"Sorry, Charity, what?" Adam asked.

"Nothing, Adam. So you're going up to the ER?" Charity asked.

"Yeah. Ash said he feels responsible, seemed worried about her."

"We're almost done at the salon. We'll swing by there when we leave. So she was cursing a blue streak?" Grace asked.

"Yeah. She was pretty upset. I'll bet she gave Ash a good tongue lashing in the truck." Adam sighed, so he didn't hear Charity when she sputtered in her Coke.

Grace rolled her eyes at her sister. "Oh, honey, I hope not. He's so sweet."

With a laugh, Adam said, "Well, you might not think so if you heard what he told her after he loaded her in the truck."

The room got quiet. "What did he say?" Grace asked.

Now it was Adam's turn to snicker. "He told her he was going to take her to the hospital since it was his fault she got hurt. He told her she was in no condition to drive herself, and if she didn't *shut the fuck up,* he was going to duct tape her pretty little potty mouth closed."

Giggles erupted and filled the room. Grace asked "What did she say?"

Adam replied, "She opened her mouth to pop off at him again, and he slammed the door in her face. I'm not sure why, but I get the impression he *likes* her."

Grace pressed her lips together. "Maybe so. We'll talk about that some more later, honey. Are we all still on for supper, or should we—"

"Oh, yeah. They both said to go on ahead without them, but we're going up there first anyway. *So, you're about done?*" he asked in a deeper, sexy voice. Grace immediately reached for the cell phone and took him off speaker.

"Yes, you're off speaker now." Teresa noticed Grace's voice took on a huskier, dreamy quality. "Yes, we are. Mmm-hmm, I sure did. Just like you asked, baby. I think you *will*. No, not that bad." After a sharp intake of breath, Grace giggled delightedly. "Really? Oh, *Mama*! I live in heaven. Uh-huh, I love you, too, baby." Grace ended the call with a smile on her face and a blush in her cheeks.

"You two are nauseating." Charity chuckled, examining her fresh manicure.

Chapter Twenty-four

Grace gazed out of her dining room window with satisfaction. The wedding was going to be absolutely beautiful. Tables and chairs had arrived and were already set up. The layers of the wedding cake were waiting on the breakfast bar, ready to be assembled into a tiered cake. Dave, the DJ from The Dancing Pony, was setting up his sound system, and the musicians who would be playing the wedding processional were preparing. Ethan was directing his helpers in the kitchen and out at the smoker pit. The weather had even cooperated. Sunny and unseasonably warm with a high of seventy degrees.

Rachel and Kelly's decorations were bright and cheery, making up for the lack of greenery in the trees and on the shrubs. Grace had been able to arrange for a large white tent to cover the area in the backyard where everyone would be seated for the meal and reception. The portable dance floor was to be under the stars, assembled in the level-flat area in the ranch house's large backyard.

Teresa's parents were in Jack's bedroom, napping in preparation for the festive evening. Jack and Angel had picked them up from their nursing home in Tillman the day before, and they'd all had a wonderful meal at Grace's Friday evening. It was the first time her parents had ever seen Michael. Because she suffered from Alzheimer's, Mr. Palacios had to remind Teresa's mother several times why they were there and who Michael was. Teresa seemed joyful at seeing her parents, but Grace had noticed her wiping her eyes on several occasions.

Angel and Joaquin's family arrived Friday night and were all staying at a bed and breakfast Grace had arranged for them in Divine.

Maria, Eleazar, Ricardo and Marco seemed captivated by Michael and hung on his every word.

Grace went upstairs to check the bride's progress. Teresa sat at Grace's vanity in her bathroom as Serena from Madeleine's worked on her hair and makeup, while Teresa and Grace chatted.

Grace looked out of her bedroom window as she asked, "Have you noticed what flirts Luka and Matthias are?" They were currently chatting with Ethan's younger sister, Erin.

"*Yes!* Angel warned me about them. Luka asked last night, if, 'when he's finished growing up,' would I consider allowing him into our marriage."

"No he did not! What did you say?" Grace giggled.

"I asked him what he meant by 'finished growing up' because he's in his early twenties now. He confessed he meant 'finished sowing his wild oats.' Joaquin knocked the back of his head for being disrespectful, but he still blew me an air kiss, the scoundrel."

Grace had never seen a bigger pair of flirts than those two handsome devils working in tandem with each other. No single women were safe from their charms at the reception tonight.

* * * *

The gathering was surrounded by tall oak trees whispering in the wind. Angel remembered wondering what it would be like to be the bridegroom waiting at the end of the aisle when Teresa participated in Grace's and Rachel's weddings. He and Joaquin experienced it firsthand now as the musicians began the processional. Angel and Teresa had suggested an instrumental version of "Remember When" by Alan Jackson because of its beautiful melody.

Grace appeared at the open back door of the Divine Creek Ranch house. She made her way slowly forward and took her place opposite them beside the pastor.

Next, Rachel appeared escorting Michael as he reprised his role as ring bearer, opting to be carried in his 'Rachel-baby's' arms. She set Michael on his feet as she reached the end of the aisle. Michael approached gamely with the rings pinned to his tuxedo. His little chest stuck out proudly as he beamed at Angel and Joaquin.

The music increased in volume to signal the arrival of the bride. He groaned appreciatively as Teresa appeared in her simple, white satin v-neck gown. She carried a bouquet of white lilies and wore the turquoise necklace, bracelet, and earrings Joaquin had given her for Christmas. Her face shone with joy as her father escorted her down the aisle. A breeze caught her veil and it billowed behind her as she moved forward. Her hair was in a style Angel particularly liked, done up, but with tendrils left curling down to her shoulders. He grinned when he heard Joaquin give a whistle of admiration.

* * * *

Tears flowed from Teresa's eyes as her men both took a knee in front of her. She trusted that the binding ceremony would be similar to the wedding that had just occurred downstairs but was unprepared by the way both of them kneeling reverently in front of her, affected her.

Their eyes brimmed with unshed tears as they looked up at her, ready to begin. After the public ceremony, Teresa, Angel, and Joaquin had been joined by Angel and Joaquin's parents, Grace and her men, and Rachel and Eli in the sitting area of Grace's mistress suite upstairs.

Rosemary, Kelly, and Charity kept the event downstairs moving forward as they relocated the folding chairs under the tent for the meal.

A good friend of Ethan's, Blake Gray, had driven down from Dallas to perform the binding ceremony. He stepped forward to stand beside Teresa, also facing the men.

Blake gestured toward the men. "Teresa, these men desire to enter into marriage with you. They profess to love you and want you for their own. Is this what you desire?"

Her heart throbbed as she nodded. "Yes, it is."

To the men before her, he said, "Do you understand the sacrifice Teresa is willing to make to be with both of you? Will you protect her, provide for her, and love her every day for the rest of your lives? Will you claim her son, Michael, as your very own and help him to grow into the man he is destined to become?"

"I will," both men replied in unison.

Blake turned to Teresa and said, "Will you love these men for the rest of your life, seek to honor them by your actions, and care for them to the best of your ability?"

"I will," Teresa replied. Joaquin's mother and Grace both quietly sniffled in the background.

Joaquin repeated the vows Blake spoke and placed his ring upon her right ring finger, now complete with the attached diamond wedding band. He turned her hand, kissed her palm, and laid his cheek in it. He stayed that way for a moment, and Teresa could feel his hand tremble as it held hers. A tear slipped from the corner of his eye and ran between her fingers.

She received Joaquin's ring from Grace and repeated her vows to him. She slipped the wedding band on his finger then kissed his palm. Still kneeling in front of her, he drew her to him solemnly. Wrapping his strong arms around her waist, he looked up at her with adoration burning intensely in his eyes and whispered, "I love you, Teresa," as his family stood proudly by.

Angel repeated his vows to her and kissed her palm, placing his cheek in it as well. Teresa's hands were both damp with their tears, which she allowed to dry there. She repeated the same vow to Angel. They rose to their feet and kissed her.

Returning downstairs, they found that the guests were all seated under the tent, eating the evening meal. The DJ announced the happy couple's arrival, and all the guests applauded. The music started after Teresa and the others had eaten, and Angel stood and held out his hand to her.

"May I have this dance, beautiful?" His eyes glowed with love. Placing her palm in his, she allowed him to lead her to the dance floor where they danced to Keith Urban's "Making Memories of Us."

After their dance finished, Teresa's father claimed his turn and danced with her to a slow love song.

"Your mother and I are so happy for you. There are so many things I would change, looking back over the years, but I'm so glad that life has brought you the love and devotion of such a fine man. You've done well. He obviously adores you and Michael."

She smiled and kissed his cheek. "Thank you, Dad. You don't have to worry about me anymore." Before she could say more, the song had ended, and Eleazar approached them to claim a dance with her. Soon, everyone joined them on the dance floor which was strung with brilliantly twinkling little lights.

"Teresa, you know that if there's anything you ever need, you can call on us, yes?" She nodded as he continued. "We are proud of Angel and Joaquin's choice for a wife, and we consider your little Michael as our first grandchild."

"Thank you, Eleazar." A little bowled over by his words, Teresa stumbled a bit when her toe bumped his dress shoe. Her cheeks tingled with heat, and she apologized as he kindly helped her get back into the rhythm of the dance. As the last chorus played, she knew what she needed to say to him. "Eleazar, I owe you my gratitude for raising such wonderful sons. I feel very blessed."

Eleazar smiled and kissed her cheek as he looked over her shoulder. "The other half of that charming duo has come to claim his dance." He gently turned her as the last note played, and she went more gracefully into Joaquin's waiting arms.

She looked into his twinkling green eyes and smiled dreamily. She heard the opening strains of Andrea Bocelli's rendition of "Besame

Mucho" as it began to play. Her heart felt like it might burst with love for him and she couldn't help the tears that welled in her eyes. His features were schooled because she was supposed to be dancing with her brother-in-law, but she never wanted to kiss him so badly as she did right then.

"Do you think anyone will wonder why you're dancing with your brother-in-law to a song about kissing you…*a lot*?"

She sniffled and replied, "I don't mind. I love you, Joaquin," she said, her bottom lip trembling slightly.

His deep voice resonated with feeling as he said, "I love you, sugar." Then he sang along with Andrea Bocelli, whispering the words to her. Tingles went up her spine as she listened to him.

"Has Angel ever told you how he got his name?"

"No, he hasn't."

He chuckled. "Well I'll tell you. My mother said Eleazar charmed her into falling in love with him by singing love songs to her. She said he sang like an angel. Long story made short, she married him and his brothers, and a year later it was time for their first baby to be born. Her labor was difficult and painful. He was her first baby, and the only thing that would calm her was if Eleazar sang to her. The midwife wouldn't allow him in the bedroom with them, so he stood beneath her open window while she labored.

"Angel was born that night and she took one look at him after the midwife presented him to her and wept, calling him her sweet little angel. We all grew up on the ranch, singing like our fathers. It calms the horses, as well. Anytime they are in the doghouse with our mother, my dads sing to her. It never fails to break down her defenses."

"I hope you'll sing to me, too. I never knew you had such a beautiful singing voice."

Joaquin's lips twitched with a hint of a sexy grin. "Thank you, sugar. I guess we got out of the habit. If it makes you happy, we'll sing for you."

Marco tapped Joaquin on the shoulder as the song ended, a teasing twinkle in his eye as he murmured a warning to Joaquin to be "less obvious" in the way he charmed his new bride. Teresa smiled, knowing he was right but she was like putty in Joaquin's hands.

"So, you have succumbed to the charm of *both* my boys?" Marco asked as he guided her smoothly around the dance floor. He led her in the dance as though this were the hundredth time she'd danced with him and not the first.

"Yes, sir. I love them very much," she murmured happily.

"I can see how much they love you. They certainly have a way with your son," he said, indicating Michael who was busy talking to both Angel and Joaquin. Both men took a little hand and led him to the drink table for a glass of punch. Teresa laughed with Marco as Michael studiously attempted to walk the same way they did.

She smiled up at Marco and said, "Michael adores them both."

"Joaquin told me he fell in love with you the moment he saw you standing in the doorway that night."

"Yes," she replied, feeling her cheeks heat.

Marco nodded, a tender, faraway look in his eyes. "It was that way for me and my Maria. Eleazar introduced us at a dance. She looked up at me and smiled with fire in her eyes, and I was lost to her from that moment to this."

"Now I know where Angel and Joaquin get their romantic ways from."

"I merely tell the truth, Teresa. Ah, here is Ricardo, ready to push me aside," Marco murmured as he twirled her into his brother's arms.

Ricardo bore the closest resemblance to his brother, Eleazar, just as Joaquin most closely resembled Angel of all his brothers.

"Now, little angel, you promise to call me and tell me if my sons step out of line, won't you?"

Teresa giggled. Of the three brothers, Ricardo was the also least formidable to her. The playful twinkle in his eye reminded her of Joaquin. "Oh, they would *never* do that, sir. They are kind and gentle with me. Very chivalrous, like their fathers, I'm sure," she replied coquettishly.

"*Ah! She flirts!* I remember meeting a shy and demure little Teresa at the hospital a few months ago. What have you done with her?"

"Angel and Joaquin have charmed her from her scared little shell into the light."

"So, they have been as good for you as you have been for them. We love you dearly, Teresa, and we welcome you to our family," Ricardo said affectionately, and she hugged him tight.

"Thank you," she whispered against his lapel as he hugged her back then led her to her men. Her men.

Chapter Twenty-five

Teresa was pleasantly surprised when she, Angel, and Joaquin returned to their home to find a fire lit in the front fireplace. Michael was staying at Grace's house, playing and getting to know his newest set of grandparents. Angel set her down after carrying her over the threshold, and they looked around in wonder at all the twinkling lights which led back to the master bedroom. Joaquin lifted her and carried her down the hall to the bedroom. A chilled bottle of wine and one wineglass sat on one of the bedside tables in the bedroom, and a fire flickered in the fireplace there, as well. Candles flickered everywhere.

Teresa asked, "Would you mind if I took a shower?"

"If you want to," Angel replied before kissing her tenderly. "Can we help you out of this dress?"

She giggled. "If you do, will I still get my shower?"

"Of course, sugar," Joaquin murmured in his deep Texan drawl as he began kissing his way down the back of her neck to her shoulder. As Joaquin loosened the bow that secured the ties for the corset-style closure at the back of her gown, Angel knelt before her and slipped her white satin peep-toe pumps from her feet.

Teresa gasped as he slid his hands up her calf and thigh. He gazed up at her while releasing her stockings from the garters on the white silk corset and then smoothed them slowly down her legs. Her pussy pulsed with warmth, and a needy ache ignited within her. Joaquin continued working the laces at the back of her dress as Angel slipped the stockings from her feet, one at a time, leaving them where they lay. He drew a whimper from her as his searing fingers moved upward until they reached the tops of her thighs and grasped the G-string she wore beneath her corset.

His eyes and his words were warm and tender. "I promise you'll get your shower, beautiful. But I want to feel your silky skin beneath my fingers. We've missed you since Wednesday morning, haven't we, Joaquin?" At Joaquin's silent nod, he continued. His fingertips were right there, about to discover if waxing really had made her pussy as smooth as a baby's bottom.

Another rush of hot moisture flowed to her engorged pussy lips as Angel's fingers neared their destination. "He and I want to feel your sweet—*oh god...*" He groaned as he pressed his mouth to her thigh through her gown. She was sure she felt his teeth nip lightly at her through the fabric. He'd found the completely bare lips of her pussy. His fingertips sifted through the neat patch of curls that pointed the way to her slit, which was abundantly slick with her juices.

The dress drifted from her body in satiny waves as Joaquin slid the shoulder straps down her arms, and then he was on his knees before her as well. The hunger in their eyes as they feasted them on her throbbing pussy gave her a feeling of heady power.

Desire shot through her as they stroked her thighs. Her pussy trembled as they caressed her sensitive, bare lips. Her knees almost buckled when Joaquin trailed his fingertips through the slippery moisture that seeped from her. She watched breathlessly as he slid his fingertips between his lips, and he growled softly.

She reached up and unfastened the hook and eye closures at the side of the corset as her men watched on their knees before her, enthralled.

They rose to their feet as the corset fell away and led her to the bathroom where more candles burned. Angel turned on the shower for her and whispered, "Hurry, beautiful. We ache for you, both of us."

When she returned mere minutes later, Angel and Joaquin lay beneath the covers on either side of the bed, waiting for her to fill the center between them. The hard ridges at their groins could be seen even through the sheet and blanket. The sight sent an exhilarating thrill through her. She smiled at them, relieved now that they hadn't waited for the first time to be tonight. There were no nerves for her tonight, only eagerness for the pleasure she knew was to come.

As she moved toward the bed, the feathery tufts on her little white mules tickled Teresa's insteps. She was clad in the white satin gown and sheer robe they'd given her. The way it moved around her made her feel exotic, self-confident, and worthy of these men.

"You look...stunning," Joaquin murmured. As they sat up, the sheets dipped to their hips, forearms on their knees, just drinking her in. One of them had opened the bottle of wine and poured some in the wineglass on the table by the bed.

She stopped at the foot of the bed and slipped her feet from the mules, lifted the hem of the gown, and went on her hands and knees to them, her heart thumping and her pussy aching for the touch of their fingers again.

"Thanks for being patient," she whispered as she undid the bow that held the front of the robe closed under her bust.

"You were so lovely tonight in your bridal gown, and now in this." Angel reached for the shoulders of the robe as she settled between them, facing them on her knees. "I'll never forget the day you came to the ranch that first time. Do you remember?"

"When I brought you the pie?" She smiled, remembering like it was yesterday.

Angel smiled and nodded he carefully drew the robe from her arms. "I almost fell over I was so happy to see you."

She blushed. "You squatted down and put your hand on my door. I wanted to reach out and touch you, but I couldn't do it."

"You were like a scared little rabbit. I *wanted* to reach out and run my fingers along your pretty pink cheek." He caressed her cheek as if making up for that missed opportunity.

Teresa turned her misty gaze to Joaquin. "Remember standing in the doorway, Christmas Eve?"

"Yeah. I felt like you were looking right into my soul," he said, chuckling as he twined her fingers with his.

"I loved you both, practically since the moment I met you." She gazed into Angel's golden eyes. "Angel, thank you for being so patient with me, for teaching me to trust, and for allowing Joaquin…"

"To love and adore you, too?" Angel finished for her when her words trailed off.

"Yes. Thank you." Teresa's lip trembled as she laid her fingertips on their handsome cheeks.

She slowly lifted the gown from her body and felt a tingle of heat in her cheeks as they gazed at her with appreciation. They drew her to recline on the piled-up pillows with them.

Angel offered the wineglass to her. She took a long sip and handed it to Joaquin to share with him. He drank from the glass as his fingertips traced her upper arm, over her shoulder. He handed the glass to Angel, who finished what remained and set the glass aside.

Angel turned back to her and rested his cheek in his palm as he said, "Teresa, do you want our wedding night to be like our first night together was? Or would you like to try something new?" His fingertip made a slow trek over her collar bone, sparking a tingling sensation as it slid downward toward her nipple.

She giggled at his tickling touch. "You're my husbands now, and I want my husbands to teach me every position they know. I imagine you know quite a few?" Her cheeks grew warm as other parts of her tingled at the thought.

Joaquin chuckled sexily. "Angel, I love our kitten's frisky side."

"Me, too. But before we teach our wife something new, I want to more closely inspect that smooth pussy of hers," Angel stated as he sat up and ran a hand down one of her thighs. Joaquin mirrored his motions until they reached her ankles then she realized their intent.

Teresa's heart thumped at the carnality of what they intended to do. "You mean you want a *really* good look?" she asked as they lifted her ankles and spread her legs, tracing their knuckles down her inner thighs and making her shudder in anticipation of their touch. Their eyes were riveted on her denuded skin.

Joaquin slid a finger over her smooth outer lips as he murmured, "This will make your pussy even more sensitive to our touch." Teresa gasped as he stroked a fingertip over her perineum and her asshole, obviously noting that she'd gone the "extra mile" for them. "Completely bare, our kitten was brave," he added in an admiring tone.

He skimmed his fingertips over her bare skin and into the shorter curls that formed the triangle above her slit.

"We love your pussy this way. Thank you," Angel said, tracing her slick inner pussy lips with his fingertips then dipping into her entrance, swirling her juices around her clit in a circular motion before sliding in again. Her pussy muscles tightened on his finger, increasing the pleasurable sensation. "You're going to come so many times tonight you'll lose track."

Angel sweetly tortured her with his tongue, flicking her clit teasingly as Joaquin whispered in her ear, "You might as well leave your panties off this week, sugar, because we won't be able to keep our hands off of you. I can't wait to have my turn at that bare, beautiful cunt. I want to feel it pulsing under my tongue while you come for me."

"Oh, Joaquin. Anything, *anything* you want," she whispered as the heat in her pussy flamed higher. Waxing the hair away did indeed make her much more sensitive to their touch. She felt every puff of Angel's hot breath on her skin and the fullness of his lips against her wet flesh.

Angel laved her clit, and it seemed to swell much more than she remembered from last time. Even his finger still pumping into her pussy felt different, bigger. When he added a second finger and the two digits curled inside her cunt, finding her G-spot, she wanted to scream in pleasure.

The moment he found it, he chortled softly because her back arched and her head pressed against the pillows, which were evidently his telltale signs. A breathy moan escaped her lips. Joaquin took that opportunity to plunder her mouth, and his kiss was passionate. She pressed her wet cunt against Angel's mouth and fingers as he mercilessly stroked her G-spot and clit simultaneously.

Joaquin's lips were against her ear as he whispered to her, "We're all alone, sugar. There's no reason to hold back tonight. Let go when you come for us."

The reminder of freedom from the mandate to keep quiet sent her arousal shooting higher. She reached for Joaquin and gloried in the sensation of him kissing her lips as Angel kissed her pussy. Joaquin's plucked at one of her hardened nipples, rolling it firmly between his fingers in a touch that was gentle enough to be pleasurable but firm enough to almost border pain. Teresa moaned as the electrifying current of pleasure and pain shot straight to her clit.

Joaquin's fingers were replaced by his hot lips over the turgid nipple, and he slid his fingers farther south. He trailed a hand over her hip and slid it up the back of her thigh, holding her open for Angel's easier access. Joaquin rolled the other nipple between his fingers, repeating the demanding caress from earlier while sucking hard on the nipple in his mouth.

Teresa thought she might scream as her nipples sensitized into tight points that felt like electrical currents were attached between them and her clit. Angel's fingers were a tight fit in her cunt, but the copious moisture there made for a slick, easy slide as he continued pumping her. Orgasm barreled down on her. A few more thrusts and she'd go over.

She moaned in disappointment when he withdrew and rose over her. *So close.*

"Up on your knees, beautiful." Her pussy quivered deliciously as if it realized he intended to take her from behind.

Teresa was assailed by a tremendous sense of vulnerability as she exposed this most intimate part of her in an act of total trust. An incredible sense of submission came over her, and she was overcome by the urge to surrender completely to them. Rather than feeling alienated from Angel, she felt a greater sense of connection, showing him her trust and deference. Her pussy pulsed again at her not being able to see what he was doing.

Angel stroked her ass, grounding her as she shifted restlessly. Joaquin caressed her arms, evidently sensing that she needed his contact, as well.

Joaquin's lips found her cheek, and he gazed into her eyes as he murmured, "We have something new for you to try, Teresa." His green eyes were alight with love and mischief. He looked over her shoulder at Angel and gave a slight nod.

Her pussy clenched at his words and playful tone. "What are you going to do?" she asked breathlessly. Her thighs trembled as Angel caressed the inside of each one.

"When went shopping for you and found some toys we thought you'd enjoy experimenting with."

She looked Joaquin in the eye and then turned to look back at Angel. Her pussy pulsed and clenched again, quivering in frustration and renewed arousal as she whispered, "Toys? For me?"

Angel smiled at her, not revealing what he held in his hand. "Yes, beautiful. Nothing wild and crazy or too big. Although, if you like what we got, we can always shop for more."

She giggled and leaned forward to kiss Joaquin, still on her hands and knees. "Whatever it is, I trust you. Can I play while you play?" she asked suggestively, eyeing Joaquin's erection.

Both men chuckled, and Joaquin replied, "Let Angel get you accustomed to this little toy, then if you want to suck on my cock, I'd be most obliged, sugar." Joaquin's lips plundered hers, his tongue sliding with hers in a silken duel as she giggled and arched her back for Angel, presenting her ass and pussy to him for his own play. She spread her thighs a bit and even wiggled her ass at Angel. She smiled when she heard him chuckle behind her in obvious admiration of her playful provocation.

"I see you wiggling your pretty little ass at me. Joaquin, I'm going to play with her pussy while you keep that hot mouth of hers busy. Sweetheart, no coming until I give you permission, understand?"

She let out a distraught but compliant squeak as Joaquin kissed her lips and tweaked both nipples gently, renewing the twin spears of lust connected to her pussy.

"Good girl," he growled in approval. She wanted to play more than she wanted her way.

Teresa heard a click and a whirring sound, and she practically sucked the oxygen out of Joaquin's lungs, making him chuckle as she felt a low, deep vibration on her pussy lips. Whatever Angel had been warming in his hand was poised at her cunt, sending pleasant vibrations through her pussy lips, which communicated themselves up to her clit. It was a teasing sensation and felt good, but not nearly enough and not where she *really* wanted it. He slid the vibrator back and forth through her tingling pussy lips, picking up more moisture as he did.

Teresa groaned as Angel teased her cunt, and the toy slid an inch into her pussy, sending vibrations in a different direction. She wanted it in farther, and she arched, trying to take more of it. Angel chuckled and withdrew it. She groaned piteously into Joaquin's mouth, hoping Angel would have mercy on her. The toy slid along her lips again, and her pussy clenched as it vibrated closer to her clit this time.

Joaquin released her lips, and she moaned out loud. "That's right, sugar. We want to hear how good it feels to you."

"More, Angel, please," she whispered as she looked over her shoulder at him, chasing the vibrator with her pussy as he evaded her clit. He smiled in obvious pleasure at her uninhibited enjoyment as he teased her.

"Damn, that's a pretty sight. Your little pussy is soaked and such a pretty, dark rose color. You must like this a lot. Tell you what, beautiful. I'll give you more if you'll suck Joaquin's cock for him."

Teresa smiled at Joaquin. "Would you like me to suck on your cock?"

Joaquin growled deep in his chest and held his cock for her. She dipped her head down to his distended shaft and licked the head playfully. "I love the way you taste. I love to feel you in my mouth." She licked her lips and closed them over the top, allowing the head to slide slowly between them. Joaquin hissed in pleasure.

Joaquin's voice shook slightly. "Damn."

Her mouth watered at the erotic taste of him, the silken feel of his flesh, and the hard, heated feel of his erection between her lips as they slid over him, taking him to the back of her throat. He moaned when she suckled on his length as she came back up. She shuddered in pleasure as Angel continued to stroke her pussy with the vibrator while she moved over Joaquin's cock, acclimating to experiencing two pleasurable sensations at once.

Angel slid the vibrator a couple of inches into her pussy, making her cry out, which sent another vibration through Joaquin's cock, causing him to respond with a groan of his own. As Teresa sucked on Joaquin, she noticed Angel copied her motions. When she bobbed over Joaquin's cock, Angel pumped more of the length of the vibrator into her, setting up spasms in her pussy with each pass over her enflamed G-spot.

Joaquin's sounds became panting growls, and she groaned over him in response, loving him with every pass of her tongue and lips. She felt the undeniable rise on the wave of her orgasm. Her moaning took on a higher pitched, more desperate quality. She was going to come soon, whether she had permission or not.

Angel pumped the vibrator deep, thrusting it against her G-spot with every pass. He reached for her clit and flicked it with his fingertips. Her hips flexed against him in a rhythm of their own, and

Joaquin thrust into her mouth. His hand was gentle in her hair as he whispered encouragement to her, his thrusts becoming more powerful as he neared his climax. Abruptly, he whispered, "Baby, it's good, but let go. I want to come in your pussy. Let go, and take your orgasm. I want to hear you come for Angel."

She released Joaquin, and he groaned in frustration, gripping the base of his cock. Bucking on the toy as Angel continued to fuck her with it, Teresa released a triumphant yell, all her inhibitions gone. Her pussy clamped down on the toy, increasing the pressure it delivered over her G-spot.

"Come for me now, beautiful one." Angel growled

"Oh, Angel, don't stop! I feel it coming! It feels so good!" Her hips churned against his hand in tighter movements, and her head fell to Joaquin's abdomen. Joaquin cupped her breasts, flicking and then pinching and rolling her nipples, setting off the explosion deep inside her. Teresa came with a panting scream of ecstasy that built and crested along with each wave, higher and higher, until the pulses receded within her. Angel never stopped the motion or his relentless touch over her clit until she was finally finished.

The vibrator was gone and she was shocked by the sudden lack of sensation, but her body quickly compensated with a pulsing vibration of its own. Angel stroked her lips, not allowing her to come down too much as she moaned.

Her hitching breaths rose again as she realized there was movement on both sides of her. Angel took Joaquin's place before her and she heard the tear of foil. Joaquin sheathed his cock then pulled her toward him. She rose back up on her knees, and her arousal escalated again with the knowledge he would now take her from behind now. Her pussy quaked in an echo of the still receding orgasm while another one signaled its imminent arrival.

"Joaquin, it's coming already. Please fuck me. I want you inside me now when I come. Please *hurry*," she whimpered, undulating her hips against him.

"Not yet, sugar. Hold it for me." His steely voice sent a thrill down her spine,

Oh fuck no! Not again!

"I can't!"

"You will. I'm taking you slow and deep. I don't want to rush. Hold it for me," Joaquin ordered. Teresa had momentary thoughts of revenge directed at her sweet lover. Two could play that game, and she'd remember this the next time she had his cock between her lips.

"Mmmm!" She gulped air and swallowing convulsively, trying to hold off the rushing tide that threatened to overtake her.

Joaquin groaned in pleasure. "That's it, sugar. I'm going to slide in now. Wait until I tell you, and I promise I'll fuck you just the way you want it. Suck Angel's cock for him, and that will help both of you."

Did it ever. Angel held his rock-hard erection for her, and she licked her lips and suckled him into her mouth, swirling over his head. He groaned euphorically as she laved him with her tongue, and it gave her enough distraction that she no longer focused quite so hard on her need to come.

She groaned desperately over Angel's cock when she felt Joaquin's blunt head at her slick entrance. She pressed back against him, welcoming him into her wet cunt as he hissed at her sensual embrace. Joaquin's cock stretched her entrance tight, the muscles clamoring and quivering as he slid inside her another inch or two before pulling out and thrusting back in. Arching her back, Teresa groaned at the feel of each inch of him pushing into her cunt. She took Angel in her mouth and reveled in the dual pleasures she was receiving.

Lowered down onto her elbows to free her hands, Teresa lifted Angel's cock in one hand. She played with and caress his balls with the other, making him groan loudly. Angel caressed her cheeks as she sucked his cock, relishing every inch of his manhood. She craved the feeling of him inside her, as well.

Joaquin gripped her hips, and she whimpered as he pulled her back onto his long cock, stretching her tightly and filling her with his thick length. Joaquin growled near her ear, and she felt his back against hers, covering her. He wrapped his arms around her and pumped his hips against her, fucking every inch of his girth into her until he was lodged deep. She felt utterly consumed. Shivering ripples began in her pussy as he pumped powerfully against her. He rose up and gripped her hips and began to thrust and withdraw in long, deep sweeps.

"Oh, fuck, sugar. The way your little body takes every inch of me, it's too fucking much."

Reluctant to release Angel's cock, Teresa moaned in ecstasy to let him know she loved the way his cock hammered into her. Every sensation was intensified by her bare pussy and the sheer eroticism of his words. She pictured his cock, as it pistoned into her pussy, coating him with the slick moisture that they drew from her body.

Angel pressed his fingertips at her chin, stopping her. "Later I'll let you suck me until I come for you. Right now, let go, so you can enjoy your pleasure."

"But—" she said breathlessly, wanting him to have his, too.

He smiled down at her tenderly, taking her chin in his fingertips. "I know, sweetheart. Soon enough. Is it good, Joaquin? Are you fucking that slick little pussy just the way she likes it?"

She braced herself and moved with Joaquin as he pumped into her. Angel stealthily slid his fingers down her abdomen. Two fingers found their way into her slit and stroked each side of her clit, building pressure against it until it was gripped between them. The pressure of his fingers combined with the pummeling of Joaquin's cock caused her pussy to run with more of her juices. Both men felt it, and one, she wasn't sure which, growled in satisfaction.

"Come for us, sugar. You feel so fucking good," Joaquin drawled, releasing her from his earlier mandate. She'd lost sight of the fact she was holding her orgasm for him, waiting for him to release her when the time was right.

A keening wail began in her throat. Relief flooded through her. Angel's fingers lightly pulled and stroked on her clit, stealing her breath.

Joaquin murmured in her ear as he came back down over her, his sexy voice devastating her senses. "Soon, we won't need to use these rubbers, sugar. I'm going to fuck you until you come so hard you think you died and went to heaven. Then Angel's going to fuck you, too. You'll know you're ours, and so will we." He punctuated his words with his strokes as he drew her back up to his chest.

Each word sent her into a heightened state of arousal. He was wrapped around her and she was still on her knees with her legs spread wide, but now she was pulled upright over his lap, his arms around her. In this position she felt both powerful and vulnerable.

Raising her arms over her head, she gripped his shoulders behind her and a wail broke from her as she arched her back. She could feel his hips against her ass, moving against her, and the erotic sensation broadcast an image to her mind of how they must look together. The unspeakable intimacy of the act tugged at her heart, and tears overflowed from her eyes. She was theirs.

His cock pistoned into her three more hard times, and they both came together, her sobbing in ecstasy and him roaring as he held her tightly to him, his cock pulsing deep inside her. Angel's fingers against her clit gentled as she sobbed with each hitching breath.

"Damn, that was hot to watch." Angel murmured, groaning as Teresa melted in Joaquin's dominating embrace.

Joaquin nuzzled Teresa's throat under her ear and held her tightly to him. "It's like there is heaven inside her."

"All yours," she whispered with her eyes closed. Her lips trembled as she added, "Only for you." Tilting her head, she looked up at Joaquin.

Joaquin smiled at his brother and nodded at him to come near. Angel took her upper body in his arms, supporting her as she wrapped her arms around him while Joaquin took his time withdrawing from her. He caressed her pussy lips, drawing a little shuddering sigh from her as Angel enveloped her and tucked her into his arms. Joaquin rose from the bed and went to the bathroom.

When he returned to the bed, Joaquin stroked her back, sitting down next to them.

Raising her eyes to them both, she smiled, feeling in utter bliss. She rested her head on Angel's chest and held onto his forearm as she caressed Joaquin's hip.

"I think she needs a little break," Joaquin said, and kissed her cheek.

Angel nodded as she looked up at him through half-shut eyes. "I think so, too. Grace told me there's a tray in the refrigerator with some fruit, cheese, cold-cuts, and crackers on it. I'll pour us some more wine. Why don't you get the tray, Joaquin?"

Joaquin rose from the bed and walked nude down the hall to the kitchen and retrieved the thoughtfully prepared snack.

They tucked her in under the sheet between them and took turns feeding her little tidbits from the tray. Teresa never had to lift a hand except to drink from the wine glass they shared. Her inhibitions vanished as she talked with them, giggling at their touch, opening to their kisses and responding to their erotic words. There were no walls, no traces of fear, only trust and love. A great, heart-rending, beautiful love.

"Feel up to some more loving?" Joaquin asked, his voice a seductive murmur. "I'll bet Angel wouldn't turn down the opportunity to make love to you right now."

"Mmmm, I don't think I would turn him down, either," she replied as Joaquin placed the tray and the glass on the bedside table. Turning in Angel's embrace, she kissed him as she straddled his hips. He hissed at the contact her pussy made with his bone-hard erection.

"You feel good there, beautiful," he drawled sexily, pressing up against her as he held her hips.

"Angel, I owe you a lap dance, don't I?" She smiled playfully and then reached for the lubricant. She looked at Joaquin and smiled sexily. "Tell me, Joaquin. Do you think Angel might enjoy a lap dance?"

"Speaking from experience, I think he'll be your willing slave if you'll dance for him."

"You think so? After he gets his lap dance, maybe he'd like it if I slid down on his big, thick cock that's pulsing against my pussy right now."

With eyes practically aglow with lust, Angel finally piped up, "I think '*he'd*' fucking love sliding every *rock-hard inch* into your teasing little pussy."

Feeling a little wicked, she leaned down to him and caught his lower lip between hers and sucked on it, flicking it with her tongue playfully before releasing it with a pop. "You sound enthusiastic about it. Are you sure that my inexperienced little lap dance will be enough to satisfy your tastes?"

"I think your lap dance is the *only* one that *could* satisfy me. I've developed quite a taste for your little body," Angel drawled.

She squeezed a generous amount of lubricant onto her fingers and spread it over her bare folds and into her opening before spreading a little more over his erection. Her heart throbbed with love for this man, even as her pussy clamored to be filled with him.

"Sugar, it's going to feel even better to you, too, with your pussy nice and bare now. I wouldn't be a bit surprised if you come before he even gets inside of you," Joaquin murmured in a deep, sexy voice that set her insides to wobbling and quivering.

"I hadn't thought of that. Yum!" Giggling, she centered her open slit over his thick, hot length, and he groaned in pleasure. She was grateful again for the most recent candid, and frankly, entertaining, conversation she'd had with Grace on the subject of pleasuring a man.

Bracing her hands on his thick pecs, Teresa asked, "Does that feel good on your cock? Nice and hot?" As she spoke, Teresa arched her back slowly which slid her pussy down Angel's long, hot shaft to his balls. She heard Joaquin groan softly beside her and reach out to caress her hip and ass.

Angel moaned and drew out the words, "Yes, baby."

Teresa leaned slightly forward, brushing her outer lips over his cock in a circular motion, swirling over him. Her long black hair fell in waves over her shoulders. Her pussy was definitely more sensitive now, especially since making love with Joaquin, but her bare skin was hyper-sensitive, and she could feel him all over her pussy and not just in her open slit. The sensation of her body slickening his and his hardness brushing against her tender flesh sent waves of pleasure to her clit. It was entirely probable that she would come during this lap dance. Her mind embraced the thought and her body raced to catch up as she settled more firmly on him. He groaned in pleasure as she established her rhythm.

Rising into a more upright position, her hands slowly slid up her flanks. The backs of her nails raked over the sides of her breasts as she sighed in pleasure, her fingers drifted up into her hair. With her arms over her head, she thrust her breasts out invitingly.

Joaquin sounded a little strained as he said, "Look at the way she moves. Our shy dove is a tempting vixen when the mood strikes her."

"Mmmm, the way she moves. She's more graceful and talented than any dancer, and she tells us she's *ours*. These hips," he murmured sexily, stroking her hips but not inhibiting her movements.

Their words were having a powerful effect on her heart and her body. She was about to come any second, and her heart leapt with pleasure to know how much her body pleased them. Their words made love to her soul, just as surely as their bodies made love to hers.

"Ours." Angel groaned.

Moaning as she changed her rhythmic strokes to undulating figure-eight movements, Teresa stretched her arms up and curled her forearms behind her head. Angel groaned in response to the change.

"Such full, beautiful breasts," Angel whispered, stroking her swaying breasts. He gave a deep growl of approval as the juice flowed over his cock from her pussy. She never would've thought she'd enjoy listening to them talk this way.

"Ours," Joaquin murmured sexily as Angel's hands firmly cupped her breasts, stroking the nipples with his thumb and drawing a moan of pleasure from her. Covering his hands with hers, she returned to the circular motion, grinding over him with slow, wet strokes of her pussy. Beneath her, his cock grew harder.

* * * *

"These luscious thighs," Angel whispered, reveling in the feel of Teresa's satiny flesh spread wide, straddling his body as she pleasured them both. He could tell by her breathing that she was approaching climax.

Angel intertwined his fingers with hers when she reached for his hands. She held on and used them to brace herself as she found the rhythm and stroke that would bring her to orgasm, her body taking over. Her head fell back, and a low groan escaped her open lips as her movements became smaller and more focused.

He exerted every bit of control he had not to come, as she rocked her pussy against him. Flooded with her juices, she leaned forward and braced her little hands against his chest and slid up over his cock to the head. Her beautiful face was ecstatic as her orgasm overtook her. With a sobbing scream, she undulated wildly over him.

The split second before it happened, he knew what was coming and barely had time to brace himself, too late to still her motions. His cock jerked hard when she slid up to the head, and instead of grinding back down his length, his cock slid right inside her pulsating, coming pussy. She screamed again louder at the invasion and ground harder against him, unable to stop herself and quickly seating him to the hilt inside of her, her rapturous sobs of ecstasy telling the tale.

Angel's back bowed and he gritted his teeth at the sudden hot embrace of her pussy around his cock, trying desperately to stem the erupting tide as his body fought to explode inside her. He wasn't wearing a condom.

"Holy fuck!" he ground out, gripping her thighs desperately. She toppled over on him, her breath coming in great heaving sobs.

Joaquin silently retrieved another condom from the drawer, not breaking their fragile moment together with words. Angel gathered her limp form to him and rolled them over. Regretfully, he pulled out from the heavenly wet recesses of her body. Joaquin handed him the torn wrapper, and he sheathed himself quickly in the condom before returning to her. She reached for him silently and lifted her knees as he settled in the warm cradle of her body, his cock nudging her entrance. Teresa gave a mewling cry as his cock slid slowly back into her pussy.

Seated to the hilt, he stayed that way with her, gazing into her love-dazed eyes, his hips motionless as he nuzzled her throat.

He whispered, "You think her pussy is heavenly now, Joaquin. Wait until you can slide into her with no barrier. I think I died there for a few seconds being bare inside her like that." She was so hot and silky inside. He could have stayed that way with her for the rest of his natural life.

Teresa whispered shakily, "I'm sorry, Angel. I completely lost control, forgot all about the condom. It—it was so *good*."

Angel pressed a finger to her lips. "Don't, beautiful. That was easily the most incredibly erotic thing I've ever experienced, if unexpected."

Joaquin stroked her arm and the side of her breast as he lay alongside them. "Sugar, that was wild. You are the sexiest thing I've ever seen. I thought for sure I was going to come just watching the two of you."

Her tingling cheeks became even hotter. "Really?"

"Without exception." Angel murmured and rolled his hips against hers, making her gasp.

"Oh, Angel. You feel so good inside me," she said as she held tightly to him, flexing her hips against his.

Angel groaned and said, "Ready to ride, cowgirl?" He gave her a lopsided grin and made her squeal as he rolled them back over, never breaking the connection. Carefully she rose up and pulled her knees up under her with his help then lay back down over him. Joaquin smoothed his hand along her naked back and over her rounded tush.

"This is a pretty sight, sugar. You tucked up nice and tight over Angel with his cock buried deep in your pussy, ready to be fucked."

She smiled at him and gave an experimental grinding move with his cock deep inside her. They both groaned at the unbelievable feel of it.

"Beautiful, do that again." Angel rolled his hips against her in counterpoint as she moved over him, continuing the circular grinding motion. She smiled ecstatically, and her eyelids slid closed as she rose up over him. Bracing herself at his shoulders, she moved sinuously, practically purring for them as Joaquin stroked her back and her ass.

"Damn, that feels incredible. Oh, *damn baby*, what the—" He growled as she lay down on him and began a reverse thrusting motion over him. Her pussy muscles gripped his cock hard as she came off of him then slid back down again. It felt like a fist gripping him then allowing him to slip back into her liquid depths. On each downward thrust, she ground her lips and her clit against his pubic bone and was rapidly gasping as her body took control of her motions again. Angel glanced over at Joaquin to find that he was lying there unmoving, as he watched her. His brother glanced into his eyes and mouthed one word. "Perfect."

Angel thrust against her, cooperating with her movements and timing his strokes with hers so she received the stimulation and contact on her clit that she needed. He growled as her body tensed. Her pussy drew up tighter, and her breathing turned to panting.

Angel whispered, "Damn, she's a natural. Baby, you make love to me like you're reading my mind."

Grinding hard on him in an upright position, her pussy clenched tight as a vise as she screamed herself hoarse in her ecstasy. Pulling her to him, he rolled them so she could lie back. He lifted her hips, tilting her to him, and pumped into her, rubbing against her clit on every thrust, glorying in her cries as her fading orgasm was chased quickly by another. Her pussy clamped down on his cock harder than before as she wailed. Growling in satisfaction when he saw her cream gush from her and coat his cock, he grasped her hips hard and pummeled into her several more times before roaring with his own release. He thrust hard with each pulse as she milked his cock of every drop of his cum.

When Angel was able to move again, he slid from her body and lay down at her side. He nuzzled her throat and her shoulder and allowed Joaquin to draw close as her breathing returned to normal. She tipped her face to Joaquin and kissed him then Angel, and her warm lips felt fragile.

"Thank you. You've both made me *so happy*. I love you both so much...I—" Her eyelids slid closed over escaping tears as her lips trembled.

"Sugar, don't cry," Joaquin whispered.

She sniffled against Angel's chest. "If I cry, it's because you make me so happy. They're a good thing."

"We just need to kiss them away and love you more then, shouldn't we?" Angel murmured as his fingers gently wiped them away and kissed her again more deeply.

After disposing of the condom, he returned with a fresh glass of water. She took it from him, drinking half of it before handing it back and thanking him. He knew it pleased her when they looked after her like this, and he could see the appreciation in her eyes.

She laid back down and snuggled back to Angel as he spooned against her with Joaquin cuddled to her front.

"Teresa, I think Angel would agree with me when I tell you that you're our every fantasy come to life."

She blushed as she replied, "I was worried that I wouldn't be…*enough* for you."

Both men chuckled, and Angel said, "Beautiful, you're more than enough. You're everything."

Chapter Twenty-six

Teresa smiled up at Joaquin as he wrapped her in a wool blanket where she sat on the beach towel next to Angel. He plopped down in the sand on the other side of her and helped Angel rub her to warm her up.

"Thank you, Joaquin. It's cozy under here if you both want to join me," she said then yawned sleepily.

Returning to their guesthouse a little while ago from the deep-sea fishing excursion, Teresa had noticed the brilliant hues of pink, orange, and purple as the sun set. On the boat, the first mate had mentioned that a storm would be blowing in during the night, and she was fascinated by the line of dark clouds that encroached on the brilliant sunset, leaving just a patch of a brilliant white cloud. She'd sat on the porch, taking it in until they'd suggested walking to the beach access point then finding a good spot to sit and watch.

They had the beach all to themselves. The wind that blew in over the water was chilly, but Teresa had asked to stay out a while longer, watching the billowing clouds as they rolled in, and the men had smiled and let her have her way.

They tucked the blanket in more securely around her and pulled it up to cover her ears. Teresa smiled at both and snuggled down against them.

"You take good care of me. Thank you," she murmured, her eyes drawn by a flash in the dark clouds on the distant horizon. "Beautiful," she whispered, waiting expectantly for the next flash.

"Yes," one of them replied quietly, and she realized they were looking at her. Angel tucked a stray lock of her long black hair behind her ear that had blown loose in the wind.

She returned her eyes to the horizon and leaned into him. His lips brushed her temple in a light kiss.

Twilight arrived, and though she loved watching the light show from the vantage point of the beach, she knew they were cold, so she asked to go back to the house. Sharing the large walk-in shower in the master bathroom with them, she allowed them to wash her body while she shampooed the salt from her hair.

The men shooed her from the kitchen, and while they cooked the fish, she watched the lightning flash across the sky from the big picture window in the upstairs home theatre room. Every so often, she would hear a low rumble and surmised the storm was getting closer. The house they were renting had a metal roof, and she looked forward to hearing the rain pelting against it later.

The early morning was catching up with her, and she yawned as she heard footsteps on the stairs. She called out from the darkened room, and Angel appeared in the doorway.

"Hey, beautiful? Are you all right in here?"

His voice was low, and she could hear the love in his tone. "Yes," she replied softly. "I'm watching the lightning. Come sit with me?"

"Sure," he murmured. He sat down on the sofa and drew her easily into his lap, cuddling her to him. "Did you enjoy the dolphins today?"

"I loved it. I'm so glad I brought my camera. Today was so much fun," she said, covering a big yawn with her hand.

Angel chuckled indulgently and squeezed her. "We'd better feed you, sleepyhead. You need to get tucked into bed."

"It's because I was sitting here in the dark. I'll be fine once I get some food in me. Is there anything I can do to help?"

"No, it's all ready. Come on," he said and helped her rise from the sofa. They'd been in Port Aransas for three days, and her body and mind had finally agreed to unwind and relax a little.

Port Aransas was quieter in the winter months, which meant less traffic, but also less to do. They were all okay with that, preferring to spend the time exploring together on the beach and in the little tourist town. The men had been willing to go somewhere more exotic for their honeymoon, but Teresa had been reluctant to be too far away from Michael for that long.

Angel and Joaquin seemed to take great delight in discovering what she wanted from them as lovers. She talked openly with them about her needs and theirs, and they taught her what they liked. She loved their reactions each night when she would emerge from the master bathroom dressed in a different nightie.

She yawned again as Angel led her from the dark room and went downstairs. Joaquin came in from the back porch with a roasting pan laden with grilled fish and skewers of grilled shrimp. They had set the table, poured wine, and even lit candles.

As they enjoyed the meal, Teresa playfully said, "What color do you prefer tonight? Red or Pink?"

The men grinned at each other, and Angel said, "Joaquin and I talked, and we think it might be good if you rested tonight."

Joaquin nodded and stroked her shoulder. "Every time we've been with you, you've taken us both. We love it, but you need time to adjust, and we realized we haven't been as diligent as we intended because we want you so much." Through the glass of the table top she saw for herself this was a sacrifice on their part.

She looked into their eyes and could tell that they were sincere, despite the demanding bulges they were both dealing with at the moment. "Oh. Well, all right. You're sure?"

Angel shifted a little in his seat and smiled devilishly at her. "Despite what my cock wants, beautiful? Yes, I'm sure."

"That doesn't mean we don't want you to have fun, though," Joaquin said, the twinkle in his eyes speaking volumes.

"Oh? What did you have in mind?" she asked, shivers racing up her back as she felt their hands gliding over her, Joaquin's at her shoulder and Angel's over her thigh.

"We thought you might enjoy a massage," Angel replied. His fingers left a tingling path as they stroked her upper thigh. A massage sounded perfect.

"I would as a matter of fact. I noticed my shoulders have gotten stiff and tense from the fishing trip today."

Joaquin rubbed her shoulder, murmuring, "Well, we'll just have to see if we can't work the stiffness out of them."

Maybe if I play my cards right, they'll let me work their *stiffness out.*

"I'd love that. Can I still dress up for you?" she asked as she rose from her chair.

Angel grinned happily and said, "Sure. We enjoy seeing you model all your lingerie for us."

Stepping out of the master bathroom every night dressed in something sexy had been an adventure for Teresa. The same went for her daytime lingerie, as well. They seemed to take great delight in seeing her in her push-up bras and lace thongs or panties before she dressed in the morning. She loved teasing them with reminders during the day about what lay beneath her clothing. "I really do love all of it. I may never wear plain white cotton briefs ever again."

Joaquin said, "Sugar, we don't mind what kind of underwear you wear, but it sure is fun when we're wondering what you have on under your clothes."

"Even more fun to find out," Angel said, chuckling. "Why don't you go change while we clean up down here, and we'll meet you in the bedroom in a few minutes?"

"You don't need my help?"

"No, sugar. You go make yourself pretty for us. We'll be along shortly."

"I'm spoiled rotten."

"Just how we like you," Joaquin responded before kissing her tenderly.

She went upstairs to the master bedroom, opened the dresser drawer that contained her lingerie, and began sorting through the selection she'd packed. She stepped out to the landing and called out.

"Red or hot pink?"

"Hot pink!" they both called back.

She gathered what she needed and went into the bathroom to get ready for bed. After brushing her teeth, she wrapped herself in her dark-pink, silky chenille robe and returned to the bedroom. She lit candles, turned off the lamps, and opened the blind over the large picture window that faced the gulf. The lightning had increased and, combined with the romantic candlelight, set the mood for what was to come. Climbing on the turned-down bed, she arranged herself in the middle.

Teresa appreciated the obvious care that they had for her, and although she didn't physically feel like she needed the night off, she did look forward to receiving a massage.

* * * *

Twenty minutes later, Joaquin came quietly up the stairs, finding Angel standing in the doorway gazing at Teresa. Joaquin thought she was the most beautiful woman he'd ever seen, clad in a pink satin nightie, bathed in golden candlelight, lying on the bed sound asleep. Her hair was fanned over the pillow in the middle of the king-size bed, the robe open to the waist, revealing the tempting swell of her cleavage. As he stood by the bed with Angel, love swelled almost painfully in his heart. He looked up at his brother and saw the same love showed in Angel's eyes.

Carefully, Joaquin and Angel slipped her robe from her exhausted limbs and covered her with the blanket. Angel blew out the candles then they both undressed in the dark and slid in the bed on either side of her.

During the night, a brilliant flash, followed by the crash of thunder and rain pelting the metal roof, woke her from a sound sleep. Disoriented, she bolted upright in the bed. Joaquin reached out to calm her as he whispered to her, "Shh. It's all right, sugar. It's just the storm passing over," he murmured as he stroked her hip.

Teresa sighed and lay back down with him, snuggling back to him. Even straight from a sound sleep, her smallest touch affected him as his cock stirred and throbbed. He continued stroking her, and his hand itched to wander farther. He could tell by her breathing that she was alert, and she hummed softly, and pressed her ass against his hardening cock.

The bed dipped, and Angel drew close to her, as well. Joaquin caught the smile in Angel's eyes as he looked at him and then leaned down to kiss her bare hip. Teresa moaned when she felt Angel's lips, and the sound was like a siren song to his cock. Joaquin stroked along the back of her thigh then drifted upward to her cleft and growled at finding her slick, hot, and aroused. She whispered, "Please," as she arched her back and pressed her ass against Joaquin's cock more demandingly.

Angel nodded at him to suit up and give her what she wanted while he stroked her and kissed her. Joaquin sheathed his cock in a condom then returned to stroking her pussy with his fingertips. Soon she was begging for him to take her. Joaquin tilted her back against him and lifted her upper thigh, thrusting into her silky wet pussy from behind. Holding her thigh elevated, he nodded at Angel and said, "Angel is going to stroke your clit while I make love to you, sugar. Sound good?"

Teresa panted and moaned in pleasure. "Yes, Angel, please." She shuddered as he pumped his dick deep inside her. Her pussy contracted tightly on his cock the moment Angel's fingertips stroked her clit. She arched her back when Joaquin played with her nipples, which always drove her wild. She came with a wail as a lightning bolt streaked across the sky outside the window. Joaquin thrust hard into her clenching pussy one last time and came with a deep growl that was echoed by the rumble of the thunder as his cum jetted from him in long, hot streams.

Brushing her silky hair from her cheeks, Joaquin nuzzled her throat as Angel rose up and kissed her. After disposing of the condom, Joaquin cuddled up to her in the bed and listened as her breathing gradually slowed, and she drifted back to sleep. He stroked her deep into the night, unable to sleep as he marveled at the woman in his arms. She was coming into her own, beginning to understand she could ask for, or demand, what she needed from them without fear.

Chapter Twenty-seven

Teresa tried to hide her grin with difficulty. The joyful, expectant smiles on Angel's and Joaquin's faces were cuter than she could resist. They were sitting on the back porch, tools ready, instruction sheets spread out, and green molded plastic parts laid out neatly.

She couldn't suppress her chuckle as she said, "He's three."

"The box said ages three to five. It's perfect for him," Joaquin said, his eyes twinkling as he watched her fight her amusement.

Gesturing to the large cardboard box that had been laid aside on the porch, emblazoned with the image of a pint-sized green tractor, she said, "This is too much for a three year old. It's too expensive."

Angel rose from his spot and hugged and kissed her. "We'll teach him how to use it."

His scent enveloped her and made her mouth water. She was going to have to get her responses to them under control otherwise they'd be getting their way every time. Heck, what was she thinking? She didn't mind them having their way as long as she was who they were having.

"What if he damages something?"

"It doesn't go that fast, and he can't really damage much in the backyard. We'll have a talk with him and deal with any damage if and when it happens. This is perfect for a boy his age."

His fingertips stroked her hips through her silky skirt, and she knew her capitulation was complete. They used "sexy" like a weapon on her to get their way. "I suppose you're right, honey. It just surprised me that you would spend so much for a toy."

"It wasn't that bad," Angel replied. "It will be great for teaching him about responsibility and that he'll have to be careful."

Teresa smiled, finally won over. "Plus, you two big boys will have a lot of fun playing with him."

Joaquin grinned triumphantly. "Well, it does look like fun. I can't wait to see him behind the wheel."

Teresa held up an index finger to make a point. "Fine, but you know this is going to lead to bigger and more dangerous toys like motorcycles later."

She'd thought that might give them pause, but the opposite was closer to their response. "Cool! We can teach him about those, too. In a few years, he's definitely going to need a dirt bike."

Teresa rolled her eyes and threw her hands up in the air as Angel laughed and hugged her tight and kissed her. She chuckled and said, "Fine, but it's all fun and games until someone loses an eye."

"Okay, we take full responsibility for emergency rooms visits."

That was supposed to instill confidence?

She sat down on the porch and watched her men put together the child-size version of a big green tractor complete with front-end loader. Angel and Joaquin were planning on surprising Michael with it for his birthday the following day. He was with Grace at the moment, allowing them a chance to get it put together and hidden out of sight.

Teresa gazed at her men, overwhelmed by their generosity toward her son. *Their* son, too, they made clear.

Michael had taken to their attention and instruction like one of the colts under their care, ready to be taught. He followed them around the ranch whenever it was safe for him to do so. The men told Teresa it was that way for them growing up on their parent's ranch. They caught as much as they were taught, and they were confident Michael would, too.

The ranch hands were patient with Michael, taking time to talk to him and giving him little simple jobs to do when they could. One time she caught Ash Peterson in the act of giving Michael a piggyback ride while an ever more articulate Michael babbled on to the tall, muscular cowboy about the horses. Teresa could see how important to Michael it was that they included him in the way his little chest would puff up and how he tried to emulate their movements and actions. What a blessing that her son would grow up surrounded by his heroes.

Angel and Joaquin taught him first to respect the horses and to stay away from all the vehicles. That was another reason they'd gotten him his own little tractor because the vehicles and heavy equipment were off limits unless he was in their arms. He wanted to be with them as much as possible and so he respected and listened to their instructions.

* * * *

They'd been home from the honeymoon for almost a month. It was a tight fit in the two-bedroom house, but they were making it work for now. Jack and Angel were planning to sit down soon and draw up plans for a new house.

Her work at Stigall's continued on at the usual pace. Angel and Joaquin made sure she knew that it was not necessary that she continue on at Stigall's but that if she enjoyed her job, they didn't mind if she kept it.

She still felt amazement at times that they preferred to have Michael with them and not in daycare while they worked and that he obeyed their rules so readily. Teresa questioned why they didn't expect her to contribute toward living expenses, and Angel told her it was important to them that they were able to provide her everything she needed. Honestly, she heaved a great sigh of relief as the burden of making ends meet for her and Michael shifted from her shoulders.

Joaquin committed to the Divine Creek Ranch when he committed to Teresa and was now working fulltime with the breeding operation.

Angel was working steadily toward turning over foremanship of the ranch to Ash Peterson.

The rodeo would come to Morehead in late February, and Teresa did her best to hide her unease when Joaquin registered in the bull-riding competition. The rodeo was a three-day event, and he told her he wanted to do it just for fun and promised her he didn't intend to load up and follow the circuit. He just wanted to keep active in his sport, at least locally.

Angel had competed in bareback bronc riding in years past, but when Teresa asked him about it, he'd told her he was too out of practice to compete. He'd told her he would sign up if the desire was strong enough, but he thought it more important that they both not compete in the rodeo on the off chance they might both be seriously injured.

Angel said he knew it meant more to Joaquin than it did to him because Joaquin loved competition. Angel would sit in the stands and hold her hand while they watched. Ash was registering in the bareback bronc riding event.

They were looking at a calendar early one morning in February with Teresa, trying to determine a weekend they could take off in the spring or early summer to return to Port Aransas. This time they wanted to take Michael with them.

All three looked up when they heard a sleepy little yawn from the entrance into the kitchen. Michael stood there bleary eyed with his jet-black curls mashed sideways and standing up all over his head. He came to Teresa and climbed up in her lap and rested his head against her breasts as she looked at the calendar.

Michael was growing up and getting big so fast. She knew moments like this were numbered, and one day he would be too big to want to cuddle in her arms like this. She thanked God for the blessing of the moment and hoped that someday she'd have another raven-haired infant to cuddle close in her arms. She pressed her lips to Michael's fragrant head and squeezed him gently.

She glanced up and caught both men gazing at her. The tenderness in their eyes made her wonder what they were thinking at that moment. Were they thinking the same thing?

She asked, "Are you sure you want Michael to stay with you today? I don't mind taking him with us."

Angel shook his head with certainty. "The point of going with Grace today was so that you could stop by Discretion. You won't have much fun shopping with one hand over his eyes the whole time, will you?"

"Oh right, that would *not* be fun, would it? Are you sure it will be safe for Michael?"

"Absolutely safe," Joaquin reassured her. "Ethan and Jack are going to be here also. Michael will probably ride my shoulders the whole time, and I won't be in the corral if that has you concerned. If Michael is going to become part of the operation some day, now is as good a time as any to begin teaching him horses including their breeding. He won't be down running loose. I promise."

That wasn't the only reason she needed to be sure he was properly watched over. "How long will those men be here?"

"Del Valle and his brothers are supposed to arrive around nine, and we should be finished by two or three," Angel replied, pouring milk in Michael's cereal and helping him into his booster chair. His next words were directed at Michael. "Come on, buddy, if you're gonna help today, you need to eat a good breakfast."

Teresa and Grace were going to have breakfast together at Rosalie's Café, a new venture in town owned by a woman who had recently moved from Del Rio to Divine. The girls were enthusiastic about visiting the new café.

"Thanks for understanding about this morning," Angel said, stroking her thigh.

"I trust your instincts, Angel."

"We just think it might be better if you and Grace were away from the ranch today while Del Valle and his men are here. Something about them doesn't sit quite right with me and Jack. This way you both get to have some fun, and maybe you'll come home with a few surprises?"

"I'm looking forward to shopping at Discretion. I wonder if there is any particular 'surprise' that you're hoping I'll bring home," she whispered in Angel's ear as Joaquin grinned at her while he poured Michael a glass of orange juice. "I would be open to *suggestions*. I'll be in the bathroom," she offered then slipped out of the kitchen to finish getting ready for the excursion.

Angel and Joaquin had spoken with her about a group that would be coming out the following morning to obtain stud service for their mares. The Del Valle family would only be there for the day and might possibly be returning once more later in the week. Grace and Teresa had decided to take the opportunity to visit Discretion Boutique in Morehead.

Teresa was applying her makeup when Angel came and rested a shoulder against the master bathroom door. There should be a law against men looking that sexy with almost no effort.

"Any special requests? Clothing? Toys?"

"I want you to buy something you'd like to experiment with in the bedroom. Jack tells me the ladies also stock pretty evening wear and accessories. I want you to buy yourself something sexy, for a nice evening out and whatever you'll need to go with it."

She still had the mindset of a single mom on a ferociously tight budget and was so accustomed to keeping the purse strings tight that she still needed reassurance sometimes. What he was asking for would be fun, but expensive. She glanced at him hesitantly.

Angel had that look in his eyes like he knew what she was thinking. "Since we are responsible for sending you out this morning, the shopping spree is on us. You should feel free to use your debit card for anything you purchase. Anywhere you go, all right?" She knew Angel and Joaquin did not have to worry about money. They were invested in the ranch and earned a healthy income plus the return on their investment.

"Thank you, honey. I appreciate it. I don't mean to seem so miserly."

"I know it will take time, beautiful. You're with us now. We're going to take good care of you."

"You do. I love you," she murmured then kissed him. Angel wrapped her in his strong arms and she rested her cheek against his chest, breathing in his clean scent.

"Joaquin wants to check in with you, too. I think he's hoping you'll bring home something in particular, as well. Speak of the devil," he murmured as Joaquin came up behind him in the doorway. "I'll go help Michael get dressed," he said, pecking her nose and leaving Joaquin alone with her.

Teresa felt the heat of Joaquin's gaze as he looked her over from head to toe with a wolfish smile on his face. Glancing in the mirror, she noticed the prominent bulge at his groin and knew he'd given some *hard* thought to what he hoped she'd bring home from Discretion.

Carefully applying her eyeliner, she murmured, "Got a shopping list for me, husband?"

A slow smile spread across his lips, and he gazed back in the mirror with his bedroom eyes. "It's a short list."

The deep tone of his voice and the sexy way he said it led her dampening pussy to believe that while the list might be short, the night would definitely not be. "What would you like?"

"Remember when we talked during the honeymoon about making love to you at the same time?"

Her heart lurched a little in her chest, and her cunt clenched in an ecstatic spasm. "Yes," she whispered, applying her mascara. "You meant both of you penetrating at the same time, right?"

"Yes, did you still want to try that?"

Like you read about, baby! Her pussy welled with hot moisture at the thought.

"You know I do. You said we'd work up to it later. Is this 'later?'"

"Yes, but only if you still want it."

Like people in hell want ice water!

She'd had plenty of time to fantasize about it after they'd told her how they planned to take her. They'd experimented with light anal play ever since, and she had come to crave that little pinch of pain that anal penetration delivered, which escalated her pleasure.

"Joaquin, I think I'm ready."

Joaquin slipped into the bathroom and closed the door in case little ears were nearby. "When we've played anally, it's only been with fingers or the small vibrator. Taking one of our cocks anally is going to require some preparation."

"Would it help if I bought plugs? Grace told me that was what she did—Oops! Maybe I shouldn't have told you that," she whispered, her hand going to her lips.

"It's okay, sugar. Married to three men, both Angel and I already assumed that she would know a thing or two about anal sex. Buy a series of plugs. But I want you to remember something. If we get started and you're uncomfortable, if it hurts or you decide you hate it and don't want to do it, all you have to do is tell us. It wouldn't be the end of the world."

Oh, yeah it would!

Sometimes she still shocked herself with how uninhibitedly she lusted after them both now. Once they got started, she wasn't going to be satisfied until she had both of them inside her at the same time.

"I'll remember, Joaquin, but I'm going to love it. I'll get Grace to help me pick the right ones. Anything else?"

Teresa's enthusiasm seemed to stoke a fire in his brilliant green eyes. "Lubricant. Lots of lubricant. Beyond that, I want you to get anything else you want to try. We're totally open."

"Oh, boy. At this rate, I'll be horny and needy all day." She whimpered. Hearing a metallic click, she glanced in the mirror and hummed in need when she saw the heat in his eyes as he locked the door to the bathroom.

"Have I told you how much I love being able to fuck you without a condom on?" he murmured as he slipped behind her and gazed into her half-lidded eyes. His hands slid around her and cupped her breasts, and brushed his hardened cock against her ass.

She moaned in need, wanting to feel that hot length thrust inside her. "Um, repeatedly."

"Going skin on skin with you is the hottest thing I've ever experienced, sugar. I'm your willing slave."

She gave him a seductive smile in the mirror. "Well then, my sweet slave, your mistress needs a quick, hard fuck from behind if you're up for it." Her vocabulary had evolved in recent days.

Joaquin pressed against her again, grasping her hips so she could feel how hard he was then quickly freed her from her jeans. "*I live to serve*," he murmured, kissing her shoulder as he released his solid erection.

He flicked on the vent to mask any sounds and slid his fingers down her abdomen. She leaned back against him with his cock resting against the cleft of her ass. His fingers traced the wispy black curls at her mound before sliding slowly into her bare, wet slit to find she was dripping and ready.

Joaquin growled softly in her ear. "Oh, holy fuck. I want to eat you up."

She chuckled quietly. "No time. That'll have to wait for tonight. Mmmm, yes, honey."

One finger delved into her opening then swirled up around her clit, zeroing in on it and drawing a husky moan of pleasure from her. He was persistent, swirling a fingertip around it, stroking one side then the other in a relentless rhythm that had her rising inexorably toward crescendo. Teresa's hips flexed, and just as that assurance washed over her, signaling her release, the head of his cock nudged her cunt.

His fingers never wavered in their tempo, and her orgasm broke over her in a tumultuous wave as his cock slid home in one firm thrust. She panted loudly out as she came. The feel of him stroking his long, hot length into her caused her hips to grind against him while he continued strumming until she came a second time even harder. The orgasm was almost overwhelming in its burning intensity, and he growled as her pussy clamped down on him. He thrust gently, whispering words of encouragement as she rode each pulse.

As her whimpers and cries faded, he thrust hard, pulling out and plunging in over and over. She braced herself on the counter, and he thrust directly against her G-spot, and the cry built inside her as he punctuated every word with an earth-shattering stroke. "Love that little *sweet spot*." Her pussy reacted by tightening like a fist.

Covering her mouth with her hand, Teresa tried desperately to muffle her cry and at the same time wanting to shout the house down. They'd unleashed a shrieking banshee when they conditioned her to not hold back her orgasmic cries over their honeymoon.

Her pussy clamped down on him again as she came, and this time he followed her with his own release, letting loose a husky growl as his cock pulsed inside her. He rested his chest lightly against her back as he caught his breath. Joaquin wrapped his arms around her, and she was glad he stayed that way for a minute. Teresa needed the quiet contact with him as much as she'd needed the release.

Resting her cheek on her forearm, Teresa closed her eyes as she caught her breath. She loved the feel of him still so huge inside her, always amazed by his stamina and his willingness to go out of his way to please her. An aftershock flowed through her at the thought, and he thrust against her in response, growling softly in pleasure.

Finally he stood, his hand pressing on the small of her back. Teresa watched his handsome face in the mirror, knowing how much he loved this. She arched her back so he could see better and squeezed him with her pussy muscles as he slowly withdrew, making him hiss in response.

She was gratified when his cock finally slid from her, and he smiled with absolute male satisfaction. The look on his face proclaimed *mine,* and she knew he could see his seed filling her opening. Teresa moaned when her pussy clenched in his absence, wanting him back. Her cum and his mixed together trickled from her pussy, and she gasped when he slid his finger through her pussy lips. She arched a bit more, and he slid his thumb into her opening then brushed her clit tenderly, like a promise of more to "come" later, *literally.*

"I love your pussy so much, Teresa. I wish I could plant myself here and never leave it." He groaned as he brushed his thumb over her sensitive lips one last time.

"Well, my pussy loves you, too. *Come* as often as you like," she quipped and giggled. He snickered good-naturedly at her double entendre.

"That's Gracie's influence on you, right there."

"What a nice thing to say! Well, I'd better get cleaned up." She glanced at her watch. "Oh *shoot,* I lost track of time. Grace is probably waiting for me."

He helped her get cleaned up and redressed. A few minutes later, she left the bathroom with him and ventured down the hall to the living room. Heaving a sigh of relief, they saw Angel out on the front porch with Michael, talking with Grace.

She didn't often get time alone with just one or the other of her men. Each night, all three shared the master bedroom, and there were times, other than at night, when she wished for the chance to be alone with each of them, talking and making love one on one. She'd have to ask Grace how she communicated that need to her men without making the others feel rejected. She hoped Angel wasn't feeling left out right now.

Grabbing her purse and jacket, she kissed all her men out on the porch and then climbed into the BMW convertible with Grace. Grace looked over at her as she pulled away and gave her a knowing smirk. "You just got laid, didn't you?"

"Huh?" *Oh gosh, did they hear me when I came?*

"And I'm willing to bet you came good and hard by the looks of things," Grace said as she snickered knowingly.

Oh gosh! Exactly how loud did I scream? "How—how can you tell?"

Grace flipped open the mirror on the visor. "Look in the mirror. Your throat and upper chest are beet red."

Teresa looked and gasped. Grace was right. And the more she looked, the redder she got. "Oh, goodness! You can tell by that?"

"It's a pretty good indicator. Let me guess, three times altogether. And twice *really* hard? Yeah?" Grace snorted and cackled at Teresa's deer-in-the-headlights look.

When she recovered her voice, she chuckled and said, "Yes, you're exactly right. *I live in heaven!*"

"That's what I've been talking about!"

Chapter Twenty-eight

"Holy moley. Would you look at that?" Teresa whispered as Grace pulled up into the parking lot. The neat and pristine building looked like a quaint little ladies' boutique from the outside. There were planters intermittently along the sidewalk and heavy lace curtains lined all the windows. More lace lined the glass front door.

Mirroring the lettering on the store sign out at the street and the sign over the marquee, there was a clearly printed sign done in beautiful calligraphy on the door:

Discretion
You must be at least 18
years of age to enter.
We reserve the right to check
your identification.
Absolutely no children
N o E x c e p t i o n s
Thank you,
Discretion Management

"Goody. No teeny-boppers allowed," Grace said with a giggle as they entered the store, which was fragrant with the aroma of essential oils.

"Indeed," said a sexy, chuckling voice. "I cannot abide teeny-boppers."

Grace and Teresa looked to the left and right, finally spotting the owner of the sexy voice rising from the tall rolling chair behind a large antique lingerie-display cabinet, which doubled as a sales counter.

"Hi, I'm Summer Heston," the woman said, stepping out from behind the counter. "Welcome to Discretion."

Grace struck up the conversation and Summer told them a little about the shop and showed them around. She and her sister, Margot, co-owned the boutique which had opened in November of the previous year.

By today's standards, Summer would be considered overweight just as Grace and Teresa would be. If Teresa spent her time looking at fashion magazines and watching reality TV, she would probably believe that as well. But she spent her time in the real world with real people who regularly ate a little more than a cube of cheese and a baby carrot at a meal and enjoyed their food.

Consequently, she felt reasonably happy with her figure and could see in Angel's and Joaquin's eyes that they felt *slightly more* than satisfied with how she was built. She could hardly turn her back without one of them pressing up against what *they* described to her as her sweet little ass.

Listening to Grace and Summer talking, Teresa experienced a self-affirming moment of realization. Life experiences had tried to frighten her into living her life tightly bound in her shell, protecting herself. What she had experienced the last eight months was all about her breaking free and doing more than just forgetting the past. It was about embracing the future and becoming the person she was meant to be and spending time around other people who wanted the same thing, like Grace.

Grace had not always been so talkative and sanguine, so filled with a zest for life that you felt it when she was near. She was on the same journey as Teresa, in her own way. Teresa had doubted at one point that she would ever be as open and sociable as she'd become.

Summer gave them a tour of the store. The little boutique was a sexy, eclectic mix of fanciful items. Of course there was the requisite collection of lingerie, corsets, bustiers, panties and other bedroom attire. But Summer and her sister gave the shop an added edge by stocking a wide selection of sexy evening wear designed with *easy access* in mind. They stocked handmade costume jewelry with a sexy twist, including intimate jewelry. They carried a wide variety of sex toys and a collection of scented and flavored massage oils, body lotions, and lubricants. There was a selection of sexy clothing in leather, vinyl, and latex as well as bondage gear. She showed them books on topics ranging from the evolution of lingerie in the modern world to resources for BDSM, dominance, submission, and a wide variety of erotic romance novels. Summer told them that their inventory was geared toward women, but they also boasted an enthusiastic male clientele.

"So, Teresa. Grace tells me you're both newlyweds," Summer said. "Do your husbands know where you are today?"

"Yes. Our husbands suggested we come and do some shopping. Grace's husbands had shopped here before Christmas and told my husbands about it. Mine gave me a shopping list," Teresa said, taking a big chance with the reveal about multiple partners. She was testing the waters with Summer, and it didn't take long for her to respond.

Summer looked back and forth between them, and a twinkle lit her eye. "*Back the hell up.* Did you just say husbands as in *plural?* More than one?"

Grace grinned at her and elbowed Teresa. "Want to hear all about it?"

A broad smile crossed Summer's face. Her cheeks even pinkened a little. She held up one manicured index finger and took a small "back in thirty minutes" sign from under the cash register. Slipping it in front of the lace curtain on the front door, she twisted the latch, locking it.

"Come with me. This sounds like a sit-down conversation." Summer beckoned them through a doorway that led into a little kitchen area.

"Have a seat," she said, indicating the bistro-style table and chairs near a rear window, which looked out on a rosebush in a flower bed. She brought a tray that had sugar, creamer, spoon, and napkins on it then brought over a pot of coffee and placed it on a trivet. She handed them each a pretty ceramic mug and said, "The coffee is fresh."

Reaching in the refrigerator, she pulled out a glass dish. "Margot makes a tiramisu that is to die for." She got plates and utensils from the cabinet and cut all three of them a piece of the delicious looking dessert.

After they poured coffee, she sat down and looked at them with eyes twinkling with enthusiasm. "Okay. Dish. I am *all ears.*"

"I'm married to three smoking hot cowboys," Grace said happily. "Jack has thick, wavy black hair and blue eyes. Ethan has longish, dark brown hair and blue eyes and is tall. Adam has short brown hair, captivating pale green eyes, and he's—"

Summer gasped. "Enormous! I knew it*! I knew it! I knew it.* I should have guessed. Peppermint, Hot Cocoa, and Honey Lemon!" Teresa looked at Grace because Summer had just lost her. She listened quietly, eventually surmising that Summer referred to the scented and flavored lotions and lubricants Grace's men must have bought for her.

"Yes!" Grace giggled. "You must have waited on them!"

"They seemed too good to be true. I thought *you* must be too good to be true. They told me you were their wife. I did my best to help them, but I have to confess I was a little twitter-pated by the thought of the three of them—well, you can guess, and I don't rattle easily. They went on and on about you once they got started talking. It was like something out of an erotic romance novel."

"Grace and our friend Rachel are both writers." Teresa said. "This tiramisu is delicious."

"Really? Oh, thank you. I'll pass your compliment on to Margot. She's going to be so pissed she missed your visit. I told her about your men, and she didn't believe me at first. So, Teresa, what's your story?"

"My husbands, Angel and Joaquin, are brothers and longtime friends of Grace's men. They handle the horse breeding operations at the Divine Creek Ranch. Grace's men own the ranch, and Ethan also co-owns The Dancing Pony nightclub in Divine."

"Oh, I've heard of that club. I always wanted to see what it was like."

"Well, now you have friends to visit there."

"Any of these guys have other brothers tucked away somewhere?"

Grace shook her head but smiled. "We know several eligible bachelors, and Jack does have three handsome cousins who just moved back to Divine. If you don't mind me asking, how old are you?"

"Thirty."

"I'm going to give you my number, and when you think you might want to visit The Pony, you call me, and we'll come in, too. Do you like to dance?"

Summer chuckled happily. "I love to dance. I have the feeling this is the beginning of a great friendship. So what's it like? Are you tired all the time?"

"Oh, no," Teresa said dreamily.

"But I'm sure the sex is demanding, isn't it?" Summer's cheeks flamed crimson and she put her hands over her mouth and said, "I'm sorry. That was so inappropriate of me."

Grace patted her arm. "Summer, if we're willing to talk about being married to more than one man, we're certainly willing to talk about sex. You didn't offend either of us."

Teresa chuckled. It felt good to embrace the future.

"Okay, so how is it?"

Teresa volunteered the answer. "Well, it definitely takes energy, but they're careful to not overdo it. And it's not sex with multiple partners every night, just some nights."

Summer asked a few more questions which Grace and Teresa answered with candor. "So, Grace? Teresa mentioned you were a writer? What do you write?'

Grace smiled like a Cheshire cat and blushed a little. "A great author once said, 'Write what you know.'"

"Oh! So you write erotic romance? Are you published yet?"

"Not yet. All my friends keep getting engaged and asking me to plan their weddings," she said, elbowing Teresa who grinned sheepishly. "Now that life is settling down a little, I'm planning on submitting a manuscript."

"Well, I hope someday I get to read your stories."

"That's my hope, too."

They talked more and finished their snack and coffee. Summer quizzed them about what they hoped to find in the store that day as they left the kitchen, and she took down the sign and unlocked the door.

Teresa said, "I want to try on evening dresses, but you're going to have to show me how the 'easy access' features work. Joaquin asked me to bring home something new to experiment with."

Summer asked nonchalantly, "In bed, you mean?"

"Yes," Teresa said with a smile, trying to imagine the old Teresa having this conversation.

"Grace?"

"I need undies and lingerie. I want to try on dresses, too."

"Then let's start there. Tell me your sizes, and I'll get you set up in the dressing rooms."

Teresa narrowed the selection down to the gown she liked the best and let Summer deck her out, including shoes. She stepped out to show the beautiful, slinky black dress, shoes, and jewelry off. Summer showed her how to unhook the hidden closures on the bodice of the dress, which opened all the way down the front but overlapped enough that no one would know the dress opened with a simple flick of the wrist. The ultimate in easy access.

Grace came out in a silky, dark purple dress with a jeweled bodice and empire waist. Hidden in the bodice of the dress were snaps that could be taken loose.

After they made their clothing selections, Summer took them around to the antique glass sales counters that displayed all the sex toys.

Teresa mentioned to Summer that she'd like to look at anal plugs in graduated sizes.

"Okay, Teresa, let me show you what I have," Summer said nonchalantly. "These are the different sizes," she said, indicating silicone anal plugs lined up in a row inside a glass case. "Look at the thickest part of each plug, and tell me which is closest in girth to the thickest part of your men's cocks when erect." *Wow, way to put it out there!*

Teresa glanced at Grace uncertainly. Grace said, "It's okay, Teresa. Summer's an expert at this stuff." Grace turned to Summer and said, "Would you mind if she handles some of them?"

"Sure," Summer replied easily. She removed the compartmented display tray and put it on the glass countertop. Grace lifted one from its nest and placed it in Teresa's hand. It felt flexible and a little squishy, not hard like she'd expected. She wrapped her hand around it.

Summer asked, "Teresa, can your thumb and index finger touch each other when you wrap your hand around either man?"

"Almost, but not quite," she answered, knowing immediately the one in her hand was too small.

"*Mama*," Summer whispered, handing her a blue jelly plug. "Try wrapping your hand around that. Okay, try this one." And Teresa quickly found the maximum size she would need. It looked gigantic. The look in her eyes must have spoken volumes.

Grace smiled encouragingly. "Don't worry, honey. It'll fit. Remember, you're working *toward* that size, not starting there."

"You're right. What now?"

Summer helped them pick out four different plugs in graduated sizes. She recommended a good lubricant and set aside two bottles of it for Teresa then made some suggestions for other toys she could use along with the plugs.

Grace looked over her selection of intimate jewelry, settling on a couple of pieces. Blushing, Grace fingered one of the silver wrap-around cock rings and picked one out silently but never hinted to Teresa which man it was for. She knew Grace would tell her if she wanted Teresa to know.

Saying that her men might love it, Grace talked Teresa into purchasing pussy dangles with black onyx beads. "It'll go with the jewelry Angel gave you for Christmas. Summer, do you have anything in a bright blue turquoise?"

"Teresa, your skin tone would look perfect with turquoise dangles.

If your men like turquoise, I have a turquoise clit clip, a magnetic belly ring, and nipple dangles. I could order extra dangles and make you a nipple dangle chain that can be worn with the nipple rings. It attaches right on to provide extra weight." *Ooh, extra weight, there?* The thought made Teresa a little wet imagining what that would feel like.

Teresa felt a little daring. "I think they would love that. Yes, Summer. I'll take those, and order the extra dangles. I want to look at your books," Earlier she'd been curious to look at the titles Summer had available but had been too self-conscious. Their conversations had loosened her up considerably. "Grace?"

Grace shook her head. "You go ahead, Teresa. I'm going to chat with Summer for a few minutes."

Teresa wandered over to the large bookcase display and began leafing through the erotic romances. She'd never owned a book like these before. Some of the covers were very erotic and downright shocking, others were simply beautiful. She found several whose back cover descriptions were intriguing and returned to the sales counter. Grace grinned as Teresa showed her the covers.

Summer smiled and said, "That's one of my all-time favorite authors. If you like that book, she is releasing a sequel to it in a couple of months."

Teresa had never felt so at home in such an unusual place as Discretion.

Chapter Twenty-nine

Teresa slipped into the supple leather seat of Grace's convertible BMW Z4 and buckled her seatbelt, looking over at her friend. "I'm not sure what I was expecting, but *that* was fun!" Teresa had gotten all the things her men had asked her to get, plus a few fun surprises they weren't expecting.

Grace laughed and said, "I hated to leave. She was so fun to talk to. We're going back sometime soon and we're bringing Rachel and Rosemary with us." Grace turned the key in the ignition then popped her Miranda Lambert CD into the player. Grace had gotten Teresa hopelessly hooked on her. "Only Prettier" played in the background.

Teresa suggested, "If we time it right, we could take her out to lunch or supper."

Grace said, "Can you imagine how *fun* it would be to work in a shop like that?"

"Once I stopped blushing when someone asked to handle the dildos." Teresa said.

Just like that, the seed was planted. What if, down the road, Margot and Summer needed help, or what if the opportunity to invest in a great little boutique like that presented itself? She enjoyed dealing with customers at Stigall's. The idea wasn't that far-fetched.

"Maybe they might be interested in Harper's doing some embroidery work for them," Grace speculated.

"Overnight bags for holding toys and other 'goodies' monogrammed 'Discretion'." Teresa replied.

Grace gasped and got a sparkle in her eyes. "Lingerie cases for traveling, monogrammed garment bags for submissive wear, duffle bags for equipment. *You're brilliant.* I'm going to do some research and get back with her. I think we just made a good friend."

"I'm so glad we *came!*" Teresa said then laughed when Grace snorted and cackled.

"Yeah, *some* of us more than others."

They cruised down the state highway headed toward the Morehead historical district.

"Grace, I want you to know how much I appreciate your help and encouragement. You've taught me how to have fun with you and the girls."

"You're welcome. You remember how it was for me with Owen. Once I was free from that and found out what real love felt like, I wanted for you to be that happy, too. Remember the first time you laid eyes on Angel in the store?"

Laughing, Teresa said, "I'll never forget. I lost the ability to speak."

"You fell in love with him the moment you saw him. Too bad he was still bound to that freaking psycho. When I visited him after she shot him, he asked me about you. He wondered if you might be interested in him, knowing he'd allowed someone like her in his life and his home."

Teresa replied, "Angel told me he knew she didn't love him. I know there were benefits for him with her. Angel is very…virile," Teresa said as her cheeks got hot. "I can't hold that against him. He didn't know me. It's easy for both of us to regret our pasts. We both trusted people we shouldn't have and paid a heavy price. But how can I regret it if it ultimately caused us to cross paths and, thanks to a *certain matchmaker,* to fall in love with each other. The same goes for Joaquin about regretting his past."

Teresa groaned and shook her head, chuckling. "You know, he finally sat me down a few weeks ago and told me his conscience was bothering him and could he come clean to me about something."

"Gracious! What did he do? Murder somebody? Make a porn movie?" Grace snickered when she said the last one.

"I know! I was imagining all kinds of awful things, bracing myself for some disaster."

Grace glanced at her as they neared the restaurant they planned to eat lunch at. "What could he possibly have done?"

"He was worried that I'd find out what…"

"Holy crap! What?"

Teresa broke out in uproarious giggles. "He was afraid I would find out what a *buckle-bunny-slut* he was!"

Grace's jaw dropped open and they both broke out in laughter. "A what? Does that mean what I think it means?"

"Yes. I mean, can you imagine someone who looks like him, unattached and available, not taking advantage of any decent offer that came his way? He felt guilty about Christmas Eve, though."

Grace's eyebrows drew together and she asked, "Why? He loved you the moment he saw you. Anything he did before was in his past. It wasn't cheating. It was being a normal, handsome, horny male. What would he feel guilty about?"

Teresa smiled and said, "Well, he feels guilty because Christmas Eve morning, when Angel talked to him, he said he was tied up there, and he'd be along a little later in the day than he'd originally planned. What we didn't know was that he really *was*."

"Was what?" Grace squealed, evidently having an idea, going by the laughter in her tone.

"*Tied up in El Paso*. He was tied to some gal's bed in a hotel room while she took advantage of his vulnerability with his full consent."

"*Sweet merciful heavens*. What did you say?"

Teresa stifled her laughter. "I asked when would *I* get to tie him up."

Grace shrieked and cackled like she was about to lay an egg. *"Who are you,* and what have you done with my friend, Teresa? You did not say that! What did he say?'

"He said that did *not* help his guilt at all, but he smiled when he said it. He was afraid one of the buckle bunnies at the rodeo coming up in a few weeks might…remember him and make an offer. He felt bad about being such a horn dog with all of them. Evidently, he had quite a prolific reputation. Anyway, when he met me and started feeling like it could lead somewhere, he went to see Dr. Guthrie and got tested to make sure. He was clean and clear, but he even felt bad for going to the doctor and not telling me about that."

"So he got it all off his chest?"

"Yes. Bless his heart." Teresa replied, taking out her cell phone when it chirped. It was a text message from Angel.

Hey, beautiful. How's your morning so far?

Teresa quickly typed a reply. *Hi, Angel. We're stopping for lunch downtown.*

Her phone chirped almost immediately with his next message. *Find anything you liked at Discretion?*

Teresa giggled and decided to tease him a bit. *Wait until you see the naughty things I'm bringing home with me..*

Her phone chirped again with Angel's response. *We'll look forward to you modeling for us.*

She was still concerned about the men visiting the ranch and hoped that Michael was behaving. *How is Michael doing?*

Angel's reply was swift. *He's doing great. Another hour or so and we'll be done here. Have a nice lunch.*

Teresa answered, *We will. I love you.*

Angel came back with, *Love you, too, beautiful. Be careful.*

We will. Teresa typed as Grace pulled into the parking lot of a cute little tea room tucked into old downtown Morehead.

"Angel said they'll be done soon," Teresa said as she climbed from the convertible.

"Good. That whole deal kind of…creeps me out a little."

"Me, too."

Chapter Thirty

Teresa squinted from the bright sunshine as she and Grace approached the old-fashioned double glass doors of the tearoom. The doors opened inward as they approached, and a petite young woman greeted them. "Hello. Welcome to Nikolai's!"

The hostess led them to a table near one of the windows looking out over the garden that grew in the little space between the tearoom and the building next door.

The alleyways had been permanently closed and were repurposed by the downtown revitalization committee as outdoor rooms and gardens. Several restaurants in the area used them as outdoor dining rooms, like Nikolai's, while other businesses used them as venues for live music and open-air shopping markets.

After looking at the menus, Teresa and Grace placed their orders with their waitress.

Grace removed her phone from her purse when it chimed and looked at the display. Grace looked up at Teresa and said, "It's a text message from Ethan. Do you mind?"

"Of course not. Go ahead," Teresa said. Grace texted back and forth with Ethan for a minute or two, and Teresa watched with amusement as Grace occasionally giggled and her cheeks turned a rosy color over the course of the conversation with him.

When Grace set her phone aside, Teresa asked, "Was Ethan telling you what he's going to do to you when you get home?"

Grace chuckled as she put her phone up. "Yes, how could you tell?"

"You kept giggling and squirming in your seat. I'm glad I'm not the only one who blushes so easily. Were you teasing him?"

"I was giving him hints about the cock ring I bought him at Discretion."

That got Teresa's cheeks burning! Her best friend was talking about penis jewelry for her husband, with Teresa, and she wasn't running from the room.

"I'll bet he's going to love that. Do Jack and Adam go for things like that?"

"I don't know, but we're gonna find out. He'll probably run it by them privately and then let me know. They've never denied me anything I've asked for, even if they aren't sure it's something they'll enjoy."

"Like *bondage*?" Teresa asked quietly, curiosity spurring her to come right out and ask.

Grace looked carefully at her friend, probably searching for a trace of unease or judgment, then said, "You know I wouldn't want you to feel embarrassed, right?"

"You haven't steered me wrong so far. I'd never judge you if you were seeking to please your men. So, let me guess, it's Ethan, isn't it?"

Grace nodded. "Yes. He tends to be more toward the *edge*."

"Does he tie you up?" Teresa asked. She pictured Angel and Joaquin in control of her like that, and her pussy echoed a responding pulse.

"Not yet, but we're curious about things like that. He spanks me, though," she whispered so softly Teresa could barely hear her.

"Do you…like it?" Teresa asked. Grace might be the one embarrassed and shocked if she knew how the thought of Teresa's men doing that affected her.

Grace whispered, "Like you would not believe!"

Teresa patted Grace on the shoulder as she rested her forehead in her hands briefly. *"Damn, that good?"* she asked as Grace nodded with her head down.

When Grace looked up, Teresa couldn't deny the glow she saw in Grace's eyes. "It's amazing. It's like I go to a different place. It's euphoric…and comforting."

"Comforting?" Teresa echoed, thinking she was missing the connection. Getting spanked could be comforting? "Okay. I'm gonna trust you on that."

At that moment their waitress delivered their meals. Other diners were seated at the tables surrounding them, so they were unable to finish their conversation. Teresa waited until they were back in the convertible and quizzed Grace all the way home about what it was like to be spanked. Teresa was breaking all kinds of new ground today. Butt plugs, erotic romances, and spankings, oh my.

Chapter Thirty-one

Teresa heard singing and laughter from the backyard as she and Grace unloaded her purchases from the trunk of Grace's convertible. Teresa beckoned to Grace, and they went in the house, put the shopping bags on the couch then headed for the back door. The house was immaculate, just as she'd left it, if not better. She loved that her men cleaned up after themselves. The two of them peeked out the window in the back door and giggled.

Angel and Joaquin sat on the back porch. Michael was in the backyard riding around on his little green tractor. His mouth was moving, but the sound was muffled, so they quietly opened the door.

Michael's vocabulary had grown considerably, and Teresa had noticed he'd become more articulate. She attributed some of that to his precociousness, but knew that Angel and Joaquin could take credit as well. When he was with them, he was always asking questions, and they took an active role in instructing him.

Joaquin and Angel looked up, smiling happily when they saw them, and motioned them to come out and sit.

Joaquin put his finger over his lips and chuckled as he whispered, "Listen to what he's singing." Teresa and Grace silently took seats on the glider and at the table.

"...*take you for a ride on my big green tractor.*
We can go slow or make it go faster."

Michael was going around in circles, singing "Big Green Tractor" by Jason Aldean at the top of his lungs. He was toggling the lever for the front-end loader, so the little shovel on the front of the toy vehicle was moving randomly up and down.

"Climb up in my lap and drive if you want to.
Girl, you know you got me to hold on to."

Teresa tried unsuccessfully to stifle her giggles as she watched her little boy have fun. Grace had tears in her eyes she was laughing so hard. Teresa looked over at Angel and caught his eyes. He smiled at her and indicated with his chin to the camera he was holding to show her he was shooting a video of Michael singing.

"That's ten thousand dollars for his college fund, right there," Joaquin whispered in her ear as he sat next to her on the glider. "Earlier he was doing his Kenny Chesney impersonation, singing 'She Thinks My Tractor's Sexy'."

The scene was even funnier because Michael was, of course, dressed in the obligatory hat, chaps, and spurs that had become a favorite part of his daily attire. Most kids outgrew those parts of a cowboy dress-up costume, but it was clear he was going to wear his out.

"Just let me dust off the seat.
Mmmm, put your pretty little arms around me.
Here we go."

* * * *

Angel parked in the Morehead fairgrounds parking lot, the first night of the rodeo. Teresa allowed Joaquin to help her climb from the front seat of Angel's truck, placing her on the ground as if she were fine china.

"You doing okay, sugar? You were awful quiet on the way into town." He tilted her chin up and looked into her eyes. Teresa looked down because she knew she couldn't hide the worry there.

"Just promise me you'll be careful and stay focused. Please, Joaquin."

"It'll be fine, sugar. I've done this hundreds of times."

Two more big Dually pickup trucks parked next to theirs, and Ethan, Jack, and Adam jumped out of one of them to help Grace down from her seat, much to her obvious enjoyment. Teresa smiled at the way the men always watched out for her. Ash and several ranch hands piled out of the other truck, which pulled a horse trailer loaded with three of the mares from the ranch. Ethan and Adam were going to be working as pickup riders during the events. Teresa looked over at Grace, and Grace smiled encouragingly at her.

Teresa tried to get all this into perspective. Joaquin had done this before. Being fearless like that was one of the reasons she loved him, and rejecting this part of his life would be rejecting part of who he was. She couldn't do that. Sucking up her fear and worry, she smiled up at him. He kissed her before leaning into the truck to lift out the canvas duffel that contained all his gear.

The night before, he'd shown her the Kevlar-lined vest he'd be wearing. Joaquin also explained that two pickup riders would be mounted and ready in the arena to pick him up if the bull bucked him off and charged him, and also to redirect the bull from the arena. It had helped to know that he would not be completely alone in the ring with the bull and that there would be bullfighters to distract the bull, as well.

Teresa smiled and said, "I'll be cheering for you with Angel and the others. You just stay focused on that bull."

"Yes, ma'am. You want to walk with me to the registration booth?" he asked as he strapped on his leather chaps. Teresa watched him as he did up all the buckles and straps, glancing over at Grace, who was watching her men appreciatively as they did the same, catching her eye. Grace's lip was caught between her teeth as she made eye contact with Teresa. Teresa suppressed a snicker when Grace mouthed "O.M.G." to her then looked back.

Grace leaned in to whisper something in Ethan's ear as he stood up, adjusting the buckle to the chaps that was located over his fly. Ethan went motionless and gave her a sexy smile then whispered something back and kissed her neck. He released her to Adam, who had come up to stand beside them, speaking softly. Grace's arms snaked around Adam, her fingers sliding into the top band of the chaps.

Teresa returned her attention to Joaquin as he stood up, adjusting the fit on his chaps, and smiled at her. "What, sugar?"

What? He knows exactly what. Handsome devil.

She bit her lip, unsuccessful in stifling a sigh of longing. "I've never seen you in chaps before."

"And?" Joaquin asked knowingly. He gave her a sideways twinkly-eyed grin as he fastened the buckle.

"No wonder the buckle bunnies swarmed around you." Giggling, she slid her arm around his hips.

He chuckled, kissing her cheek. "But I'm all yours now, me *and my chaps.*"

"Yes, *mine*. All mine."

The horses were unloaded, saddled, and all the gear was gathered.

"You didn't answer me earlier," Joaquin said, sliding a hand around her hip and squeezing her to him as their group made their way to the main entrance of the arena.

With all the ogling, she'd forgotten he'd asked a question. "What question? Oh! Yes, I'll be happy to walk with you."

Angel lifted Michael onto his arm. "I'll take Michael with me and help Grace find us good seats. After you get done with Joaquin, call me, and I'll come get you." Angel kissed her as the group split up. The spectators headed toward the stands, while the men participating went to the registration area which was set up at the rear entrance of the facility.

The crowd was thick, and the fragrance of funnel cakes and popcorn filled the cool afternoon air as they worked their way to the end of the arena. A couple of times, they stopped, and Joaquin introduced Teresa to cowboys and their wives or girlfriends, who were longtime friends of Joaquin from the rodeo circuit.

Teresa noticed calculating looks from several young women as they passed. Joaquin appeared to not notice them as he conversed with her and his friends. Those young women were all dressed the same, in skintight, colorful jeans, low-cut tops, hats, and boots. Several sported large, polished silver buckles on their belts.

Teresa felt confident enough to handle whatever came her way today with regards to these women that followed the rodeo circuit. When she'd come out of the bedroom dressed and ready to go earlier, Angel and Joaquin had complimented her and caressed her ass and breasts, making their point clear that she was the one they saw.

They were speaking with a cowboy dressed in a red plaid shirt when, from somewhere nearby, a female voice squealed, "Cowboy!" Joaquin's head swiveled, and Teresa saw him cringe.

His friend turned toward the source of the squealing voice, looked at Joaquin, and said, "Oh shit." The cowboy turned to Teresa and quickly said, "It's a pleasure to make your acquaintance, ma'am. Enjoy the rodeo."

She smiled at him distractedly and shook the hand he offered before he hightailed it out of there. Teresa knew it was just a matter of time before one of these buckle bunnies made a bold move. Grace warned her that not all of them would keep their distance, regardless of whether a woman walked beside him or not. Some of them were that brazen, others just unobservant.

This young woman was evidently of the unobservant variety. That or she was making a concerted effort to ignore the possessive hand Joaquin had wrapped around Teresa's hip. Either way, she was about to embarrass them all.

Teresa finally spotted the squealing young woman as she came at Joaquin at a dead run. Teresa felt the eyes of all those who stood nearby.

Oh no.

This buckle bunny was going to make a scene out of her reunion. Joaquin looked at Teresa imploringly and said, "Sugar, I'm sorry," as the buckle bunny made full, crashing body contact with his left side, practically knocking Teresa to the asphalt on his right side. Only Joaquin's hand on her hip steadied her.

Teresa was sincere when she'd told him she didn't hold any of his sexcapades against him. That didn't mean she wasn't feeling more than a little territorial about his arm and hip that the young woman was currently *mashed* up against. The young woman giggled shrilly and clutched at him, pressing her breasts and hips against him.

In a loud voice, she said, "Cowboy, I'm *so happy to see you again!* I thought you'd fallen off the face of the planet!"

In a moment of clarity, Teresa realized something. This girl didn't even know his name. Or didn't remember it.

"Um, hey," he said half-heartedly.

The young woman rubbed her breasts on his arm as he tried to slip away from her grasp unsuccessfully. "Listen, my daddy bought me a brand-new trailer. You should see it! I'm parked—"

He turned to the buckle bunny and quickly, but gently, removed her hands from his arm and closed a protective arm around Teresa.

"Hey, it's—uh—good to see you. But I'm newlywed. This is my wife. I'm sorry, but—"

The buckle bunny looked at him, stunned. She opened her mouth, then slammed it closed again. Finally, she smiled and summoned the grace to say, "No, cowboy. I'm sorry. Congratulations on getting married."

She lowered her eyes, gathered her tattered pride about her, and sauntered away, her long, straight blonde hair wafting on the breeze.

Joaquin gazed at Teresa in surprise. "I'm so sorry, sugar. *Damn it.* Are you okay?" he asked, tilting her chin up to look in her eyes.

"I'm sorry, Joaquin. Maybe I should have gone with Angel. That would have been less embarrassing for you."

"You don't have to apologize to me, sugar. I should be apologizing to you for being such a —"

"Don't you dare say it," she whispered, placing her fingers over his lips. "It's in the past."

"I should call Angel to meet us and walk you back to the seats. There will probably be others like her," he murmured, embarrassment coloring his cheeks.

Teresa shook her head. "No, I don't want you to be late getting checked in, Joaquin. I'm a big girl."

Joaquin smiled down at her, and they moved along toward the short line at the registration booth where all the riders and workers needed to check in. Adam and Ethan looked back at them as they approached, but said nothing of the exchange they had no doubt witnessed.

After check-in was finished, they proceeded to the area where Joaquin would leave his gear. He needed time to stretch out and prepare. He held Teresa to his side for a few minutes, introducing her to other riders and their wives, who were all friendly toward her.

One of the wives told her there was a prime location in the arena from which family members and other VIPs could watch the action at a closer vantage point than the other spectators, the best seats in the house. That must be where Angel and the others waited for the rodeo to begin now. Numerous buckle bunnies hung out on the periphery of the behind-the-scenes area. Several of them made eye contact with her, challenge gleaming in their eyes.

Fiona Wills, one of the wives, said, "Don't let them bother you, honey. Joaquin was prime-cut tenderloin to those gals for years. They're trying to piss you off and make you defensive. You just hold tight to his hand and ignore them. It's obvious he's only got eyes for you by the way he looks at you. It's good to see him like this."

Joaquin was deep in a conversation with Fiona's husband and did not appear to be following the ladies' conversation.

Curious, Teresa asked, "Like what?"

"Showing his feelings. His eyes are sort of tender when he looks at you. He's always been a happy-go-lucky ladies' man having a good time. But there was never anything in his eyes, no feeling, no real enjoyment, just gratification. I can see in his *eyes* that he's happy."

"Thanks, Fiona. I appreciate that." Glancing at a group of young women that walked by, she frowned.

Fiona curled her lips at them as the girls passed her. "Don't let them see that they get to you. And don't trust a thing any of them say to you. They'll wait until you're alone and act like they're trying to befriend you, but they work together at 'divide and conquer.' Stick with your man or one of us, and you'll do fine. So how is Angel doing? I haven't seen him in a couple of years."

A happy smile came to her face as Joaquin turned and looked back at her and grinned. She looked at him, unsure how to answer. He said, "It's okay, sugar. Fiona knows Mom and the dads, known us all our lives. You can talk freely with her, though probably not around any others," he said, glancing around.

Teresa released his hand for a moment and held it paired with her other hand with the tops facing out, showing Fiona the pair of wedding bands. Fiona's eyes went a little bulgy.

"Well, honey! You hit the jackpot, now didn't you? I hope they are taking good care of you?"

"Oh, absolutely, Fiona," Teresa said dreamily, making the older woman giggle.

"Uh-oh. I think you're about to be claimed," Fiona said, chuckling as Teresa was startled by a large hand sliding around her waist. A hard male body pressed against her backside, and she felt caressing lips at her temple. She couldn't stifle the feeling of euphoria that came over her at Angel's touch. Joaquin smiled and nodded when he saw him. He must have called Angel while she was talking with Fiona to walk her back to the stands.

"Those are good men you have, honey, watching over you like this," Fiona said. Then she turned to Angel, and he gave her a friendly hug. "It's so good to see you, Angel. I see you learned well from your daddies." They made small talk about the families and life in general for a few minutes.

"Well, sugar, it's about to start in a few minutes. If you want to be able to see, you'd better go with Angel and Fiona. I'll see you afterward. Pray for me," he said in a whisper as he gathered her in his arms and kissed her fiercely. She felt a little dazed when he released her.

"I promise I will, honey. Do good. Be safe."

"I'll make you proud. Thanks, Angel," he added, bumping fists with his brother before Angel drew Teresa away, with Fiona walking along beside them.

Teresa looked back at Joaquin as she twined her fingers with Angel's. She felt her face blush slightly when she caught him ogling her ass as she walked away. He gave her a lopsided grin and waved before turning to put on his gloves and approach the area where the rest of the cowboys were congregating.

"He feels pretty guilty for putting you in an uncomfortable situation. You okay?" Angel asked. Teresa noted the calculating looks of several young women hanging around the area as they observed her close proximity to Angel, his fingers intertwined with hers. She wasn't about to pull away from him for anybody else's benefit.

Quietly, she asked, "How can they be happy doing this? Following the rodeos, looking for one-night stands."

"The chance to say they've been with someone who could be famous. Bragging rights. They come into these towns like tourists, spending their daddies' money. They have anonymity except amongst us. Maybe they enjoy the 'freedom.' Some of them just like the lifestyle and men in chaps."

Teresa's lips twitched. "Well, there's definitely something to be said for the chaps."

"I'll remember you said that, beautiful," he whispered in her ear. Teresa felt herself grow wet and throb a little at what he intimated. She bit her lip and glanced at him, her cheeks tingling with warmth.

Angel's eyes were locked on her, a knowing smile on his face. "Hmmm, interesting."

Thankfully, Fiona spoke up, "Joaquin drew a challenging bull."

"Which one?" Angel asked her as they walked along together, weaving through the crowd.

Fiona replied, "Joe Peterson's CC."

Angel nodded his head positively. "Good one. Joaquin has a chance at a good score with him if he stays on."

"What does CC stand for?" Teresa asked, not sure she wanted to know.

"Crazy and cantankerous," Angel replied. He evidently noted the worry in her eyes when the name registered. "Don't worry. It's a good, hard-bucking bull. I'll bet he does well tonight."

"He was in the running for 'Texas Bucking Bull of the Year' last year, in the top ten," Fiona said. "Joaquin seemed real pleased with his pick."

Angel explained to Teresa that the bulls were scored on how hard a time they gave the rider and on their overall agility, kicks, and drops. At the end of the season, the best bulls would be brought to the rodeo finals.

Part of her felt excited to watch him ride this challenging bull, and part of her was terrified. Teresa hoped she didn't make a fool of herself in the stands. She didn't want to embarrass her men.

Fiona joined her kids and her brother-in-law in the stands, and Angel led her to where Grace and Michael were sitting. Rachel and Eli had also joined them. After exchanging hugs, Teresa sat down next to Angel, and he reached for her hand, slipping his other arm over the backrest of her seat. She looked at him and smiled tremulously then leaned into his shoulder.

"He'll be fine, beautiful."

She smiled up at him and squeezed his hand. A few minutes later, right after Jack joined them in the stands, the rodeo began with the grand entry of all the riders and mounted competitors. Michael was enthralled by the horses and riders making their galloping entry into the arena, carrying all the flags.

He looked at Angel with big, trusting brown eyes and asked, "Daddy, am I gonna do that someday?"

"Yep, you are son. If you want to, we'll let you."

"Cool!" Michael said, clapping his hands with the spectators as everyone stood for the national anthem. Her heart pounded with gratitude for Angel and Joaquin taking the time with him that they did. Michael would grow into an amazing man with them guiding him.

As announcements were made, people streamed into the arena, parading back and forth on the wide aisle at the foot of the stands.

A beautiful blonde strutted down the aisle. Her hair was styled, nails done, and makeup perfect. She was gorgeous and just a little voluptuous, but she was clad in a strapless sundress that was smocked at the bust, tube-top style, and only reached mid-thigh, with fancy cowgirl boots on.

Sympathetically, Teresa whispered, "I'll bet she's cold. It's too chilly to be dressed like that,"

Grace chuckled and said, "I think she's probably planning on having a cowboy keep her warm."

The rodeo queen, junior miss rodeo queen, and little rodeo princess were all introduced then the timed events began. The women's barrel racing was exciting to watch. Teresa wondered if one of the young women racing was the one who'd had Joaquin tied to her bed Christmas Eve morning. Surprisingly, she didn't harbor ill feelings for that particular woman. Joaquin had access to that kind of carefree nightlife and lifestyle but had fallen in love with Teresa on sight. She was confident in where she stood with Joaquin.

Steer wrestling and team-roping competitions were next then mutton busting. Angel walked Michael down lower into the stands for the mutton busting, so he could watch close up. Each child was secured on their sheep then they held on for dear life as the animal tried to buck them off. The top two little riders were awarded the right to claim a small cash prize or to keep the sheep they successfully rode, plus the obligatory winning ribbons.

"Ladies and gentlemen, that's some redneck child abuse for you, right there. You can't spank your kid in Wal-Mart, but you can tie 'em to the back of a half-wild sheep and *let 'em run.* Give 'em a round of applause, folks!"

The crowd cheered for all the little ones as they lined up for a quick photograph for the *Divine Courier* newspaper.

"I'm gonna be a mutton-buster boy!" Michael crowed when they returned to their seats.

Angel grinned and said, "You're eligible after you turn four."

Teresa laughed gaily when Michael did a triumphant fist pump and climbed into Angel's lap.

Soon the rough-stock competitions began, with bareback bronc riding, followed by saddle bronc riding. The top riders would ride one more time on the third night in the "short go" round. The cowboys with the highest total scores would claim the cash purses offered for those competitions.

Teresa watched, riveted, as the first bucking horse was loaded into the chute and a cowboy climbed in and mounted the animal. The side door was pulled open, and the horse erupted from the chute, leaping in the air and bowing in two, all four feet off the ground.

Their seating was close enough to the bucking chutes that the sounds the animals made and the vibrations from their hooves could clearly be heard and felt. Six and a half seconds into his first ride, the cowboy was bucked off but landed on his feet. One of the pickup riders shooed the bronc back to the exit with little difficulty. Because he'd not stayed on for the requisite eight seconds, the rider received no score, which Teresa soon realized was not uncommon.

Most often, it seemed the rough stock won this competition between man and animal. Teresa recognized Ash as he climbed onto the pipe fencing around the bucking chute then moments later the announcer called his name. Waving when the crowd cheered for him, he mounted the horse. His movements as he readied himself were swift, tight, and confident. Teresa briefly glimpsed Joaquin on the pipe fencing before Ash gave a sharp nod, and the gate swung open.

The horse and its rider lurched from the bucking chute. The horse sounded infuriated as it leapt in the air, landed as though spring-loaded, and all four feet went flying, twisting and trying to buck Ash off. The cowboy moved with fluid agility, finding a rhythm with the wildly bucking, twisting, turning animal. Ash's free arm flew through the air, staying well away from the animal and himself just as the regulations stipulated. The motions of the pair were by turns abrupt and violent but also smooth and graceful.

Ash lasted the full eight seconds, released the surcingle, and leapt to the back of Ethan's horse as the other pickup rider herded the still-bucking horse to the exit. At the last second, the horse turned from the exit and streaked across the arena, still bucking to the cheers of the crowd, which seemed to egg it on. The pickup rider finally roped the uncooperative horse and led him toward the exit.

The announcer picked that moment to chime in. "That brings back memories of me trying to get my wife outta Wal-Mart."

Even to Teresa's untrained eye, his performance had been a good one. He moved on the horse as though he were comfortable, if that were possible, finding a rhythmic counterpoint to the violent attempts by the animal to unseat him.

Angel was appreciative when they announced Ash's score of 86.5. The next rider was not so fortunate. He was unable to achieve a good bucking rhythm with his horse and got his bell rung when he rocked forward as his horse bucked back, popping him in the forehead and knocking him semi-conscious. Ethan and his horse leapt between the wildly bucking animal and the rider, giving the rodeo clowns a chance to assist him out of the arena so he would not be trampled by the animal. By the end of the first night of bronc riding, Ash had earned a place in the top five.

The bull riding was the finale of the evening, prior to the concert afterward. Joaquin was the last to ride, so Teresa was certain she would have a chance to acclimate herself to the sight and sounds of the bulls as their riders attempted to cheat them out of eight seconds astride their bucking backs. It was no easy feat, and the first rider was thrown almost immediately.

She'd grown accustomed to watching the horses as they came from the chutes but was assailed by the difference as the second bull, which the announcer said was a 1,800-pound veteran of the rodeo circuit, pounded from the shoot. The ground thundered under him, and the crowd went wild as the rider, a well-known cowboy from Colorado, did his best to spur him on, establishing that same graceful fluidity, riding counterpoint to the bull's bucking.

It all went well until the last second, when he lost his rhythm and was almost unseated as the snorting beast changed directions suddenly, and he was unable to regain his seat atop the bull. He made the full eight seconds, but the last second wasn't pretty. He looked pissed off as he caught Adam's hand to get away from the bull while Ethan worked to haze the bull into the exit chute.

Rider after rider gave it their all as their turn came. Teresa noticed some wore helmets and others merely wore cowboy hats. She knew Joaquin was only wearing a hat, but she was grateful for his sport foam and Kevlar vest.

One of the riders avoided injury thanks to his protective vest when he was thrown from a bull that attempted to gore him. The rodeo clowns distracted the bull, and Ethan herded it away. His horse proved its own tremendous athletic ability as it avoided the bull's horns, as well. Teresa noticed Grace's knuckles were white as Jack held her hand, but her face betrayed no emotion.

Teresa's heart lurched when she saw Joaquin leap up to the pipe fence and swing a leg over. He looked in the direction of the VIP seating. She prayed and gripped Angel's hand tightly, mesmerized by the sight of the huge bull they had just fought to load into the chute.

"All right, folks. Y'all be honest with me now," the announcer began in his west-Texan twang. "How many of you are *really* rooting for the bulls tonight?" The audience laughed and many cheered. "Our final competitor of the evening is up now. Y'all cheer for Joaquin Martinez as he takes on CC, or vice versa, cheer on CC as he takes on Joaquin!"

The crowds roared as Joaquin prepared to ride the humongous beast. Angel leaned to her and said, "I know you're scared, Teresa. Joaquin knows you're scared. He wants to show you what he loves to do. It's violent and often ugly, but he's *good*. Listen, you can tell by the applause they know he's going to do well on CC. Smile real big and wave. Show Joaquin you're *proud* of him. You want him focused on that bull. Give him what he needs, beautiful," Angel said, urging her.

Teresa burst from her seat as Joaquin perched on the rail, and put her index and ring finger to her lips, the hand that displayed his wedding band, and gave an eardrum-shattering whistle.

Anyone would have thought he'd won the lottery. An idiotic, lopsided grin split his face, and he grasped his chest with both hands over his heart. All the cowboys around him laughed and then looked into the stands for the source of his goofy behavior. She waved at him and blew a kiss before sitting next to Angel again.

"That there, ladies and gentlemen, is the look of a newly-wedded *man in love* as he is cheered on by his lovely new wife and his brother, Angel, whom you may remember as saddle-bronc champion from two years ago. Give 'em a round, folks."

Joaquin blew her a kiss then turned very seriously to the business at hand. She glanced uncertainly at Angel, but he smiled and shrugged.

"Don't worry about it, beautiful. If anybody says something, we'll just tell them the announcer misspoke. It doesn't matter to us what any of them think. We like to see you happy and free like this."

Joaquin mounted the bull, and his motions as he adjusted the rope over his riding hand were tight and energetic before becoming motionless. He gave a small nod, and the gate was yanked open. The massive, 1,800-pound bull exploded from the chute, and Teresa could have sworn she felt the vibration of his angry snorting, and pounding hooves in her chest as he thrashed and bucked.

CC's massive rear legs shot off the ground, and he began a twisting, rolling motion, turning and bucking in a tight circle to the right then twisting again, and began an even faster twisting motion to the left. Joaquin rode him with athletic elegance, his free arm swinging wide and clear, balancing him as he stayed astride the bull.

He spurred the bull, which switched directions again, snorting furiously as all four hooves left the ground, and he arched and twisted again. Each time the great beast made contact with the compacted dirt of the arena, Teresa felt it in her chest. She sat in awe, watching as Joaquin rode out each bucking wave, his arm stretched out long behind him over his head. The bull pitched forward, trying to buck him over his horns, and Joaquin held on tight and spurred him into another rolling circle.

The buzzer sounded, and the arena erupted in cheers as he leapt triumphantly from CC right behind Ethan on his horse and rode back to the gate as the bull was rousted out of the arena by the other rider.

It was then that Teresa noticed she was standing, along with Angel, who had Michael in his arms. Michael was yelling and waving at the top of his lungs. She sent up a grateful prayer to God that Michael hadn't seen Joaquin get hurt tonight.

Then the thought struck her.

Michael was probably going to want to do this, too. Teresa filed that away for later thought. *Later* she would ponder how she'd be able to watch her son ride an 1,800-pound bull. She was just grateful Joaquin had been successful.

Feeling like a limp noodle, she sat back down. Grace caught her eye and gave her a wink and an exaggerated sigh of relief. Angel hugged her and said, "That's how it's *supposed* to look. That was a good ride, all eight seconds. I'll bet he tells you later that ride was for you."

"Wow," she said feebly. "That was amazing."

The arena broke out in wild applause a second later when his score flashed on the scoreboard. Ninety-one point five. Everyone from the Divine Creek Ranch leapt to their feet, cheering and hollering.

Down on the dirt in the arena, Joaquin did a triumphant fist pump and looked up in the stands. Teresa waved and blew him kisses, and his face glowed with happiness as he blew a kiss back to her before sauntering from the dirt floor of the arena, his chaps waving and flapping with each movement.

"Daddy rode that bull good, huh, Mommy?" Michael said, his eyes glowing with excitement.

Two more riders took their turns, finishing out their eight seconds, but with less stellar scores.

Michael turned to Teresa. "Mommy, I need to use the potty."

Angel offered, but Teresa assured him they would be fine, and she led Michael from the stands. He had, of course, worn his full cowboy outfit. Hat, bandana, plaid shirt, denim vest, jeans, belt, chaps, spurs, and boots. Several friendly people called congratulations out to her as she hurried him to the potty. Like any other red-blooded American boy that age, he'd waited until the last second to tell her he needed to go. She hurried him into the restroom as he hummed desperately. She helped him with his chaps and then let him do his thing.

"Holy guacamole! Ay! Chihuahua!" he exclaimed as he tinkled. She doubled over trying to hold in her laughter.

Teresa heard the scuffle of several pairs of boots approaching outside. A dulcet, sexy voice said in a steely tone, "Oh, no you *don't*, Judith. Why can't you leave well enough alone? You've had him, and now he's off the market."

An angry-sounding, whiney voice replied, "Don't act all high and mighty with me, Gwen. Seems I recall it was you going back to the hotel with him at Christmas. You're not going to dictate to me what I can or can't do. It's not fair, and it's not right that she claims them *both*. I'm giving her a *piece of my fucking mind*." Teresa felt chills go up her back. Thankfully, Michael was singing to himself, unaware of the exchange taking place outside the ladies' room entrance.

"Oh, no, you're not, potty mouth. Turn around. See? We've been keeping an eye on you and your group of cohorts from backstage. Joaquin knew her little boy would need the potty sooner or later, and we knew you all would try something if everyone was distracted. Mmm-mmm, what a shame. Look at all those prime, *single, available* cowboys watching all of *you* make asses of yourselves. We had our chance, and he made his choice. As to whether or not she claimed both of them, that's none of your business. Hmm," the unknown voice chuckled before continuing, "interesting how fast your friends scatter, Judith."

"It ain't right!"

"And you're such a good judge of what's wrong and right. Puh-lease! Go find another man, and leave them alone."

The whiney voice growled something, which Teresa was glad she couldn't understand, and evidently walked away.

The rest of the exchange had been clearly audible, but thankfully, Michael had not paid any attention as he sang "Big Green Tractor" while he finished his business. Boot heels made soft, leathery sounds as a beautiful woman in her early thirties came slowly around the cinder block partition that formed a privacy barrier to the outer concourse. She was blonde and dressed in jeans, royal-blue western shirt, cowgirl hat, big silver buckle, and boots. When Teresa saw the blonde's reflection in the large mirror, she realized the young woman had a numbered placate pinned to the back of her shirt. The barrel-racer girl.

"You okay in here?" she asked, sincerely smiling at Teresa. Teresa nodded silently as the woman continued, "We've been watching out for you. Joaquin's helping at the chute, but he saw you leave the stands with your little boy and got my attention. I saw how the girls were acting toward you earlier and overheard some things they were saying. I got over here as fast as I could." She grinned as Michael exited the stall while zipping up then she squatted down. "Well, hey, little-mister-cowboy-man. You riding tonight?"

Michael smiled and went right up to her, giving her a high five. "No, ma'am. I'm a little too little, just yet. But Joaquin and Angel are gonna teach me how. You rode the barrels real good earlier. Shootfire, you're fast, pretty cowboy lady!" he said and smacked his hands together in a sliding motion. Teresa definitely detected an exaggerated version of Angel and Joaquin's Texan twang in his speech.

Then he did something that shocked Teresa and the girl both. Giving the young woman a twinkling, flirtatious grin, he put his arms around her neck and hugged her.

"Well, thank you, little-mister-cowboy-man."

He allowed her to lift him as she stood up, holding him on her left hip before handing him to Teresa. They looked at each other and had to laugh. Just like that, a friendship was born.

The cowgirl put her hand to her blushing cheek and said, "Oh, you *so* can tell he's been hanging around Joaquin and Angel. The women are going to be defenseless against that charm. I'm Gwen Henderson, by the way," she said, holding out her hand, which Teresa shook. Teresa couldn't help but take a liking to the girl.

"Congratulations on your performance in the barrel racing. Looks like you're going to win it."

"Well, it's not over yet. Those other riders may do better tomorrow night. We'll see. I apologize that you had to hear that confrontation. I thought that it was better to stop them before they got in here, especially with the boy around. You probably heard more than you wanted to, though," Gwen said, averting her eyes as a rosy blush stole over her cheeks.

Teresa patted her forearm. "The past is the past. Joaquin thought it best that I know a little of his 'prolific' history so I would be prepared for tonight. He and Angel warned me about those women and that they are…territorial. I appreciate you stopping those girls. Little cowboys don't need to know about all of that," she said as she helped Michael wash his hands in the sink.

They exited the bathroom together, and Gwen chatted with her for a few more seconds, walking her back to the spectator stands. Michael went to Gwen, and she squatted down to him.

"Good luck tomorrow night, pretty cowboy lady. I'll be cheering for you," he said and gave her a quick peck on the cheek, batting his eyelashes and flashing his twinkly-eyed grin again.

Gwen hugged him and pecked his cheek. Still squatting, she said, "I'll see you on the back of a bull one of these years, little-mister-cowboy-man. I'll be cheering you on, too. Take good care of your mama."

"Yes, ma'am. I will," he said and tugged on his hat.

She rose and said, "Congratulations, Teresa. Thanks for not holding the past against me. He deserves a good woman like you. They both do. See you later."

"Thanks for watching out for us, Gwen. We'll be cheering for you tomorrow night."

"Thanks!" she called as she sauntered away, a big smile on her face.

Chapter Thirty-two

Adam Davis strode down the concourse, locating Gwendolyn easily in the thin crowd. The spectators in the stands roared with laughter and applause at the rodeo clowns' comedic antics.

"Hey, sweetheart. Everything okay with Teresa?"

Adam had been helping Joaquin when Joaquin happened to look up into the stands and saw Teresa helping Michael down the aisle to the exit. They had been keeping an eye out for her after the other girls made it clear that they resented her presence there. Gwendolyn looked triumphant and a little smug.

"Yeah. You were doing right to keep an eye on Teresa. A whole shitload of buckle bunnies were ready to go in the ladies' room after her. Seems they think that it's unfair she claims both handsome Martinez men."

Adam scoffed. "I was there Christmas night, Gwen. From the looks of things, it was more like *they* claimed her."

"She's beautiful. And that little *cowboy* of hers! *Dayum*! You can tell who he's been hanging around. He's gonna be just like all the other men from the Divine Creek Ranch. Chivalrous, handsome, and flirtatious. Speaking of chivalrous, thanks for coming to check on me, but I had them in hand."

"We should have sent reinforcements with you. I hope those gals are not going to be a problem every night."

"Probably best to escort the ladies when they're in the concourse. Those gals wanted blood with little Michael nearby. I want to go *slap* them all now," she said, getting herself worked up all over again.

Adam grinned at her. "Wow, you're a little bloodthirsty. I'm sure Joaquin and Angel will keep an eye on Teresa from now on."

"You should probably escort your wife, as well, Adam. Wait till the bunnies get wind that she's *claimed* the three of you. Life's not fair to the loose and slutty, I guess." She laughed with him as they headed back to the area behind the chutes.

* * * *

Joaquin groaned loudly as he settled his aching body into the tub of hot water Teresa had drawn for him and dissolved Epsom salts into. He groaned again as he sank down, submerging himself to his chin. The heat soaked into his sore muscles, and he let out a sigh of relief.

"Feels good," he murmured before he slipped under the water's surface, his long hair floating in the water around him. He came back up, smoothing his hair back from his forehead. Teresa sat down on the toilet seat as Joaquin sank under the water again, smiling at him when he opened his eyes as he emerged.

He sighed as he sat against the sloped backrest of the Jacuzzi tub and grinned back. "Care to join me, sugar?" he asked in a husky drawl.

Teresa grinned and said, "You're incorrigible. Don't you think you should rest?" The words were coming from her mouth, but he didn't think she really believed them. Her gaze strayed down his body like a caress he could actually feel.

"I consider baths to be very restful and a bath with a sexy woman *particularly* regenerative. See? I'm feeling like a new man already," he said playfully, gesturing to his rapidly hardening cock. "Michael's already in bed, and there's plenty of room in this tub."

"Not really," she replied doubtfully, but he noted the look of longing in her eyes. She was definitely coming in the tub tonight. Literally.

"When we build the new house, we're going to get you an even bigger tub, one that will hold all three of us."

"Promise?" she asked, blushing as he turned up the high beams on his charm.

"Of course. Please? It's *lonesome* in here without you," he cajoled, aches and pains all forgotten. He chortled happily when she stood up, slipping out of her blue jeans. "That's my girl. I'm feeling *better all the time*." He palmed his cock, stroking lightly as she lifted the hem of her top, revealing her transparent, black lace bra beneath.

His cock grew heavy and twitched in his hand. Damn, he loved that bra. It was black but sheer, so he could see every detail of her breasts. The underwire was disguised by a wide band of pretty lace as if it were offering her breasts up to be worshipped. She blushed again as she watched him stroke his cock.

Quickly pinning up her hair, she removed the bra and her black lace thong and stepped carefully into the hot water, sighing luxuriantly. He loved the sight of her pretty waxed pussy.

"It got chilly sitting in the spectator stands all evening. The hot water feels so good," she crooned as she carefully sat down and laid her calves outside of his, easing back against the other end of the bathtub. She sighed as he caressed her little feet, massaging her arches, enjoying the delicate feel of the little bones and tendons beneath her skin. After strapping himself onto nearly a ton of raging bull, she felt even more precious to him, her dainty feet like the finest china in his hands.

Teresa gasped when he gently tugged her toward him in the tub. He pulled her over him in the water as he slid down a little until she was straddling his hips, his pulsating cock pressed against the satiny flesh of her pussy. She splashed a little as she moved closer over him, bringing her knees farther forward. He'd never grow tired of the feel of her hot, silky cunt pressed to him. Never.

His eyelids slid closed in pleasure, and he moaned as she moved against him, saying, "I thought you were amazing tonight. So strong and in control. I was proud of you, proud to be yours," she murmured as she kissed his chest above the water line.

"You about bowled me over, blowing me kisses and whistling like that." He swirled hot water over her and stroked her back and ass. "I gave that bull every bit I had just for you."

She rubbed her breasts against his chest and giggled when he growled softly.

"Joaquin, when you get off of each bull safely, *that's* what you're doing for me. So tomorrow night will be the same routine?"

"Pretty much," he murmured, pressing against her as his hands swept over her ass. He needed inside of her more than he needed to breathe at the moment. "How about you raise up a little bit there, where you're rubbing so sweetly, slide down, and take a little ride of your own?" he asked, watching as the flames of lust lit in her eyes at his sultry words.

Biting her bottom lip, she slid forward against him in the water, brushing his lips with hers, before sliding back when he flexed his hips. His cock obligingly bobbed up, positioning the very engorged beast at her slick entrance. They both groaned as her wet heat enveloped him tightly. She pulled up and slid down again, farther along his hard length each time.

"We're going to flood the bathroom, sloshing water everywhere," she said then moaned as she undulated sexily, seating him to the hilt and smiling when he groaned loudly in bliss.

"Not if we move nice and slow, sugar. That feels so good right now."

"Does it?" she asked, grinding her hips against him, swirling her pussy around the base of his cock over and over, and drawing a deep moan from him.

With her face tucked against his throat, she whispered, "Have I told you lately how much I love your long, thick cock inside me? I adore every irresistible inch. A perfect fit."

His heart pounded in his chest at her words, keeping time with the throbbing in his cock as he slid inside her slick pussy with her movements. He slid his hands over her back and down to the delicious curve of her ass, squeezing gently.

"Thank you, sugar. Your snug little pussy feels like I'm sliding into hot, slippery satin. I want to stay inside you forever and just feel you move against me. Mmmm, like that. Yeah." He sighed deeply as she moved over him in a slow, grinding circle again. Joaquin felt her pussy slip against him as her body released another rush of honey, and he knew she must be enjoying his whispered words.

Enjoying the little shuddering moan that escaped her lips, he thrust into her in small, insistent movements. Teresa moved with him, lightly tugging on his cock with her sexy, sensuous body, the hot water swirling around them. He kept his movements small and allowed her to move on him at her own unhurried pace.

He groaned in pleasure, encouraging her with more whispered erotic words as her pussy drew tighter on him, a sure sign she was about to come.

Joaquin let her have her way, watching as she moved gracefully over him. Teresa looked down at him, her eyes filled with rapture, her pussy rippling intensely around his cock. She threw her head back and bucked her hips against his, grinding her clit at the base of his cock. Her breath came in little staccato, high-pitched pants as she finally gave into her orgasm, a heartfelt moan rushing from her lips.

He growled approvingly as her pussy pulsed and contracted around him in caressing waves, timed with the undulations of her hips. After she finished, she fucked him in graceful, fluid strokes, gazing languidly in his eyes and leaning down to kiss him.

Joaquin swept his hands over her ass in a caress. She shuddered, which made her pussy clench on his cock again. He slid his fingers down the cleft of her ass, and she moaned again as he pressed a fingertip to her asshole. He massaged the tight ring of muscles, and her body responded by flexing and tightening on his cock.

Encouraging her as her eyes lit once again with the promise of an orgasm, he growled deeply and whispered erotic, naughty things to her as the second wave overtook her. This time, the tightening pulses of her coming pussy pulled him under with her, and the wave of ecstasy shot down his spine as his release streamed into her pulsing cunt.

After they'd wrung every ounce of pleasure from every last surging wave, he drew her to him tightly as they both caught their breaths. Damn it felt good to hold her against him like this, so warm and yielding. Her breath tickled in the hairs on his chest, and he sighed at the feel of her fingertips lightly caressing his back in the hot water.

Teresa shivered lightly, and he remembered that the half of her not pressed to him was exposed to the cool air while he was engulfed in the hot water and her silky heat. Holding her hips, he withdrew from her and slid her down in the water beside him to warm her. She smiled up at him, the water coming up to her chin, and she lifted the hand he'd used to hold the rope on the bull.

She twined her fingers with his. "It already looks better, not quite as swollen around the knuckles," she murmured, then pressed her lips to his knuckles.

"The hot water and Epsom salts helped."

Looking up at him, she changed the subject. "You should have seen Michael *flirting* with Gwen tonight. Three years old and flirting with a grown woman," she said, laughing good-naturedly.

Joaquin chuckled and scrubbed a hand over his face. "He's been hanging around us, learning how to treat the ladies."

"Michael gave her your little sideways, twinkling grin, and she was putty in his hands and even kissed his little cheek. He called her 'pretty cowboy lady'," she said with a soft chortle. "We're going to be cheering for her tomorrow night."

"Wow, baby, you're really something," he whispered, squeezing her gently.

Teresa nuzzled his chest. "Forget the past, and embrace the future, honey. I made a new friend tonight."

"You know, I'm embarrassed to say it, but I didn't even know her name until today." Regret made his chest ache, which he tried to rub away.

"Honey, she's our friend, Gwen, now. We move forward, and don't feel bad about what we can't change." Teresa snuggled to his chest and soaked with him quietly for a minute.

"Angel says Michael talked him into taking him on the kiddie rides and the ponies tomorrow."

"Yes. He's excited about it. I'll let you finish your soak and go see what Angel is doing," Teresa said as she kissed him, her breasts pressed against his chest. He enjoyed the sight of the water sluicing off her body as she stood in the tub.

"I'll be out in a bit," he said. After pausing to watch her, he reached out to her. "Teresa?"

He caressed her delectable ass as she bent down and turned the hot water back on to refill the tub up to its previous level. She moaned as he brushed his fingertip between her pussy lips, which were already wet with her silky juices again.

"Hmmm?" She climbed carefully from the tub and looked over her shoulder as she wrapped herself in a towel. She released her beautiful black hair from its clip and shook her head so it cascaded around her shoulders. She took his breath away.

"Thank you." His heart swelled with happiness as he gazed into her loving brown eyes.

"You're welcome," she whispered back, trailing her palm over his cheek. He turned his face toward her and kissed her fingertips. She smiled and dried off then slid into Angel's thick fleece robe and winked at him before leaving the steamy bathroom.

* * * *

The bedroom was dark as Teresa entered it. The fireplace provided the only illumination, the heat thankfully taking the damp chill from the room. It had begun raining on the ride home from the fairgrounds. Her eyes adjusted quickly, and she chuckled when she saw Angel lying in bed looking out the window at the starry sky. He turned and smiled at her as she padded barefoot to the bed, drawing the covers back for her. She allowed the robe to slide from her arms and laid it over the end of the bed. When he drew her to him, the first thing she noticed as he kissed her was his thickened cock pressed against her thigh.

"The sound of you coming earlier with Joaquin got me very hard, and I've been fantasizing about you ever since." He brushed his lips over her collarbone and slid his fingers up to the lower swell of her breast, his thumb teasing her nipple.

"About me?" Her pussy quivered with need for him. "What were your fantasies like?" More moisture flowed to her aching slit as his lips followed his hand over her breast.

Angel pulled her beneath him and kissed her throat again. Her hands slid up his rib cage, over the thick muscles of his back, then down to his hips and ass.

He spoke as his lips continued to trail over her throat, sending shivers up and down her torso. "You have no idea how beautiful you were to us tonight. You *radiate* love."

Her heart throbbed as she listened to his words, and she couldn't find her voice.

Drawing her even closer, Angel murmured, "You make me want to take you to bed and lay you under me. I want to kiss my way down your body until I reach the sweet place between your thighs. I want to hear your sighs, moans, and little cries as I lick and kiss your pussy until you come, moaning my name. After you're finished coming, I want to lick my way back up your body and worship and suckle at these lovely breasts." Angel murmured as he suckled a nipple. His sensual words were making her mindless in her arousal.

"Th-then what?"

"After your nipples are nice and pink, I want to lift your delicate little feet and place one on each of my shoulders. You'll open your knees for me to make sure I can see your pussy as it opens for my cock and allows me to slide into your silky body. The way your wet heat surrounds me as I slide into you is incredible, Teresa. I don't know if words can describe how you feel to me when I push my cock inside your tight little cunt and the way it feels when your muscles grip me when you come. I love the way your little pussy runs with your juices for me, especially when I tell you what I'm going to do to you. I'll bet you're dripping with it right now, aren't you?"

Teresa was red hot for him, right now. A moan of need escaped from her throat as she nodded, her hips thrusting against him.

His voice grew deeper with need as he whispered to her, "I'd watch as my cock slides deep, then comes the best part, when I slide out, drenched in your cream. I'd fuck you nice and slow, enjoying pushing every inch inside you until I have chills running up and down my spine from fighting my own release. I'd take hold of your hips and hold you *just right* so my cock is rubbing your G-spot, and I'd fuck you until you come so hard you scream. Then I'd spread your legs wide in my hands and fuck your hot, wet little pussy." He groaned, sliding his fingers through her extremely slick slit. "And I'd fill it full of my cum. After we were both satisfied, I'd stay buried deep inside you and roll us over. I'd make sure you're comfortable then I'd let you fall asleep on me and let you stay that way all night."

His fingers slid again through her warm slit but avoided her clit. Shakily she murmured, "That sounds beautiful. I think I almost came when you talked about it."

"Well, then you should let me see to that. I'd love to make that fantasy a reality, although it's not much of a fantasy if you ask me. Pretty tame, but it's what I'm thinking about right now. What about you? Do you have any fantasies you're entertaining?"

Oh, hell yes! Let me get my list!

"You know I am. I've been thinking about making love with both of you, together," she said. Her cheeks warmed at the sexy grin he gave her. Clearly, he was on board with that fantasy. Her pussy throbbed when he stroked a fingertip lightly alongside her clit.

"Oh yeah? You've been using your plugs?"

They used them sometimes when they made love, filling her ass with one while one made love to her and she went down on the other. Another shiver ran down her spine as she recalled how hard she came when they did and how much they'd enjoyed it, as well. Teresa loved it because the sensation of being filled that tightly intensified her orgasm but also because she knew it moved her closer and closer to being able to take them both at the same time.

"Yes, Angel. I've been using the thickest one all week. I think I'm ready for you both."

Angel looked into her eyes and said, "Let one of us take you anally a couple of times, and then we'll see about the next step."

"But the plugs—"

"Please trust me. It'll hurt a little, and you'll need time to adjust. I want the first time we both take you to be pleasurable for you because, once we both take you, we'll want you that way on a regular basis for the rest of our lives."

His words sent a shiver down her spine, and wetness flowed from her pussy at the erotic image playing through her mind. The moisture slipped down to her anus, sensitizing it, and she undulated against him.

"Tonight?" she whispered hopefully. She moaned when he shook his head.

"I was the first to make love to you," he whispered as his hand slid down her torso. Panting, she moaned again in bliss when his fingertips slid into her slit and one finger dipped inside her drenched pussy. "Sliding into your tight little cunt for the first time was an incredible privilege for me. I want you to have another memory of a first experience that you share with Joaquin. I had your first kiss. He had your first orgasm. I made love to you first. I want him to have this," he said as his finger slipped from her pussy, drenched in her juices. He slid down to her asshole and gently massaged and pressed on the tight ring of muscles. She moaned as every nerve ending there flared to life.

Speaking up before she was no longer capable of speech, Teresa said, "You're right, Angel. It should be his, but—"

"But we both know Joaquin needs his rest now."

Teresa nodded with a little pout, which made him chuckle. "He's giving us time alone while he soaks in the tub. Why don't you let me do as I told you earlier, and I'll talk to him about it afterward or in the morning?" he said as his tongue followed the path of his hand down her quaking torso.

Angel kissed his way down her body and worshipped her just as he told her he would, bringing her to three heart-rending, beautiful orgasms.

* * * *

Joaquin joined them later, feeling relaxed and sleepy. He smiled at the replete image of Teresa, already sound asleep, lying nestled on his brother's body as he stroked her back, her long black hair spread around him like a shawl. The covers still lay bunched at the foot of the bed where they had kicked them during their lovemaking.

"*That* is a beautiful sight," Joaquin whispered as he came to the foot of the bed. In the dim glow from the fireplace he could see his brother's cock was still buried to the hilt inside her. Her body was still flushed from the orgasms he'd had the pleasure of listening to from the bathroom. Joaquin had enjoyed each little panting cry and moan when she came as though she were about to die from pleasure.

Joaquin joined them in the bed and got comfortable.

Angel smiled at him and said, "You did well tonight, Joaquin. Do you need to ice your hand again?"

"No, it should be fine. Soaking it helped take down the inflammation. Tonight's ride was good," he whispered, flexing his hand carefully. "Our little kitten's a tiger when she wants to be, isn't she?"

"She sure is," Angel whispered, kissing the top of her head lightly as he continued stroking her back. "Teresa was so excited for you once she got over her fear. She surprised me earlier. She's ready to take the next step with us. She wants to try anal sex, and we both agreed you should be her first."

"Me? But—"

"That's what we want. You should be her first there."

"She say when?" Joaquin asked, gazing down at her relaxed, trusting form. He caressed a lock of her silken hair between his fingertips.

"Soon. It makes her pretty hot to talk about it. Discuss it with her in the morning, and you'll have an idea of when."

"I love her so much," Joaquin whispered, reaching out to stroke the curve of her back down to her ass.

"Me, too. I can't imagine life without her and the little man," Angel murmured back, stroking her hip.

"We got lucky, didn't we?" Joaquin said over the lump that had formed in his throat.

"Damn lucky." Angel yawned.

Teresa shivered as the flush left her and the cool of the room started to sink in. Joaquin pulled the covers from beneath their feet and covered the three of them then lay back as the crackling flames in the fireplace died down. Contentment flowed through him.

Teresa's breath hitched in her sleep, and she sighed softly and snuggled closer to Angel, drawing her little hands under her cheek.

Joaquin glanced at Angel, saw the sappy grin on his brother's face, and chuckled. "Just like a sick kitten to a hot brick."

Chapter Thirty-three

Joaquin stood with Angel outside the little fenced enclosure, watching as the owner of the tame little ponies helped Michael onto the pony's back and stayed by him, leading the animal around the circle.

Joaquin observed Michael in his perch. "You know, he looks almost…bored," Joaquin noted as Michael confidently leaned forward to pat the pony.

Angel chuckled and nodded in agreement. "Michael feels comfortable up there. We've gotten him used to being on the back of a horse," Angel said as he whistled appreciatively at Teresa, who was returning from buying more ride tickets.

She blushed as Angel said, "You sure do look beautiful tonight, Teresa."

Joaquin wholeheartedly agreed. "Mmm!"

They pulled her in between the two of them, and she leaned on the fence, watching Michael as he conversed happily with the owner. Angel wrapped an arm around her hips and hugged her to him. Joaquin slid his hand through her hair, sweeping the thick, jet-black length over her shoulder as she turned her face to smile up at him. He leaned down and kissed her gently then clasped her hand in his. They stood there like that in companionable silence for a few minutes while Michael finished his ride.

Once he had exited the little corral, Michael made a beeline for the tent where a small mechanical bull had been set up for the kids to ride.

When the man at the entry gate told him he wasn't tall enough, *by a lot,* Michael didn't pitch a fit but merely pulled them all around to the side where he could watch through the nylon netting of the tent. A worker helped a boy onto the mechanical bull.

The boy held on for several seconds before sailing through the air and landing on the mats, giggling. His older brother helped him up and then climbed on himself. He seemed more confident and stayed on the bull for quite some time. For his age, Joaquin thought he did well.

Michael's eyes were big and round as he turned to his parents and said, "Man, did you see that? I'm gonna ride that bull when I get taller, just like he did."

"Yes, you are, little dude," Joaquin said, lifting Michael onto his shoulders. He grinned when Michael automatically balanced with him and braced against his daddy's hands at his ankles.

"How about a corn dog, Daddy?" Michael said, leaning to the side to look at Joaquin then over at Angel.

"Sure, let's all get one," Joaquin said. They walked to the vendor and placed their orders.

Joaquin looked over Teresa's shoulder and saw three of the girls from the other night walking by, giving her the evil eye before noticing that he was watching them. His heart plummeted in his chest as he recalled that he was better acquainted with each of them than he *ought* to be. What had he been thinking? He lost his appetite on the spot.

One of the girls, a rail-thin brunette, raised her voice a little as she drew near Teresa's back and sniped, "She should be ashamed of herself." The young woman threw her hair over her shoulder and would have sauntered away, but her path was blocked by Gwen Henderson.

"Who I feel ashamed of is your mama for not teaching you better manners, Judith Bowers. You needed more whippings when you were little and never got them. By the way, that drunk cowboy you took back to your trailer left the door hanging wide open when he finally climbed out of it a little while ago. You *might* want to go check on it. Close your mouth before you catch flies, honey. Leave decent married folks alone."

Joaquin noticed Teresa's smile as she looked on in awe at Gwen Henderson, who wasn't finished yet. To the other girls with Judith, she said, "You girls need a new role model." In dismissal, she turned her back and smiled. "Hey, how's my handsome little-cowboy-man tonight?" She shook Michael's hand from his perch on Joaquin's shoulders.

"Doing good, pretty cowboy lady," Michael answered jovially. Joaquin wished he could get a look at Michael's face, but he'd be willing to bet Michael had the high beams turned on, going by the daffy charmed grin on Gwen's face. "Been riding the rides and getting a corn dog now."

"Ooh goody! I think I'll get one, too. How're you doing, Teresa? Don't mind those girls. Judith can't resist getting a dig, and I couldn't ignore her catty remark. Not all the girls are that mean, by the way."

Teresa introduced Angel to Gwen. Joaquin thought he might have seen a shadow of guilt in Gwen's eyes when he greeted her. He could see that she genuinely liked Teresa.

Jack, Grace, Ethan, and Adam happened upon them in the midway, and Gwen had a chance to get to know her a little. Joaquin was comforted by the thought that Teresa was right. He could keep feeling guilty, or he could suck it up and embrace the future.

* * * *

The second night of the rodeo was as exciting as the first and not quite as scary for Teresa now that she knew what to expect. She'd brought her camera and was able to get a few good photographs of both Joaquin and Ash in action. Their scores meant Joaquin and Ash made it into the short go-round the following night.

Teresa was pleased to see Juliana Meyer show up. Juliana was unable to watch Ash compete the previous night because she had to work. Teresa commiserated with her, watching the horrified look on Juliana's face when Ash's bronc had bolted upright off of all four hooves out of the chute before going nuts trying to buck him off. The cast was off her wrist, and she confirmed that her back was completely healed.

After the rodeo, their group went to the dance for a little while. Teresa noticed that Angel and Joaquin and Grace's men never let them out of their sight. They weren't bothered by any of the girls from the carnival midway. Neither did they see the mouthy Judith again.

Juliana seemed to enjoy herself at the dance with Ash afterward. Teresa noticed that Juliana also garnered her share of dirty looks from some of the buckle bunnies at the dance. Ash kept her close at his side the whole evening.

* * * *

On the third night, Teresa protested when Angel escorted her to the food vendors for a soda refill then to the ladies' room for a bathroom break once they were inside the arena building.

"Angel, you don't have to do this. I'm a grown woman."

Angel gave her a flirtatious smile. "I know, beautiful." His eyes took on a harder gleam, and he continued, "But those girls could have cornered you in the ladies' room the other night when Michael was with you. I take that seriously. I'm not doing this because I don't think you can handle yourself. I'm doing it because I don't trust that girl, Judith, or her friends. I *need* to protect you."

She could hear the sincerity in his voice and knew there was no point in arguing.

Grace joined them with Adam close on her heels. The men waited on the concourse while the women went into the restroom. One of the stalls opened, and Grace entered then Teresa waited for the next one. Unfortunately, it became available because Judith Bowers exited it.

The thin brunette did a double take, and her lip curled as she said, "Oh, crap. *You* again. Where's your buddy to take up for you, huh? Not around to save your *little feelings* this time?" Judith glared as Teresa closed the bathroom door behind her to take care of her business. Not feeling the girl deserved any respect, she spoke to her over the stall door.

"I don't *need* anyone to take up for me. I haven't done anything wrong." Teresa heard Grace gasp from the next stall. This situation was utterly ridiculous. It took a lot to piss Teresa off, but she knew she'd just reached that point.

"You say I've 'claimed' them as though they wear my brand. They both pursued me and convinced me that they loved *me*. You tell me where that's unfair to you."

"It's not fair, you takin' two eligible bachelors like that. It's immoral. And you're all BFF with Gwen Henderson when she just *had* Joaquin at Christmastime!"

Teresa slammed open the stall door and came out ready to have this out. "Not fair to who? *You?* I doubt the notion they were single even came into your thoughts until they weren't. If you adored Angel so much, why didn't you make a play for him two years ago? You've already had Joaquin. If you were so good, why didn't he keep you? You are one of those people who wants what you can't have.

"And as for Gwen herself, the big difference between her and you is that she understands that Joaquin has a commitment to me, and she's not acting like I *stole her man* from her."

Judith's plan had backfired if she had hoped to inspire an indignant response from the women over her declaration that Teresa had two men. Teresa felt Grace's reassuring presence beside her as she had her say once and for all. She was surprised by how calm she felt.

"My friend and I have had to be escorted every second that we've been here because you can't resist backbiting," Teresa said evenly as she approached the red-faced Judith. "But I'm here to tell you right now, Judith Bowers, you'd better back off from me—"

"Tell her, honey!" Fiona Wills said, laughing from one of the sinks.

Teresa continued, "Because I have had—"

"Go girl," a woman she didn't know said.

"—*just* about enough—"

"Tell her how you *really* feel," Grace said then giggled.

"—of you!" Teresa finished with her finger right in Judith's face.

Judith gave a hateful glare to the other women while backing out of the restroom then yelled at them, "Y'all are all a bunch of fucking idiots! You don't even know! Both these bitches are married to more than one man. That slut has two husbands, and this *whore* has three. That's immoral!"

The woman who spoke up earlier, whom Teresa didn't know, said, "Judith Bowers, you gotta lot of damn gall accusing someone else of immorality. If you had as many sticking *out* of you as you've had stuck *in* you, you'd look like a porcupine. I don't know these ladies, but I do know their husbands and that they're involved in committed relationships, the circumstances of which are none of *my* business."

Commanding respect as she stood there with her hands on her hips, she pointed her finger at Judith and said, "I don't cotton to being called an idiot, nor do I think their husbands appreciate you calling their wives names. You should've stayed to the periphery where riffraff like you belongs. Pack up that tramp trailer and be out of here within the hour." The serious look in the woman's eyes changed to humor as she directed a grin over Judith's shoulder. "Oh, *hello*, Angel. Hello, Adam. Good to see y'all!"

Teresa watched as Judith turned and looked up into Angel and Adam's faces, their eyes glowing with anger at having heard the names she'd called Grace and Teresa. Judith wisely ducked her head and strode from the arena.

The woman gave a friendly hug to both men and said, "I am so sorry that happened. If we'd known she was harassing y'all, we would have asked her to leave sooner. I'll tell Caughlin, and he'll make sure she leaves and doesn't cause any more trouble."

Angel said, "Thank you, Mrs. McIntyre. We appreciate that. Until we heard Teresa give her a piece of her mind, we didn't realize that girl was in there."

Mrs. McIntyre cackled happily. "Woo! Did she ever! So, these are your lovely brides, huh?" she added, turning to Teresa and Grace.

"That they are, ma'am," Adam replied as he introduced Grace and Teresa to the wife of the rodeo's operator, Caughlin McIntyre.

Several women exited from the bathroom as they stood there talking and nudged Teresa or Grace and gave them the thumbs-up or shared a kind word with them before walking away. Mrs. McIntyre departed to seek out her husband, and the four of them returned to the VIP seating.

The evening got exciting as Ash took second place in bareback bronc riding, which also carried a hefty purse. The short bull-riding round began when the seven top-scoring riders from the previous two days all had a third chance to add to their scores.

Angel groaned when the commentator announced the name of the bull Joaquin would be riding. Teresa looked at him nervously, waiting for a response.

"Texas Bucking Bull of the Year two years ago. I've ridden him before. He's rough and…hooky."

Hooky? That couldn't possibly be a good thing when he was referring to an animal that had horns. "What does 'hooky' mean?"

"Battleship will likely give chase after Joaquin jumps off. He'll try to catch Joaquin with his horns. Joaquin knows him, so he'll stay light on his feet. He's probably pumped about the draw because it could mean a good score for him."

Teresa took Angel's hand and started praying as Joaquin settled onto the bull's back and tightened down the flat rope that would be the only thing keeping him astride the bull. Joaquin and one other rider were in close competition for the first-place prize, and this ride would make the difference.

Michael puffed out his chest and hollered along with everyone else. "Come on, Daddy! You can do it! Ride that bull!" Joaquin became very still as he prepared to ride Battleship. Teresa felt her phone vibrate in her purse at her feet but ignored it, in no frame of mind to answer it.

The gate swung open, and the crowd went crazy. The 1,600-pound bull erupted from the bucking chute, making up what it lacked in weight with a tenacious ability to buck, roll, and twist, rotating back and forth from left to right with no predictability whatsoever.

Teresa kept her eyes on Joaquin and was mesmerized by the way he rode the bull. Exuding confidence, he spurred the bull and *grinned*, moving with the animal like he was a part of him, as though they'd rehearsed beforehand. Nothing Battleship did could unseat his rider. He twisted and turned, kicked his back legs, rolled and even leapt in the air, all to no avail.

The bull snorted angrily and switched directions. Joaquin evidently anticipated it and moved with him in the right direction. The spectators went wild as the buzzer sounded. Teresa watched on, wanting to see for a fact that he would be okay. Joaquin released the tether rope and leapt to the pickup rider's horse and clung to the back of its saddle.

The bull turned angrily and charged, catching Joaquin below his knee and attempting to flip him off the back of the horse. The horse proved to be the better athlete though and maneuvered the rider and his passenger out of the way while the rodeo clowns distracted the bull. The other pickup rider herded Battleship to the exit. Teresa was worried about his knee, but Angel assured her he probably only suffered bruises. Joaquin jumped down, showing he was all right as he landed without difficulty and collected his hat, which had come off in the wild ride.

His score of 92.5 flashed up on the screen, and he jumped in the air triumphantly as the crowd cheered for him. Loud music played as they applauded, and Joaquin did a little victory dance, locating Teresa in the VIP seating and blowing her a big kiss. She smiled and cheered, blowing kisses back to him, and read his lips as he yelled, "I love you," to her. She yelled back and waved as he made his exit while the next rider prepared for his ride.

Gwen joined their group in the stands, excited about Joaquin's high score. Michael got down from Angel's lap and went to sit in Gwen's, giving her a big hug. "I cheered hard for you! You won big, didn't you?"

Gwen kissed his cheek and said, "I sure did! Thank you for cheering me on, little-mister-cowboy-man."

"Yes! Congratulations, Gwen! We're so proud of you," Teresa said, patting her shoulder.

The tension in the arena increased as the final rider of the evening prepared to ride his bull, a massive 1,800-pound monster named Ricochet. Teresa watched with a strange mix of emotions. Obviously, she wanted Joaquin to do well in the scoring, but she didn't want to see this rider get hurt on the back of that bull, which seemed to dwarf the little cowboy. She'd seen him ride the previous nights, and his size seemed to work to his advantage, and he held on with a tenacity that was admirable.

The gate swung open, and his ride started out on a high note, the bull bucking and weaving, trying to get the irritating nuisance off his back. The diminutive cowboy spurred him on, angering him further, and the bull began twisting and rolling. The ride was stellar until the last second when the bull bucked in the direction opposite of what the cowboy anticipated, and he was unseated.

He flew through the air and landed on the dirt floor of the arena. He'd just jumped to his feet as the bull charged and nailed him between his shoulder blades, trampling him ferociously into the dirt.

Screams erupted from the crowd as the rodeo clowns distracted the bull from the rider beneath his hooves, but he returned moments later for another shot at the cowboy, pummeling him again with his heavy horns, knocking the rider unconscious.

Everyone in the stands was on their feet, watching in shock as the rodeo clowns tried with limited success to distract the bull into chasing one of them. He followed one, but then returned for a parting shot to the cowboy's head with his horns. The cowboy was moving, struggling back to consciousness, and was able to curl into a ball and shield his head. The bull rolled him with his horns one last time before taking off for the exit gate.

There was a collective groan and sigh as the bull finally moved off. The rodeo clowns ran to the cowboy, who was curled up on his side, while the paramedics entered the dirt arena rolling a gurney. All the other riders, including Joaquin, were either in the arena with them or perched on the pipe fence. Several took a knee in the arena, removed their cowboy hats, and lowered their heads, praying for the rider who had slumped back, unconscious again.

Teresa saw stars and sat down, taking a deep breath, realizing she'd been holding it since the first impact. Angel sat with her, whispering to her to put her head down and take some deep breaths. Luckily, Michael was still in Gwen's arms, watching the action unfold below them. The thought kept going through her mind that it could have been Joaquin under that bull, and chances were good that someone who loved that cowboy had watched him get savaged by it.

"Just keep breathing, Teresa. I'm sure Rusty will be fine. He has years of experience, and he had his protective gear on. I've seen the same sort of thing happen to Joaquin before."

"Oh, *so not helping* with telling me that," Teresa said weakly as Angel rubbed her back.

He pointed out into the arena and said, "See? Rusty's awake and moving around. His wife is right beside him there. He's talking to her and hugging her. It looked a lot worse than it was."

"Oh, good," she murmured, looking up as the cowboy struggled to his feet amidst cheers from the stands, raising a fist into the air. The cowboy went to Joaquin and shook his hand then gave him a hug before he allowed him and another cowboy to help him from the arena on his own two feet.

Teresa smiled at Angel as he looked over at her, concern on his face. "You okay?"

"Note to self. Don't forget to breathe," she said sheepishly as he slid an arm around her and kissed her cheek.

Angel said, "This sport takes some getting used to. You've been brave."

"*Puh-lease!* I'm the biggest chicken-heart that ever walked the planet," she said, flapping her elbows like a chicken, trying to laugh at herself. He just gave her that flirtatious grin and kissed her again.

"Naw, I think our *kitten* proved earlier that she has the heart of a lion."

Unfortunately, because he didn't last the full eight seconds, the rider received no score for his last ride. The top scores were flashed on the scoreboard screen, and everyone cheered wildly. Joaquin had taken first place. Caughlin McIntyre announced the standings and congratulated all the participants.

Teresa felt her purse vibrate again and reached for her phone. She glanced at the screen, and a chill ran through her as she recognized the phone number. It was a text message from her friend, Delores. Her go-between for communicating with the nursing home in Tillman about her parents.

She tapped her fingertip on the touch screen to open the message.

Honey, you need to call me right away. It's about your mom. Love you.

Angel must have noted the sudden tension in Teresa's body and the change in her demeanor. His arm slid around her waist. "What is it, Teresa?"

"My mom," she whispered with a tremor in her voice as she allowed Angel to look at the message.

"Do you think it's bad news?"

"She wouldn't call in the evening if it wasn't important."

Angel nodded and hugged her. "Then you'd better call her back right away. Joaquin will understand." Teresa tapped the screen on her phone to dial Delores' number, grabbed her purse, and exited the stands, leaving Michael with Angel.

* * * *

Joaquin looked up into the stands, trying to find his family. He located Teresa as she made her way from the stands. Her phone was held to her ear, and the worried look on her face and the hint of concern in Angel's body language told Joaquin something was wrong. He slipped out of the dirt arena and gathered his gear, stuffing the five-thousand-dollar check into his shirt pocket. He grinned and smiled to everyone that patted him on the back and shook his hand, but he felt a deepening sense of urgency to get to his wife. Something was definitely wrong.

He hefted the duffel with his gear in it onto his shoulder and hotfooted it onto the concourse, making his way toward the VIP stands.

Chapter Thirty-four

Teresa sniffled as she gathered clothing and other necessities into a bag for Michael. Angel watched from the door, the concern obvious in his eyes, but left her to her own thoughts. Her mother had a massive stroke earlier that evening, and the eventual outcome was clear. The doctors did not expect her to recover from it, and they were honoring her mother's request to not use heroic measures. Joaquin and Angel promised her that they'd do their best to get her to Tillman in time to see her mother before she passed away.

Zipping up Michael's little suitcase and his backpack, she handed them to Angel as Joaquin brought Michael in to change his clothes. Michael was coming with them because Teresa could not bear to be parted from him, regardless of any circumstances in Tillman.

She left Michael's room and returned to their bedroom, where Joaquin's and Angel's duffels and a garment bag were already packed and ready on the neatly made bed. Teresa tried to think of what she would need to bring with her. She battled with the urge to simply run out of the house, jump in the truck, and speed down the highway to Tillman.

A strange numbness descended as she showered and dressed for the trip. Moving like an automaton to the closet, she methodically pulled out a black outfit and several changes of clothing. Angel and Joaquin had not pressed her to talk unless it was necessary. They seemed to understand that she was preparing herself to say goodbye to her mother. Teresa's heart lurched painfully at that thought. Joaquin's large hand grasping hers drew her from her painful reverie, and she turned to him. He squeezed her hand comfortingly.

"Do you have everything you need?"

Teresa nodded. As she went out the door with Joaquin, she saw Jack standing by the truck talking to Angel, nodding and shaking his hand. Jack gave Teresa a hug, and she got into the truck.

Climbing into the driver's seat, Angel said, "Grace will let the girls know. They'll head out to help in a day or so when we know what is going on. I asked Jack to get hold of Ace and have him come out if he's available."

"Why?" she asked numbly, smoothing her fingertips over Michael's brow as he slept in his car seat.

"Ace has connections, as a private investigator. He helped Jack when Grace's ex-boyfriend was harassing her. Jack said Ace handled another investigation recently with good results. He wasn't real specific, and I didn't want to pry. I think it would be helpful to have him do a little snooping while we're there. While we're in Tillman, I don't want any mishaps with *him* or his parents. I have a feeling that if they get wind you're in town, they may try to make contact with you, which I'd like to avoid."

"Me, too," she quietly murmured. Teresa was sure they would show up at some point in the guise of being "friends" of her mother and father. Selective memory seemed to work for them.

* * * *

Upon arrival at the nursing home in Tillman around four o'clock in the morning, Joaquin helped Teresa from the big truck and kissed her tenderly then climbed into the driver's seat. He watched as Angel and Teresa went into the nursing home to check in with the staff and then drove on to the hotel they'd made reservations at, with Michael still slumbering in his car seat. Joaquin would lie down with Michael for a few hours then they would drive the short distance back to the nursing home to be with Teresa and Angel later in the morning.

Joaquin carried a slumbering Michael into the lobby and got them checked in with no problem. Michael was restless in the unfamiliar bed but curled up to Joaquin, tucking his hands under his chin just like Teresa did when she slept.

Drowsily he said, "Mama sad?"

Joaquin kissed the top of his head and whispered, "Yeah, but she'll be better. You sleep, and then we'll go see her."

"'Kay," Michael murmured around a yawn.

Joaquin caressed Michael's head, and they both eventually drifted off.

A little while later, Joaquin rose from the bed. After tucking a snoring Michael in under the covers, he locked up the room securely and took a quick shower to revive himself. When Michael woke up, Joaquin ran a warm bath for him. It helped Joaquin to have Michael to take care of, and he wondered how Teresa was faring. Allowing Michael to play with the bubbles for a minute, he retrieved the five-thousand-dollar check from his other shirt pocket and placed it carefully in his wallet.

After dressing Michael in jeans and a shirt, Joaquin helped him into his pint-sized barn jacket. Michael popped his cowboy hat on his head, just like he saw his daddies do, and he held Joaquin's hand as they left the hotel room. Joaquin drove them to a *taqueria* that had a drive-thru window and ordered breakfast tacos and orange juice for everybody.

"So, Granny is sick?"

"Yeah, son. She's real sick."

"She gonna go be with Jesus?"

"Maybe so. What do you think about that?"

"Okay, I guess. I don't really know her, but if she's Mommy's Mommy, then I'm gonna be sad. I heard Mommy crying last night. I think I might cry, too. Mommies are special," Michael said softly, then sighed heavily, his breath hitching a little.

Joaquin looked at his son sitting in his car seat, his little hands resting on his knees, and felt the lump in his throat double in size. "Your mommy could probably use a hug when we get there."

"I'll give her lots," Michael responded. Joaquin noticed that Michael's little eyebrows were drawn together with a little crease between. He silently wiped a tear from his chubby little cheek. Seeing that brave display caused a painful hitch in Joaquin's chest, and he wiped a tear from his own cheek. Michael hadn't had enough time with his grandmother.

They drove to the nursing home and located Teresa and Angel in the room her parents shared. Angel sat talking quietly with Teresa's father on one side of the bed. Teresa sat on the other side with her head on her mother's pillow, brushing her fingertips over her mother's brow. Teresa crooned to her as they entered then sat up and went to Joaquin and Michael. Michael hugged her and kissed her forehead then got down and went to Angel and Mr. Palacios, who seemed so happy to see him. Joaquin held her securely in his arms, and she shook and sobbed softly as the men looked on in concern.

He pressed a kiss to her brow and said, "Tell me what the doctor said."

"Her organs have begun to shut down," Teresa whispered in a trembling voice. "She's not expected to last the morning. I've been listening to her, and I can tell her breathing has begun to slow down. *Thank you* for getting me here in time."

"Sugar, we'd do anything we can for you. Has she regained consciousness?"

"No, they don't expect her to. At least I got to see her one last time at the wedding." She rested her head against his chest and held on to him. He would have given her his strength if that was possible. Joaquin couldn't fix this, but he could help her as she faced the inevitable parting.

"Want me to let Grace and the others know?"

She nodded. "Yes, would you? Call Grace, and she'll know what to do."

"Sure thing, sugar."

* * * *

Teresa tried to eat but lost her appetite after a few bites. Even though she was sure the taco was delicious, it felt like sawdust in her mouth. She returned to the bed and stayed by her mother's side the rest of the morning.

Mr. Palacios sat holding his wife's hand and humming to her as she slowly faded from the world. The nurses came to check on her several times, and near mid-morning, one of them nodded at Teresa, the glimmer of tears in the nurse's eyes.

The nurse stayed and turned off the alarm on the monitors when it sounded as Mrs. Palacios's respirations decelerated. Teresa's father ignored them and kept singing to his wife until her heart ceased to beat and her chest no longer rose in shallow breaths.

Teresa couldn't control the trembling in her limbs and turned her face toward her mother's pillow and allowed a long, quavering sob to spill from her throat. She was vaguely aware of gentle hands in her hair and around her torso. Teresa heard murmuring in her ear, the press of lips on her hair. Allowing her to cuddle against her mother as long as she wanted to, they never lost contact with her, grounding her and letting her know they were there. Her heart was shattered in her loss but held together by the love that surrounded her.

Eventually she sat up, having had the time with her mother that she needed. With a painful ache in her chest, she turned to her men. Michael was perched on Angel's forearm, and all three of them gazed at her with soulful eyes. She was so grateful that she had them. Her father still sat at the bedside, his fingers drifting through the silver hair at his wife's temple. Tears streamed down his weathered cheeks, but his face was peaceful.

Her father had been awake all night and was exhausted, so they left him at the nursing home after he promised to lie down and take a nap. They met with the mortuary director to plan the funeral. Teresa asked Joaquin to call Grace back to let everyone know.

Teresa felt like she was walking through a dream. Part of her was rejoicing because her mother no longer suffered in the muddled world that Alzheimer's had relegated her to. She was glad her father would no longer need to answer the same questions over and over again, though he swore it never bothered him all that much. Teresa was relieved that her father seemed to accept her mother's death so easily and wondered if he thought he would follow her soon. She hoped not. Memories kept coming to her, and it made her feel like she had an anvil on her chest.

Once the choices were made and the paperwork signed, the four of them left the funeral home and returned to the nursing home. Delores met them in the hallway. After hugging her while they both cried, Teresa introduced Delores to Angel and Joaquin.

Grace, Jack, Ethan, and Rachel arrived later in the afternoon. The men spoke quietly to each other for a few minutes while Grace and Rachel visited with Teresa.

Teresa had always envisioned herself going through this process when her parents passed away on her own, with no one to hold her hand or help her make decisions. Now the exact opposite of that was true. Everywhere she turned, there was someone to help with Michael, commiserate with her, or offer a shoulder to cry on. There were surreal moments where Teresa felt almost euphoric for all the support she received, in a way.

Then it would hit her that she'd only seen her mother once in the last three and a half years and that there would be no more opportunities. Teresa felt she and Michael had been robbed of those opportunities by Ranulfo and his horrid parents. At other times, she would worry because she had no doubt that they would show up at the visitation or the memorial service. No burial was to take place.

Her parents had decided they wanted to be buried together and so whichever of them died first would be cremated and their ashes stored in an urn. When the remaining spouse passed away, the urn would be placed in the arms of the spouse and they could be buried together.

Her father had already seen to the sale and dispersal of their house and worldly goods at an auction. He'd given Teresa the key to a storage unit packed full of all the things her parents had thought she might like to have. With nothing else to do, they went out to the storage facility and loaded a moving van Angel contracted to deliver all the items to the ranch.

Teresa was happy to discover heirloom linens, a set of china that had belonged to her grandmother, and many other keepsakes. There were also several pieces of valuable antique furniture.

Teresa helped her father pack the few belongings he had at the nursing home. Her father would be returning to Divine with them. Mr. Palacios had nay-sayed the offer when Teresa suggested one of the rooms in the new house would be specially earmarked for him. He insisted on moving into a room at the new assisted living facility in Divine.

Her father clasped her hands in his wrinkled ones. "A young family needs their privacy. I should know. Your grandmother lived with us for five years after your grandfather died. We were still newlyweds. She snored, *loudly*. It was criminal. I'll be happy knowing that you'll be able visit me. Plus, I could use a little time to myself to just 'be'."

The following day, Adam, Juliana, Rosemary, Charity, Eli, Eleazar, Marco, Ricardo, Maria, Luka, and Matthias all arrived. Ash agreed to stay behind to run the ranch but sent his condolences with Juliana and Adam.

Teresa was filled with dread as the hour for the visitation drew near. As there was no burial or funeral procession to plan for, people would come and go as they wished for the visitation then return for the memorial service in the morning.

Michael perched on either Joaquin's or Angel's arm as visitors arrived. Teresa was miserable standing around being sociable with people when she secretly wanted them all to go away. Juliana provided a nice buffer at times since she, too, was from Tillman, making small talk beside her with some of the visitors. A few good friends of her parents and old classmates of hers showed up, and she realized she was glad that she had agreed to have a visitation time.

Teresa would retreat at times to Joaquin and Angel, needing a few private moments here and there, when the crowd got thick around her. She noted with consternation that her habit of keeping her eyes downcast seemed to be re-emerging in the presence of all these acquaintances from the past. Noting her unease, Angel and Joaquin flanked her, allowing Eli to handle Michael, keeping him well away from most of the strangers.

Folded in the pocket of Eli's slacks was a photocopy bearing the images from photos Delores had given to Angel of the Ferraro family. Eli scanned the crowd vigilantly, knowing that he and Rachel would retire to a private room with Michael if any of the three of them made an appearance.

Allen, who was now the county sheriff, showed up early in the evening and greeted her, hugged Juliana, and then shook hands with both Angel and Joaquin. Teresa wondered if they'd already met, the way that they comfortably entered into conversation with each other.

Teresa felt so much more comfortable with Angel and Joaquin at her side, though she detested introducing Angel as her husband then having to relegate Joaquin to the status of brother-in-law. She grimaced at one point as she caught Grace's eye after having to give the inaccurate introduction. Grace shrugged philosophically and gestured with a wave of her hand back and forth between the two of them, meaning that she knew how Teresa felt.

Teresa noticed Allen scanning the crowd then he suddenly turned to Angel and Joaquin and nodded. She turned to find Eli in the rear of the room and saw that he'd gotten the message and was already making an exit with Rachel. She knew their silent communications meant that the Ferraros had entered the room. Anyone observing might have assumed that the tall, handsome couple were exiting the room with their own dark-headed son.

* * * *

Angel leaned down and whispered in her ear, "Would you like to take a break in the private room with the others?" Feeling as protective as he was, that would have been what he preferred, but he wanted her to have the choice.

Teresa looked up at him with determination in her eyes. "No, Angel. I'm not running from them anymore. I allowed their ugliness to run me out of my hometown. I'm standing my ground right here with you all beside me. I want to say my piece."

Angel gazed at her warmly. "We're not going anywhere, beautiful. Isn't that right, Joaquin?"

"We're right by your side the whole way, sugar," Joaquin murmured in her ear. His brother placed a comforting, but platonic, hand on her shoulder.

Jack murmured in agreement, "We're all here for you, Teresa." She looked over her shoulder and smiled up at Jack and seemed encouraged that all of the men were standing directly behind her, even his fathers. "Teresa, you say the word or give a look and we close ranks," Jack added, with nods of affirmation from all of them.

"I love you all so much. You're truly men of worth," she said as she looked at each of them. Joaquin, Jack, Adam, Ethan, Allen, his fathers, Eleazar, Ricardo, Marco, and even Ace Webster was there with him in the midst of the group backing her.

Angel stood at her side, next to Joaquin, and stroked her back comfortingly. He heard her sigh deeply, and she seemed to be mentally preparing for the confrontation. He glanced at the older couple that cut a swath through the room as they approached. The crowd watched curiously, and many whispered amongst themselves. Angel noted the older couple's superior air as they approached. Glancing at his brother, he knew by the look in Joaquin's eyes that he itched to be the one to speak to the couple as much as Angel did.

Angel noticed that the sheriff's features were coldly neutral as Ace spoke quietly to him, a large envelope in his hand. Ace had an uncanny ability to dig up information on people that they would have preferred stayed hidden.

Dressed in garments that could not have been purchased at any of the local stores, Mrs. Ferraro looked chic in her black pantsuit. Mr. Ferraro was dressed immaculately from the collar of his white dress shirt to the soles of his dress shoes. The predatory gleam in their eyes, however, spoiled the solicitous, mournful look they were evidently going for.

In this setting, they must have expected Teresa would behave in a congenial manner. Angel suppressed the urge to speak up right then as the couple scanned their group, obviously looking for a child around the age of three.

Not on your fucking life.

Mr. Ferraro spoke first. "We are *so* saddened by your loss, my dear. How *painful* it must be for you to have lost her after abandoning her three years ago." He shook his head sadly. "Now there's no way to get that time back. What a shame you did not accept our generous offer *then*." His tone implied that she must have come to her senses and planned to take them up on it now.

Only Teresa's statement that she wanted to have her say kept Angel from throttling the man for his cruel words. That and the fact there was a lawman standing three feet away.

"The offer still stands, my dear," Mrs. Ferraro assured Teresa in a condescending tone. Her accented, cultured voice sent chills up and down Angel's spine.

"What offer was that, Mrs. Ferraro?" Teresa asked. Angel noted that Allen leaned forward slightly in his peripheral vision.

Mr. Ferraro replied craftily, "You know of which offer we speak."

Mrs. Ferraro's eyes scanned the vicinity again.

"No. I'm afraid I don't remember. My memory needs refreshing. They're curious, as well," she added, gesturing to Angel and the others. *Go, kitten.*

"We merely offered you a way to make your life easier. The *needs* of a toddler must be exhausting for you as a *single* mother," Mrs. Ferraro said, emphasizing the word "single" as though it were some distasteful, socially damaging condition. Angel heard Joaquin exhale through his nose angrily.

Teresa nodded. "Yes, a toddler does make a lot of demands, which I've weathered quite well since my departure from Tillman. But as a happily married woman," she said, gesturing with a loving caress to Angel and clutching at Joaquin's hand at the small of her back, "I can assure you that all my child's *needs* are well met." Dropping all pretense of not remembering the offer of which they spoke, she added, "I have no need of the shameful cash offer you made to buy my child from me. I would never give my child up to you for any amount of money."

Mrs. Ferraro tsked haughtily. "We would have reimbursed you handsomely for your…'pain and suffering' as it were." Mrs. Ferraro emphasized the words pain and suffering as though she doubted Teresa experienced either, going so far as to use air quotes around the words. "For the inconvenience of birthing the baby, we'd have paid your expenses. You could have moved forward with your life unscathed," Mrs. Ferraro said carefully, aware that the sheriff was listening.

Teresa's fingers intertwined with his and squeezed gently. Her fingers were cool, but her voice was steady and calm as she spoke. "I did move forward with my life, but there is no way you could ever repay me for the pain and suffering that monster you bore inflicted on me. The child *I bore* resembles none of you in either looks, personality, or behavior. My child is the image of his stepfather's name, an angel and a pleasure to have in our lives. I would fight you with the very last breath in my body if you ever come near my child."

"My dear, we had no idea you would be so...*maternal*," Mrs. Ferraro replied disdainfully. "We merely sought to provide a proper upbringing for our grandson, provided that he's actually *ours*, of course, rather than relegating the young innocent to a substandard future."

Angel could feel the anger radiating from the men who surrounded her, not just from Joaquin. Teresa's hand had tremored slightly when Mrs. Ferraro intimated that Michael might not be Ranulfo's son. Teresa blushed at her insinuation, but she answered the woman confidently. His respect for Teresa skyrocketed.

"I can assure you that I was not entertaining any other boyfriends while your son *assaulted* me," Teresa responded quietly but clearly. This was a revelation to Angel's fathers, and he clearly heard a growling sound come from his father, Eleazar, who stood behind Teresa. "And as far as providing a proper upbringing, I believe my husband and I are more capable of providing that than you. Thank you for reminding me that you had made a *cash offer* to *buy* my child from me still stands, but I must decline."

Allen spoke up then, acting in his official capacity as Sheriff. "Mr. and Mrs. Ferraro, I need to speak with you privately. Mr. Webster here has some information he'd like to share with you *and me*. This way, please," he said, gesturing to the front entrance through the curious crowd. His words and tone gave them no options as they arrogantly moved through the crowd.

The men all looked at Teresa with pride shining in their eyes. Even Allen looked back at her and grinned, giving her a thumbs-up as he escorted the Ferraros out. Teresa turned back to thank the men standing around her, so she missed the look of love and regret on Allen's face, although Angel saw it. Allen didn't try to hide it but instead nodded at him. Angel hoped he never knew the regret of letting down the woman he adored. It looked painful, judging by

Allen's eyes. He nodded back before turning to her and giving her a hug and a tender kiss. She sighed like the world's weight had fallen off her shoulders.

"Well done, sweetheart," Angel said. "This seems to be your week for confrontations."

"Next person who messes with me gets a black eye and a fist in the mouth," she said, balling up her delicate little hand. "Thank you for standing with me and for letting me get that said. I'm sure that was probably more information than any of you wanted," Teresa added, a blush staining her cheeks.

Jack smiled at her reassuringly and said, "Trust me, Teresa, when I say that we take care of our own, and you are definitely one of our own. If we could get to that rotten bastard in jail, we would."

"We still might be able to," Adam muttered. "I've got duct tape in the truck, and Ace has connections."

Angel and Teresa both looked at Adam, and Teresa tilted her head in confusion. Jack said, "You really don't want to know, honey. Let's just say we avenge our own and leave it at that."

Chapter Thirty-five

Teresa took the color snapshot Ace handed her and looked at it then squinted her eyes and looked closer at the photograph. She glanced at Ace and tilted the photograph so Angel and Joaquin could see it as they leaned over to get a peek.

She glanced at Ace in confusion and pointed at something in the face in the photo. "Ace, is that…?"

Ace nodded and handed her another photograph. "Mr. Ferraro? Yes, Teresa, it is."

"And that—Is that a Halloween costume he's—" Looking closely at the second photograph, she gasped and averted her eyes from it. "Oh! Angel is that his—?" Teresa felt her cheeks go red hot.

Angel took the second photograph and groaned then handed it to his brother. Teresa looked at her men and surprised herself by giggling when Joaquin gave a full-body shudder.

Teresa asked, "Why is he dressed like a dog? And why are his…privates exposed? Is Mrs. Ferraro doing…what I think she's doing to him?"

Do I really want the answer to that question rattling around in my head?

Ace took the photographs they handed back to him. As he placed them in the manila envelope, he answered her question. "It's called puppy play. There are people who get turned on by the thought of being someone's puppy. For some, it can be very erotic, even. That must be the case for Mr. Ferraro and Mrs. Ferraro. Now, what grown adults want to do in their private time is nobody's business. A lot of people get enjoyment from this sort of play, and I say more power to them," he said, holding up his hands in a nonjudgmental gesture. "You needed leverage and, speaking for my own self, a little revenge on them. These pictures provide that leverage. My guy found the stash in their hiding place and brought these to me. I showed the Ferraros last night. Besides the fraud charges they are now dealing with, thanks to Kemp's efforts, they have this little information leak to worry about. I have a video, as well. Knowing these were in our hands provided just the right amount of motivation." Ace smiled and handed her an envelope. "It gives me tremendous pleasure to hand these over to you, Teresa."

Removing the papers from the envelope, she looked at them, at Ace, and at her men. The papers were signed documents relinquishing any and all rights to Michael, signed by the Ferraros *and* their son.

Teresa burst into tears and hugged the big private investigator.

* * * *

Teresa spent the mild March morning in the backyard, pruning shrubs. Trimming dead branches from a rosebush with a pair of shears, she was startled when strong hands slid around her hips, pulling her back against a hard body. A cool breeze blew through the yard, and she shivered slightly. Angel's warmth shielded her as he wrapped those big arms around her and pressed his erection against her ass.

His hands slid up over her abdomen and ribs to gently cup her breasts. Her pussy clenched and pooled with hot moisture as she heaved a sigh of longing and chuckled. "Angel, it's not even lunchtime yet." She ground her hips back against him, and a shudder went down her spine when she heard him growl invitingly in her ear.

He chuckled deeply and said, "Close enough. I even know what I want to eat." He slowly slid a hand into the waistband of her jeans, making her press her hips back against him. He allowed his fingers to wander clear down to her bare, newly waxed mound. A sense of power swept over her when she heard his breathing increase, and he groaned. "Since you told us you were going to Madeleine's first thing this morning, *this right here*," he whispered sexily, his fingers sliding into her quickly liquefying slit, "is all I've been able to think about." Teresa groaned when his callused fingertip stroked over her clit. "You're soft and smooth. And so wet," he murmured, nuzzling her cheekbone with his lips.

"I thought maybe you'd like to know what I was up to on my day off," she whispered teasingly, panting when his finger slid over her clit again.

"I like that you enjoy taking care of yourself like this."

Teresa huffed and said, "Let's set you up with an appointment to get the hair on your privates ripped off and see how much you *enjoy* it."

"Do you need me to kiss it and make it better?"

"Mmm. I think I might like that." He slid a finger deep into her pussy.

Flexing her hips against him, she moved on the finger currently fucking her. His cock was a rigid length in the cleft of her ass, and she wanted it inside her in the worst way.

After kissing her, he asked, "Would you like to take a little break with me? Inside?"

"Where is Michael?" Having a toddler around limited any "alone time" they had during the day.

"Grace claimed him from me a few minutes ago. She wants to feed him lunch, and then they're going to watch a movie and take a nap."

That girl is worth her weight in chocolate.

Angel continued to play with her body, and Teresa was grateful that the perimeter of the fenced in yard was solid with thick shrubbery. He allowed her to turn in his embrace then his hands slid back into her jeans over her bare ass, his fingers straying into the cleft.

She smiled when he chuckled and said, "Well, well. What do we have here?"

He pressed on the anal plug lodged in her ass, and she nearly purred. "You know what you have there. Now you know the reason I went to get waxed this morning. I wanted to be nice and neat for you, all over."

"Using your plugs like a good girl."

"That's not all. Something that Summer ordered for me came in. I'm going to model it for you tonight," Teresa said as she led Angel by the hand to the back porch. "Right now, I have an ache."

"An ache?" Angel replied sympathetically. "Can I help you with this ache?"

"Yes, since you're the one who caused it." She giggled and led him in the backdoor, the pruning all but forgotten.

* * * *

Teresa's body was still humming as she set the table for supper. Michael sat at his little activity table in the living room, drawing on a pad of white paper. She tossed a romaine and tomato salad then returned to the oven to check the garlic bread. Joaquin startled her when he snuck up behind her and wrapped his arms around her waist.

"I heard you had a nice time this afternoon," he murmured before kissing her lips hungrily. "I wish I could have gotten away to join you."

"I'm sorry, too, but there's plenty more love where that came from," she whispered, kissing him again. "I have a surprise for you tonight. Something you'll like."

"That's what Angel tells me. He told me you had your plug in earlier. He can't wait for tonight."

"You think *he's* excited? I'm all aquiver." She giggled quietly, resting her head on his chest. "The anticipation has been half of the thrill." She trembled against him a little as she hugged him.

"For us, too, sugar." He tipped her chin up for another kiss. "Promise me that you'll stop us if it's too much?"

Speaking in a whisper, she said, "Yes, if you'll promise we can move to the next step sooner when this turns out to be wonderful tonight. I don't want to wait."

"We'll see how it goes. Maybe tonight?"

She groaned when Joaquin squeezed her ass cheeks firmly. Her pussy practically vibrated with need. "Yes, yes! Tonight, please," she whispered excitedly, just about done with waiting.

"Supper is all ready. Where is Angel?"

"He was just finishing up. Should be in soon," Joaquin said as he released her and went to the bathroom to wash up.

Michael brought his tablet of white paper into the kitchen. "Mommy, look what I drew."

Teresa took it from him and sat in a chair at the dinner table, drawing him into her lap. "Can you tell me about this picture?"

He pointed to the smallest stick figure in the stick figure family portrait. "This is me. You can tell because I'm the littlest. Here is Angel and Joaquin. You can tell them apart by their hair, and here is you." He pointed at a little stick figure with lots of squiggly black hair and a red mouth. "I made you extra pretty, Mommy, because you're extra pretty now."

"I am?"

"Oh, yeah! Everyone says so." In a conspiratorial whisper, Michael said, "Angel told Joaquin today that you're so pretty you make his eyes hurt. Mommy, since we came here, you're just extra, *extra* pretty. And look," he went on, pointing to red blobs over the stick figures heads, "you can tell how much Angel and Joaquin love you and me because of all the red hearts I drew. See? I also drew Coraggio and Valiente in the picture, too. This one is for you to keep." He pulled the paper from the tablet and handed it to her, kissing her on the nose. "Love you, Mommy."

"Well thank you, baby. We'll put it on the refrigerator," she said. Her heart throbbed, and she murmured to herself, "Don't cry, don't cry, don't cry." This was why all the pain and hardships she'd endured were somehow redeemed in the end. She felt victorious because she had this wonderful little boy in her life and the love of the two incredible men who would raise him. Her heart felt like it might burst from her chest, so much love for all of them filled it.

"Did you sign it somewhere?"

"Yep, right there." He pointed to a big, squiggly M on the page. Michael climbed down from her lap to pick a magnet to hang it, and Teresa took a pen from the kitchen counter and quickly wrote down what he'd told her on the back of it, with the date, so she'd never forget this moment.

Chapter Thirty-six

Teresa was in the tub soaking when Joaquin slipped into the bathroom after knocking. "Michael is in bed and sound asleep now. We've lit the fireplace and everything is ready. Do you want a glass of wine? It might help you relax."

The ache in her cunt increased at the thought of what was to come, and she smiled at him. "I'd love a glass of wine." She slid down into the bank of scented bubbles that surrounded her until her eyes and her hair pinned on top of her head were all that was visible. Closing her eyes, she sighed in contentment.

A sound caught her attention, and she looked up. Joaquin was still standing there, watching her as he leaned against the door. "I love seeing you so happy. It feels good to think I helped to put that smile on your face. You're always beautiful, Teresa, but tonight your especially gorgeous, sugar. I'll be back with your wine."

Smiling at him, she said, "Thank you, Joaquin."

A minute later, he returned with her wineglass and kissed her on the forehead as he handed it to her. "Take your time."

She heard the shower running in the other bathroom as she settled back in the tub. The loving attention her husbands paid to her made her feel like a princess. Sighing dreamily, her breath hitched in her throat, and her heart ached with happiness. So beautiful she made his eyes hurt. That's what Angel had told Joaquin. Tears formed in her eyes.

How strange life was, the places it took you. A year ago next month, she'd met Angel for the first time. Attracted to the point of utter speechlessness, in that moment she would never have believed she would be here tonight. If anyone had told her she'd share her life with him and his brother, she would have told them they were insane. It was Angel's unswerving patience that had gotten her here, eased her into this state of bliss she now reveled in. A small sob escaped at the thought of a lifetime spent in the arms of two men who loved her with a passion that made her ache with need for them.

Her cunt clenched and pulsed as though a miniature orgasm brought on by her thoughts had just come over her. She smiled and sipped her wine, closing her eyes and sinking deeper in the foamy hot water.

The shower shut off in the other bathroom, and she heard a deep, muffled voice. The sound of that distant tone made her pussy quiver. A minute later, the shower started again as her other man got ready. Finishing her wine, she laid her glass aside and rose from the tub. She rinsed the bubbles from her flushed skin then dried off.

She drew on the long, diaphanous robe that she'd worn over her white satin nightgown on her wedding night. It seemed appropriate that she wear the robe, which was completely sheer, *without* the nightgown for this evening. Nothing was held back from them anymore after they took her in this manner. She'd left the ties to the robe undone and then put on the silver nipple rings with the attached chain that would drape down between her breasts. Five dangling turquoise charms swung playfully from it, adding a delicious weight to the rings tugging at her nipples.

Pressing her lips together to stifle a breathy sigh, she slid the silver clip down over the hood of her swollen clitoris and then slipped the dangles onto her inner lips, tucking the little sparkling crystal and polished turquoise beads inside her lips for them to be surprised by later. After it was on, she rested her hands on the bathroom counter and waited for the tremors in her pussy to fade.

When she'd purchased it, she thought the men would love it but had no idea how incredibly wanton she would feel putting it on. Her pussy welled with moisture, and her clit throbbed against the heavy turquoise bead. With the clit clip and dangles in position, even walking was going to be an erotic experience.

She shut off the light and opened the bathroom door. The room glowed from the light of several candles and the merrily crackling fireplace.

Over the sound of her pounding heartbeat, she heard the rustle of fabric and a shaky exhalation. "Damn." Joaquin.

"Beautiful," Angel murmured as they both climbed from the bed.

"What do we have here, sugar?" Joaquin asked as he drew her closer to the glow of the fire instead of to the bed. The light from the dancing flames made the clear crystals and polished beads sparkle. Her breath hitched at the green lust that glittered in his eyes for her.

Angel's eyes smoldered as she faced the fire, and they drew her sheer robe from her breasts, revealing her jewelry. Angel slid a hand along her abdomen and over her ribs to cup her breast in his calloused hand, admiring the turquoise and silver beads that dangled there.

"Well, isn't this pretty?" Angel strummed her nipple, and she shuddered as the erotic sensation communicated itself to the jewelry hidden between her legs, making her throb even more.

Joaquin cradled her other breast in his hand. "I like your new jewelry, sugar. This is so pretty. How does it feel?" His finger slid down the chain that draped between her nipples and gave a light tug to set all five charms swinging. More heat bloomed in her pussy and spread outward through her body.

Quivering, she murmured, "Mmmm, it feels even better than I imagined it w-would." Being near the fire made her nipples tingle. Her clit and pussy engorged from the luxuriant heat and her juices trickled.

She allowed the robe to slip from her shoulders and land in a puddle around her feet. "There's more." She traced her index fingers over their pectoral muscles down to their abdomens. She bit her lip as she gazed at their fully engorged, firmly erect cocks. Power surged through her when she licked her lip, and Angel's cock twitched, and he groaned. They were as desperate for her as she was for them.

A tear of pre-cum seeped from Joaquin's cock as he asked, "Any hints?" His eyes twinkled as he lightly stroked her nipple.

"No. I know you'll probably find it the first place you look." Teresa allowed them to lead her to the bed.

"Teresa seems to have a lot of confidence in us, that we'll find this other jewelry pretty quickly," Joaquin said, kissing her fingertips one at a time. "Where do you think we should start?"

Angel answered without hesitation. "At her toes. Lots of ladies wear rings on their toes nowadays. We should start there and work our way up *very carefully*." Angel smiled wolfishly at the look she gave him.

Oh! You big tease!

"Yeah. We wouldn't want to miss it. It *pays* to be thorough," Joaquin said wisely with a nod as he moved with Angel to the foot of the bed, leaving her all alone up at the pillows piled against the headboard.

"Hey, now I'm *lonely!*" she pouted as she teasingly lifted a turquoise dangle from her chain and twiddled it.

Angel chuckled. "Oh, we can't have that. Let's try divide and conquer, Joaquin. You start at the top and work your way down, and I'll meet you in the middle." Teresa giggled and nodded enthusiastically. "Teresa's frisky tonight, isn't she?"

"I fricking love it when she's frisky!" Joaquin chuckled as he nuzzled at her throat and shoulders, making a show of checking her for hidden jewelry. He stretched his big, muscled body out beside hers and fanned her hair on the pillows. Licking her earlobe, he moved downward and left a trail of wet kisses from her collarbone to between her breasts. He paused at the chain and nipple rings.

"Do you want me to remove this?" he asked, then flicked a hard peak with the tip of his tongue. "Or would you prefer I leave it on?"

Joaquin smiled when she moaned at the dual sensations as Angel sucked on her toes. Teresa had no idea how erotic *that* would feel.

"I wore it to please you, but I have to admit I like how it feels, especially when the charms are swaying. But I don't want it to be in the way, later," she murmured as her fingertips slid through the silky, long strands of his hair.

Joaquin flicked her nipple with his tongue again. "I'd love to fuck you from behind while you wear this jewelry. I bet it would feel amazing, all these little charms swaying as you move with me." He carefully loosened the silver ring with his fingertips before sucking it off of her nipple.

Teresa gasped as the blood flow returned, making her nipples feel even more sensitive and engorged. The insistent throbbing in her clitoris increased in response. Angel made his way up her calves, caressing her ankles and the back of her knees. She wrapped her hand around Joaquin's cock, delighting in his erotic growl.

Forging on, he laid the nipple rings and chain aside and proceeded to her bellybutton, caressing her abdomen and her hip bones as he stroked the indentation with the tip of his tongue.

Smoothing his hands up and down her thighs, Angel lifted one and murmured, sounding casual, "Joaquin, I haven't found anything. Maybe our lovely wife was pulling our leg?"

"*Oh, no*, I would never do that," Teresa said in an innocent voice. "There's one place you haven't looked yet. Remember, it pays to be thorough." Levity and desire warred for dominance in her tone.

Angel and Joaquin smiled at each other then looked to her. Stretching out on either side of her, they each palmed a hip bone and gazed into her eyes. She was bewitched as they leaned toward her, first one kissing her then the other, in no particular hurry for the game to end. They moved down her throat to her still throbbing nipples and suckled before laying a trail of wet kisses to her completely bare mound.

Angel hummed in admiration. He trailed a finger over her mons and her outer lips then surprised her by laying a light kiss there. Joaquin followed Angel and nuzzled her mound with his lips, kissing her and licking in small light strokes directly over her slit. The beads shifted, and she gasped as the movement tugged slightly at her clit.

Joaquin's eyes met hers in triumph. "Wait, Angel. What do we have here?" Joaquin asked as he nuzzled against her outer lips, causing the bead to shift yet again. Moisture seeped from her slit as they took turns nuzzling her there without going deeper. Both men reached for the back of a thigh and lifted slightly before palming her thighs open. Moaning rapturously, she felt her outer lips part.

Joaquin drawled sexily, "Well, now isn't that a pretty little thing she's got there."

Angel chuckled. "It's *always* been pretty. Now she's got it decorated for us, don't you, beautiful?"

Panting softly, she nodded, arching as Joaquin touched the clip.

Oh! One touch! One touch! Please!

Joaquin's slid s fingertip over her clit, and she spasmed a little at the electric sensation, crying out.

"You okay, sugar?" he asked, smiling at her.

"Uh-huh!"

"Can I kiss you?" Angel murmured as he kissed the junction of her inner thigh and her mons.

"Oh, please, yes!"

Turning his head slightly, he nuzzled her swollen flesh, his tongue slowly smoothing over her clit in a long, leisurely lick, causing another quivering spasm in her pussy. Teresa felt sure she'd come any second. Her clit felt so swollen, and Angel was the giving type as his tongue lovingly stroked her again, flicking the beads dangling from her pussy lips and clit back and forth, rubbing them against the side of her clit, which drove her wild.

Joaquin's fingertips slid up her inner thigh, seeking her slit, but careful to not dislodge the clips. He dipped a finger into the well of her pussy, causing her to moan and clench hard on his fingertip before he slid out and smoothed her wetness over her anus.

As his fingers brushed that virginal opening, all the nerve endings came alive, making her as acutely aware of it as she was of her clit. The ring of muscle clenched then relaxed as she reminded her body to allow his penetration. His fingers circled on the tight rosette, pressing firmly as Angel's tongue became more insistent with each pass.

Working in tandem, they brought her to the pinnacle where she flew free, her orgasm tumbling her into a warm pool of ecstasy. Once she was finished and every pulse had washed through her, Angel lifted the bead with his teeth and tongue and carefully loosened the dangles, freeing her lips and clit and sending a powerful aftershock through her. She stretched luxuriously for them, practically purring.

"The way you arch your back is so sexy," Joaquin said admiringly.

Kissing him, she looked up into his crystalline green gaze. She licked his lips and flicked his tongue with hers as he parted his lips for her. "Joaquin, I'm ready. Angel, I want it all. Now."

Joaquin paused and turned to make eye contact with his brother. She waited, heart and pussy throbbing through their silent exchange, then Joaquin turned back to her.

"Thank you, sugar," he said deeply as he rose to his knees. "Up on your knees, straddling Angel."

His voice was rough with desire, but his hands were gentle, helping her into position. Angel moved to the center of the bed, and she climbed astride his hips. Angel's cock lay completely engorged against his belly, ready for action.

Angel covered her hands with his, where she braced them on the thick muscles of his chest. "You're sure?" He gazed seriously into her eyes.

"Yes, Angel. Completely," she whispered back as she leaned forward to kiss him tenderly. He was almost worshipful as he caressed her waist and hips.

"Angel is going to help you stay relaxed," Joaquin said as Angel pulled her onto his chest for a kiss, his pulsating cock trapped between them. Joaquin applied a generous amount of the lubricant to her asshole and the area around it. He pressed some of it into her, making her groan and flex against him. She arched her back to give him as much access as she could.

"Mmmm. Easy, sugar. You're anxious for my cock, aren't you?"

She whimpered against Angel's lips and then looked over her shoulder at him. Joaquin took the time to apply a generous amount of the lube to his cock. Resting her cheek against Angel's broad chest, she felt him shift into position behind her Angel pulled her to him and put his strong arms around her, not trapping her but merely grounding her. Joaquin lifted her hips so she was in position for his cock. Making a sound that was half moan and half sob, she murmured, "Joaquin, yes!" Her heart throbbed, desperate for them both.

Joaquin's staying hand was warm on her tailbone. "I'll be moving slow, sugar. Breathe for me, okay?"

"Listen to Joaquin, beautiful. Relax for him." Teresa rested her cheek on Angel and nodded, taking several deep breaths.

"That's good, baby," Angel whispered. His heart pounded beneath her ear, letting her know how much he was affected by the moment.

Joaquin's hands slid in soothing firm strokes over her ass. "Such a gorgeous ass, sugar," he whispered as he caressed her quivering opening. He must have felt her trembling because he asked, "You're not afraid, are you, sugar?"

"Of you? No, I can't help it. I need you."

She was startled when the blunt head of Joaquin's cock brushed against her lubricated opening.

Angel stroked her back then slid his hands down to hold her ass cheeks. His callused fingertips pressed near her anus felt so intimate.

The butterflies in her stomach disappeared, and she was filled with a feeling of rightness in this moment. Her body relaxed as Joaquin pressed for entrance, giving her body a chance to adjust to his size. Her asshole burned, but she knew there was enough lubrication. Her body just needed to give in, like with the plugs.

The muscles finally relaxed under his insistent pressure, and Joaquin's cock slid into her a fraction. He hissed and groaned, and she clenched against the burning pinch of pain. Joaquin softly cursed, and Angel stroked her ass, which helped her to focus. She breathed deep and willed her body to relax and accept Joaquin there, and he hissed in pleasure.

"You all right, sugar?" he asked, breathing roughly as he caressed her hips and gave her time.

Sensations swirled over Teresa all together. Most obviously, the small pinch of pain as he took her ass for the first time but also the electrifying, intense pleasure of being filled in a place that was largely considered taboo was a dark, thrilling rush, and she reveled in it. "I love it, Joaquin. I want more." She flexed against Joaquin, trying to take what she wanted. Angel stopped her.

"Joaquin wants to last until we're both inside you. You keep moving like that and you'll make him come too soon. We want you to feel what it's like to come so hard you see stars while we both make love to you together."

Teresa lay against Angel's chest, breathing deeply and willing her body to open for Joaquin. She moaned happily when he advanced another inch, then withdrew, then repeated the motion, never pulling completely out and gaining a little more ground with each thrust.

"Thank you, sugar. This is so beautiful what you're giving me, giving us, by trusting us like this." Joaquin arched over her and kissed her shoulder. His hips were pressed fully against her ass. He ground the thick root of his cock against her, and her pussy pulsed in response. She felt consumed by the immense fullness in her bottom. Joaquin slid out a few inches then thrust back in and growled then did it several more times as the stirring of her orgasm began already.

"I'm going to come, Joaquin," she whimpered, realizing that when she said it she was allowing him control of when she came.

"Hold it for me, sugar. Wait until Angel slides in, too. Don't let it go. Hold it for me." There was no way her body could've denied his request.

She moaned in assent as she nuzzled Angel's chest.

Joaquin pumped a few more times then wrapped his arms around her and lifted her off of Angel so he could position his cock at her pussy. Angel's hands were on her thighs as he pressed for entry, as well. Her breathing turned to frantic panting as Angel's lubricated cock slid somehow into her overcrowded cunt. Her pussy throbbed as his heated length found its home inside her. Feeling completely overwhelmed by her love and lust for these men, she held onto both of them and experienced the storm as it swirled inside her.

"Oh, Angel," she whispered in awe. "It's beautiful." She tried to stay still but found that her hips were flexing and squirming on her men's cocks whether she wanted to or not as instinct took over.

"Yes, it is," Angel said as he gazed at her with smoldering eyes, smoothing her hair back from her hot cheeks.

"Oh, fuck yes," Joaquin said as he withdrew a little and allowed Angel to thrust then countered as he thrust and Angel withdrew. Quickly they had a rhythm going so that she was always filled with one or the other. Bearing her weight on her hands, she rocked with them and quickly found her place in the rhythm, her orgasm spinning out of her control.

"Yes, sugar, come hard for us. Don't hold it back." Joaquin growled. Even though his voice and his grip were intense, Teresa could still tell that he was under control and thrusting as gently as possible. The realization that, even in this explosive moment, he cared so much for her wellbeing that he held back sent her skyrocketing. Her orgasm built to a burning intense crescendo, and they all came at once, their cocks filling her with their seed as they undulated and bucked together in an orgasm that seemed to go on and on until all three collapsed in a panting heap.

After kissing her between her shoulder blades, Joaquin carefully withdrew and left the bed. Teresa heard water running and felt his return when the mattress shifted behind her. Teresa felt the heat of a washcloth at her throbbing entrance, and she squirmed slightly.

Joaquin placed a hand on her hip and stayed her movements. "No, sugar. When we take you like this, we will always do this afterward. It's the least we can do." He wiped the lubricant from her ass cheeks and cleaned her up.

Angel kissed her lovingly. "It would be inconsiderate of us to do otherwise. You'll get used to it."

"Truthfully, I probably couldn't stand now if I tried. I seem to have lost the ability to move." She chuckled as she wiped a lock of hair from her forehead.

With satisfaction thick in his voice, Angel said, "Then we know we did it right."

"I'll say," she moaned. "That was intense," she added drowsily. Sighing as Angel's cock slid free from her pussy, all she cared about right then was sleeping tucked between the two of them. While Angel cuddled her into his solid embrace, Joaquin lifted the covers over them before he left the bedroom to take a shower.

"How do you feel?" Angel asked as he stroked her back lightly. Snuggled up to him, she pressed a kiss at the base of his throat.

She felt like the blissful smile on her face must be a mile wide. "Good. My body is humming. Thank you for helping me relax."

"The privilege was mine, Teresa. That was another fantasy fulfilled." He brushed her hair from her cheek, and she cuddled closer to him, struggling to stay awake, nuzzling his chest with her lips.

"I love you so much, Angel."

"You are my heart. Everything good in my life."

Joaquin returned to the bed after showering and spooned to her back, providing his biceps for her pillow as she preferred. As she drifted to sleep, she felt their hands stroking her. Her last waking thought was a feeling of completeness, looking to her future.

Chapter Thirty-seven

Two Weeks Later

Angel looked up when he heard a car door close and smiled. Michael shifted and balanced on his shoulders and looked in the same direction.

"There's my *pretty* mommy," Michael murmured as Teresa walked into the barn greeting the ranch hands as they walked past her to the corral.

"She sure *is* pretty today."

Lately, Teresa seemed to glow with happiness. He could recall a time when she would have been afraid to walk through the barn by herself, being noticed by the other men. Now she sauntered through proudly, her eyes on her destination. It was good to be her destination. Real good. As she drew closer, she eyed both of her men and winked at Angel. Her eyes flicked to his groin, at the tingling bulge that developed there any time she was nearby, and she didn't suppress the urge to lick her lip. Little vixen.

"Damn," Joaquin muttered quietly from where he stood beside Angel. "How does she manage that?"

"Manage what, Dad?" Michael asked as he tilted forward to look into Joaquin's face.

Angel suppressed a chuckle. *Manage to get us hard with a single look or flick of that little pink tongue of hers, that's what.*

Joaquin chuckled and stumbled for a reply. "Oh, um. How does she always manage to look so beautiful?" his brother said as Teresa went into his arms, a knowing smile on her face.

Michael chirped. "Oh, that's *easy*! It's cause she loves us so much. It spills all over on her face."

Ah, the wisdom of children.

Joaquin hefted Michael from Angel's shoulders as Teresa came into his arms and encompassed him in her fragrant warmth.

She rose on her tiptoes and kissed him. "All right, I'll be back after lunch. Remember, don't lift the lid on the cake in the refrigerator. It's a part of your birthday surprise."

Angel grinned, "I promise, beautiful. Enjoy your lunch with Grace." Angel kissed her, and she blushed as he caressed her hips. She went to Joaquin and kissed him then squatted down so Michael could give her a kiss, too. He promised to be a good boy.

Angel stood with Joaquin and watched as their beautiful woman walked back to her car and got in before driving up to the ranch house to pick up Grace. All Angel knew of their excursion today was that Teresa and Grace were visiting Discretion and then planning to take the owner, Summer, out to lunch.

When she arrived home later in the afternoon, Angel brought Michael in to use the potty and to say hello to her. She hastily hid something in the closet and greeted him with a kiss and a hug.

Michael came into the bedroom yawning, which caused her to yawn, and she didn't deny it when Angel asked her if she was sleepy and wanted to take a nap. Michael had been active that morning and so he didn't complain too much as his mommy slipped his hat and cowboy boots off then trundled him onto their bed to lie down for a while with her. Angel kissed them both and covered them with a blanket and closed the bedroom door.

A few hours later, she emerged from their bedroom looking dazed but well-rested, her cheeks rosy. Michael sat in Angel's lap with a storybook open. He looked at her over his son's head and smiled tenderly at her as he recited the story for Michael from memory while Michael turned the pages.

Joaquin looked up and smiled when she cuddled into his arms. Angel and his brother were both in agreement in how much they both loved the way she would melt into their arms like this. She stayed that way with him for a minute, her face hidden against his brother's chest. Joaquin whispered quietly to her, and Teresa nodded as Joaquin stroked her and kissed the top of her head.

Joaquin invited Michael to come out and hold the pan while he placed the shrimp skewers and corn on the grill, giving her a moment alone with Angel. Teresa climbed into Angel's lap, and he wrapped his arms around her as she settled.

"Hey, sugar, what's this?" he whispered, seeing the tears that welled in her eyes.

She smiled, one tear escaping and skating down her cheek. "I'm just…in the moment, Angel. It needs an outlet sometimes. I'm so happy with you and Joaquin. I never imagined I'd be this happy in my life. *Never*."

Angel held her little body to him tightly then tilted her chin and kissed her. Her lips were tender as her velvety tongue stroked his. The kiss went on and on as he expressed his love to her without words.

Angel cleared his throat, his voice husky with emotion as he clasped her to him and said, "I understand what you mean. I sat and watched you sleep for a little while this afternoon. My heart felt like it was gonna burst from my chest."

She nestled quietly to him for a few minutes. He would sit there with her snuggled in his arms all day if it was up to him. Then he heard her stomach growl. Chuckling, he patted her bottom and said, "It's time to feed you."

She helped him set the table while Joaquin and Michael kept an eye on the shrimp and vegetables outside on the grill.

"So how was your first day of freedom?" he asked, nuzzling her throat, breathing in her womanly scent then kissing her beneath her ear. She was now officially a stay-at-home mom and no longer worked at Stigall's.

"Wonderful. How about your day, birthday boy?"

"This birthday is completely different from last year's. I don't need big celebrations or grand gestures, but as I recall, I got a phone call from several of my family members wishing me happy birthday, and I sat in front of the TV and ate a frozen dinner I heated up in the microwave."

"Oh," she said sympathetically. Teresa made no comment about the past, only said, "Well, those days are over, Angel. The day you were born is a big cause for *me* to celebrate."

After supper, Joaquin helped Michael take his bath. Angel heard muffled laughter coming from the hallway and went to check on them.

"Little dude, trust me. You'll figure it out in a few years," Joaquin said as he sat on the toilet talking to Michael while he played in the tub. Joaquin had his hand over his mouth, shaking his head and chuckling. He grinned at Angel and rose to go out in the hall. "Be right back. No standing in the tub."

"'Kay." Splash.

Angel whispered, "What's so funny?"

Joaquin gestured farther down the hall as Michael began singing "Stuck on You" by Sugarland in the tub.

"Michael was getting undressed to get in the tub."

"Yeah?"

"He took off his underwear, showed me his penis, and said, 'Daddy, how come I got this big ol' long thing for peeing?' *Showing it to me.* You've seen him, right?" Joaquin asked, holding back more laughter.

"Kid's hung good," Angel said simply with an affirming nod.

"So he says, 'Seems a waste just for peeing. What am I supposed to do with this thing?' I almost fell off the toilet trying to keep from laughing."

Angel was sure Michael had already had the same conversation with his mommy who would have cautioned him about asking just anyone. Teresa must have told him it was all right to talk to Angel and Joaquin about such things. Michael asking that question of them was a show of trust on both their parts.

They both walked back down the hall and Angel almost choked when they saw what Michael was doing in the tub. Joaquin slapped his palm over his mouth and held up a finger. Michael was making so much noise he never heard them as Joaquin pulled Teresa down the hall and they all peeked in the bathroom door together and watched Michael. He was, *of course*, standing up in the tub, his head covered in fluffy bubbles, with more clumps of bubbles dotting his little body. He was singing and dancing.

"Whoa-oh, whoa-oh, stuck like glue. You and me baby, we're stuck like glue. Whoa-oh, whoa-oh, stuck like glue, You and me baby, we're stuck like glue"

"Hey, that boy can dance," Angel whispered with a chuckle.

"Let's hope he's a little more manly like his daddies when he's dancing with girls," Teresa whispered, covering a giggle with her hand as Michael wiggled his little tush to his tune.

Epilogue

Angel put Michael to bed and then returned to the living room. Teresa brought a wrapped gift and birthday card to the coffee table after both men were seated. The special cake lay under its cover on the counter. Joaquin presented his gift to his brother, a nice hand-tooled leather wallet which Angel loved. Michael's gift to Angel, received before bedtime, was a picture he'd drawn of Angel with Michael on one of the stallions taking a ride. Teresa surprised him with a hand-tooled leather case for his laptop computer.

"You have one more surprise, my sweet Angel." She rose and went to the counter. She lit sparkling candles on the cake and dimmed the light, then gave him the card with trembling hands. He opened it in the dim light and a slip of paper fell from it. She approached with the cake as he tried to discern what was on the piece of paper. The light from the candles illuminated it as she placed the cake in front of him.

"Make a wish, Angel," she murmured as he looked up at her, confused, then smiled and turned to blow out the candles. His breath left him in a little, fruitless puff of air as the light from the candles shown on the lettering on the cake.

He read the words aloud, "Happy Birthday, Daddy...*to be*."

Realization flashed through his brain, and he glanced again at the slip of paper, understanding what it represented. Joaquin's sudden inhalation coincided with his own.

"No! *Yes? Oh God,*" he whispered. "You're pregnant? Really?" He didn't care that his voice shook, and he rose from his chair and swooped her up into his arms.

Her eyes glowed as she smiled at him. "Yes. I am, honey."
She turned to Joaquin and said, "Congratulations, daddy-to-be."

THE END

www.heatherrainier.com

ABOUT THE AUTHOR

Heather Rainier lives and writes in South Central Texas. Her stories offer up the content of her fantasies, with autobiographical humor, triumph and tragedy mixed in.

Heather believes that life doesn't always present love to us in neat little sanitized packages. Sometimes we have to seize the day, live life with no regrets, forget the past, never give up, learn to trust, and dare to live, even in outrageous circumstances.

When not happily typing at her keyboard, Heather is usually busy corralling her kids, volunteering at local schools, or loving on her smokin' hot husband, who thankfully loves to cook.

Also by Heather Rainier

Ménage Everlasting: Divine Creek Ranch 1: *Divine Grace*
Everlasting Classic: Divine Creek Ranch 2: *Her Gentle Giant, Part 1: No Regrets*
Everlasting Classic: Divine Creek Ranch 2: *Her Gentle Gian, Part 2: Remember to Dance*
Ménage Everlasting: Divine Creek Ranch 4: *Rosemary's Double Delight*

Available at
BOOKSTRAND.COM

Siren Publishing, Inc.
www.SirenPublishing.com

LaVergne, TN USA
14 March 2011
220043LV00004B/22/P